⚜

"Oh, boy," Alicia groaned. "Why am I the only one who rates this kind of attention?"

"Because you're the one who talks about romance and elegance, yet you live a life without either one." Lauren looked around the room, waved her hand. "I mean, you have all the trappings but no one to share them with."

"Haven't we beaten this horse out of existence yet?"

"No."

"Terrific." Alicia's face fell.

Lauren wasn't finished. "I know you had a great thing going with Kurt, that he was your Mr. Darcy. But I think there's someone else out there for you now."

"You're talking about Nathaniel, aren't you?"

"Yes. He kind of fits the bill, doesn't he? He's tall, dark, handsome and somewhat brooding—like Mr. Darcy."

"And he does drive you crazy." Lauren winked.

Alicia said, "Okay, okay. I appreciate your enthusiastic approval. I promise I'll be nicer to Nathaniel but that's as far as I'm going."

"Well . . . ," said Lauren. "We'll see."

⚜

WAITING FOR MR. DARCY

CHAMEIN CANTON

Genesis Press, Inc.

INDIGO LOVE SPECTRUM

An imprint of Genesis Press, Inc.
Publishing Company

Genesis Press, Inc.
P.O. Box 101
Columbus, MS 39703

Copyright © 2009 by Chamein Canton

ISBN: 13 DIGIT : 978-1-58571-351-6
ISBN: 10 DIGIT : 1-58571-351-1
Manufactured in the United States of America

First Edition

Visit us at www.genesis-press.com
or call at 1-888-Indigo-1-4-0

DEDICATION

This book is for all those hardworking women (and Austen lovers) who are looking for their own Mr. Darcy. Open your eyes and your heart. He may be closer than you think.

ACKNOWLEDGMENTS

I want to thank all the many readers who have welcomed me and my words into their lives and hearts. Your support has meant the world to me and I think of you when I type every word. I would be remiss if I didn't mention my fantastic family, beginning with the best dad in the world, Leonard F. Canton, Jr. I couldn't have gotten a better father if I had mail-ordered him. Then there is my mother, Mary E. Wallace, whose wit and down-home Southern sayings continue to inspire my humor. I again thank my sister Natalie and my brother-in-law Donell for always being in my corner. Again there's my brother-in-spirit, Joel Woodard, who always cheers for the big girls. I again thank Mrs. Frances Watkins who taught me how to find joy in every day, even when there is physical pain. I also am grateful to my sons, Sean and Scott, who have grown into fine young men. I also thank my uncles, Calvin and Cecil Canton and Charles Salley, for being fantastic uncles. Thanks also to the man that makes my heart skip a beat, Michael Bressler, for being the sweetest (and cutest) boyfriend a girl could hope for. As always, I also want to thank those I've lost but carry in my heart every day: Dorothy Donadelle; my great-uncle, Ernest "Unc" Donadelle; my

Auntie Ruth, Uncle Willis, and Aunt Edna. Thanks also to my friends, near and far: James Weil, Eric Smith, Pearl Alston, Sheri Collins and Kim Bettie. Thank you all for being in my life. I also want to say something about those of us who are living with disabilities. Although our bodies' may betray us, we still have the expanse of our hearts and minds with which to explore the world. Don't let anything keep you from living and loving to the fullest.

Finally, thanks to the wonderful folks at Genesis Press: Deborah, Valerie, Diane, Brian, and Sidney. You are a terrific team and I thank you from the bottom of my heart!

CHAPTER 1

Alicia Archer looked as if she were about to faint under the hot lights on set. *If they don't wrap this up the soufflé won't be the only thing to collapse.* The show was going on hiatus and it was the last of the block of shows she had to tape. If it were any producer other than her best friend Lauren, Alicia would have had their head. A foodie since childhood, having her own lifestyle/cooking show was a dream realized. The heat on the set, however, made it difficult to remember that.

Alicia checked the clock. "How long are the commercials?" she said impatiently. "It must be a thousand degrees in here today."

"You're back in forty-five seconds," Norman, the production assistant, answered.

"Thanks." Alicia dabbed her brow. *Maybe if I weren't in long sleeves and dark slacks I'd be cooler, but I'm the one who came up with this classic image and now I'm paying for it.* She let out a soft sigh.

Hair pulled up in an elegant upsweep, 46-year-old full-figured Alicia looked good in her cotton long-sleeved shirt and slacks. Born in Amityville, New York, Alicia was the older of Walter and Loretta Carlson's two daughters. Her sister Samantha was two years younger and nearly a half foot taller than her five feet, eight inch older sister.

So being a big girl was something Alicia knew about from birth. Her mother Loretta was from a family of big and tall women. Loretta liked to say she had a round butt in a town of square asses and it was a good thing Alicia's father had a thing for circles.

"And we're back in four . . . three . . . two . . . one . . ." The director pointed to Alicia.

"Now that we've completed a perfectly luscious lemon soufflé, all we need to do is garnish it with a little mint." She turned to the camera. "There we go. Doesn't it look great?" She smiled as she picked up a spoon. "Now we'll have a taste." She took a spoonful. "It's lovely, light and best of all, the recipe is on our website."

Norman gave her the wrap-up sign.

"Well, that's all the time we have for today. Thanks so much for joining me, and remember that it doesn't have to be a special occasion for a little everyday elegance."

"And we're out." Simon, the director, clapped.

Alicia made a beeline for the refrigerator, grabbed a chilled bottled of water and drank deeply.

"Is there another one in there?" Norman asked.

She handed him a bottle. "Here you go."

"Thanks. You feel better now?"

"Much better, thanks, Norman." She paused. "It's been a long week."

"Tell me about it."

Alicia looked around. "So where is our erstwhile producer?"

"I'm not sure. Do you want me to page her?"

Alicia checked her watch. "No need. I know where she is." She looked directly into the monitor.

Alicia, Lauren Jules Jones and Gabrielle Blanchard had been friends since ninth grade, when they met at boarding school. Three big girls in a sea of skinny girls, they became fast friends and roommates. But they had more in common than just their size. The girls shared a love of classic romance novels by Jane Austen. On Friday nights the Austen Aristocrats met in the boarding school kitchen, where Alicia got to indulge her passion for cooking while they discussed love and romance with the likes of Jane's Mr. Knightley, Edward Ferrars and, of course, Mr. Darcy. As adults they would go on a quest to find their own romantic heroes and, for a time, Alicia found hers. Lauren, however, was on her third try.

∽

I know that look on Alicia's face is for me, Lauren thought as she crouched in the corner on her cell phone. *So what if I'm on the phone?*

A shooting star producer in the television industry, 46-year-old Lauren Jules Jones was a force to be reckoned with. Born in Bayside, Queens, Lauren was raised by her grandmother. Her father died in a car accident before she was born and her mother decided she couldn't handle life as a single parent. Grandma Lee worked hard to make sure her son's only child grew up well educated. When the opportunity presented itself to get her granddaughter out of Bayside and into a prestigious preparatory school, she made sure Lauren got there.

Miss Porter's Boarding School may have been like life on Mars, but Lauren's grades and academic standing got her a full scholarship to Dartmouth, where she majored in film and media studies.

Upon graduation she earned her stripes doing odd jobs in public television. She caught her first break as an associate producer for a local television station in New York. A friend talked her into leaving the security of local television to become an executive producer for In the Mix Productions, an upstart company that wanted to shed its basic cable roots for national syndication. After she led them to a few industry nominations and a couple of awards, they gave her the green light to sign *Everyday Elegance with Alicia*, which became an instant hit. Now Lauren was light years away from the dowdy, drab, boarding school uniforms and flannel shirts and jeans of Dartmouth. She was a top producer who embraced her curves and cut a sexy and sharp image whenever she entered a room in her designer ensembles. However, while terrific at work, her personal life was another story.

Finding her own Mr. Darcy was a challenge. Twice divorced, her third marriage was to former NFL defensive tackle Kenneth Jones. Ken had never really adjusted to civilian life married to a non-sport mortal. He enjoyed the attention playing for the New York Giants got him, especially from women. Nevertheless, there were benefits to being married to a producer. Lauren helped him land a spot as a commentator on the network's highly popular football program and, combined with his appearances at fan events, Ken wasn't far from the gridiron he loved so much. For a while it had looked as if the third time was finally the charm for Lauren. She and Ken were the golden couple when they appeared at network, charity and sports events. Wherever they went, Ken was bombarded by men seeking autographs and pictures with an NFL great, including many of the buttoned-up network executives she worked with.

Then the New York Giants made Ken an offer he couldn't refuse. They wanted him to be a goodwill ambassador of sorts to their season ticket holders, which meant Ken did a lot more up close and personal meet-and-greets with the fans. Even when the job description expanded to include more travel and later hours Lauren didn't mind. She knew it made him feel as if he were still contributing to the organization. However, when she began to notice more female fans in the mix, she was less comfortable. Ken tried to tell her they were really into football but Lauren knew football groupies when she saw them. While many of them could recite stats, most didn't seem to know a touchdown from a home run. It didn't take long before it got to be a problem between them. Ken reverted back to his bad boy ways and Lauren got tired of keeping better tabs on him than the Secret Service did the president, so they got a legal separation. Still, Lauren held out hope he'd come to his senses despite all evidence to the contrary. "Damn! It's his voice mail again," she muttered as she waited to leave yet another message. "Hi, I'm just confirming dinner tonight at Ricardo's at six thirty. Call me when you get this message." She closed her phone. *God, I hope I didn't sound too anxious. . . .*

"Voice mail again?"

Lauren jumped. "Alicia! You startled me. How long have you been standing there?"

"Long enough," she said as she sat down.

"Wait a minute, how did you get up here so quickly? I just saw you on the monitor."

"Wouldn't you like to know?" She smirked.

Lauren didn't want to hear it from Alicia so she changed the subject. "Are you feeling okay? You looked like you were getting a little hot on the set."

"I was getting overheated, but I'm okay now." She took another sip from her water bottle.

"Are you sure?"

"Yes." Her tone was a little short.

"Don't bite my head off. I'm just asking. You do have MS, and I know what heat does to you."

Alicia got up and quickly shut the door. "Announce it to the whole world, why don't you?"

"The whole world isn't up here. It's just you and me. You have to stop being so paranoid."

"I don't want everyone to know my business."

"I know. I don't understand why you want to be so covert about it. You have MS. You don't have the plague."

"I just want to keep it quiet, okay?"

"Okay. So how are things going?"

"Not bad. I just started a new treatment regimen, so now I give myself an injection every Friday evening."

Lauren winced.

"See why I don't want anyone to know about this? You've known me over thirty years and you're freaked out."

"I'm sorry, but it wasn't about you having MS. You know I don't like needles."

"Neither do I, but what choice do I have? At least we're on hiatus now, so I'll have the summer to get used to this routine while I relax."

"Ha!" Lauren scoffed. "You relax? I give you three days before you start climbing the walls out there in Scarsdale."

"Naturally it won't be total relaxation. I still have magazine, kitchenware and housewares lines to worry about."

Lauren shook her head. "You just said you were going to relax this summer. You're such a workaholic."

"Oh well." Alicia shrugged her shoulders. "Speaking of climbing the walls, did you get Ken?"

Lauren sighed aloud. "No, I didn't get him, but you already knew that."

"Don't get snippy. It was just a question."

"I'm sorry. We're supposed to meet for dinner at Ricardo's tonight."

"Dinner at Ricardo's, I'm impressed. They're usually booked up at least a month or more in advance. How did you manage a reservation?"

"Ken made it. The manager is a big Giants fan."

"I see. Membership does have its privileges."

"Yes, it does." Lauren looked at her phone.

"So what's the occasion?"

"I don't know." She flopped into a chair.

Alicia shook her head.

"Don't give me that look, Alicia."

"What look?" Alicia played innocent.

"The look of disapproval. He's still my husband."

"In name only, Lauren. You've been legally separated for a year now."

"I know, but that's not to say we can't work it out."

"That's exactly what it means, Lauren. You've been to marriage counselors, pastors and therapists galore. Hell, you even saw a rabbi! When are you going to wake up and move on with your life? God knows he has."

"Then why did he call me to have dinner at a romantic restaurant like Ricardo's?"

"You've got me there." She shook her head, puzzled. "I still believe you deserve better than the likes of Kenneth Jones."

"Maybe so, Alicia, but this is my third marriage. I've already struck out twice and I'd rather not be a three-time loser."

"It's the twenty-first century, Lauren. No one is going to make you wear a scarlet 'D3' on your chest. Besides, not wanting to get another divorce isn't a reason to stay married."

"Not everyone is as lucky as you were with the perfect marriage."

"Oh, please, don't start that again. Kurt and I didn't have a perfect marriage. We had our ups and downs like everyone else."

"Well, it always looked like you had more ups than most people."

Alicia couldn't help but smile. "We had a lot of good times together but we liked a good fight, too. It kept things interesting," Alicia said wistfully.

"Does it get easier?"

"There isn't a day that goes by I don't think about him. Some days I smile and other days I cry. So I guess the answer is yes and no."

Kurt Archer had been the love of Alicia's life. He was a tall, skinny, fair-skinned black man with reddish hair and nearly green eyes. When they met at Dartmouth they took an instant dislike to each other. They were complete opposites. Alicia was an economics major who understood she would have to play the game in order to succeed in business. Kurt, on the other hand, majored in environmental studies. He was "green" before it was chic. Alicia thought he was nothing but a tree hugger. Kurt thought she was a corporate raider in training. Her one redeeming quality for him was that she was minoring in creative writing. At least three times a week she and Kurt turned the pavilion dining hall into a debate forum. They said they couldn't stand one another, but no one believed them. Kurt and Alicia were the last two people to figure out they were in love. They married a year after graduation.

Two years later Alicia gave birth to their only child, Kurt Jr., in the idyllic Westchester suburb of Bronxville. At that time Alicia worked as a lifestyle editor and contributor for a major magazine, which allowed her to combine her business and artistic side to create features that entertained while keeping her group on task and under budget. Kurt managed a successful landscape design firm. Life was wonderful until Kurt was diagnosed with pancreatic cancer when Kurt Jr. was a senior in high school. Alicia dropped everything to take care of her husband. She knew Kurt wanted to hang on long enough to see their son graduate and she was determined he'd make it to graduation. Her care through the many pain-filled nights was rewarded when he beamed with pride at graduation as he watched his namesake take his diploma. Unfortunately Kurt didn't live long enough to see his son follow in his footsteps at Dartmouth.

After Kurt's death Alicia didn't fold in on herself. She used her grief to fuel her ambition and moved forward to build her own lifestyle media company, Archer Omnimedia, which included cookbooks, her show *Everyday Elegance with Alicia*, and a magazine of the same name. As CEO she took her company public and became the queen of branding with a kitchenware line in two major store chains. The only kink in the plan came when she was diagnosed with MS two years ago, information she somehow managed to keep from the public, press, her magazine staff and her shareholders. Only a select few knew about her condition and they weren't telling. However, the diagnosis meant more than just a change in Alicia's body. If her friends and family had any glimmer of hope she'd try to find love again, it faded. As far as Alicia was concerned, she'd found her own Mr. Darcy and didn't believe lightning would strike twice, nor did she want it to.

"So how's my godson?"

"He's good."

"Is he excited about grad school?"

"I think so. He has a new girlfriend." Alicia rolled her eyes a little.

"What's wrong with her?"

"Nothing, she's a perfectly nice young lady."

"But . . ." Lauren said.

"She's just blah. There's nothing to her."

"What do you mean?"

"She's not ambitious." Alicia sighed. "She seems content being a legal secretary, even though she has an associate degree in criminal justice." Alicia shook her head.

"So what's wrong with that?"

"Nothing, I guess." Alicia shrugged.

"Not every woman can be as driven as you, Alicia."

"Now if that isn't the pot calling the kettle black."

"Point taken."

"I'm going to leave it alone. It's his life and he loves her just the way she is."

"Now if you'd only follow that advice when it comes to Gabby and me, we'd be set."

Before Alicia could respond 52-year-old Ron Wilder, a slim, brown-skinned man, knocked on the door, out of breath. Ron was one of the executive features editor at *Everyday Elegance With Alicia.*

"Ron? What are you doing here?"

He caught his breath. "I wanted to be sure to get these papers to you." He handed Alicia a folder.

"Thanks, Ron, but you could have messengered them up to the house."

"I know, but I think Barbara needs your signature on them now."

Alicia looked the papers over and signed them. "Here you go." She handed them back to him. "Ron, you know Lauren."

"Oh, hi, Lauren, I didn't see you there."

"Obviously. How are you, Ron?"

"Not bad." He took a deep breath. "I guess I'd better run back to the office. Have a good vacation, boss." He turned to Lauren. "Nice seeing you again, Lauren."

Lauren waved as he dashed out. "You know he has a crush on you, don't you?"

"Don't be silly. He likes Barbara. Why else would he run over here to get papers signed for her?"

"I don't think that's the case, Alicia." Lauren shook her head.

"Stop with your speculating already," she said, grinning. Alicia looked at her watch. "I'd better get going. The car will be here in a minute." She paused. "What are you wearing?"

"Do you really want to know?"

"Of course. I might not like him but that doesn't mean I don't want him to drool over the mere sight of you."

"I'm wearing the Goddess Dress by Abby Z in chocolate brown."

"Nice."

"Are you doing anything special tonight?"

Alicia stood up. "Gabby's supposed to come over for dinner. If things wrap up early you're welcome to join us for dessert and coffee. We haven't had a meeting of the Austen Aristocrats in a while."

"Thank you for the invitation. However, if things go well, dessert is covered tonight."

"Entirely too much information." Alicia kissed her on the cheek. "Tell Ken I said hello."

"You know you don't mean that."

"Of course I do. I'm nothing if not polite. Even if he is a three-timing bastard who doesn't deserve you."

"Alicia."

"Sorry." Alicia knew to back off. "You know I only want the best for you." She kissed Lauren on the cheek again.

"It's a good thing I love you like a sister."

"I know." She waved as she left the production booth.

Lauren stared at her cell phone. *Do I call him again?* "Oh, the hell with it." She dialed the phone.

Just then Norman knocked.

"Lauren?"

"Yeah, Norm." She closed her phone.

"Simon wants to see you on set."

"I'll be right there." *Simon saved me from myself. I need to relax and get ready to go to dinner.*

✑

It had been a long day at the Blanchard Gallery and it showed on Gabrielle's face the moment she sat down on the sofa in her office. A natural blonde with blue eyes, Gabby was a curvy size sixteen and although she looked more like a benefactress than hip gallery owner in her navy blue suit, complete with pearls and an updo to match, she'd made it look sexy all day long. She'd seen fifty up-and-coming artists over two days who were competing to fill a mere fifteen slots for her gallery's annual exhibit of new artists, and she couldn't wait to get some peace.

"Gabby?"

"Yes, Robin?" She pressed the intercom button.

"I have to go into the file room for a few minutes."

"No problem. We're done with artists for the day."

Robin Pope was Gabby's executive assistant of seven years. A beautiful bronze-skinned woman of thirty-four, she was married to a successful architect on the West Side. A graphic designer herself, she'd given it up to take a job that would be more conducive to her ultimate goal, having a baby.

Although she wasn't an artist herself, Gabrielle Blanchard, nicknamed Gabby, had had an appreciation for and love of art since she was a little girl growing up in her family's posh townhouse on the Upper East Side. Yet Gabby was different from the rest of the pretty blonde, reed-thin girls she grew up with. She was always a little more "voluptuous," as her dad put it. Her mother, however, didn't subscribe to her father's terminology or lax attitude about her size. Bunny Blanchard put Gabby on every diet known to man before she shipped her off to Miss Porter's Boarding School in Connecticut, where she met her best friends, Alicia and Lauren. They were big girls, too.

"Ms. Blanchard?" a male voice asked.

Gabby opened her eyes. "Yes?"

Her assistant Robin rushed in. "I'm sorry, Gabby. I told him you were done seeing artists and he snuck back here anyway."

Gabby's eyes focused on the man who'd interrupted her solitude. He was very tall and thin with a rich, dark, cocoa brown complexion, but he didn't fit the usual artist mold. She was used to seeing artists in chic bohemian clothes and not expensive Italian suits.

"Are you representing a new artist?" she asked, puzzled.

He laughed as if he'd heard this question before. "No. I am the artist."

Her assistant Robin looked equally puzzled. "Really?"

"Yes."

Gabby was intrigued. "It's okay, Robin."

"I'll be at my desk if you need me," Robin said as she walked out.

Gabby stood up and straightened out her suit. "So Mr. . . . ?"

"Clark. My name is Nigel Clark."

"It's a pleasure to meet you, Mr. Clark," she said, putting her hand out.

He shook it. "Please call me Nigel."

"Okay, Nigel. You can call me Gabby, but I'm still sorry to say that I've already picked the artists for our exhibit."

"I know I'm late getting here but I would really like you to look at my work. I brought one of my paintings with me."

"I don't know what good it will do. Our next new artists exhibition is next year."

"Maybe so, but I would really like it if you took a look. I've heard terrific things about your gallery, and your reputation for having a good eye for the next big thing precedes you."

Gabby smiled in spite of herself. "Flattery will get you everywhere, Nigel." She picked her glasses up from the desk. "Bring it in."

"Thank you," he said as he left the room.

I hope I don't regret this, she thought, crossing her arms.

The minute he walked through the door, her eyes were drawn to the canvas. It was a scene depicting life in Africa with all its hustle and bustle. Gabby was captivated by the vivid way he captured his subjects with color. The painting spoke to her.

"Is this Cotonou, Benin?"

"Yes." He seemed genuinely surprised she recognized it.

"My ex-husband and I visited West Africa many years ago and Cotonou was one of our stops. It's quite a city. Is that where you're from?"

"No, I was born here. My mother is from Cotonou. She came to the States to study and then she met my father."

"I see. Do you often go back to visit?"

"I used to visit my grandparents every spring but they passed away when I was in college." He sighed. "I can still see the place in my mind."

"I can see that." Gabby pressed the intercom button. "Robin."

"Yes?"

"Call Victor and tell him we have one more artist for the exhibit."

"Okay, but you know he's going to complain."

"Victor complains if it's Tuesday. He'll get over it."

"Okay."

"Thank you." Nigel flashed a megawatt smile.

"You're welcome. Just be sure to see Robin on the way out and she'll give you the details."

He put his hand out. "You won't regret this."

"I'm sure I won't." Gabby leaned back in her chair. "I guess we'll be in touch. I'll see you."

Gabby watched him leave. *He's good looking, talented and charming. He should do well with our patrons, particularly the female ones. He can brush my canvas anytime.* Gabby raised her eyebrow. *This is business, Gabrielle,* she chided herself. *What would Bunny think?*

⟳

The car pulled into the winding driveway of Alicia's little piece of heaven in Scarsdale. At over 4,500 square feet, the stone/stucco Tudor-style home suited Alicia's image, even if it was too much house for her with its six bedrooms, six bathrooms, powder room, gourmet kitchen, pantry and every other amenity imaginable. It was private, sort of, with the exception of the Becker place next door.

Harrison opened the car door. "Hello, Alicia. How did it go today?"

"Not bad. It's hard to believe we're going on hiatus."

He closed the car door. "Time does fly by."

At sixty-four, Harrison Kendall was Alicia's executive personal assistant, which, as far as he was concerned, was a glorified way of saying butler. The only hint of Harrison's age came from his silver hair. He was average height with just a hint of post-middle-age-spread around the middle. He had a tan complexion, which he credited to his Italian mother. Alicia met Harrison and his late wife Martha, who'd had a more progressive form of MS, at her neurologist's office just after her own diagnosis. It didn't take long for them to become fast friends, and, with no children of their own, they treated Alicia like a daughter. When Martha passed away, Alicia invited Harrison to live with her under the guise of being her second set of feet and hands in the house.

They walked into the foyer. "So how are you feeling?"

Alicia looked at her watch. "Wow, you went a whole three minutes before you asked. You're getting better," she said facetiously.

"I know you like to make light of it, Ms. Alicia, but your neurologist did say you need to be mindful of your body and rest every now and then."

"I am resting. We are on hiatus for the summer."

"You know what I mean."

"Of course I do. I'm fine. I promise." As she walked into the living room her right foot dragged a little. She plopped onto the sofa. "That's much better."

Harrison zeroed in on it. "I'll get your cane."

"What for?"

"You're beginning to drag your foot because you're doing too much."

"What am I doing now if it isn't resting? Leave the cane where it is."

Harrison ignored her and took it out of the closet. "I'm leaving it right here for when you get up." He set it next to the sofa.

"Fine. Has my son called?"

"Yes. He's coming up this weekend."

"Great. Is it just him or is she coming, too?"

"Her name is Sally."

"Yes. Sally. Is she coming?"

"He didn't say."

"So there's hope." She grinned.

Harrison shook his head. "No woman is ever good enough for a woman's son."

"You got that right."

"But your late husband's mother loves you."

"That's because I'm special." She smiled as she flipped the television on.

"Your parents called today."

"They did? Why didn't they call the studio or my cell phone? They knew I was at work."

"They're roaming the countryside in that Winnebago you and Samantha bought them."

Her father was a 70-year-old retired schoolteacher and her 69-year-old mother was a retired cafeteria lady. They had been married forty-eight years. While most of their friends had sold their homes to move into expensive retirement communities or down South, they'd stayed in their home in Amityville. Alicia's parents still had quite a bit of zip left in their step and enjoyed being on the move, but they didn't trust the cleanliness of hotels or other people. Therefore a Winnebago seemed the perfect gift to give them the comfort of home while allowing them to have an adventure.

Alicia laughed. "It's what they wanted."

"I know."

"Where were they calling from?"

"They were at the Grand Canyon."

"That sounds nice. I bet they're having a great time."

"They are, but they really called to check on you."

"You told them I'm fine."

"Yes. However I wouldn't be surprised to see their Winnebago pulling into Scarsdale sometime this summer."

Alicia chuckled. "Oh, won't the neighbors love that."

"Oh yes." Harrison picked up her briefcase. "Can I get you anything?"

"Just a seltzer with a twist."

"No problem. What about dinner? I'm planning steaks."

"Good. Gabby's coming for dinner."

"Great. What about Lauren?"

"Lauren is having dinner with Ken at Ricardo's."

Harrison's ears perked up. "Dinner at Ricardo's. Is there something going on you haven't told me?"

"Nope."

"Well, even I know Ricardo's is known for its romantic ambiance. Is reconciliation in the air?"

Alicia shrugged. "Who knows? Your guess is as good as mine."

"I'm asking what you think."

"To tell you the truth I know that's what Lauren wants, but I have a bad feeling about it."

"You don't like Ken."

"No. I don't like him, and I don't think he's the one for Lauren. I've never made any bones about it."

"She loves him."

"The Beatles did say love is all you need. Who knows? Maybe he'll surprise me."

"Maybe." Harrison was about to walk away when he said, "Oh, there is one thing I forgot to tell you."

"What's that?"

"Your favorite neighbor is back in town."

Alicia's face fell. "Why did you have to go and ruin my dinner? When did he get back?"

"I'm not sure exactly. All I know is the parade of women has already begun."

"Great." She hung her head in disgust. "I manage to find a half acre of quiet and it has to be next to Scarsdale's own version of the Playboy mansion."

For any other woman, living next to Dr. Nathaniel Becker would be a treat. A confirmed bachelor at age forty-eight, he was six feet, four inches tall with an athletic build, a full head of wavy dark hair and crystal blue eyes. It also didn't hurt that he came from old WASP money and, though he didn't need to worry about making a living, was an Ivy League educated doctor who was a part of a thriving medical practice in Scarsdale. What wasn't commonly known was his involvement in pediatric AIDS research and Doctors Without Borders, through which he traveled the world helping impoverished communities get the care they needed. He also gave his time to several clinics throughout the five boroughs. Most people, including Alicia, believed he was an international playboy and he did nothing to discourage it. He gave parties and always seemed to have a parade of women in and out of his place whenever he was in town, which annoyed Alicia to no end. So to say he delighted in pulling her chain was an understatement.

Harrison walked back in the living room. "Here you go." He handed her a glass.

"Thanks." She took a sip.

"So what's on the agenda for the Aristocrats tonight?"

"I don't think we're going to have a meeting tonight since it's just Gabby and me."

"You can't fill Lauren in later?"

"No. It's one of the rules we set up for our little club. In order to have a proper meeting of the Austen Aristocrats all three of us have to be there."

"I guess that means you're sort of the charmed ones of classic romantic literature."

"Yes, it's the power of three." She chuckled.

Even though it had been thirty-two years and a few divorces later, they still had meetings, although now they had the added choice of movie DVDs of their favorite author's work.

"Are you going to show the footage from your last trip to England for the next meeting?"

"I was thinking about it. I had a lot of fun touring Austen's stomping grounds."

He chuckled. "You mean The Virgin Suicides Tour."

"Oh, that's not nice. Jane Austen died of Addison's disease."

"She lived in the eighteenth century, same difference."

"You might have a point." She laughed.

He looked at the clock. "I'll go fire up the grill."

"Thanks." *Hopefully this is only a pit stop for Nathaniel. The idea of that man being here for the entire summer is more than I want to think about. . . .*

♋

Dressed to kill, Lauren nursed a martini alone at her table. She checked herself in the reflection of the silver. *Glad I decided to wear my hair down. It looks better with the dress.* She ran her fingers through her dark, shoulder-length hair. Everywhere she looked there were happy couples and groups enjoying the modern yet romantic elegance of Ricardo's. She stared at her cell phone. *Why he hasn't he called? Where is he?*

The waiter interrupted her thoughts. "May I get you something else?"

"No." She picked up the menu. "I'm sure my husband will be along soon and then we'll order together."

"Very good." He walked away.

Lauren continued to stare at the entrance, hoping to see Ken walk through the door.

"Pardon me?"

She looked up to see a nicely attired gentleman standing next to her table. He was tall, broad-shouldered, with dark good looks. In fact, he was just the type of man she usually was attracted to, but she was in no mood to be hit on.

"May I buy you another drink?"

"No, thank you, I'm waiting for someone."

"Okay then. How about an appetizer while you wait?"

Is this guy for real? "Listen, I'm waiting for my husband."

He smiled. "And I will extend the same offer to him. I'm Randy Rivera. This is my restaurant."

Lauren turned red. "Oh, I'm sorry. I thought you were . . ."

"Trying to pick you up? Not at all, although you are a very attractive woman."

"Thanks." She paused. "Aren't you the executive chef, too?"

"Guilty. I'm usually behind the scenes, but the manager called in, so I'm front of the house tonight. Speaking of being a good host, may I ask your name?"

"I'm Lauren Jones."

"It's very nice to meet you, Lauren Jones." They shook hands. "So how about that drink?"

"Why not? I'll have another pomegranate martini."

"You got it." He called the waiter over. "She'll have another one of these."

"No problem." The waiter scurried away.

"Do you mind if I have a seat?"

"Please do."

"Thanks." The minute he sat down, he looked as if he'd taken a load off. "I thought it was tough being on my feet in the kitchen, but the front of house is no picnic either."

The waiter brought her martini back.

"Thank you." She took another sip. "It's good."

There was awkward silence between them.

"Are you hungry? We have the best tapas."

"I know."

The sound of a little commotion grabbed their attention.

"I wonder what's going on," Randy said as he strained to see.

There was Ken signing autographs with a group of people around him. At six feet, five inches and 275 pounds it was hard not to miss him, surrounded by fans or not.

"It looks like my husband is here." She beamed.

"You're married to Kenneth Jones? I'm a big fan of his. He's one of my favorite defensive tackles."

"Mine, too."

Randy stood up as Ken approached. "Mr. Jones, I'm a big fan."

"Thanks." He smiled and shook his hand. Kenneth looked good in his custom-made Armani suit. He bent over and kissed Lauren on the cheek. "You look great, babe. Is that a new dress?"

"Thanks, and as a matter of fact, it is new. You like it?"

"It looks great on you."

Randy held the chair for Ken. "Can I get you something from the bar, Mr. Jones?"

"I'll have a scotch, neat."

"Coming right up. I hope you two have a pleasant evening. Enjoy."

"Thank you." Lauren grinned like a schoolgirl.

Randy walked away. A minute later the waiter returned with Ken's drink.

Ken took a gulp and set the glass down. "You look good, Lauren."

"You already said that but I won't complain."

Ken fidgeted in his seat.

Lauren found it endearing. "What's the matter, Kenneth? You look as nervous as you did on our first date."

"Do I?"

"Yes. It was cute then and it's still cute." She sipped her martini.

Ken rubbed his forehead. "I guess there's no easy way to do this."

"Easy way to do what?"

He reached into his pocket, pulled out an envelope and put it in front of her on the table.

"What's this?"

"Divorce papers."

Lauren's heart fell. "What?"

"It's been a year since the legal separation and now I'd like to proceed with the divorce." He waited for a response from Lauren, but she was dumbfounded. "All the terms are still the same. You can have the apartment lock, stock, and barrel. You don't have to buy me out. I think that's only fair."

"Do you?" she asked, still stunned.

"Yes. We had our moments but it didn't work out. I have no hard feelings."

"So what is it you want in return?"

"It's in the papers." He pointed to the envelope.

"I don't want to look at the damn papers, Kenneth, just tell me." She tried to control her anger.

"All you have to do is sign off on the no spousal support clause and we're done."

"That's stated in the prenup agreement I signed before we got married."

"You know how lawyers are. They have to prove they're earning their fee." He gave her a weak smile.

Lauren tore open the envelope and unfolded the document. "Do you have a pen?"

"Don't you want to read it?"

"You're kidding me, right? It's obvious you invited me to this romantic setting so I wouldn't make a scene. Well, you're getting your wish. Give me a damn pen before I change my mind and start bucking for the cover of the *New York Post.*"

Ken handed her a pen.

Lauren quickly signed it and threw the pen down. "Are you happy now?"

"Of course I'm not happy. My lawyer told me to use a process server but I thought you deserved to hear it from me directly."

"Why? So you could see my humiliation up close and personal?"

"No. Maybe I shouldn't have asked you here." He put the envelope in his jacket.

"You think?" she asked sarcastically. "You're a real piece of work, Kenneth."

That was Ken's cue to get up. "I'm sorry. I know you don't believe me but it's the truth. Dinner is on me tonight."

"That's the least you can do." Lauren felt herself choking up.

When Ken tried to kiss her on the cheek, she turned away. "I am sorry, Lauren. You're a great lady. You deserve better than me." He walked away.

Lauren sat in stunned silence. *How could I have been so stupid? I'm such a fool.*

Randy walked over. "Will your husband be coming back to order?"

"No, I'm afraid not. You're stuck with little old me."

Although he didn't know her personally, Randy could see something was different. "Is everything okay?"

She gulped down her martini. "Everything's just fine. Can I get another one of these?"

"Sure." He stopped a waitress who was carrying a tray of martinis and took one off. "Just get another one for your table and tell them this round is on the house."

"Okay, boss."

"Here you go."

"Now that's what I call service." She took a big gulp.

"How about some appetizers, something to wash it down?" He smiled.

"You're the chef. I'll follow your lead."

He called the waiter back over. "Trey, we'll have the *pincho de datiles* and *patatas bravas.*

"Don't forget another martini. I'm almost finished with this one." Lauren was beginning to get a buzz.

"Yes, bring her another drink and a seltzer with a twist."

"I'll have you know I can handle a few martinis. I'm not a 110-pound model who gets drunk from fumes. I'm a big girl, in case you haven't noticed."

"All I see is a beautiful woman who deserves to have a good time. The seltzer is for me. I'm still working."

She smiled.

"Now that's more like it."

"Don't you have to run your restaurant? You shouldn't be babysitting patrons."

"What's the point of being the boss if I can't switch it up every now and then? Someone else will just have to take over my duties for a little while."

"If you say so."

"Are you staying for dinner?"

Lauren looked at her watch. "Sure. I don't have any place to go, except for my apartment." Her martini buzz was fast becoming a martini haze. "I'll have you know I have a great big three-bedroom apartment and it's all mine."

"Terrific."

"It was a real bargain, too. You know what it cost me?"

"No, I don't."

"My dignity, that's all. It doesn't get any cheaper than that."

Trey brought the drinks back.

Randy raised his glass. "Here's to you and what I hope is a new friendship."

They put their glasses together. "Cheers," Lauren said as she sipped her martini. *Here's hoping the martinis can cover my humiliation or at least get me drunk enough so I don't notice it anymore. Ken may be retired, but he still knows how to get a quality sack. I didn't see it coming.*

CHAPTER 2

Seated at the island in her kitchen, Alicia chopped vegetables for the salad, while Harrison set the table in the atrium. Gabby decided to go for a little walk on the grounds before dinner.

"Has the sorbet set?"

"I made it yesterday. It should be fine."

Suddenly Gabby burst into the kitchen from the backyard, out of breath. "Oh my God!"

Alicia was alarmed. "What's wrong, Gabby? What happened?"

Gabby collected herself. "Dogs. I just saw two of the biggest rottweilers I've ever seen in my life."

"Dogs? On my property?"

Harrison looked up. "Nathaniel has two dogs."

Alicia looked disgusted. "I'm not home one day yet and he's already terrorizing the neighborhood." She got up and took her apron off.

"Where are you going?" Harrison asked.

"I'm going to get a leash."

"Don't you mean two leashes?" Gabby asked, puzzled.

"No, I mean one leash. It's not for the dogs." She picked up her cane.

"The dogs are still on the loose, Alicia," Harrison warned.

"I know, but my cane is pretty heavy."

"You're taking your cane outside?" Harrison asked pointedly.

"No. I'd like to, though." She put it back.

"The dogs didn't chase me. They just scared me, that's all," Gabby noted.

"Don't worry, Gabby, if I did take my cane outside, the dogs wouldn't be my target." She walked out the glass door and made a beeline for Nathaniel's.

Nathaniel put the dogs on their leashes as Alicia walked over.

"Better late than never, I guess, Mr. Becker."

Alicia and Nathaniel made a game of referring to one another by their surnames, which definitely had a certain *Pride and Prejudice* quality to it that didn't go unnoticed by Alicia.

"Well, if it isn't Scarsdale's own diva of domesticity. How nice to see you, Ms. Archer."

"I'd like to say the same, except you've managed to scare my company to death with your dogs."

"Rocky and Bull? They wouldn't hurt a fly. They're just stretching their legs."

"Mr. Becker, they're rottweilers, not lap dogs, and they scare the crap out of people."

"Why Ms. Archer, such language. What would your viewers think?"

"Grow up!" she huffed.

He chuckled.

"Do me a favor and use the leash." She looked him over. "And don't forget one for yourself."

"Nice return, Ms. Archer."

"By the way, what brings you back to Scarsdale this summer? I thought you preferred summering in some European or Mediterranean hideaway."

"I'm not exactly an expatriate, Ms. Archer. I do enjoy living in the good old USA."

"I see. I guess you were caught diddling someone's wife or girlfriend in international waters and decided to lay low." She snickered.

"You wound me, Ms. Archer." He feigned being shot in the heart.

"Oh please, Mr. Becker, you don't have a heart, remember? That's what you told me. Or did you pick one up in the duty-free shop on the way back to the States?"

"Still as sharp as ever, Ms. Archer. You know it turns me on when you mix just the right amount of reserve, disdain and raw animal attraction," he said seductively.

Alicia shook her head in disgust. "You're incorrigible." She turned on her heel. "Just remember to keep the dogs away from my property."

"So does that mean they can't cool off in your pool?" he called after her.

"Put a sock in it, Mr. Becker," she called back.

Smiling, Nathaniel watched her as she stormed back to her house.

A minute later, she was back in the kitchen. "The man is a menace."

"He really gets under your skin, doesn't he?"

"The man is a Neanderthal, Gabby."

"I see."

"What do you see?"

"Why are you getting so testy? I'm just saying . . ."

"I've known you since we were fourteen so I know that tone. You might as well say it."

"I seem to remember another Neanderthal that got under your skin."

"Oh, no, you don't. Kurt wasn't anything like this guy."

" 'Methinks the lady doth protest too much,' that's all I'm saying. Am I right, Harrison?"

"Leave me out of it."

"Smart man, Harrison."

"That's okay, Harrison, I've got your back. Alicia knows she married the last man who got under her skin like this."

"Enough already." Alicia was clearly vexed. "Let's change the subject, shall we?"

"Fine with me."

"How's your Fifteen to Watch new artist exhibit and reception coming along?"

"It's coming along, and this year there will be Sixteen to Watch."

"Sixteen?"

"Yes."

"You know Victor's going to throw a fit."

Interior designer Victor Long had worked with Gabby on setting up the gallery from its inception and was involved in staging every exhibition within an inch of total perfection. At forty-one he was one of the most sought-after interior designers in New York. Victor was a combination of *Project Runway's* Tim Gunn and Michael Kors and *Flipping Out's* Jeff Lewis. Most people needed half a Xanax just to speak with him over the phone.

"I know. He'll get over it," Gabby said dismissively.

"Must have been some painting."

"It was." Gabby had a little twinkle in her eye.

"Scratch that. It looks like the artist caught your attention more than the work."

"Why would you say that?"

"It's written all over your face."

"Shouldn't you be checking on the steaks or something?"

"Harrison, would you do the honors for me?"

"No problem." He went outside to the grill.

"We're covered. Now spill it."

"There's nothing to tell. His name is Nigel Clark and he brought a canvas he'd painted of West African street life in a port city."

"Uh-huh. What did this Mr. Clark look like?"

Gabby looked lost in thought for a minute. "He was tall, muscular and clean shaven. He came in dressed to impress in an expensive Italian suit, which kind of threw me for a loop, since I'm used to more Bohemian-looking artists."

"I see he made an impression on you."

"The painting was amazing," she protested.

"So was the painting tattooed on his head or something?"

"Don't be silly."

"He was cute." Alicia winked.

Harrison came back in with the steaks. "All done."

"Terrific. Saved by the dinner bell." Gabby was relieved.

"Aren't you lucky?" Alicia handed her the salad bowl. "Can you put this on the table, please?"

Gabby placed the bowl on the table and then Harrison seated them.

"The steaks look and smell divine. Too bad Lauren isn't here."

"Don't feel too bad for her. She's having dinner at Ricardo's."

"Wow. I've heard good things about that place. Getting a reservation is a bear, though. How did she manage one?"

"Ken got it. It's one of the perks of being a former NFL player."

"Do you think he wants to get back together?"

"To be honest I don't think so, but I could be wrong." Alicia sipped her water.

Gabby picked up her bag and began rifling through it.

"What are you looking for?"

"My calendar. I want to mark the day Alicia Archer said she could be wrong."

"Ha, ha. I'm not that bad."

"I'm just teasing you."

Harrison put his fork down. "So which movie is it going to be, ladies? *Pride and Prejudice, Sense and Sensibility, Mansfield Park* or *Emma*?"

"Lauren isn't here. Should we watch a movie?" Gabby asked.

"I suppose it wouldn't hurt."

Gabby looked at Harrison. "You must think we're pathetic," she laughed.

"No, not at all."

"And even if he did think we're pathetic, he wouldn't tell us. Isn't that right, Harrison?"

"I plead the fifth."

"You're batting a thousand tonight." Alicia smiled.

"You'd think that now that we have the money, power and, dare I say it, the celebrity, we'd be out partying every weekend to make up for all the weekends we spent pouring over Austen novels in high school. Yet even though the digs are way better than the dorms, we're still nerds sitting at home on a Friday night."

"Well, at least one of us is out having a good time." Alicia lifted her glass. "Here's to Lauren. I hope she's having fun."

✑

Lauren quickly threw all her clothes on the floor and wrapped her arms around Randy's neck as he lifted her onto the bed. Her body pulsated with anticipation as he lowered his body onto hers. She wrapped her legs around him and their bodies began to rock. Her inhibitions were released and they made feverish love over and over throughout the night. Lauren was having fun. Whether she'd remember it in the morning was another matter entirely.

CHAPTER 3

It was early Saturday morning and Alicia was already doing laps in the pool. Although never a hardcore exercise person before being diagnosed with MS, Alicia hadn't sat around on her butt doing nothing, either. She'd practiced yoga, pilates and tai chi. Now she modified them for her condition. Luckily for her she didn't have to change her other physical activities, walking and swimming. Swimming was Alicia's favorite form of exercise. There was an indoor pool in town for the colder months, but the idea of wearing a bathing suit in front of that many people had never appealed to her. Besides, Alicia reveled in the time she spent swimming in her own pool far away from prying eyes.

As Harrison sat in a lounge chair nearby as the de facto lifeguard on duty, Nathaniel walked over.

"Good morning, Harry, my man."

He looked up. "Good morning, Nate. What has you up this early on a Saturday morning?"

"I took Rocky and Bull for a walk. Don't worry, they were on a leash." He studied the pool more closely. "I see the lady of the manor is taking a dip this morning."

"Yes."

"I didn't think she was allowed to take her clothes off." He chuckled.

Harrison didn't answer.

Nathaniel watched for a few minutes. "Wow. How many laps does she do?"

"Sixteen. She does four laps each of the breast stroke, butterfly, back stroke and freestyle."

"Impressive."

Before Nathaniel could get another word out Alicia emerged from the pool in a red crisscross one-piece suit with a little retro sweetheart neckline that showed off her assets nicely in a "less is much more" way. Nathaniel couldn't take his eyes off her.

Harrison handed her a towel and she covered up quickly.

"Thanks. Good morning, Mr. Becker."

He was still speechless.

"Mr. Becker? One of your rottweilers got your tongue?"

"No, I just assumed you swam fully clothed."

Harrison cleared his throat to keep from laughing. Alicia glared at him.

"Very funny," she said dryly.

Harrison composed himself. "Will Kurt be joining us for breakfast?"

"I'm not sure. He didn't say what time he was coming up."

"How is your son? I haven't seen him in ages."

"He's great. Thanks for asking."

"Maybe I'll see him around."

"Maybe." She paused. "Okay, Harrison, I think we should let Mr. Becker get back to whatever."

"I wasn't doing anything."

"Well, I wouldn't fret. It's Saturday. I'm sure one of your playmates will show up once the morning cartoon shows wrap up."

Covering his mouth, Harrison chuckled.

"Touché." Nathaniel smiled.

Satisfied that she'd gotten the last word, Alicia turned toward the house. "I'd better get going if I want to be ready when Kurt gets here. Have a nice day, Mr. Becker."

"You too, Ms. Archer. I'll see you around, Harry."

"Later, Nate."

Harrison was close behind Alicia as she headed inside.

"Is Lauren coming over today?" Harrison asked as he opened the sliding doors.

"I doubt it. If she had her way she's in the midst of a long love hangover."

❧

The morning sun shone on Lauren's face and she slowly opened her eyes. "Oh, it hurts to blink," she groaned as she shielded her eyes. The night before was a blur with the exception of her massive headache. *If I never hear the words "pomegranate martini" again it will be too soon. God, my head is pounding.* As she began to scan her bedroom, she noticed her clothes were strewn about.

She sat up slightly. "What the devil?" She looked under the covers and discovered she was nude. *I never sleep in the buff.* A feeling of dread came over her. *What did I do? Oh, my God!* Lauren panicked. "Get it together, girl," she said aloud. *I was drunk. I probably just took my clothes off and crawled into bed, that's all,* she rationalized.

"You're up."

Lauren grabbed the covers. "Yeah. I'm up." She tried to play it off.

Randy had a tray in his hands. "How's your head feel?"

"It feels like it weighs a ton." She fidgeted. *Oh, my God. I can't believe I have to play it cool like I'm not totally freaked out he's here.*

"Four pomegranate martinis will do that to you. Try this. It might help."

She looked at the tray with eggs Benedict with hollandaise, Canadian bacon, whole-wheat toast and orange juice. "You made all of this? I didn't think I had anything for a PB & J sandwich, let alone all of this."

"You didn't have anything in the kitchen. I made a couple of calls for ingredients and voila, I made breakfast." He put the tray down on her lap.

"Thank you. It beats hair of the dog."

"Those hangover cures never work. The best thing to do is to eat. Eggs contain an amino acid called cysteine, which steps up liver function and will help your body to break down the alcohol toxins faster."

"Wow. You're a regular *Iron Chef* meets *Good Eats* meets Bill Nye, the science guy." She smiled.

He laughed. "Maybe so. I learned all about hangover cures in culinary school."

"So you were a party guy in college."

"Let's just say I was a very popular quarters player in those days."

She laughed, even though her head still hurt. "You make it sound like a lifetime ago."

"Now that I'm over forty it seems like it."

"You're only as old as you feel." She grabbed her head. "Oh boy," she groaned.

"Eat your eggs before they get cold."

Lauren relaxed enough to eat, but not so much that it loosened the sheet wrapped around her.

He looked at his watch. "I'd better get going. I've got to head to the restaurant."

"Okay. Thanks again for breakfast. It's great."

"I'm glad. Just so you know, I cleaned up after myself in the kitchen."

"That's really nice of you but if you didn't notice, my kitchen doesn't get much use."

"This from the producer of a cooking/lifestyle show," he joked.

"Alicia is the one with the apron."

He smiled.

Maybe nothing happened last night after all, she began to think.

He came closer to her. "Pardon me for a minute." He put the tray on the floor and then he leaned over and kissed her. A jolt of electricity surged through her body and curled her toes. There was no doubt she and Randy had done more than exchange recipes the night before. "I'll call you later."

"Mmm hmm," she muttered, still in shock.

The sound of the door closing unlocked Lauren's memory of the night before. She remembered how it felt to run her hands from Randy's broad shoulders to the small of his back, the feel of his lips as he kissed every inch of her skin. Her heart pounded at the memory of the two of them locked in seamless pure passion. "Oh, my God, not only did I sleep with him, it was amazing!" She stopped to think. "Now what happens?" She finished her gourmet breakfast and headed for the bathroom. She planned to answer that question, but she wouldn't do it alone.

❦

Gabby was already out and about on Saturday morning to check out some of New York's street artists who displayed their talents in and around Central Park. Dressed casually in jeans and a denim shirt with her blonde hair in a ponytail, she strolled leisurely through the outdoor gallery of artists without a thought to time or schedules. It was a far cry from the way she used to spend her weekends.

Once upon a time she had been a busy wife and mother splitting her weekends between her son Ian's lacrosse matches, daughter Lizzie's equestrian events and husband Bill Van Essen's busy social calendar. For all appearances the Van Essen family was the epitome of an upscale Norman Rockwell painting. When Gabby met Bill he was an intern at her father's advertising firm. Bill was a Nordic god with his tall, trim build, blue eyes and blond hair. After he worked up the nerve to ask the boss's daughter out, they dated for a little less than a year before he popped the question. Her mother Bunny was over the moon, thinking that Gabby had hit the jackpot. Bill had the right pedigree and his family was connected. However, while the Van Essen family represented an old money name, the family's fortune had gone the way of the horse and buggy two generations prior, so it was Bill who hit pay dirt.

After a lavish wedding with a veritable who's who of the social register, Bill became an associate at the agency, and Gabby put her art history degree on the shelf to raise a family on Long Island's north shore. To everyone it appeared they had a lock on the perfect life. But life inside of the bubble was far different. Although Bill eventually earned a partnership in the firm, his role at the firm was that of the schmoozer; he wined, dined and got potential clients to sign on the dotted line, usually with his beautiful wife on his arm. A lot of women would have enjoyed being a part of their husband's business life, but Gabby always felt that she was trapped in a sixties time warp, where women were expected to look the part of the perfect mate and never open their mouths.

Gabby struggled not to gain weight so she could be the perfect Barbie to Bill's Ken. Even though Gabby liked her curvy body, they had an image to uphold as the golden couple. Despite their carefully maintained façade, eventually she and Bill grew apart and lived separate lives that only intersected for the children's sake. Once Lizzie went off to Dartmouth, Bill announced he wasn't in love anymore. Yet in spite of this declaration he was still very much in love with the lifestyle being married to a

Blanchard afforded him. Unfortunately for Bill, the Blanchard family attorneys made sure he was a lot less comfortable.

On the positive side the divorce allowed Gabby to start her life anew at forty-plus. She sold her place on Long Island, bought an Upper East Side townhouse and put her art degree and the cache of her maiden name to good use as the curator of the Blanchard Gallery. Best of all and much to her mother's chagrin, she got her voluptuous size sixteen body back, along with the freedom to do what she pleased on her Saturday mornings.

"Gabby?"

Surprised to hear her name, Gabby turned around.

It was Nigel Clark and he wasn't wearing an Italian suit. He looked quite yummy in jeans and a fitted Polo shirt that drew attention to his toned arms and chest.

"Nigel. How nice to see you again." They shook hands.

"Fancy meeting you here, Gabby. Are you out looking for undiscovered talent?"

"Sort of," she said as she brushed her bangs from her eyes. "I like to get out of the gallery to see how new artists are pushing the boundaries."

He seemed impressed. "That's nice to hear."

"Not all of us live in an ivory gallery," she said jokingly.

He laughed. "Do you mind if I join you?"

"Not at all."

They started walking together.

"So you're in my exhibition but I don't know much about you. Tell me a little about yourself."

He paused for a moment. "I'm not sure there's that much to tell."

"Humor me." She smiled like a schoolgirl.

"Well, for starters I'm an investment banker at Longford and Lowe."

"Wow." *Color me surprised.*

"Does that make me a bit strange?"

"Actually, it makes you an anomaly. Most of my artists take the starving part quite literally."

"If it hadn't have been for my parents, I might be one of them, too."

"How did they feel about art?"

"They didn't have any problems with me picking up a brush, but they told me I'd better have a day job to buy my supplies."

"Smart people, your parents."

"I know. What about you? What's your medium?"

"I wish I had the kind of talent it takes to create art." She paused. "You know the saying those who can, do, those who can't, teach?"

"Yes."

"In my case it's those who can't do either help those who can."

"Your eye for talented artists is reflected in the gallery."

"I chose you, didn't I?" She grinned.

"While I believe that attests to your good taste," he joked, "the fact is I've been to several exhibitions and I've always felt that way about your gallery."

How in the hell did I miss him? "Thank you, Nigel."

They were coming upon another row of artists. "It looks like we've hit the mother lode. Do you mind if I continue with you?"

"Not at all."

The two went off at a leisurely pace until they were engulfed by a sea of people, only they didn't seem to notice. It was as if they were the only two people in the world, which was pretty amazing, considering they were in the middle of Central Park on a beautiful Saturday.

CHAPTER 4

Harrison finished setting the table for lunch while Alicia finished making one of Kurt's favorite dishes, seafood jambalaya.

Harrison took a whiff. "Mmm, it smells good in here."

"Thanks." She looked at the clock. "Kurt should be here any time now."

Before he could open his mouth, the doorbell rang. Besides his father's good looks, Kurt had also inherited his knack for losing keys. Alicia had given him several keys over the years and he'd managed to lose every set. So he rang the bell like any other guest.

"I rest my case." She smiled as she removed her apron. "Just a minute!" She rushed to the door. There stood Kurt Jr., a carbon copy of his father with his light skin, soft curly hair and bright green eyes. At six feet, five inches, he towered over Alicia.

"Hey there, gorgeous." She lit up.

"Hey, Mom." He hugged her.

"I'm so glad you're here." Alicia had her eyes closed and imagined him as a baby for a moment.

"Is that jambalaya I smell?"

Alicia grinned. *As tall as he is, he's still my baby.* "Yes, it is."

"You didn't have to make anything special for me, Mom." He put his arm around her and they began walking to the kitchen.

"I didn't. I just happened to have the ingredients in the house."

"If you believe that I have a bridge in Brooklyn to sell you," Harrison piped in.

"Hey, Mr. H." They hugged. "I guess Mom had you running to the store."

"Yes, but I was happy to do it. You know your mom loves to spoil you."

"Ahem. I am still in the room."

"We know, Mom." He kissed her cheek. "I'm glad I didn't eat breakfast." He rubbed his stomach.

"Now you know you shouldn't skip breakfast. It's the most important meal of the day."

"I know, Mom. But I was in a hurry this morning."

"I'll let it go this time."

Lunch was already on the table when they walked into the dining room. Alicia was tickled to have Kurt home and even more tickled that he had a second and third helping of jambalaya.

Finally full, Kurt pushed his plate away. "I think I've had enough."

"Are you sure, sweetie? I made a ton."

"She's not kidding," Harrison said as he sipped his soda.

"I'll take some home with me. I know Sally loves Creole-style food."

Alicia's good feeling deflated slightly but she tried to cover with a grin. "Oh, sure. How is Sally?"

"She's good, Mom."

"Still working in Garden City?"

"Yes, Mom." Kurt knew that tone all too well. "She's still not going back to school."

"Did I say anything?" She tried to sound innocent.

"You don't have to, Mom. I'm your child, remember."

"I know."

"She's happy working in her firm, and I support her decision, just like she supports my decision to go to grad school."

Harrison got up to clear the table to escape the line of fire.

"Okay, Kurt, you made your point."

"Thank you. So how are you feeling, Mom?"

"I'm good. I did laps in the pool this morning."

"Great. What happened on your last visit to the neurologist?"

Alicia was surprised he knew of her visit. "Harrison!"

"Don't blame him, Mom. I'm your son. I want to know, and I should know what's going on with you."

"Everything is fine. He started me on Avonex. It's only one injection a week as opposed to the others, which were every other day and every day. This fits into my life a little better."

He winced. "You have to give yourself a shot? Are you okay with that?"

"Yes. The nurse showed me how to do it."

"Are there any side effects?"

"They say I might have flu-like symptoms for a couple of days, but so far I've been fine."

"What about stress and working too much?"

"Good grief, Kurt, are you asking questions or interrogating me?"

"I want to know. Did he tell you to take it easy?"

Kurt knew his mother was a workaholic.

"I'm on hiatus for the next eight weeks. I promise I'll relax."

"And let Taylor Dawes do her job as managing editor of your magazine, right?"

"Of course." She crossed her fingers under the table.

"Did you hear that, Mr. H?"

"Yes, I did."

"I have a witness and I'm going to hold you to that."

"Fine," she grumbled.

"I want you to relax and have some fun, Mom. Maybe even go out on a date."

"A date?"

"Yes, Mom. In case you don't remember, a date is where a man asks you out and you go and have a good time together."

"Don't be a smart ass. I know what a date is."

"When's the last time you went on a date?"

"What kind of question is that to ask your mother?"

"It's a fair question. I'm not a kid anymore, Mom, and you need to date."

"No, dear child of mine. I need to eat, drink water and breathe. I don't think dating qualifies as a need."

"You're avoiding the question." He was getting impatient.

"That's because the answer is she hasn't been on a date, period," Harrison chimed in.

"Were we talking to you, Harrison?"

"No, but it's the truth."

"Now that's a shame. You're still a young woman."

Alicia grinned. "Listen to how cute you are." She got up and kissed him on the cheek. "I got my Mr. Darcy when I married your dad."

"I know, Mom, but I'm sure Dad would want you to find someone and be happy."

"I am happy. I was lucky enough to marry the love of my life, and even though he's gone I can still see him in you. What more could I want or need?"

"Game, set and match, Mom. How am I supposed to answer that?" He looked down at his cell phone. "I have a text here from Sally. Listen, Mom, I think my phone is about to die. Can I use yours to see what's happening?"

"Sure."

"Thanks." He got up and left the room.

Harrison waited until it was clear. "What kind of BS are you handing your son?"

"Excuse me?"

"You know what I mean. Why don't you tell him the real reason you're not dating?"

"I just did."

"We both know that's not the whole reason."

"Leave it alone, Harrison."

"Why? Why are you so scared?"

"What am I supposed to tell him? Should I tell him I'm scared to date because I'm diseased?"

"Don't say that."

"It's the truth. I don't want the people who work with me to know I have MS. How can I possibly start dating?"

"Martha had MS, too, and I didn't run away. I loved her completely, no matter what."

"I know. But you were already together when she was diagnosed. I mean, what's the proper etiquette on when to tell someone you have a chronic disease with no cure? Is it the third date or the fifth date? Frankly, I'd rather not call Emily Post. I'll take a pass."

"You're taking a pass on life, you know."

Kurt Jr. walked back in.

"Everything okay, honey?"

"Yes." He looked at Harrison and Alicia. "Did something happen while I was on the phone?"

"No. Everything is fine," Alicia lied.

The doorbell rang.

"Were you expecting anyone else today?" Harrison asked as he headed for the door.

"No."

A minute later Lauren walked in.

"Hey, Auntie Lauren. How are you?" Kurt got up and hugged her.

"Kurt, it's good to see you." She kissed his cheek. "Let me look at you." She smiled. "You're still as handsome as ever."

"Oh, Auntie, you have to say that, you're my god-mother."

"No, I don't. It just happens to be the truth."

"What brings you over today? I wasn't expecting to see you," Alicia said.

"Can't I just pop by? Do I need a reason to see my best friend?" She sat down.

"Of course you don't need a reason. Except you look like you just flew out of your house and past all mirrors."

"Excuse me? Are you saying I'm a mess?"

"No, you look fine." She came closer. "But there is something up. Are you hung over?"

Lauren seemed shocked Alicia was so dead on, but she tried to play it off. "I may have had one too many martinis, but I'm fine."

Lauren could see from the expression on Alicia's face that she wasn't buying it.

"Can I talk to you in my office, Lauren?" She stood up.

"Why?"

"Okay. Would you rather I continue in front of Harrison and Kurt?"

"No." She got up.

"Be strong, Lauren," Harrison said.

"I'm not going to the principal's office, Harrison."

She and Lauren left the kitchen.

"Your mother has that look on her face. Whether or not Lauren knows it, she really is going to the principal's office."

"Glad it's not me." Kurt grinned.

"Me, too."

As soon as Alicia closed her office door, Lauren flopped onto the sofa.

"Okay, we're alone now. What's really going on?" Alicia looked her over carefully. "You look like hell."

"Thanks."

"Sorry, but you do. What happened to you?"

Lauren looked down at the floor to keep from seeing Alicia's expression once the words were in the air. "You want the long or short version?"

"I'll take either. Get to the point."

"Ken invited me to Ricardo's and served me with divorce papers. Is that to the point enough for you?"

Eyes wide and mouth agape, Alicia flopped onto the sofa next to Lauren. "That son of a bitch . . ."

"I know."

"Well, you weren't on page six this morning, so I know you didn't make a scene. What did you do?"

"I signed the divorce papers. What else could I do?"

"You could have told him what a piece of . . ."

"What good would that have done me? Besides, aren't you the one who always tells me I deserve better than him?"

"I knew he didn't deserve you. Still, he could have handled this better. What was the point of taking you to a romantic restaurant?"

"He said he didn't want to use a process server. He felt he needed to deliver the papers in person."

"What a jackass," Alicia fumed. "If he was worried about your feelings, he should have come to the apartment and handed them to you privately."

"It's water under the bridge now." She sighed heavily.

"What did you do after you signed the papers?"

"I stayed and had a pomegranate martini to numb the pain."

"From the looks of your eyes I'd say you had several martinis."

"I lost count after four."

"Whoa." Alicia was taken aback. "Why didn't you call me instead of drinking alone? I would have come."

"Who says I was alone?"

"Oh, excuse me. Who was your drinking buddy?"

"Randy Rivera."

Alicia's eye's lit up. "Randy Rivera? As in the owner and executive chef of Ricardo's?"

"Yes, but he wasn't exactly my drinking buddy. He kept me company."

"That was nice of him."

"He's a nice guy."

"So how did you get home? You obviously didn't drive."

"I think Randy drove me."

"You think he drove you home?"

"I did have a few martinis. Last night is a little fuzzy." *There is no way she's buying this.*

"Is that right?" Alicia asked suspiciously. "Look at me."

"What?" Lauren started to fidget.

"Oh, there is far more to this story than you're telling me and don't deny it."

"There's nothing else to tell." She wouldn't look at Alicia.

"Oh, yes there is. I've known you for thirty-two years, Lauren, and whenever you're lying or avoiding something, you get fidgety. And right now you look like a Mexican jumping bean. What gives?"

Lauren put her hands over her face. "I can't even look at you."

"Why? What did you do? Sleep with the guy?"

She didn't say a word.

"You slept with him?" she asked excitedly.

"Keep it down. My head still hurts."

Alicia started laughing. "That's why you came rushing up here, you naughty little girl."

"Stop it, Alicia, I feel bad enough."

"You feel bad about the hangover or getting it on with the chef?"

"Stop making fun of me. I'm still a married woman."

"Oh please, give me a break! Ken handed you divorce papers and you've been separated for a year now."

Lauren sank down on the sofa.

"So?"

"What?"

Alicia nudged her. "You know what I'm asking."

"No, Ms. Prim and Proper, I'm going to make you say it."

"So how was it?"

"You're not going to ask me what he looked like or anything?"

"No, I've seen Randy Rivera's picture before. I know he's gorgeous. But I want to know if he curled your toes."

"Stop that, Alicia. You are so silly." She laughed.

"Well, did he?"

Lauren's mind flashed back to his lips on her stomach. She fanned herself.

"It looks to me like he curled more than your toes."

"It was really good." Lauren couldn't contain herself.

"Oh, wow," Alicia playfully punched her in the arm.

"Ouch."

"It's just like my grandmother used to say. The best way to get over a man is to get under another one."

"Ms. Archer, your grandmother, said stuff like that?"

"Oh, yes, my father's mother was a real character. She was completely ahead of her time. But she didn't talk to me like that. I used to stay up to listen to her on the phone with her friends."

"She may have had a point." Lauren stopped to think. "But now it's the light of day and who knows what Randy thinks now."

"Did he sneak out before you woke up?"

"No. He stayed and made me breakfast to help my hangover."

"He made you breakfast in your kitchen?" Alicia was shocked.

Lauren rolled her eyes. "If you must know, he made some calls to get some provisions."

"I bet he did. Your kitchen is practically a museum."

"Very funny," she said dryly.

"It's the truth." Alicia leaned in. "So how did you leave things?"

"He kissed me and said he'd call me later."

"That's promising. He didn't exactly blow you off."

"I don't remember if I gave him my number. Hell, I didn't remember I slept with him until he kissed me good-bye."

"And it all came flooding back, did it?"

"Oh, yes." Lauren relished the thought.

"If it was that good, Lauren, I'm sure he has your number."

"Then why haven't I heard from him yet?"

"He's a guy. I know it's been a while since I dated but I'm pretty sure guy time hasn't changed much. They never call when you think they should."

"You're right about that."

"Do yourself a favor and stop sweating it. He'll call. It hasn't been that long, and he does have a restaurant to run."

"True," she sighed.

"Did you call Gabby?"

"I tried to call her on the way over here but she didn't pick up. I halfway expected to see her here."

"It's Saturday. This is her day to check out the latest works from some of Central Park's finest street artisans. We'll probably hear from her later."

"Right."

Alicia stood up. "Are you hanging out here for a while?"

"Yes. I'd like to catch up with my godson and maybe have some of that jambalaya." She stood up.

"Be my guest."

Lauren looked a little worried for a moment.

"Don't worry, your new little love muffin will call," Alicia teased as she opened the door.

"Oh, you are never going to let this go, are you?"

"Are you kidding? This is way too good," Alicia said devilishly.

"You know, you really need your own love life."

"Why? When I can have more fun living vicariously between you and Gabby, it's all the drama I need."

CHAPTER 5

After a morning of artist watching, Gabby and Nigel got a couple of ice cream sundaes and found an empty bench.

"Now this is what I call a great lunch choice," Nigel grinned.

"Yes. I'm happy to say I have three of the basic food groups, cream, sugar and chocolate."

"Here, here." They toasted with their sundae cups.

Gabby looked around the park. "Now this is what I love about Central Park. Where else can you dine a la carte and still get the best seat in the house?"

"True." He had another spoonful of ice cream. "So is this how you always spend your weekends?"

"It is for the last four years since my divorce. Before that my weekends were all about my family's activities, especially my children."

"How many children do you have?"

"Two. My son, Ian, and my daughter, Lizzie."

"A perfect set. How old are they?"

"Ian's twenty-three and he's in NYU Law. Lizzie's twenty-one and she just graduated from Dartmouth with a degree in English."

"You don't look old enough to have children in grad school."

Gabby blushed. "Thank you, but my birth certificate would beg to differ."

"What type of law is your son thinking of going into?"

"He's been talking about environmental law and civil rights law a lot. I'm not sure which one he's leaning toward these days, but I know he's going to be an amazing lawyer."

"I know it sounds like an oxymoron, but both fields could use more good attorneys."

She laughed.

"What about your daughter?"

"She's traveling through Europe with her friends for the summer before she begins teaching ninth grade English in the city this fall while she goes to grad school for her certification."

"Oh, that's great. The city can use as many teachers as it can get."

"I think so, too. Her grandmother, on the other hand, is completely mortified at the idea of a Blanchard teaching in an inner city school."

"Really?"

"Oh yes, but my mother is from a different generation. She went to college to find an eligible husband. The degree was secondary."

"Is that how it was for you?"

"No. I wanted to do something with my art history degree, and then I got married after college and the rest, as they say, is history." She reflected for a moment. "That's enough about me. Do you have any children?"

"I have a fourteen-year-old son, Nigel Jr. He lives in Chicago with my ex."

"Fourteen, I remember that age. How long have you been divorced?"

"His mother and I weren't married."

"Oh, I'm sorry. I just assumed when you said ex . . ."

"No harm done. We were going to get married, but it didn't work out."

"Sorry."

"Don't be. She married a nice guy and everyone gets along."

"You're a regular Bruce, Demi and Ashton." She grinned.

"I wouldn't go that far." He laughed. "That's a little strange."

"I agree."

He looked down at his watch. "I didn't realize the time. I have an appointment in about an hour."

"Oh, don't let me keep you."

"You're not. I really enjoyed it."

"Me, too."

They got up and began walking.

"How did you get here? Can I hail a cab for you?"

"Thank you, that would be great. You have an appointment, so would you like to share a cab?"

"No, that's okay. My appointment isn't too far from here. I can walk."

"Oh, all right."

They walked toward the entrance to the park.

"Before you go I'd like to ask you something."

"Sure."

"Would it be inappropriate for me to ask you to dinner?"

"No. Why?"

"I am showing at your gallery. Some people might think it's a conflict of interest."

"It wouldn't be. I added you to the exhibit based on your artwork before we had this pleasant little afternoon."

"Good. Then would you like to have dinner with me tomorrow evening?"

"I'd love to."

"Great. Shall we meet, or would it be okay to pick you up?"

Gabby was tickled. "You can pick me up." She rifled through her bag to get her notebook to write down her address. "Here you go." She handed him the paper.

"Thanks." He studied it for a moment. "If you could write down your telephone number, too, that would be great. In case I run late with traffic or something."

"Oh, sure, how silly of me." She took the paper and jotted down both her numbers.

She handed him the paper again. "Thanks."

"No problem."

He turned and flagged a cab down, then opened the door. "Here you go, Gabby."

"Thank you. I guess I'll see you tomorrow."

"Yes. I'll be there around six if that's okay with you."

"Yes, that's fine." She got into the cab.

He leaned down. "So I'll see you."

"I'm looking forward to it." She waved as the cab pulled away. Contented, Gabby settled in for the ride home.

∽

Despite the 86-degree reading on the thermometer, Alicia and Lauren relaxed on the chaise lounges with a glass of lemonade, while Kurt tried to get some color a little closer to the pool.

"Are you sure you have enough sunblock on?" Alicia called.

"I'm fine, Mom," Kurt said, exasperated.

"Leave him alone, Alicia. He's a grown man."

"I know. But do you remember how quickly his father burned? Kurt's got skin just like him."

"Kurt was the only black person I've ever seen turn into a lobster in under ten minutes."

"Exactly."

"For God's sake, Alicia, you gave him SPF 50 and that's essentially long sleeves in a tube. I think he's good."

Just then a Frisbee flew into the yard, followed by a topless blonde.

"Sorry." She waved and ran back to Nathaniel's yard.

Alicia sat up and felt her forehead. "I don't think I have heatstroke. That was a topless woman that just ran in my yard, right?"

"Yes. I'm surprised they allow such things in uptight Scarsdale. But that can only mean one thing, naughty Nate's back in town," she sang.

"Don't remind me." Alicia groaned. "Mr. Becker is up to his usual shenanigans."

"Listen to you with all this Mr. Becker stuff."

"That's his name."

"His name is Nathaniel Becker, and most of us call him Nate."

"So what? He calls me Ms. Archer."

Lauren shook her head. "You don't see it, do you?"

"What don't I see?"

"The sexual tension between you two. You can practically cut it with a knife."

Alicia burst out laughing. "That is completely ridiculous. We can't stand each other."

"There's a thin line between love and hate, Ms. Archer."

"Put a sock in it, Lauren," Alicia warned.

Lauren continued undaunted. "What's wrong with Nate? He's successful, educated and God knows he's not hard to look at, in case you haven't noticed."

"In case you haven't noticed, I seem to be living next to the Westchester version of the Playboy mansion. He's got women coming in and out of there at all times of the night and day. It's a wonder he has the time or energy to practice medicine."

Just then a volleyball bounced into the yard and two topless women came over to retrieve it. They waved at Kurt. He waved back and turned to Alicia. "Mom, I didn't know you had a semi-nudist colony next door," he joked.

"It would appear so." She huffed and turned to Lauren. "I rest my case."

Ten minutes later the volleyball rolled over again and this time Nathaniel was behind it.

Alicia leaped up. "Mr. Becker!" she called as she walked toward him.

He smiled. "Good afternoon, Ms. Archer. It's a lovely day, isn't it?"

"It was. Are you holding the games for the topless Olympics?"

"We're just having a little outdoor fun. Care to join us?"

"No, thank you. Where are their tops?"

"In the house, I guess."

"I'd appreciate if they'd put them on if they're going to come into my yard. I prefer not to see so much silicone after lunch. It spoils my digestion."

"What makes you think they're not the real thing?"

"Come now, Mr. Becker, you're a doctor."

"I'm interested to hear your take on why you think the boobs aren't real."

"I don't know, maybe gravity for one thing. With the way they're scampering about, real boobs would have at the very least bruised their chins, put an eye out or caused them some other kind of discomfort."

Nathaniel chuckled. "I guess I can't argue the point."

"Thank you."

He looked over and saw Kurt. "Are you sure it's a problem? I'm positive your son didn't mind." He walked away from her. "Excuse me, I'm going to say hello."

"You leave my son out of this." She was on his heels.

"Hey, Kurt."

Kurt sat up. "Hey, Nate." They shook hands.

"How are you?"

"Good. I'm starting grad school in the fall."

"Cool." He nodded. "Your mother tells me you're bothered by my guests coming over here."

"They don't bother me."

"Kurt!"

"I've seen topless women before, Mom. It's no big deal."

"What!"

"That's not an image you want to leave your mother with, Kurt," Lauren said loudly.

"Hey, Lauren." Nathaniel waved.

"Hey, Nate." She leaned back in the chair.

"Kurt, while I appreciate your open-mindedness, I will try to keep the scampering to a minimum."

"Thank you," Alicia said.

Nathaniel looked over at the sliding doors and saw Harrison carrying a tray. "Here comes Harry with some more lemonade for you and your guests, Ms. Archer. Why don't you have a glass and cool off?"

She made a face.

"Enjoy the day, everyone." He turned and walked back to his bevy of still-topless beauties.

Alicia shook her head in disgust. "God help me! I'm living next to a booby wonderland." She sat back down in her chair while Harrison refilled her glass. "Thanks, Harrison." She took a long sip. "Not a word, Lauren!" she warned.

"What did I say? I didn't say a thing."

"No, but I can hear you thinking."

"Well, as long as I'm going to get in trouble for thinking it, I might as well say it. He really gets under your skin."

"You see what I have to deal with. The man has no couth."

Kurt walked over to get some lemonade. "Nate's a fun guy."

"In a *Penthouse* kind of way," Alicia scoffed.

"It's obvious he likes you, Alicia. Why else would he take the time to bother you?"

"You should see the way he looks at her when she turns her back," Harrison interjected.

"I've seen it, too, Harrison," Lauren agreed.

"What kind of conversation is this to have in front of my child?"

"I'm not a kid, Mom. Besides, I think he likes you, too."

"Don't be silly. Nathaniel Becker has his hands full with nubile twenty-something women keeping him busy."

"So you've thought about it," Lauren teased.

"I've done no such thing."

"Maybe he's just passing time with these young things until you come around," Harrison said.

"Are all of you suffering from heatstroke?"

Lauren's cell phone rang.

"I think you like him, Alicia."

"I think your cell phone is ringing, Lauren."

She jumped and then rifled through her bag for the phone. "Hello?"

"Hi." It was Randy's voice.

"Hi," she said breathlessly.

Alicia looked at her watch. "Not bad for boy time."

Lauren started to walk away. "Can you hold for a second?"

"Sure" he answered.

"I'm going to take this in your office."

"Be my guest."

"By the way, you're not off the hook. I'll be back." Lauren walked away.

"Take your time," she called after her.

Kurt sat in the chair next to her. "There is something between you and Nate."

"The sparks always fly when they're around each other," Harrison said casually.

"Stop encouraging him. There is nothing between Nathaniel Becker and me but a shared property line."

"If you say so, Mom."

"I do." She turned to Harrison. "Harrison, can you bring those lemon drop cookies out for me, please."

Kurt's eyes lit up. Lemon drop cookies were his favorite. "You made the lemon drop cookies?"

"Yes."

He jumped up. "I'll get them."

"They're in the white cookie jar."

"All right." He ran into the house.

Harrison clapped. "You are something else, Alicia. You got him off the subject and onto lemon cookies."

"What can I say? I'm his mother and no matter how old he is, he still loves it when Mommy makes cookies." She sipped her lemonade.

❧

Seated comfortably at Alicia's desk, Lauren nearly bubbled over with enthusiasm. "So how are you, Randy?" She could hear the bustling kitchen in the background.

"I was about to ask you the same thing. How's your head?"

"Better, thank you. Breakfast helped a lot."

"Good. I hope something else helped, too," he said suggestively.

She felt a little hot. "It did."

"That's nice to hear." He paused. "I know this is a little backwards, considering, but I wanted to know if you'd like to have dinner with me tonight?"

"Tonight?" Her ears perked up. "What time?"

"Is eight o'clock okay?"

She looked at the clock. "Sure. That gives me enough time to get back to the city and get ready."

"Oh, listen, if it's too much trouble we can make it another night."

"No. It's not a problem."

"I'll pick you up at eight then?"

"Yes."

"Great, I'm looking forward to it."

"Me, too. I'll see you then." She hung up.

Lauren felt light as a feather as she walked from the office to the kitchen. Alicia, Harrison and Kurt were having cookies at the table.

"Hot date?" Alicia winked.

"As a matter of fact I do have a date, which means I need to get going." She picked up her bag.

"Wait up, Auntie. I'll walk out with you. It's getting late and I'd better get back."

"You're leaving me, too?" Alicia asked sweetly.

He got up and kissed Alicia. "I'll come back soon, Mom." He paused. "You know, the road goes both ways. You can visit me."

"Now that I'm on hiatus and at home for a little, I will."

Kurt looked at her in disbelief. "I'll believe it when you pull into the driveway."

"You're on."

Harrison got up and handed Kurt a bag of take-home goodies. "Here, take this home with you. Maybe Sally would like to try your Mom's jambalaya, too."

"Thanks, Mr. H." He kissed his mom again. "Remember to take it easy."

"I will."

Kurt walked out with Harrison.

Alicia turned to Lauren. "Don't forget to call me. I want to hear all the details, unless of course you're otherwise occupied." She had a glint in her eye.

"A dirty mind is a terrible thing to waste, Alicia," she said drolly.

"But it's mine to waste. Have a good time."

"Thanks." She kissed her on the cheek and headed out.

She met up with Harrison and Kurt in the driveway.

"You have a good time tonight, Lauren. I'll keep working on her majesty in there." He kissed her and hugged Kurt before he went back inside.

Kurt opened Lauren's car door. "Here you go, Auntie."

She mussed up his hair. "You're still such a good boy," she said as she got into the car.

He closed her door. "Thanks. Maybe you can help with my mom, too. It kills me to think of her alone."

"I'll do my best. You know how stubborn she is. However, I can promise you that Gabby and I will tag-team her."

"Thanks, Auntie. Have a good time tonight. Drive safe."

"I will." She put the car in gear.

∽

Gabby sat at her kitchen table going through photos she'd taken of the artists she and Nigel had seen earlier in the day. She couldn't help but smile when she came across a photo of her and Nigel one of the artists had taken for them. "He is cute," she said softly.

"Do you need something, Ms. Blanchard?" Rosie, Gabby's petite brunette maid, entered the room.

"No, Rosie. I'm fine."

"Very good, ma'am."

The phone rang. Rosie answered and handed it to her. "Hello?"

"Hey there. You've been awfully quiet today. How's it going?" Alicia lay back on her bed.

"Hey, Alicia, I'm good."

"Did you find the next big thing in art?"

"I wouldn't say that, though I did see some good stuff."

Her happy tone made Alicia smile. "I can hear you grinning. What's up?"

"How can you hear someone grin?" she asked, incredulous.

"It's just the way you sound. You always have that little lilt in your voice when you smile."

"We have known each other a long time, haven't we?"

"Yes. Now spill the beans."

"I ran into Nigel in the park."

"It must have been kismet at work. I mean, what are the chances you'd run into him in Central Park? That is where you were, right?"

"Yes."

"Go on."

"We spent the morning and some of the afternoon together, talking, looking at artists . . ."

"Did you have lunch?"

"Not exactly. We had a couple of ice cream sundaes."

"Sounds sweet. No pun intended."

"We had fun and the time flew by."

"It always does when you're having fun, my dear. So how did you leave things?"

"We're having dinner tomorrow night."

"Fantastic," she exclaimed. "Hmm, there must be something in the air this summer."

"What do you mean?"

"I take it you haven't spoken to Lauren."

"No. What's going on? Did she and Ken get back together?"

"Hardly. He served her with divorce papers."

"What? How is she?"

"She's fine. In fact, I'd venture to say she's as right as rain."

"Am I missing something?"

"She met someone who took her mind off Ken Jones."

"Who did she meet?"

"Randy Rivera."

"He's the chef owner of Ricardo's, isn't he?"

"Yes."

"Wow. Tell me more."

"I've already told you too much. Give Lauren a call and let her fill in the rest of the details for you."

"You can bet I will, now that you've whetted my appetite."

"But you're going to have to wait until tomorrow to call her. She has a date with Chef Rivera tonight."

"What a difference twenty-four hours makes."

"I know. The same goes for you, too. Nigel certainly doesn't sound like the usual hair club rejects your mother tries to pawn off on you."

Bunny Blanchard's second mission in life was to find another appropriate suitor for her only daughter. Bunny had taken the divorce harder than Gabby or even her grandchildren did. She mostly wanted to save face amongst her friends, so she set Gabby up with their

boring-as-melba-toast sons, much to her daughter's chagrin. Gabby was sure that Nigel wouldn't pass muster
with Bunny, but as far as she was concerned, he passed
with flying colors with her and that's what mattered.

"Thank God." She paused. "You know, he might
even be a little younger than me."

"Oh, you naughty little cougar," Alicia teased.

Gabby laughed.

"All kidding aside, I am happy for you."

"Thanks. You know you can get in on this action, too."

"Are you proposing a *ménage a trois*, Gabby? I'm
shocked," she said facetiously.

"Ha, ha, very funny. You know what, or should I say
who, I'm talking about."

"If you say Nathaniel Becker, I'll scream."

"Then go ahead and scream because I don't think he's
all that bad." She sighed. "Do you want to be single for
the rest of your life?"

"I'm a widow, remember? I'm not exactly an old maid."

"I know, Alicia. Still it would be nice to have
someone to snuggle up to at night."

"As Emma said, 'It is only poverty that makes celibacy
contemptible. A single woman of good fortune is always
respectable.' In other words, I have all I need to keep me
happy."

"I still think you'd be happier with Nate."

"Why does everyone assume he likes me? The man
goes out of his way to antagonize me."

"Right. Why would he bother if he didn't feel something for you? Besides, he is cute."

She relented. "I'll give him that. He has all his own hair, teeth and he's in pretty good shape."

"Sounds like the perfect man to me."

"I already met and married my perfect man."

"I loved Kurt, too, Alicia, but I'm sure he wouldn't want to see you cooped up in an ivory tower for the rest of your life. He'd want you to move on. Besides, if I remember correctly, despite her proclamation of being a single woman of good fortune, Emma wound up marrying Mr. Knightley. Isn't that right?"

"You know how much I hate it when you use Jane against me."

"I'm not so much using it against you as I am trying to make a point. I know you've got your media empire, but would it hurt to have love in your life?"

"I do have love in my life. I've got Kurt Jr., Harrison, Lauren, my parents and you. What more could a girl ask for?"

"You're impossible."

"You love me anyway."

"God help us." Gabby heard the doorbell ring and glanced at her watch. "Who in the world would come by now?"

"What's going on?"

"Someone just rang the doorbell."

"Were you expecting anyone?"

"No."

A minute later she heard Victor's distinctive voice.

"Oh, boy," she sighed. "Victor is here."

"Oh, dear, I'd better let you go see what has his silk boxers in a knot tonight. Good luck."

"Thanks. I'm going to need it. I'll talk to you later."

"Okay, baby."

Gabby hung up and made her way to the foyer where Rosie was trying to calm Victor down.

"Ms. Blanchard." Rosie looked relieved.

"It's okay, Rosie. I'm here."

"Thank you." She took off.

"Hello, Victor. What brings you by, besides getting another chance to terrorize my maid?"

At five feet, six inches and dressed like a chic preppy in a polo shirt and Dockers, Victor didn't look like a diva until he put his hands on his hips. "For one thing, you can tell me why you're making my life miserable."

"How am I making your life miserable?"

"I spent all day at the gallery trying to figure out how to stage the exhibit now that you've upset the balance of the universe."

She looked at him. "I've upset the balance of the *universe?*"

"Okay, you've upset my universe. I've done my feng shui and I finally have the perfect flow of fifteen. Then you go and add one more."

"Come now, Victor, it's not like I added twenty more. It's one artist and we have the space."

"That's not the point."

"Then tell me what the point is?"

He stopped to think.

"I'm waiting." Gabby tapped her feet.

"Okay. So there isn't a problem. I just wanted to register my complaint. We have been doing the future fifteen for six years or something, you know."

"I know, Victor, but we can embrace change, can't we?" She put her arm around his shoulder.

"You know, whenever you do that I never know whether you're going to kill me or hug me. You must be at least four inches taller than me."

"I'm four and a half inches taller than you," she corrected.

"I stand corrected. No pun intended."

She began walking him to the door. "Victor, you have plenty of time to pull it together and make it fabulous like only you can."

"Are you playing to my ego?"

"Yes. Is it working?"

"Yes."

"I'm glad we've come to an understanding."

"Me, too," he said as he opened the door. "Wait a second." He bent down and picked up a bouquet of roses. "Look what I found."

"Was that here before?"

"No, I think I would have noticed. It's a huge bouquet." He handed her the flowers. "There's a card."

The heady fragrance of the flowers overwhelmed her senses. "They're intoxicating." She opened the card.

Looking forward to tomorrow night. Nigel.

Gabby felt herself blush.

Victor was intrigued. "Oh, was it X-rated?"

"No. It was sweet."

"It smells like romance is in the air this summer."

"Indeed it is, Victor, and I for one am going to take as many deep breaths as possible." She beamed.

∽

Lauren had gone through the contents of her closet without coming to a decision. She flopped onto her bed. "What am I going to wear?" She let out a heavy sigh. "There's only one thing to do." She picked up the phone.

Alicia was working on her laptop, surrounded by reports. "Hello?"

"Help me, Alicia. I don't know what to wear." She sounded desperate.

"You're kidding me, right? What time is he picking you up?"

"Eight o'clock."

Alicia looked at the clock. "It's almost seven-thirty. You're cutting it close. Please tell me you have your makeup on."

"I do."

Alicia was quiet for a moment. "What about that IGIGI outfit with the georgette blouse and pencil skirt? I think that would be sexy and romantic."

The light went on over Lauren's head. "I completely forgot I'd ordered it. I must have blown right by it."

"You have a sickness when it comes to clothes, Lauren. How is it you can't remember what you just bought?"

"I know." Lauren looked over at her closet, which was as large as one of her guest bedrooms.

"Are you set now?"

"Yes. Thank you."

"You're welcome. Call me later."

"I will." She hung up and got dressed in a hurry. By 7:52 she waited in the living room, dressed to thrill. The intercom buzzed.

"Yes?"

"Ms. Jones, I have a Mr. Rivera here for you. Shall I send him up?"

"Yes. Thank you, Bo."

She got up and checked out her reflection in the mirror. *Should I give my hair a little shake?* She examined it carefully. *Why not?* Lauren gave it a little shake, then looked at her work. "Not bad." She smiled.

The doorbell rang.

When she opened it, there stood Randy in a beautiful chocolate brown suit that complemented his butterscotch skin tone to perfection. He looked good enough to eat and Lauren was hungry.

"*Buenos dias.* You look wonderful."

"Thank you. So do you."

He put his arm out. "Shall we?"

"Yes." She took his arm and they walked to the elevator. "I'm curious. Where does a chef go for dinner?"

The elevator opened and they walked in. "That, my dear, is a surprise." He smiled as the doors closed.

Half an hour later they were seated in at AOC L'aile ou la Cuisse, an adorable little bistro in Greenwich Village.

"What do you think?"

"It's a nice place." Lauren looked around at the comfortable, homey décor.

"The food is very good here."

"Do you know the chef?" she asked before she sipped her water.

"Yes. He's a good guy."

She opened the menu. "All right then, what do you recommend?"

He opened the menu, too. "Let's see." He studied the contents. "There are a lot of good choices here. What do you feel like?"

"I know we're in a French restaurant, but I'm in the mood for pasta."

"Ah, great minds think alike. They have some terrific pasta, with a French flair of course."

"Of course."

"How do you feel about *pasta du sud?* It's fresh pasta with green olives, a fresh tomato sauce with basil, and Reggiano parmesan cheese. It's good and it's perfect for a light summer dinner."

"Mmm, you sold me."

The waiter came over. "*Bonjour.* May I start you with something to drink from the bar?"

Lauren made a face. "I think I'll stick to mineral water with a twist tonight."

Randy laughed. "You can make that two."

"Wonderful. Are you ready to order or would you like me to bring your beverages first?"

"We're ready to order. We're both having the *pasta du sud.*" He handed him the menu.

"Very good, sir, I'll be back with your beverages."

"By the way, is Rafael in tonight?"

"No, he was here earlier."

"I'm sorry I missed him. Please tell him Randy asked for him."

"I will." He walked away.

He reached across the table and took Lauren's hand in his. "I've been thinking about you all day."

"You have?" Her heart fluttered.

"Oh, yes. I was distracted the whole day, which isn't good when you're working around hot pots and sharp knives."

She rubbed his hand. "It looks like you're still intact."

The waiter brought the beverages back.

"Thank you," Randy said.

"This is a good time to get to know each other better now that we have our land legs, so to speak." She stopped to sip her beverage.

"Indeed it is, especially without the pomegranate haze."

Lauren was embarrassed. "I'm so sorry about that. I don't usually drink that much."

"It's okay. Under the circumstances you were justified."

"Yes, it's not every day you become a three-time loser at love." She looked away.

"It was their loss."

"Thanks."

He looked around. "Are you sure Ken isn't going to come in here and tackle me for saying that?"

She laughed. "You're safe, believe me. Ken and I have been over for a while. Last night finally put a period on it and ended the story."

"I'm sorry."

"Don't be, it's okay." She exhaled.

"On that note we'll change the subject."

"Good. Tell me a little more about you."

"My father's from Puerto Rico. He and my mother met while he was vacationing in Madrid, Spain."

"That sounds romantic."

"I guess it was. After a whirlwind courtship they married and settled in Madrid. We moved to America when I was four."

"Wow." She sighed dreamily. "Spain is one of my favorite countries. It must have been a little bit of a culture shock for your mother."

"My father said she was homesick for a while, but we lived in one of Manhattan's many colorful neighborhoods and she made friends easily."

"Oh, that's good. Were your parents in the restaurant business?"

"Not exactly. My father owned a small produce market, but he always had specialty items from Spain, Puerto Rico and the Caribbean so people could bring a little of their homeland to their American kitchens."

"He was a good businessman. Does he still have the store?"

"No. He sold it a few years ago. He and my mother moved to Miami. They're really happy there."

"They're enjoying their golden years."

"It's more like their platinum years. My father made a killing when he sold the store." He laughed.

"Good for him."

He sipped his water. "So you've been to Spain."

"I fell in love with it during the Olympics in Barcelona."

He laughed. "I went to the Olympics in 1992. Or I should say I worked them as a chef."

"You did?"

"Yes. It was a part of a culinary exchange program between the restaurant I worked for and its sister in Barcelona." He paused. "The experience really reconnected me with my culinary roots."

"That sounds profound."

"It was. You see, I spent every other summer in Spain. My parents would send my older brother Thomas and me to visit our grandparents. That's where I found my love for cooking and Spanish food. I'd spend hours in the kitchen cooking with my grandmother, and then my grandfather would teach me about grapes and wine making."

"Did you work in your father's store?"

"I did. My father taught me how to choose the best produce, and I can haggle with the best of them. I guess I was destined to go into food. I was lucky to have found my passion early in life. But I will tell you I thought I'd lost it after years of breaking my neck in countless restaurants trying to make a name for myself."

"So the Olympics re-lit your torch." She regretted the sentence the moment it left her lips. "Sorry, that was totally corny."

"That's okay, I appreciated the effort." He chuckled.

"Thanks." She sipped her water. "So did you go to culinary school in the States or Europe?"

"I went to the Hyde Park, New York, campus of the Culinary Institute of America."

"That's great. A lot of terrific chefs and personalities graduated from that school."

"I know. I graduated with some of them."

"Really, anyone I know?" Her curiosity was piqued.

"I went to school at the same time as Michael Chiarello and Todd English, even though they were ahead me. Then there was Rocco DiSpirito, but he graduated a couple of years after I did."

"Those are some really big names. Did you know them well?"

"We spoke and everyone was really friendly in spite of the 'me-ism' of the eighties."

Lauren was taken off guard by the mention of the eighties. "When did you graduate?"

"In 1984. Why?"

"No reason. I thought I was older than you."

"When did you graduate?"

"The same year."

"We're both forty-six years young." He winked.

"I like the way that sounds."

"Okay, now it's my turn to ask the questions."

"All right, shoot."

"Are you a native New Yorker?"

"As a matter of fact I am. I grew up in Bayside, Queens. I'm a bridge-and-tunnel girl."

"Does that mean you're a Mets fan, too?"

"I don't really follow baseball, but I'm a traitor. I like the Yankees."

"Me, too." He paused. "You said last night you were in television."

Lauren nodded as she tried to recall their conversation.

He chuckled softly. "I take it our conversation was bathed in pomegranate."

"I'm sorry, but it was. I don't remember much of what we talked about last night. I could have told you I was the queen of England."

"That's all right. You'll just have to take my word for it." He paused. "But I have to ask, is everything from last night a hazy memory?"

"Not everything." She smiled knowingly.

"That's good to know," he said, satisfied. "To get back on track, were you always interested in a career in the media?"

"Yes, although I never wanted to be in front of the camera. To me the real power and action was behind the scenes."

"That's why you became a producer."

"Exactly."

The waiter returned with their dinner. "Here you go, *madame et monsieur*." He put the plates down. "Careful, the plates are hot. *Bon appetite*."

"Thank you." Lauren inhaled the aroma. "This smells wonderful."

"Dig in."

She curled the pasta around her fork and took a bite. "Oh, this is heavenly."

"I told you the French were pretty good at pasta."

"I'm a convert." She smiled.

They ate quietly for a few minutes.

"So continue with your journey to successful television producer."

Lauren put her fork down and wiped her mouth. "I don't know if there's much more to tell. I majored in film and television studies at Dartmouth, and after I graduated I got a job in public television as a lowly gopher, but it helped me learned the ins and outs of producing."

"You went to Dartmouth. That's a long way from Bayside, Queens. It must have been a culture shock."

"I suppose it would have been if I hadn't gone to Miss Porter's Boarding School in Connecticut for high school. After four years there I was ready for anything."

"Connecticut? That's practically another country."

"You have no idea how right you are." She picked up her fork again.

They continued eating until they both finished.

"This was a real treat. Thank you, Randy."

"You're welcome, but the night is not over yet. There is still dessert." He raised his eyebrows.

Lauren felt warm. "I don't know if I have any room for dessert."

"Then we'll share." He picked up the dessert menu. "Let's see. The chocolate mousse is incredible, although the Belgian chocolate gelato gives it a run for its money. Do you like gelato?"

"Yes."

"Good." He called the waiter over.

As the waiter cleared the table, he asked, "Would you like to order dessert?"

"Yes. We'll have the Belgian chocolate gelato with two spoons, please."

"Very good, sir. I'll be back with your dessert momentarily."

"Thank you." Randy reached over and took Lauren's hand in his again.

"How are you enjoying life on the other side of the kitchen tonight?"

His eyes locked on hers. "I love it."

The waiter returned with dessert. "Here you are." He handed them two spoons. "Enjoy."

They each raised their spoon. "Here's to more nights on the other side," he said.

"I second that."

They toasted with their spoons before digging in. It was obvious that dessert time was far from over.

❧

A little while later Lauren and Randy were locked in an ardent embrace outside her apartment door. Keys in hand, Lauren struggled to get the key in the door.

Randy pulled away and put his hand over hers. "Allow me." He opened the door.

A moment later they continued where they'd left off.

Lauren could barely breathe as he kissed her neck and shoulders. "Oh, my," she said breathlessly. Her body trembled as he slowly undid her blouse while never missing an inch of her skin with his lips until he reached her breasts. Soon her blouse and bra were on the floor. He reached around to the back of her dress and unzipped it so that it joined her blouse on the floor. He stood back to admire her. "You're so beautiful."

Although she was touched she felt a little shy. Even though they'd been together before, she put her hands over her chest.

"Let me see all of you."

Slowly she lowered her hands to the side and he took his tie and shirt off. His body was firm and chiseled. Lauren was wracked with anticipation.

"You're all mine and I'm all yours tonight." He lifted her up into his arms and carried her to the bedroom.

Randy laid her on the bed and lowered himself onto her for a kiss. Before she could wrap her arms around him, he worked his lips and tongue down her body until he reached her stomach. Then he purposefully removed her last barrier and tossed the panties on the floor. Lauren could hear her heart pounding in her ears as he removed his pants. He was as lean and muscular as a thoroughbred. Soon their bodies came together as one. The passion Lauren thought she'd lost in her life was there, pulsating through every inch of her being.

A little later Lauren had her head on Randy's chest while he gently stroked her shoulders. All the noise that usually filled her head about work and her failed relationships had vanished. She was content to live in the moment and not worry about what was to come.

"What's the going rate for thoughts these days?" Randy asked.

"Considering what the dollar's worth right now, I think a penny for thoughts still works."

He quietly chuckled. "A penny for your thoughts."

"I was just thinking how nice it feels to be in the moment."

"Me, too," he sighed. "It's nice not worrying about what's going on with the restaurant all the time. Don't get me wrong, I love what I do, but sometimes I need a break."

"I hear that." She rubbed his chest. "This is nice."

"Yes, it is." He stroked her hair. "I could get used to this."

"Me, too."

As soon as their eyes locked they kissed again. It was going to be a busy night.

CHAPTER 6

Although she hosted a nationally syndicated lifestyle show and was the creator/editor-in-chief of a wildly successful magazine, Alicia didn't consider herself to be a real celebrity in the classic sense. She didn't have an entourage, didn't fret about the paparazzi and rarely used security. In fact, she lived her life under the radar and frequented many local businesses, especially Mrs. Green's Natural Market, where she shopped early every Sunday morning.

George, the manager, walked down the produce aisle.

"Good morning, Ms. Archer. How are you?"

"I'm fine. How are you?"

"I can't complain." He turned to Harrison. "How about you, Harry?"

"I can't complain either."

Alicia examined a pint of blueberries.

"What's cooking this morning, Ms. Archer?"

"I think I'm going to make blueberry muffins. I've had an idea in my head for a new twist on the recipe and I'd like to try it out today."

"I'd like to be at your house this morning." George rubbed his stomach.

She smiled. "I tell you what. If they turn out the way I want them to, I'll have Harry here bring you a couple."

"I'd like that."

Suddenly Nathaniel appeared and rushed by them without a word.

"Long night, I guess." George shrugged.

"There's nothing surprising about that," Alicia said dryly.

A few minutes later Nathaniel emerged from the coffee aisle with a pound of Kona and the largest cup of brewed coffee he could get.

"Forgive my earlier rudeness. Good morning, all."

"Good morning, Nate." Harrison pushed the shopping cart to the side.

"Hey, Harry."

"Good morning, Dr. Becker," George said as he continued to stock a shelf.

"Hey, George. How's the family?"

"They're doing well, thank you. My wife's allergies are under control, thanks to you."

"I'm glad to hear that. How's Allan? Is he ready for college this fall?"

"He's ready. Theresa and I, on the other hand, not so much. They grow up fast."

Nathaniel was George's family doctor and had been good friends with him since the birth of his son seventeen years ago.

"They certainly do." He turned to Alicia. "And a special good morning to you, Ms. Archer. You look lovely."

She looked down at her black slacks and denim blouse. *What the hell is he talking about?* "Good morning, Mr. Becker."

Nathaniel looked at the clock. "Scarsdale's own domestic doyenne is out and about already. Where do you find the energy?"

"Clean living."

"I tried that. It almost killed me."

"That figures."

"Clean living is nice and all, but it's boring. What you need is something else to help you expend your excess energy."

Alicia chuckled. "What excess energy? All I do is focus on what I have to do and that's it."

"Do we need anything else, Alicia?" Harrison asked.

She looked through the shopping cart. "I think we're done."

George walked over to the register. "I'll take you over here, Harry."

Alicia, Harrison and Nathaniel followed George to the register.

Nathaniel stared at Alicia. "I just realized what's different about you. You're wearing your hair down."

Instead of her usual updo, Alicia had her hair pulled back in a loose ponytail.

"It's a ponytail, Nathaniel," she replied dryly. "I didn't have the patience to deal with all those bobby pins this morning. I'll pin it up when I start baking."

"Is that the main reason you always have your hair up?" He was curious.

"It's one of the reasons."

"And here I thought it was because you're uptight."

Harrison and George looked uncomfortable.

"Pardon me?"

"I didn't mean that the way it sounded," he back-tracked.

"What did you mean?" Alicia folded her arms.

"Nothing bad, I promise you."

Harrison knew from Alicia's stance she was about to let Nathaniel have it with both barrels, so he jumped in. "It looks like we're all done, Alicia. We can head back and get started on those muffins."

"Good."

Harrison looked relieved as he picked up the tote bag they'd brought.

"You have a great day, George. I'll see about sending you a couple of muffins."

"Thanks, Ms. Archer."

"Have a good day, Mr. Becker."

"Same to you, Ms. Archer," he called after her as he put the coffee down on the conveyor belt.

"Have a good one, Nate," Harrison called out.

George rang up his order. "Is that all, Dr. Becker?"

"No." He watched Alicia walk by the window. "I need a bowl and a spoon."

"Excuse me?" George was perplexed.

"For Ms. Archer." He grinned.

George smiled. "I'm afraid we can't help you there."

"It's barely seven in the a.m. and she looks amazing." He continued to stare.

"I'm no medical professional but I'd say you've got it bad, Dr. Becker."

"I know. Believe me, I know."

❧

In pursuit of blueberry muffin perfection Alicia worked her muffin technique for two hours. Finally, she and Harrison sat at the kitchen table with coffee and muffins. More specifically, Harrison actually ate his muffin while Alicia dissected hers.

"What's wrong, Alicia?"

"Are they moist enough to you?"

"Yes. They're delicious."

"You're not just saying that, are you?"

"No. I've been with you a long time, Alicia. You know I would tell you if I thought there was something wrong."

"Okay." She took a bite. "A little bit of almond extract went a long way here. I think it balances the vanilla and orange extract flavors out nicely."

"You're right." He sipped his coffee. "Would you like to me to take a few to George? Lord knows, we have plenty to spare." He looked at the counter.

"I over-baked again." She paused. "I think we have nearly two dozen muffins. Go ahead and box up a dozen for George. He has a teenage son, so I'm sure they won't go to waste."

"Good idea." He got up. "Why don't you send a couple over to Nate?"

Alicia nearly choked on her coffee. "Why?"

"It would be the neighborly thing to do."

"If he were a nice neighbor, he wouldn't have called me uptight in the store this morning."

Harrison knew it was a lost cause to continue. "Have you heard from Lauren or Gabby today?"

"Lauren had a hot date so I don't expect to hear from her for a little while. As for Gabby, it's Sunday, which means tea with Bunny, and then she has a date tonight, too."

"It's nice that things are moving along for them."

"I think so, too."

"Things could be happening for you, too, if you would slow down and let them."

"Please don't start about the dating thing again, Harrison. I'm happy with my life, and that's the end of it. I'll be in my office if you need me." She made a dash for her office before Harrison could say another word.

"That woman can't get out of her own way." He shook his head. "I know what I'll do." Harrison boxed the muffins for George and then walked over to the pantry. *I know she has baskets in here somewhere.* He scanned the party. "Ah, here they are." Alicia kept an assortment of baskets and accoutrements on hand. Harrison grabbed a basket and a couple of jars of strawberry preserves. He thought for a moment. "I've seen her do this a thousand times. Let's see if I picked anything up." He lined the bottom with a fresh white linen cloth and then placed the muffins in the center, flanked by the preserves. It was pretty as a picture. "Not bad, if I do say so myself." After admiring his work he walked over to Nathaniel's place.

Harrison rang the doorbell.

"Hey, Harry, what brings you by?"

"Hi, Nate." He handed him the basket. "Alicia asked me to bring you these muffins to go with the coffee you bought at Mrs. Green's earlier."

Nathaniel's face lit up as he lifted the cloth. "Ooh, blueberry muffins baked by her little hands. I'm touched. Please tell her thank you."

"I will."

"Would you like to come in and join me for some coffee and one of these heavenly treats?"

"I'll have to take a raincheck. I need to run some errands, but you enjoy." He started to turn away.

"Okay. I'll see you around, Harry."

"Okay, Nate."

Nathaniel still had a grin on his face when he closed the door.

He looked like a kid on Christmas morning who just found a big, bright, shiny red bike. There is something between these two and I know it. Now all I have to do is get the lady of the manor to come around. Harrison walked back home.

While Sunday afternoon meant work for Alicia, it was usually high tea with Bunny at four p.m. sharp for Gabby. However, she'd told her mother she had an early dinner engagement with a patron in order to move tea time to one p.m. It hadn't raised any questions.

Dressed in a simple royal blue sheath dress, Gabby watched as Rosie set a vase of tea roses on the table.

"Thank you, Rosie. The living room looks great."

"You're welcome, ma'am."

"Are the scones and tea sandwiches ready?"

"Yes." Rosie straightened her apron out.

"Sorry about wearing your uniform on Sundays. My mother is very old school."

"That's okay, Ms. Blanchard, I understand." Rosie continued fussing with the table.

Gabby's style of running a household was more relaxed. Her mother, on the other hand, was a full-time socialite and had a formal staff of maids, butlers and cooks to manage the house. She ran a tight ship. As a child, Gabby had heard the staff refer to her as General Patton in black pumps, an apt description that still applied.

Gabby looked at her watch. "My mother will be here shortly. I'm going to make a call."

"Okay."

Gabby dialed as she walked onto the terrace.

"Hello?" Lauren whispered.

"Lauren?"

"Hi, Gabby. Can you hold a minute?"

"Sure."

"Thanks." Lauren looked over at a sleeping Randy and slid out of bed. "Just one more minute," she whispered.

"Okay." Gabby's interest was piqued.

Lauren put her robe on and went into the living room. "Thanks. How's it going, Gabby?"

"Fine. Are you all right? It sounds like you have a sore throat or something."

"I'm okay. I had to keep my voice down."

"I see. You have company."

"Yes. Is there anything wrong with that?"

"Not at all. It's not high tea with Bunny, but it's a great way to spend a Sunday afternoon."

"Oh, my God. Is it four o'clock already?" She rubbed her eyes.

"No. I'm having tea with Mom a little earlier today because I have my own plans for later."

Lauren sat on the sofa. "Plans you don't want Bunny to know about. I'm intrigued."

"I'm sure you are, but first I want to hear about Randy Rivera."

"Alicia has a big mouth."

"Honestly, she didn't tell me much. She actually said I should call and have you fill me in."

"What's to tell?"

"I would say there's a lot to tell, considering how it all got started with that ass Ken."

Lauren's face fell. "Don't say that name to me."

"I'm sorry, but he is a jackass."

"You won't get an argument with me about that. Although if it wasn't for him, I wouldn't have met Randy, had too much to drink and wound up in bed with him."

"Jesus, Lauren, that's hardly the romantic tryst we talk about."

"I know, but last night was." She grinned.

"Oh, you got a chance for a do-over."

"And what a do-over it was," she announced.

"I'm happy for you, Lauren, but that was a little too much information."

"Speaking of information, what's happening with you?"

"I'm going out with an investment banker/artist. His name is Nigel Clark."

"He's an investment banker and an artist? That's not a combination you hear every day."

"I know." She sighed dreamily. "He's talented and he seems to have a good head on his shoulders."

"Yeah, that's nice and all, but what does he look like?"

Gabby closed her eyes. "He's tall with a chocolate brown complexion, he has dark brown eyes and he's very fit."

"Fit like a weight lifter or fit like Lance Armstrong?"

"Like Lance Armstrong, only a little meatier."

"He sounds much better than those hair club refugees your mom tries to fix you up with."

"Alicia said the same thing."

"She's right."

"He is definitely head and shoulders above them. I'm sure she has at least one candidate in mind for me today." She sighed. "Jane said it best: 'It is a truth universally acknowledged that a single man in possession of a good fortune must be in want of a wife.' God knows my mother certainly believes that."

"It seems she believes a woman in possession of a good fortune must be in want *and* need of a husband, too. So it looks like you're getting it from both sides."

"Aren't I lucky?" Gabby said sarcastically.

"I know." Lauren walked to her kitchen. "Have you talked to Alicia today?"

"No. You know she's probably working at home."

"I would say something but it would be a case of the pot calling the kettle black." She got a glass from her cabinet and went over to the counter.

"We're all guilty of that."

Lauren picked up her Blackberry. "I think she got roped into a charity luncheon on Monday." She looked through her schedule. "I don't have anything Tuesday afternoon. Maybe I'll go up."

"Me, too. I think the Austen Aristocrats are overdue for a meeting." The doorbell rang. "I'd better go, Bunny's here."

"Tell Bunny I said hello, and you, my friend, have a good time tonight."

"I will, and I definitely will." Gabby hung up and then took a minute to check her reflection before greeting her mother.

Reed thin, coiffed and perfectly attired in a black dress with pearls, Bunny looked good for her seventy-six years. Though her step had slowed, she still managed to wear three-inch pumps.

"You look well, Mother." Gabby kissed her cheek and helped her to the sofa.

"Thank you." She looked her daughter over. "So do you, dear."

Gabby took a seat as well. "How's Daddy?"

Her father, Richard Blanchard, had had a stroke two years earlier and it had left him frail and unable to travel too much. In Gabby's eyes, though, he was still the superman she loved.

"Your father is doing well. He's been asking for you."

"My schedule has been crazy, but I will be there soon to see him."

"Good." Bunny sipped her tea. "We just got a postcard from Lizzie in Milan. She seems to be having a good time."

Gabby nibbled a sandwich. "She's having a great time, and they're in Venice now."

"Venice already?"

"That's the beauty of the computer, Mother. I can keep up with her in real time. In fact, she emailed me last night with some pictures. She and her friends are having a blast in Europe."

Bunny shook her head. "I'm all for her enjoying herself, but I don't understand why she's coming back to work in the inner city schools when there are plenty of fine private schools that would love to have her."

"It's her choice, Mother. She wants to contribute something to the lives of underprivileged children."

"She did have an interview with Hudson Hills Prep School, and they were going to take her until she handed them her reading list."

Gabby tried to hide her pride.

"I know you're smiling about it, but they didn't think it was funny when she read passages from *Why Should White Boys Have All the Fun*, *Forced into Glory* and the *Souls of Black Folks* during her demonstration class."

"She said the kids liked it."

Bunny pursed her lips. "You encouraged her."

"She speaks her mind, Mother, and she always has. I can't stop that."

"Then why doesn't she work in one of the suburban schools on Long Island or in Westchester?"

"We've been around this before, Mother. It's her life."

Bunny dipped her scone into the tea. "Fine, I guess her mind is made up." She nibbled her scone. "How's Ian doing?"

"He's good. He and Emily have been splitting their time between his condo in the city and a place in the Hamptons this summer."

"Now Emily Scofield, there's a girl from a good family."

Here we go again. Gabby tried not to roll her eyes. "Ian isn't with her because of her family. She's a lovely girl."

"Yes, she is nice." She sipped her tea again. "You know who I just ran into at the country club?"

Here it comes. Gabby braced herself. "Who?"

"Terrence Talbot. He was there meeting a client for golf."

"That's nice."

"He's single."

"Terrence is a nice man and all but no thanks, Mother."

"So he's divorced. You're divorced, too."

"I've been divorced once. Terrence, on the other hand, has as many ex-wives as there are days in the week."

"Dear, you're forty-six years old. You can't be too picky."

"No, Mother, that's exactly why I can be picky. I'm too old to put up with just anything, no matter how great the pedigree is."

"Fine. Contrary to popular belief, I hadn't planned a wedding."

"Thank you, Mother. Can we change the subject?"

"Certainly. How is Alicia's little show doing?"

Gabby nodded her head. "It's not a little show, Mother. Alicia's show is nationally syndicated and she has a successful magazine to boot. I'd say she's doing very well."

"That's nice," she said almost dismissively. "How about Lauren?"

"She's good."

"Is she still married to that ex-football player?"

"They're getting divorced."

"Oh, I'm sorry to hear that. Isn't this her third marriage?"

"Yes," Gabby said reluctantly.

"So I guess being divorced more than once isn't all bad."

"No, Mother, for some people it isn't. Lauren is a romantic, that's all."

"Then why can't Terrance be a romantic?"

"Because a man who's been married six times has something to prove."

"Hmm," Bunny sighed. "How's the gallery doing?"

Gabby was relieved she'd changed the subject. "It's doing really well. There's a lot of excitement building for the Sixteen to Watch new artist exhibit."

"I thought you only showcased fifteen artists."

"I decided to change it up this year."

"I see. Is that why you're going to dinner tonight?"

Gabby's heart jumped. "What do you mean?"

"You're having dinner with a patron, so I assume it's to raise more money to open more slots."

"Right."

Bunny checked her watch. "It's nearly two-thirty and you need time to get ready. Would you mind calling Lee and telling him to bring the car around, please?"

"Not at all, Mother."

Rosie, who was standing nearby, brought her the phone.

"Thank you, Rosie."

"No problem, ma'am."

Gabby dialed. "Hi, Lee. Mother's ready to leave. Thank you." She put the phone down. "He'll be around in a minute."

"Good."

Gabby stood and helped her mother to her feet.

"Thank you, dear."

Gabby walked her mother outside to her waiting car. Lee held the car door.

"Thanks for coming, Mother." She kissed her on the cheek.

"You're welcome, dear. I'm going to tell your father that you're coming soon."

"Please do, I will be there soon."

"Be sure you are," she said as Lee helped her into the car.

"I'll call you this week, Mother."

"Okay, dear." She waved and then Lee closed the door.

Gabby watched as the car pulled off. Something inside of her wished she could have shared the news of her date with her mother, but she knew better. Bunny was only interested in men with the right family lineage for her daughter, and a black investment banker from Long Island wouldn't qualify in her book. What mattered, however, was that Gabby herself was very interested in Mr. Nigel Clark and looked forward to what the evening would bring.

༜

Once she'd had a little orange juice for energy and glanced over the style section of *The Times,* Lauren went back to the bedroom. As she walked in she heard the shower running in the master bath. Quietly she opened the door and watched Randy as he closed his eyes and let the hot water wash over his head. The suds seemed to sparkle as they glided down his broad shoulders and muscular back. Lauren dropped her robe and stepped in.

"I see you started without me."

"There's no reason you can't catch up." He pulled her close to him and lifted her slightly.

"Oh," she moaned softly as she held on tight.

Ten minutes later Lauren lay on the bed exhausted but satisfied. "I look like a prune." She looked at her fingers.

Randy was on the edge of the bed getting dressed. "Hot water will do that to you."

"It wasn't just the water."

He stood from the bed to button his shirt. "We did steam it up a bit in there, didn't we?"

"Oh, yes."

He leaned over to kiss her. "I wish I could stay tonight."

"But you have a restaurant to run and I have to work, too."

"When will you have some time to get together again?"

"Well, the show is on hiatus, which means my schedule is a little more flexible. What did you have in mind?"

"I was thinking that maybe we could have dinner at my place Wednesday evening."

"I'd love that."

"Great. I can pick you up or you can meet me at the restaurant around seven, whatever you prefer."

"I'll meet you at the restaurant."

"Good." He looked at his watch. "I really have to get to the restaurant to check on the kitchen."

"Don't you have a sous chef running things in your absence?"

"Yes, but sometimes the sous chef is treated like a substitute teacher. The class might be good for the first day, but by the second they're usually trying to see what they can get away with."

"Okay, I get it. You have to play big brother."

"Sort of." He leaned in again and they kissed. "Hmm, I'm going to miss you."

"Me, too."

"I'll call you tomorrow."

"Okay." Lauren stretched out on the bed as he left the bedroom. A few moments later she heard the door close. "I've never been so tired and so happy in my life." She sighed aloud before picking the phone up to dial.

"Hello?" Alicia answered.

"Hi, Alicia. How's it going, lady?" Lauren was upbeat.

"It's going all right. However, I dare say things are going much better for you today. I take it the date went well."

"The date went very well."

"You sound like the cat that ate the canary. You're practically purring."

"Well, a night with a gorgeous man will do that to you."

"I'll bet."

"Really, Alicia, he's a great guy. We got a chance to talk over dinner and we got to know each other."

"In something other than the biblical sense, you mean," she teased.

"Yes." Lauren laughed.

"I'm interested to know where a five-star chef takes a date for dinner."

"We went to a little place called AOC in Greenwich Village. Have you heard of it?"

"As a matter of fact I have. They're known as a great little French bistro. How was the food, if you know?" Alicia leaned back in her chair.

"You're a riot, Alicia," Lauren said sarcastically. "The food was good. We had a great little pasta dish with green olives, tomato sauce, basil and cheese. I forget what it was called."

"You had *pasta de sud*."

"It figures you'd know."

"Well, food is my thing. What did you have for dessert?"

"We had the Belgian chocolate gelato."

"Oh, that sounds fantastic."

"It was good."

"So what did you find out about your sexy chef?"

Lauren filled Alicia in on the particulars.

"I tell you there is nothing like a culinary European education."

"True. You probably know he went to the Culinary Institute here for his training."

Alicia nodded to herself. "Sure. He went to school with some pretty heavy hitters. Anyway, that's all fine and well, but what really matters is how he connected with you."

Lauren sighed. "I have to admit it's been a long time since I had a great date."

"I'd say you were long overdue."

"I'm not the only one."

"We're not talking about me."

"Okay. I'm in too good a mood to argue with you."

"Good. Are you going out again?"

"Yes, we're getting together for dinner on Wednesday."

"Cool. It seems summer has turned on the heat in more ways than one."

"I know. Gabby has a date this evening."

"I know she's excited, although I'm pretty sure she won't have the wardrobe dilemma you do."

"You just can't resist mentioning that, can you?"

"Three closets filled with clothes and you draw a blank. It cracks me up."

"You just wait until you're trying to get dressed for a date."

"I don't have that problem, nor do I plan to."

"You're impossible, Alicia."

"I know." She paused. "Well, I know one thing. Gabby's going to look great, and I'm pretty sure she's going to have as good a time as you did."

"Then I hope her AC is working, because she's in for a hot summer night."

∽

After a long leisurely evening spent over dinner, Nigel and Gabby stood outside her townhouse.

"I had a wonderful time tonight." Gabby smiled.

"I did, too."

"It's hard to believe it's after eleven already. The time just flew by."

"It doesn't feel late."

"Would you like to come in for decaf?"

"Sure."

She unlocked the door and they walked in. Nigel seemed impressed as he looked around. "You have a nice place here."

"Thanks." She put her keys on the table. "If you'll follow me upstairs, the kitchen and the living room are on the next level."

He followed her up the stairs. "Please have a seat." She motioned toward the living room.

"Okay." He went to the living room. Once he sat he noticed all the paintings and different art pieces she had. "You have a nicely rounded collection of art in here," he called.

"Oh, thank you." She opened another cabinet.

"Do you need any help?"

"No. I'm fine, I promise." She searched through the cabinet. "My housekeeper is off tonight and I think she moved the coffee." She closed the cabinet doors and put her hands on her hips. "I just have to keep looking." She bent down to check the lower set of cabinets.

A moment later Nigel kneeled down next to her. "Are you sure I can't help you?"

She turned toward him and they were face to face. He leaned in and kissed her.

When he pulled away he said, "I wanted to do that all night." He was a bit breathless.

"Me, too."

He stood up and helped her to her feet. Nigel pulled her close to him again and gently kissed her lips. Gabby felt a chill run down her spine. "Do you still want decaf?" she asked breathlessly.

"No, I think I'd like something to keep me up." He ran his hands down her back and grabbed her rear.

Gabby reached down and took his hands to lead him to her bedroom.

Once the door closed they began kissing. Suddenly Nigel turned Gabby around and unzipped the beautiful black dress she'd worn, revealing a sexy black merry widow. "Oh my," he gasped as he removed his tie. Gabby sauntered close to him and unbuttoned his shirt, which he quickly threw to the floor. His excitement grew as she pulled his belt off. Slowly and deliberately, she unbuttoned his pants and pulled the zipper down. Nigel's body tensed with each move. Unable to contain himself, he finished the job in one fell swoop and stood naked in front of her.

Gabby lay down on the bed, her heart pounding. As he drew closer, his body lingered just over hers. His eyes were so intense, she trembled with anticipation. Nigel pulled the laces of her bustier until her breasts were exposed. He kissed her neck and breasts, setting her body tingling all over. His hands made their way down and within an instant Gabby was exposed. She wrapped herself around his body and they became one flesh. They spent the night lost in the artistry of lovemaking.

∽

After she'd spent the day working Alicia was tucked in for the night. Suddenly she pulled the covers back. Her MS symptoms were interrupting her sleep.

"Not again. I hate these spasms." She sighed as she climbed out of bed to go to the bathroom to take a couple of pills. "Bottoms up." She tossed the pills in her mouth and washed them down with a glass of water. "Why can't you ever let me sleep?" she said to her reflection in the mirror.

All of a sudden Alicia's expression changed. She remembered the long nights she'd spent with Kurt as he battled with pain. "This is nothing compared to how you suffered, my love," she said as a tear ran down her cheek. "I would have given anything to take that pain away from you." She wiped her eyes and was headed back to bed when the muffled sounds of barking got her attention. She walked over to the window to investigate.

"What are Rocky and Bull doing out this time of night?" she wondered aloud.

Then Nathaniel appeared behind them. Alicia turned to look at the clock. *It's two-thirty in the morning. I know I'm up because of spasms. I wonder what's chasing Nathaniel.* Suddenly Nathaniel turned toward the window as if he saw Alicia.

She didn't move.

Nathaniel looked away and went inside with the dogs.

I wonder what's chasing Nathaniel, she thought again as she headed back to bed.

CHAPTER 7

Although Gabby was quite the romantic at heart, her bedroom displayed her modern sensibility. Her king-size bed was made of solid mahogany, which she softened with her choice of a floral duvet cover and sham. She and Nigel were resting cozily each other's arms as daylight crept through the window. Gabby studied his face while he slept. *He looks so handsome.* She tenderly caressed his cheek.

Nigel began to stir. "Good morning." He yawned, covering his mouth.

"Good morning to you."

They kissed.

"How did you sleep?" he asked.

"I slept pretty well when I did sleep." She winked.

"I'm sorry if I kept you up."

"Don't be."

He kissed her again and stroked her hair. "You're beautiful."

"Thank you," she said shyly. "You're pretty hot, too."

He chuckled and looked over at the clock. "It's already six-thirty Monday morning."

"Wow."

"How about a little orange juice?"

"Sure." She started to get out of bed.

"No. You stay here. I'll get it." Nude, he got out of bed.

Gabby raised her eyebrow. "Your body is a work of art."

He looked down. "You think so?"

"I know so."

"What time does your housekeeper come in?"

"She usually comes in at seven. But just in case I think there's a man's robe in my closet over there." She pointed.

He opened the closet and removed a plush white man's robe. He felt the material. "This is nice. You just happen to have a man's robe?"

"It was part of a set I bought before my divorce. My ex never wore it."

"I was just kidding." He put the robe on, then walked over to the bed and kissed her. "I'll be right back."

"I'll be here."

After he left the room Gabby stretched out and smiled like a Cheshire cat.

A scream from the kitchen brought her to her feet. Gabby quickly put her robe on and rushed out to investigate. There stood Rosie with a long fork pointed at Nigel.

"What's going on?"

"Ms. Blanchard, I found this man going in the refrigerator!" Rosie exclaimed.

"I didn't mean to frighten you," Nigel said nervously.

"Rosie, put that fork down. This is Nigel. He's my guest."

Rosie looked shocked. "He's your guest?"

"Yes. Now get that fork away from him. What were you planning to do with that, anyway? See if he was done?"

Rosie put the fork down.

"It's okay, Rosie. No harm done. You were just being a good employee." Nigel started laughing. "What else was she supposed to do when she saw a strange man in the kitchen?" he added.

"That's true." Gabby laughed.

Rosie began to loosen up. "I just did not know."

"How could you?"

"I'm sorry, Mr. Nigel."

"That's all right, Rosie. And you just saw me in a robe, so please call me Nigel."

"Thank you, Nigel." She opened the refrigerator. "What can I get for you?"

"Well, this all started over a couple of glasses of orange juice."

"No problem." She took the orange juice out.

Gabby got a couple of glasses and Rosie poured. "Here we go, babe." Gabby handed Nigel a glass.

"Thanks."

"Would you like breakfast this morning, Ms. Blanchard?"

"Breakfast would be nice."

"Very good. Would you like a continental or hearty breakfast?"

"I think a hearty breakfast is in order today." She smiled at Nigel.

"Coming up." Rosie shook her head.

Nigel and Gabby went back to the bedroom. The moment they closed the door, they broke into laughter.

"If I wasn't there, I would have thought I was on *Candid Camera*," Nigel joked.

"I'm so sorry. She only wanted to protect me."

"That's okay. It's a good thing you have a maid that's willing to fork someone to keep you safe."

"I know. I'm going to have to give her a raise."

Nigel took the orange juice from her hands and placed both their glasses on the table. "Well, it was an incredible night and an eventful morning, but I do have to get to work."

"Okay."

"How about we conserve water and take a shower together?"

"How green of you."

"What I won't do for the environment." He smiled as he led her to the master bath.

❧

After a morning of stalling Alicia decided to forgo her usual luncheon suit for a breezy rose pleated trapeze dress by Ashley Stewart that showed a little arm and leg. Yet despite being dressed, she was glued to the edge of her bed.

"Alicia! Are you ready to go?" Harrison called upstairs.

"I'll be down in a minute, Harrison!" She looked at her reflection. "Why can't I just write a check?" she mumbled as she stood up. "I'm not in the mood for a society luncheon, even if it is for a charity." She stumbled and held onto her bedpost to steady her gait. "Oh, what was that?"

"Alicia? Are you all right up there?"

She took a deep breath. "I'm fine! I'll be down in a minute!" Alicia took a moment, composed herself and walked out of her room and down the stairs.

Harrison looked up. "You look lovely."

"Thanks." She had her black clutch in hand.

He studied her face. "Are you sure you're feeling okay?"

"I'm fine. I really don't want to go to this thing." She groaned.

"You committed yourself weeks ago," he reminded her.

"I know. I guess I'll file this under no good deed goes unpunished."

Harrison snickered.

"An afternoon of society mavens and denizens at the Scarsdale Golf Club. I don't know if I can stand it."

"The food is pretty good there, if that's any consolation."

"That's about the only consolation."

"And it is for a good cause." He put his arm out.

"True." She took his arm and they left the house.

Half an hour later they pulled onto the grounds of the Scarsdale Golf Club. Founded in 1898, it was a mere twenty-four miles from New York City, but it seemed to be a world away from its metropolitan neighbor. With its panoramic views and manicured golf courses, it provided much more than just a place to play eighteen holes. It boasted seven different rooms for social events, from corporate fundraisers to wedding receptions.

The club's 1898 room was the site for the African AIDS Awareness charity luncheon. The formal dining room had a bay window that overlooked the club's practice putting green. When Harrison and Alicia arrived, the room was already abuzz with activity. Suzanne Addison, one of the organizers, waved.

"Oh, dear God, it's Suzanne," Alicia mumbled through her smile.

"Be nice." Harrison grinned

Suzanne Addison was a typical society woman. Petite, reed thin and over fifty-five, she wore a vintage Chanel suit and a ring that cost more than Alicia's Land Rover. Her husband's family had made their money in oil generations ago, so charity was her full-time job.

"Alicia, I'm so happy you came." She air-kissed her.

"I'm happy to be here for such a good cause." She turned to Harrison. "You remember Mrs. Addison."

"Yes, of course." He shook her hand. "It's a pleasure to see you again, Mrs. Addison."

"Please call me Suzanne."

"Thank you, Suzanne."

She checked a piece of paper in her hand. "You and Harrison are at table two right over there." She pointed.

"Thank you."

"I'll be over soon."

"Wait, Suzanne. Before I forget." She reached into her purse and pulled out a check. "Here's my contribution."

She glanced at it. "Oh my, Alicia, this is very generous of you."

"I think it's an important to raise as much money as we can to help with the AIDS crisis in Africa."

"You are so right."

Harrison and Alicia made their way through the room to their table, which thankfully wasn't too far from the door.

They were seated at a table with some of Scarsdale's gentry, a couple of lawyers, corporate VPs and an orthodontist. Alicia made small talk with them while the appetizers were served.

Harrison turned to Alicia. "It's nice to know liberal ideals are alive and well here in Scarsdale."

"It's refreshing, isn't it?"

"Good afternoon Harry, and Ms. Archer. Fancy meeting you here." Nathaniel smiled as he sat down next to Alicia.

"I was going to say the same thing, Mr. Becker."

"It's good to see you, Nate."

"You too, Harry." He pulled up to the table.

"You almost missed the appetizer, Mr. Becker. Full morning at the office?"

"As a matter of fact, it was a full morning. It seems my nurse overbooked me again, but I made it work." He unfolded his napkin.

The waiter arrived to refill wine glasses. Alicia covered hers.

"You're not partaking, Ms. Archer? I can assure you it's the good stuff," Nathaniel said as he sipped his wine.

"It's a little too early for me."

"I see."

The wait staff began serving lunch. Alicia opted for the prime rib.

As the afternoon wore on, Alicia began to feel warm despite the central air.

"Excuse me." She got up.

"Is everything all right?" Harrison asked.

"I'm just going to the ladies' room. I'll be right back," Alicia said reassuringly.

Alicia felt unsteady but she managed to walk across the room without a problem. When she arrived at the ladies' room, she checked to see if it was clear before she practically collapsed onto a chair.

She rubbed her head. *What is wrong with me?* She closed her eyes.

"Are you all right?"

Alicia opened her eyes. Nathaniel was in front of her.

"Mr. Becker, this is the ladies' room," she exclaimed.

"I know. I can read. I came to see if you were okay. You look a little flushed."

"I'm a little warm, that's all." She tried to dismiss it.

"The central air is working overtime. It's got to be sixty-one degrees in here." He felt her forehead.

"Hey," she protested.

"You have a fever."

"How do you know that? Do you have a thermometer in your hand?"

"I don't need to. I've been a doctor over twenty years. You tell your viewers you just know when the bread is just right when you knead it. I know a fever when I feel it."

"You've watched my show?" She was genuinely taken aback.

"Yes. We put it on in the waiting room at the office. I catch it every now and then."

"Oh."

He took her pulse. "It's a little fast. What's going on?"

"Nothing. I didn't sleep well last night."

"Sleeplessness doesn't usually beget fevers."

"Maybe I'm coming down with something. I don't know."

"In any case I think you should probably go home and get some rest." He reached into his pocket and took out a packet of Tylenol. "Take these. They will help bring your fever down."

"You just happen to carry Tylenol in your pockets?"

"An ounce of prevention is worth a pound of cure. I brought it in case of a headache. It is a charity luncheon in Scarsdale."

She laughed.

"She laughs. I think you're already on the road to recovery, Ms. Archer."

There was a knock at the door. "Alicia?"

Nathaniel opened the door. "Come on in and join the party, Harry."

Harrison looked shocked. "Is everything all right in here?"

"It seems our Ms. Archer has a fever. I just gave her a couple of Tylenol. You should probably take her home and make her get some rest."

"You can bet I will."

"I hate to leave before all the presentations."

"Sure you do." Nathaniel laughed. "You've got a get-out-of-jail-free card. Fly like the wind."

Harrison laughed. "You already gave them the check." He put his hand out and helped her up. "Nate, would you mind walking her out while I bring the car around?"

"Sure."

Alicia felt too bad to protest. Nathaniel walked her out of the ladies' room past the stares of some horrified attendees.

"There goes my reputation," Alicia said.

"You don't look so well at the moment."

"Gee, thanks."

"No, of course you look incredible."

"Excuse me?"

"Yes," he stammered. "I mean, you look good but it's obvious you don't feel well."

"I see."

"I do like that dress. It looks good on you. The color really complements your skin."

"Thank you, Mr. Becker." She was a little unsettled.

"You're welcome."

They walked outside. A couple of minutes later Harrison drove up. Nathaniel helped Alicia into the car.

"Now you be sure to get some rest, Ms. Archer. And drink plenty of fluids."

"I will." Alicia fumbled with her seatbelt.

"Let me get that for you." Nathaniel reached in and buckled her up. "There you go."

"Thanks again."

"No problem. Let me know how the patient is later, Harry."

"Will do."

"Feel better, Ms. Archer. By the way, thank you for the lovely basket of muffins. They were absolutely delicious." He closed the car door.

Alicia glared at Harrison. "What muffins?"

"You did say we had too many, so I took some over to Nate."

"You didn't just take some over there. You prettied them up in a basket."

"So?"

"So you wanted him to think I sent them."

"What's the difference who he thought they were from? You do pride yourself on being a good neighbor."

"That's not the point, Harrison, and you know it."

"Say what you will, I think he was really moved by it. Or didn't you notice that little 'house call' he made on you in the ladies' room?"

"How can it be a house call if I wasn't at home?"

"The man walked into the ladies' room at the country club. I think that qualifies." Harrison smiled as they drove off.

"Don't start, Harrison."

"What did I say?"

"You're thinking it. Just stop it."

He smirked. "As you wish, Ms. Archer."

"Don't be a smart aleck."

Whether Alicia wanted to admit it or not, she was a little disconcerted by Nathaniel's attention. She couldn't figure out why he'd fussed over her. *He couldn't possibly like me. Oh, that can't be it. He's a doctor. He took an oath,* she rationalized as she stared out the window.

"Are you sure you're okay?"

"Yes."

"You're thinking about him, aren't you?"

"Will you please drive?" she retorted.

Harrison chucked softly.

"What are you chuckling about?"

"Nothing, I was just thinking."

"About what?"

"It looks like someone else has it bad, too."

"What do you mean, too? Nathaniel Becker isn't thinking about me, and I am certainly not thinking about him."

"Mmm hmm."

"What do you mean by that?"

"What did I mean about what, Alicia? I didn't say anything."

"It's what you didn't say. That's what you're trying to say."

"That doesn't even make sense." Harrison looked puzzled.

"I have a fever. What do you want from me?" She rubbed her forehead. "I just want to get home and into bed so I can forget this whole thing."

Harrison didn't say another word. While he would hold his tongue the rest of the way home, he silently reserved the right to revisit the subject in detail later.

❧

With Corinne Bailey Rae on in the background and a glass of lemonade by her side, a decidedly dressed-down Lauren stretched out on the sofa with her laptop.

She hummed along with the music.

"Lauren?"

She jumped. "Ken. What are you doing here?"

"I thought I'd come by to get some of my things. I didn't think you'd be here during the day."

"I decided to work from home." She went back to work.

"I thought Alicia's show was on hiatus."

"It is on hiatus. However the production company is still working, as is the network."

"I see."

"Speaking of the network, I got an email from Tony. They want to talk to you about covering some of the football training camps in a few weeks."

"Really? What did he say?"

"I didn't get the details. I forwarded the email to Patrick."

"Why did you do that?"

"Patrick is your agent. He's supposed to handle this stuff for you."

"I know, but you usually get the rundown."

She stopped typing. "We're getting divorced, Ken. In case you don't remember, you brought divorce papers to dinner last week, and I signed them."

He looked uncomfortable. "I know."

"Then why on earth would you think I'd continue as your de facto agent/network liaison?"

"That was business."

Lauren grew hot. "You don't think my being your wife had anything to do with it?"

"Not really," he answered sheepishly.

"You know what? It's your business to handle from now on. Aren't you here to get your stuff?"

"Lauren, I know I handled it badly but . . ."

She put her hand up. "Save it, Ken."

He picked up his duffle bag and went into the bedroom.

He's got some nerve. She shook her head, then sipped her lemonade.

A few minutes later he walked back into the living room. "I think that's everything."

"Okay."

"If you find anything else I'll come and pick it up."

"Shouldn't that be the end of it? You moved most of your stuff out during the separation."

"It should be it, but . . ."

She cut him off. "If I find anything else I'll have it dropped at your place."

"What?"

"Yes, and if you'd please leave the key on the table, I'd appreciate it. You did say I could have the apartment, so there is no need for you to have a key."

Although taken off balance, he put the key on the table.

"Thank you."

"What's going on with you?"

"What do you mean?"

"You're acting so cold."

"How am I supposed to behave, Ken? Should I cry and beg you to stay? I've been there and done that. You can't have your cake and eat it, too, Ken. You wanted out and now you're out."

"I wasn't trying to have my cake and eat it, too."

The door opened and a very attractive young brunette in a barely there halter dress entered. "Ken, you said you'd only be a few minutes," she whined.

Lauren looked at her. "That's exactly what you're trying to do, Ken."

Ken looked like a deer caught in headlights. "Tina, baby, I'll be there in a second. Just wait in the hall."

"Okay." She went back into the hall.

Ken picked his bag up. "I guess I'll be going."

"Bye, Ken." She waved.

"Bye." He closed the door behind him.

Lauren got up and locked the door.

That man's ego is too much. I can't believe I twisted myself into knots for him. Well, that's over and Tina or who- ever the flavor of the moment happens to be can have him. She sat back down on the sofa. "What a jackass," she mumbled aloud as she picked up her phone.

∽

Alicia took her cell phone out. "Hello?"

"Hi. I didn't think you'd pick up. I was going to leave a message. Aren't you at the club?"

"No, I did my thing and now I'm home."

"Aren't we going to finish our discussion about Nate?" Harrison called after her.

She put the phone to her side. "There's nothing to talk about." She put the phone back to her ear. "Sorry about that."

"What about Nate?" Lauren asked. Her interest was piqued.

Alicia turned to Harrison. "Now you've got her started, too. Lauren, don't encourage him. Remember, you called me. What's up? Tell me while I climb the stairs."

"Ken was just here with one of his latest conquests."

"Why?"

"He said he was here to pick up a few things he left behind."

Alicia walked into her room. "He wanted to make sure you were home pining away for him."

"There was no pining going on here. I had some work to do."

Alicia sat on her bed. "Okay. Where's Randy?"

"I told you we're getting together Wednesday, remember? He's got a lot going on this week at the restaurant."

"Oh yes you did tell me you were getting together for hump day. Emphasis on hump." She snickered.

"I tell you, Ms. Archer, you certainly have a bawdy sense of humor. I'm sure your fans would be shocked."

Alicia lay down on the bed. "I don't know why it should be so surprising. You know, I think the sexiest generation probably lived during the eighteenth and nineteenth century. I bet you anything there was more going on underneath all that civility and clothing than we think."

"Basically you're saying they were freaks behind closed doors."

"Exactly."

"You're too much, you know that."

"As a matter of fact, I do." She paused. "You really called because you were a little bothered seeing Ken today?"

"It's pathetic, isn't it?" Lauren was disgusted with herself.

"No, it's only natural. You invested a lot of time and energy into him. It's going to sting every now and then."

"Well, I want it to stop altogether."

"Don't worry, it will. In case you forgot, you have a sexy chef in your life now."

"He is sexy."

"If that doesn't put a smile on your face, you need to see a doctor."

"Speaking of doctors, what's Harrison bugging you about?"

"I'm not going down that garden path again."

"What's the big deal? So he attended the same luncheon you did."

"It's not a big deal, which is why I'm not going to talk about it. There is nothing to say."

"I don't know, Alicia, there's more here than meets the eye."

"The only thing we have here is a woman who is very tired and ready for a little nap."

"Okay, play the nap card," Lauren joked.

Alicia got underneath her covers. "Will it get you off the subject?"

"It will for the time being."

"Then consider the card played." She closed her eyes.

"Okay, Alicia, I'll let you off now, but we will talk about it."

"That's fine with me. I'll talk to you later."

"Okay." Lauren hung up.

Lauren was still a little mad with herself for feeling a tiny twinge when she saw Ken. However, she knew Alicia was right. The feeling would lessen over time, and her good feelings for Randy were just getting started.

❦

Gabby usually dreaded paperwork Mondays at the gallery. It was the one day when time seemed to stand still and every minute felt like an eternity. Yet this Monday was different. Instead of trudging through the day, she whistled "Dixie" and managed to get a stack of work done in no time.

Robin knocked on the door.

Gabby looked up from her computer. "Hey, Robin. What's up?"

"Believe it or not, it looks like we actually caught everything up."

"You're kidding."

"No. The donor rolls are current, the mailing list is up to date, all the invoices are paid and filed and the final proof for the invitation to the Sixteen to Watch exhibit is off at the printers."

"Wow." She looked at the time on her computer. "It's only four."

"I know."

"Then I guess you can call it a day."

"Really?"

"Yes. Go ahead and enjoy some of this summer evening with Steve."

"Actually, I think I'll head home and crawl into bed." She yawned.

"You did seem a little exhausted today. Is everything okay?"

"Everything's fine. I'm just worn out from baby-making boot camp."

"Oh, you poor thing," Gabby joked.

"I know. What a thing to complain about."

"You have to relax, Robin. It will happen."

"I hope so. It just sucks all the romance right out the window. What man wants to hear 'My temperature's up, let's go! Hop to it! Now let's make sure we're at the right angle.' I can't believe my own ears when it's coming out of my mouth."

"Oh, honey, I'm so sorry." Gabby shook her head.

"Don't be. At least the doctor thinks we have a chance of getting pregnant without any surgical or medicinal intervention for now. I have to be thankful for that much."

Gabby got up and hugged her. "Don't you worry, you'll get pregnant and all of this will become a distant memory."

"From your mouth to God's ears."

"So go home, put the thermometer on the shelf and enjoy a nice evening with your gorgeous husband."

"I know there's a restaurant he's been dying to try."

"See, you can make it a date night."

"Thanks, Gabby. Are you sure you don't need me for anything else?"

"Yes. Go. I'll see you tomorrow."

"Thanks, Gabby. Have a good night."

"You, too."

Robin bolted.

Pleased with herself, Gabby went back to her desk and leaned back in her chair.

Her cell phone rang.

"Gabrielle Blanchard."

"Hi, Gabby."

She melted the moment she heard his voice. "Hi, Nigel."

"How's your day going?"

"Terrific. As a matter of fact, it's over. The gallery is all caught up on paperwork, and I can get back to concentrating on art. How's it going with you?"

"I wish I could say I was all done for the day. But this Wall Street mess is making for some very nervous clients."

"I can imagine. Have any of them been hit?"

"Not really. I stayed away from investments tied to the banking industry and all the mortgage stuff. It made me nervous, so I steered my clients away from it."

"I bet they're happy to have such a smart and skilled man in their corner."

"Thanks. Are we still talking about my clients?"

Gabby laughed.

"I really had a great night and morning with you, Gabby."

"Me, too."

"I was thinking that maybe we could catch a movie or an early dinner this week."

"I'd love to."

"Is tomorrow too soon?"

"I'm sorry, but I'm going to Scarsdale tomorrow after work."

"That's right, you're good friends with Ms. *Everyday Elegance*/Archer Omnimedia herself."

"Yes, and I haven't seen her in a little while. Lauren and I are both going."

"You're good friends."

"Thanks. Do you think we can get together on Wednesday?" She flipped through her appointment calendar.

"Works for me. I'll meet you at the gallery after work."

"Okay, it's a date."

"Can't wait to see you."

"Me, too." She grinned.

"I'd better get back to work. I'll call you later. Bye, sweetheart."

"Bye." She hung up.

Her cell phone rang a minute later. She picked up. "Couldn't wait for later either, huh?" Gabby used her sexy tone.

"What can't I wait for, Gabby?" Alicia was in bed.

"Oh, hi, Alicia. How are you?" Gabby tried to play it off.

"I'm fine, but apparently you're better. I take it you weren't expecting to hear from me. I'm sorry to disappoint you."

"Don't say that. I love hearing from you."

"I don't doubt it. Still, it would have been nicer if I were Nigel. That must have been some date."

Gabby was quiet.

"Gabby?"

"Yes."

Alicia sat straight up. "You slept with him."

"What?"

"Don't try it, sister. Fess up."

"What if I did?"

"I'm not Bunny. Exhale already, girl."

"Okay."

"Well?"

"Well what?"

"Don't play coy with me. You know what I'm asking."

"We had a good time at dinner."

"Obviously. Otherwise you wouldn't have slept with him. Who ever heard of having an awful date and then hopping into bed afterwards?"

"You've never been to a debutante ball," she answered dryly.

"I stand corrected. So tell me already."

"You want details?"

"I don't want those kinds of details. More like on a scale of one to ten."

"Twenty."

"Wow."

"I know."

"Are you going out again?"

"We're going to catch a movie or dinner on Wednesday."

"Why not tomorrow? You didn't want to seem too anxious or something?"

"Lauren and I are coming up to see you tomorrow. It has been a while since we've had a meeting."

"True, but you two are living the real thing. What do you need the club for?"

Harrison knocked. "Alicia?"

"Hold a second, Gabby."

"Sure."

She sat up straight. "Come in."

"I brought you some tea." He placed the tray on the table.

"Thank you." She put the receiver back to her ear.

"Tell Harrison I said hello."

"Gabby says hello."

"Hi, Gabby. Did Alicia tell you she got sick at the charity luncheon today?"

"Big mouth," she shot back.

"Why didn't you say you weren't feeling well?"

"It's no big deal."

"Dr. Becker said she had a fever," Harrison said, interjecting himself into the conversation again.

"Are you still here?" Alicia was annoyed.

"Alicia, you saw Nate today?"

"Yes. He was there today. He gave me some Tylenol. That's all."

"She's neglecting to say he followed her into the ladies' room to check on her," Harrison said with his arms folded.

"You can go now," she insisted.

"He followed you into the ladies' room?"

"He is a doctor."

"He must have been studying you quite closely."

"You're as bad as Harrison."

"Did someone take my name in vain?" he joked.

"You are such a troublemaker. I'm going to shoot you."

"You have to catch me first," he chuckled and bolted out of the room.

"He is such a tattletale."

"Be that as it may, you realize we're coming up there for sure now," Gabby said.

"I know. I couldn't stop you if I tried," Alicia conceded.

CHAPTER 8

In spite of Harrison's protests, Alicia was already on her second cup of coffee and seated firmly in front of her computer checking email on Tuesday morning.

"I still think you should be in bed taking it easy."

"I've noted your suggestion and I feel fine, Harrison. It was just a low-grade fever. No big deal."

"If you were anyone else I'd agree, but you have . . ."

She interrupted him. "I know what I have, Harrison."

"You know, even the good Lord rested on the seventh day," Harrison said with his arms folded.

"It's not the seventh day. It's Tuesday."

"I know, but I had to say something to get your attention."

"The good Lord didn't have to deal with 800 hundred emails."

"Good grief, Alicia, some of that has to be spam." He checked his watch.

"I wish." She sighed. "My biggest problem is trying to determine which ones are pertinent and which ones can wait." She continued to scroll through.

He looked at his watch again.

"Are you expecting someone, Harrison? You keep checking your watch."

"No, we need some things from the store and I really don't want to leave you here by yourself. What time are Lauren and Gabby coming?"

"They won't be here until later."

"Oh."

"If you have to go to the store, go ahead. I'll be fine."

"No. It can wait."

"Please go, Harrison. You're just getting a few things, right?"

"Right."

"So you'll be an hour or less, right?"

"Yes."

"I'll be all right. Go and get it over with while it's still not that hot."

"That's true. Do you want anything special?"

"Other than the three C's, I can't think of anything at the moment."

"You got it. Coffee, Coca-Cola and candy, more specifically, your wintergreen mints."

"Sounds good to me."

"Now you know you shouldn't be outside today. It's going up to 97 degrees."

"I know. I saw the weather report this morning."

"It must be at least 90 degrees already and it's not even eight thirty."

"That's global warming for you." Alicia hadn't looked up from the computer.

"Shade or not, you shouldn't go out today."

"Yes, sir." She saluted him.

"I should be gone no more than an hour, less if I'm lucky."

"No problem, Harrison. I'll be here."

Harrison walked out and she continued scrolling.

"What's this?" A frown came over her face as she opened an email from Barbara Folsom, the production manager. Barbara was a veteran of the magazine business and knew magazines inside and out. A divorcee with two grown daughters, the fifty-something Barbara had a gorgeous figure with a smooth, unlined face to match.

Hi Alicia,

I know you're on vacation from your show, but I needed to touch base about the attached layout for the magazine cover. Your signature is on it, but I know you didn't approve this version. I got an email from Taylor giving me the green light to go ahead, but I didn't want to go any further. Please advise before I send this into production.

Alicia opened the attachment. "What the hell is this? Fall gardening tips in the July issue? The tips should be in the August issue. And oven-baked pie recipes in July? This is ridiculous." In a huff she picked up the phone.

"Good morning, Production, Barbara speaking."

"Good morning, Barbara."

"Hi, Alicia. I didn't expect to hear from you so soon." She lowered her voice.

"I dialed the second I got a look at the attachment. I'm glad you emailed me."

"It just wasn't the layout you and I discussed earlier this month. You were very clear."

"Apparently I wasn't clear enough for some people."

Barbara sighed.

"I won't put you in the middle of this, Barb. You go ahead and do what we discussed. I'll handle Taylor."

"Yes, ma'am. I'm really sorry to have bothered you on vacation."

"Don't worry about it. I'd rather this than be really bothered by a screwed-up cover layout. I mean, what would I look like, since my picture is on the cover? I'm standing there barbecuing next to a caption about great autumn pies."

"Yeah."

"Thanks again for the heads-up."

"You're welcome."

"Before I go, any news on the Ron front?"

"No Alicia. I don't know why you think he likes me."

"He practically ran across town to get some papers signed for you."

"I still don't know why he did that."

"He likes you. I'm sure of it."

"If you say so." She sounded skeptical.

"Give the guy a chance to show you. I'll bet he makes a move the first opportunity he gets."

"We'll see."

"I won't push it any further. I've got big fish to fry. I'll talk to you later."

"Okay."

Alicia took a deep breath and dialed the managing editor, Taylor Dawes.

A wunderkind with a degree in English from Georgetown University, 27-year-old Taylor had joined

Archer Omnimedia as an editorial assistant to Stephen Brown, the features editor. She had worked her way up the ladder until she became senior features editor when Stephen retired. Ambitious and hardworking, she should have been a woman after Alicia's own heart. But Alicia had seen her mow down the competition for the position of managing editor by cozying up to Howard Wasser, Timothy Flaherty and Edward Maine, the three male board members Alicia referred to as the "Three Stooges." Alicia didn't think she had the experience needed for the job, and that morning's error didn't help her cause.

"Okay, be calm, Alicia," she told herself. "Resist the urge to call her a zygote." She tapped the desk somewhat impatiently.

"This is Taylor."

"Taylor. It's Alicia."

"Oh, hi, Alicia. How are you?"

"I was okay until I saw the cover layout for July."

"You saw the layout?"

"You sound surprised. My name is on the masthead."

"True." She cleared her throat. "Is there a problem?"

"Yes, there is. It seems someone got the summer and fall issues confused. There are fall gardening tips and fall pie recipes listed for the July issue, and that's just crazy."

"That is a mistake."

"I know. It's a big, glaring mistake. One might even think it was done on purpose."

"Why would anyone do that?"

"I don't know, Taylor."

"I would have caught it."

"Apparently not, since you sent it straight down to production with my signature on it." She slammed her hand on the desk. "So can you tell me why I didn't get the layout?"

"You're on vacation and I am the managing editor. I didn't think I needed to bother you."

"It's no bother, Taylor. It's true that I'm on hiatus from the show, but I'm not in a coma. I still plan to be involved in the running of *my* magazine, even if I'm telecommuting for the time being. Is that understood?"

"Yes. I will call in the changes."

"No need. I already took care of it with Production. And from now on I expect you to copy me on all editorial matters unless I tell you otherwise. Is that clear?"

"Yes, Alicia."

"Thank you." She leafed through her calendar. "There's a staff meeting on Thursday and I will be there via conference call at ten a.m. sharp," she said, asserting her authority.

"Got it."

"Thanks, Taylor. You have a good day now."

"Thanks, Alicia."

Alicia hung up. Then she began pacing. *That little know-it-all tries to undermine me every chance she gets. This is exactly why I don't take a real vacation. The minute she thinks I have my back turned, she tries to put her stamp on the magazine, which wouldn't be so bad if she wasn't so green. But how would the Three Stooges, lecherous, lewd and clueless, know? All Howard Wasser, Timothy Flaherty and Edward Maine saw was a tight black skirt and perky young tits, so that meant she was qualified to be the managing editor. Thank God for Spanx and good bras. Otherwise they'd have another perky zygote in my position as editor-in-chief.*

She walked out of her office. "I need to get some air." Alicia walked through the kitchen to the outside, where she was hit with a wall of heat. "Oh, God, it's disgusting out here." She turned to go back in, but the door was locked. "Oh, no." She tried to pull it open. "Harrison!" she called, then remembered he was at the store.

Alicia quickly got under the tree for shade, but it wasn't much help. She rubbed her forehead. She had worked herself up over the Taylor Dawes thing and her body was overheated. After a few minutes she felt dizzy. Needing to cool down, Alicia walked over to the pool, knelt down and splashed herself with water. "That's a little better." Within a moment, though, she fainted and fell into the water.

Across the way Nathaniel was walking outside and heard the splash. When he came to investigate, he saw Alicia floating in the water.

"Alicia!" He dove into the pool fully clothed. Within a minute he had her out of the water.

"Alicia!" He listened to see if she was breathing and began to perform mouth to mouth. "Come on, Alicia! Don't do this to me. Who else will I fight with, huh?" He breathed into her mouth again.

Finally Alicia coughed up water.

145

"Thank God." He pulled her hair out of her face. "Alicia? Can you hear me?"

Slowly she opened her eyes. When she saw Nathaniel, the sunlight formed a halo around his dark hair making him look angelic to her. "Am I dead?" she asked.

"No. You gave me quite a scare though."

"You're an angel . . ." She trailed off and fainted again.

Nathaniel gazed down at her and softly caressed her cheek. He pushed her hair back and away from her eyes. "I wonder what happened. Did you just simply faint from the heat or something?" Her charm necklace gleamed in the sun, which caused Nathaniel to examine it more closely. "Wait a second, this doesn't look like a charm." He lifted the square-shaped charm and discovered it was a medic alert. "It was hiding in plain sight." He turned it over. "She has MS, just as I suspected." He looked at her, then scooped her up, turned and walked back to his house.

He laid Alicia down on the sofa in his living room, then went to the hall closet to get a blanket, since it was about 61 degrees in his house and both he and Alicia were soaked through. He gently slapped Alicia on the cheek. "Alicia? Can you open your eyes for me?"

She didn't respond.

He checked her pulse. "Normal. Okay, I guess I need to get you out of these wet things." Nathaniel unbuttoned her shirt and then leaned her forward to remove it. His eyes widened to the size of saucers when he got a look at Alicia's lacy black bra. Though he'd been impressed with her in a bathing suit, this took the cake.

"Wow." He stopped to think. "I think I'd better stop here. Somehow I don't think I'll be able to explain why your skirt's off." He wrapped the blanket around her and went to the extra bedroom to dry off and change his clothes.

Just as he pulled his pants up the phone rang.

"Hello?"

"Hey there, baby."

"Hi, Vivian, what's up?" he said as he walked back out to the living room.

"Nothing much. I wanted to see if you'd like company," she purred.

"Thanks, but I'm not up to it today," he said quietly.

"Oh, what's wrong? You don't feel well?"

"I think I'm coming down with a little sore throat or something." He cleared his throat.

"Then you should write a prescription for yourself."

"It doesn't really work that way, Vivian."

"Then have one of the other doctors do it for you."

"I'll be okay."

Alicia groaned aloud. "Where am I?"

"Listen, I've got to run. I'll talk to you later." He quickly hung up. "Hey there, you're up." He walked over to the sofa. "You're in my living room."

"Mr. Becker?"

"Yes, you're in my house. Please call me Nathaniel or Nate."

Alicia lifted the blanket and realized she was wet and not wearing a top. "Okay, Nathaniel." She tried to think. "I can't remember what happened. Why am I wet?"

"You don't remember? You fainted and fell into your pool."

"And you dove in and saved me?"

"Yes. I saw you go in when I stepped outside."

"Wow. Did I stop breathing?"

"You had water in your lungs. I gave you mouth to mouth until you coughed up the water."

"Then I guess I can't be upset over my missing shirt."

"I couldn't let you stay in your wet clothes, so I took your shirt off and wrapped you up in the blanket. I didn't want you to catch cold from the AC. I am a doctor."

"I know. Thank you."

"You're welcome." He smiled. "I was going to put some water on for tea. Would you like some?"

"Yes, that would be nice."

Alicia looked around Nathaniel's place. It wasn't the den of inequity with disco lights, stripper pole and wet bar as she'd imagined. In fact, his place was tastefully decorated with a sofa, loveseat, coffee table and artwork from different parts of the globe. *This is certainly unexpected.*

Alicia put her hand over her mouth to hide her smile when Nathaniel emerged from the kitchen with a tea service.

She sat up as he placed it on the coffee table.

"I have lemon, cream, honey and sugar. I wasn't sure how you take your tea."

"I take it with sugar and lemon, thank you."

"As you wish." He poured the tea and squeezed a lemon. "How many sugars?"

"Two."

He fixed her tea and handed it to her. "Here you go, Ms. Archer."

"Thank you." She sipped it slowly. "I guess now that you've seen me in my bra, you can call me Alicia."

He laughed. "Thanks, Alicia." He sipped some tea, then put the cup down. "How are you feeling now?"

"Good. I remember what happened now. I locked myself out of the house. Then I got all bent out of shape about it and I overheated."

"I read your medic alert tag."

"You did?" she asked nervously.

"I know you have MS and that's probably why you fainted this morning. You know you really shouldn't be out in the heat. It isn't good for you."

She hung her head. "I know. I'm stupid."

"Listen, Alicia, you may have done a stupid thing, but stupid isn't a word I'd use to describe you."

"Thanks. That makes me feel better."

"How long ago were you diagnosed? If you don't mind me asking."

"Nearly two years ago."

"I see. Are you on any of the injections?"

"Yes. I started with Avonex a little while back."

He nodded his head knowingly. "Did you do an injection recently?"

"Yes, I did my shot on Friday."

He nodded knowingly. "That explains your fever yesterday. One of the side effects of Avonex is a fever or flu-like symptoms. In some patients it manifests like their skin is getting too hot, but it's actually the medication."

"My neurologist told me about it, but I thought that since it hadn't happened before, I was in the clear."

"The body is a fickle thing. One day something doesn't bother it and another day it does. That's why we doctors practice medicine."

"Good point. You're not going to tell anyone about my MS, are you?"

"No. There's this little thing called doctor/patient privilege."

"Thank you."

"You're welcome."

The way he stared at her unnerved Alicia a little. "I must look a mess." She combed through her curly auburn locks with her fingers.

"You look beautiful." He paused. "You'll have to excuse me if I'm staring. I've never seen you with your hair down before. I didn't realize how long it was."

"Wearing my hair up kind of goes along with the domestic diva image."

"You look good either way."

"Thanks," she said bashfully.

Suddenly there was a pounding at the door.

"Nate! Are you home?" Harrison shouted.

"It seems the National Guard has come looking for you."

"Oh, my God. I bet he's worried out of his mind."

He stood up. "Well, we'll just put his mind to rest." Nathaniel went to the door while Alicia continued drinking her tea.

"Nate!" Harrison continued pounding.

Nathaniel opened the door.

"Thank God you're here." He caught his breath. "I just got back and I can't find Alicia anywhere. Please tell me you've seen her."

"Come on in, Harry. She's in here. It seems she had a little accident by the pool this morning."

"She had an accident?" He sounded panicked.

Nathaniel put his hand on his shoulder to reassure him. "Don't worry, she's fine. Follow me." He led Harrison back to the living room.

"Thank God." He rushed over and hugged her. "You scared me to death. What happened? Why are you wet?"

"One thing at a time, Harrison," she said.

"If I may?" Nathaniel asked.

"Go ahead."

"She fainted from the heat outside and fell into the pool."

"Oh, my God."

"Calm down, Harrison. Lucky for me Nathaniel saw me go in and he pulled me out."

"Thanks, Nate. You're definitely a hero."

"You really are," Alicia agreed.

"I was just at the right spot at the right time. But young lady, you need to take your condition more seriously. MS isn't anything to play with."

"Yes, Doctor."

"I think I'd better get this young lady back home and into bed." Harrison stood up.

"Sounds like a good idea." Nathaniel smiled. "You need to take it easy."

"I will." She sat up and looked around the sofa. "Where's my shirt?"

"Right here." He picked it up and handed it to her. "I put it over there to dry out a little. It's probably damp."

She felt the shirt. "It's good enough." She took the blanket off.

"I'll turn away," Nathaniel said.

"I appreciate the gesture, but I think that horse has left the stable." She put the shirt back on and then stood up. Harrison helped her.

"Take it easy."

"I'm okay." They began walking to the door.

Once they got there Nathaniel held the door open.

"Thank you again," she said.

"I'm glad I was there."

"Me, too." She smiled.

They stepped outside.

"I'll give you an update later, Doc."

"I'm counting on it, Harry," he called back.

Harrison waited until they were a few steps away from Nathaniel's house. "And I thought politics made for strange bedfellows."

"Very funny, Harrison," Alicia said dryly. "Can I just go to bed in peace?"

"Sure. We'll talk about this later. You can bet on it." He helped her upstairs and into bed.

Harrison was in the kitchen when the doorbell rang.

"I'll be right there," he called as he walked to the door.

"It's us, Harrison!" Lauren called back.

He opened the door. "Hi. Come on in." He wiped his hands on a dish towel.

Lauren hugged him. "Thanks for calling us."

Gabby hugged Harrison too. "Where is she?"

"She's asleep upstairs."

"That's good. She probably needs the rest."

"There's no probably about it," Lauren added.

They walked into the living room.

"So what in the world happened, Harrison?" Lauren asked as she sat on the sofa.

"I don't know exactly. When I left this morning, she was in her office checking emails, and when I got back from the store, I couldn't find her anywhere."

"After yesterday shouldn't she have been in bed?"

"Wait a minute. What happened yesterday?"

"Gabby didn't tell you?"

"No."

"I'm sorry, I was going to tell you later. Alicia started to get sick yesterday at the luncheon. She had a fever."

"A fever? Did she go to the doctor?"

"No. The doctor came to her."

"That's right, I did hear you talking about Nate being there," Lauren recalled.

"He was there. He told her to get some bed rest."

"It appears she listened to him for a little while. She was getting ready to take a nap when I spoke to her Monday afternoon. So she actually managed to rest for a while."

"Until work beckoned her again." Gabby crossed her legs.

"We're a little off track here, Harrison. Why in the world was she outside? It's hotter than hell out there and heat isn't good for her."

"I know. When I left, she told me she was staying inside. I don't know why she went outside."

"We won't know that until she gets up. What did Nate say happened?"

"You can ask him for yourself, if you'd like. He's home."

"Maybe we'll do that." Lauren turned to Gabby. "Are you game?"

"Sure, I'm dying to know."

Lauren stood up. "Call me on my cell if she wakes up before we get back."

"Okay."

Two minutes later Gabby and Lauren were at Nathaniel's door. Lauren rang the bell.

"You know Alicia would kill us for this."

"She'll get over it."

Nathaniel opened the door. "Lauren, Gabby, how nice to see you."

"Hi, Nate. I hope we're not disturbing you."

"Not at all, come on in and get out of the heat." He stepped back to let them in.

"Thanks."

He closed the door behind them. "Come into the living room." He led them in. "Ladies, have seats, please. Can I get you anything to drink?"

"Nothing for me. What about you, Gabby?"

"I'm fine, too."

Gabby and Lauren looked around.

"You have a nice place here, Nate."

"Thanks, Gabby." He sat down. "So to what do I owe the pleasure?"

"Harrison called and told us what happened with Alicia earlier."

He nodded. "It was a little scary."

"Apparently you're a hero, diving into the water and rescuing her," Gabby said.

"I'm just glad I was there."

"So are we," Lauren added. "We came over to thank you."

"There's no need for thanks."

"According to Harrison, it's the second time in two days you've come to Alicia's rescue."

"You helped her when she got sick at the luncheon," Gabby interjected.

"Again, I happened to be at the right place at the right time." He smiled.

"That might be true, but not too many people would have known what to do," Lauren said.

"With a headache?" Nathaniel looked perplexed.

"No," Lauren laughed, "when she went into the pool."

"Oh."

"A lot of people would have panicked even if they knew what to do."

"Maybe my training as a doctor kicked in. We have to remain calm in tense situations. I simply dove in, pulled Alicia out and gave her mouth to mouth until she coughed up the water and was breathing again."

"That's all, he says." Lauren's mouth was agape.

"It's true." He leaned forward in his chair. "How is she?"

"She's sleeping."

"Good. She needs the rest. Her body had quite a shock today."

"True."

"Harry should be sure to contact her neurologist for an appointment."

Lauren and Gabby looked at each other nervously.

"Yes, I know she has MS. Don't worry, she's covered under doctor/patient privilege."

"We're not worried about that. We're just surprised she told you." Gabby said.

"She didn't tell me per se. I've had my suspicions for a while."

"You have?" Lauren was a little shocked.

"Yes. I just noticed little things, like how she modified her yoga and tai chi exercises."

Gabby and Lauren looked at each other, smiling. "You noticed how she modified her exercise routine?" Gabby asked.

Nathaniel looked a little self-conscious. "Don't get me wrong. I'm not stalking her."

"We didn't think you were," Lauren answered sweetly.

"I've occasionally seen her exercising outside some mornings. I also have a friend who's a physical therapist and he does the same routines with his MS patients."

"Oh, okay." Lauren nodded.

"Then yesterday I noticed her gait was off a bit at the luncheon."

"You noticed her gait?" Gabby asked.

"Yes. Alicia's got such a regal walk, I couldn't help but notice it wasn't quite the same."

Lauren and Gabby looked at each other knowingly.

Nathaniel looked at his watch. "Well, I hate to rush but I'm covering for one of my partners this afternoon. I really have to get going."

They stood up. "Oh, we won't keep you," Lauren said.

He walked them to the door. "I was going to stop by later to check on Alicia. Do you think that would be okay?"

"Sure." Gabby grinned. "I'm sure she'd like that."

He opened the door.

"Thanks again, Nate. Maybe we'll see you later."

"You ladies have a good day."

"We will," Gabby responded.

The door closed behind them as they headed back to Alicia's.

"Did you hear that?"

"I certainly did. It seems Dr. Becker has another concentration besides medicine." Lauren smirked.

Later on Harrison, Lauren and Gabby were in Alicia's bedroom.

"Did Kurt call back yet?" Lauren asked.

"No, they've been trying to reach him. He's off-site and doesn't seem to have any cell phone reception."

"Good grief."

"They sent someone out to let him know. I expect he'll be calling any time now."

"Good." Lauren looked at a sleeping Alicia. "I know she'll think we shouldn't have called him, but he deserves to know."

"I've been trying to call Walt and Loretta, but they haven't called me back yet." Harrison said.

"Don't call my parents," Alicia mumbled.

"Oh, she's alive." Gabby went over to the bed.

"I was only sleeping."

"You've been knocked out for a while today. How are you feeling?"

"I'm okay, Harrison."

"You certainly scared the hell out of us." Lauren hugged her.

Gabby echoed the sentiment. "That's the truth."

"I'm sorry to have scared you. I think I scared myself." She sat up slowly.

"I made some soup. Would you like some?" Harrison asked.

"You made soup in June?"

"Well, shoot me. I didn't know the right dish to serve after someone nearly drowns. So I made soup."

"Okay, Harrison, don't be so touchy. I was just kidding. I would love some soup."

"Okay, I'll be right back." He left.

"You know he blames himself for what happened."

"It wasn't his fault, Lauren. I'm the dunderhead. I'll talk to him."

"Good. In the meantime you can talk to us and tell us what happened."

"What possessed you to go outside in this heat?" Gabby sat on her bed.

"Is this an inquisition?"

"Yes, at this point it is." Lauren sat down.

Alicia knew she'd been painted into a corner. "I was going through my email and that zygote . . ."

"I should have known this had something to do with Taylor Dawes." Lauren hung her head.

"I really think she's trying to push me out."

"You have to stop being so paranoid, Alicia. She's just the managing editor."

"Who has designs on my office, Gabby. I don't trust her, and after today I really don't think I'm imagining things."

"What happened today?" Lauren asked.

"I got an email from my production manager about the cover layout and it was all wrong. They'd mixed up the summer and fall topics on the cover."

"It could have been an honest mistake."

"But it went down to production with my signature on it as if I approved it." She paused. "That reminds me, there's a staff meeting on Thursday."

"You're not going, right?" Gabby asked.

"No, I'm conferencing in by phone."

"No, you're not." Lauren sounded final.

"Excuse me?"

"You heard me. I'm sure someone will be there to take the minutes and send you a summary."

"A summary isn't the same thing as being on the phone."

"I know, but that's the best you're going to get. You nearly drowned today, and all you can think about is calling in for a staff meeting. You have to rest."

"The staff meeting isn't until Thursday. Listen, I promise I'll be a good patient until then."

"Where have we heard that before?" Lauren said acerbically.

"I really will be good," Alicia insisted.

Gabby and Lauren didn't buy it.

"Okay, listen, you two. Taylor has got the Three Stooges under her spell, which means she has the ear, or should I say pants, of three, of the twelve board members."

"That still leaves nine others who aren't ruled by their pants," Gabby reasoned.

"You know, I get the feeling there's something else going on here, Alicia," Lauren said.

Alicia looked away.

"We're prepared to stay here all day until you tell us." Gabby folded her arms.

Alicia let out a deep breath. "A few months ago Taylor walked into my office while I was in the midst of a very painful spasm, and it was all I could do to get her out of there. Ever since then it seems like she's lurking around, looking for the chance to take me down. That's why I agreed to go on the medication."

Lauren put her arm around her. "Alicia, you're making something out of nothing. Now if you'd tell everyone about your condition, you wouldn't have to worry about someone finding out."

"Do you really think the board or the shareholders would embrace an editor-in-chief and CEO with an incurable disease?"

"Come on, Alicia, this isn't the Dark Ages. If anything, you would inspire people," Gabby said cheerfully.

"You think I would have inspired people this morning? Falling into the pool like some drunken idiot?"

"You're not an idiot." Harrison entered with a tray.

"You tell her, Harrison," Gabby said.

He put the tray on the table and sat down next to her on the bed. "Move over." He smiled.

"I'm sorry, Harrison."

"You know my Martha had MS, so you know I understand what you're going through."

Alicia started to tear up. "I'm afraid, Harrison. I'm not normal anymore and I don't know what's going to happen to me."

He handed her a tissue. "You're going to be fine, sweetheart. You are surrounded by people who love and care for you, and that includes that pesky neighbor of ours."

Alicia smiled. "Who would have ever thought Nathaniel Becker would come to my rescue."

Gabby raised her hand. "I did."

Lauren raised her hand, too. "So did I."

"That makes three of us." Harrison smiled as he raised his hand.

"I guess I have to be nice to him now."

"You think?" Lauren asked sarcastically.

"All right, I'll be nice."

"Good, maybe you can be a little more than just nice. I really think he likes you." Gabby poked her leg.

"I said I'd be nice. Don't push it." She looked at the clock. "Is that the time?"

"Yes. It's almost four."

"How long have you two been here?"

"Harrison called us this morning and we got here at about noon or maybe closer to twelve-thirty. Right, Lauren?"

"That sounds about right."

"You have careers to worry about. You didn't have to run up here and check on me."

Lauren hit her leg.

"Ouch."

"That's for saying something so silly. Like you wouldn't drop everything if the same thing happened to us."

"You're right." She wiped her eyes. "So let's talk about something far more interesting, like your love lives."

Harrison got up. "That's my cue to exit stage right. Let me know if you need anything, okay?" He kissed Alicia's forehead.

"Okay."

"Have fun, girls." He shut the door.

"Now here's the deal, Ms. Archer. You already know all you need to know for now about our love lives. We want to talk about you," Lauren said and pointed at her.

"Oh, boy," Alicia groaned. "Lucky me. Why is it only I rate this kind of attention?"

"You're the one who talks about romance and elegance, yet you live a life devoid of any of it." Lauren looked around. "I mean, you have all the trappings, but no one to share them with."

"Haven't we beaten this horse out of existence yet?"

"No. "

"Terrific." Alicia's face fell.

"Both Lauren and I know you had a great thing with Kurt, that he was your Mr. Darcy. But we think there is someone else out there for you."

"You're talking about Nathaniel, aren't you?"

"Yes. He kind of fits the bill, doesn't he? He's tall, dark, handsome and somewhat brooding, like Mr. Darcy."

"And he does drive you crazy." Lauren winked.

"Okay, you two. I appreciate your enthusiastic approval. I promise I'll be nicer to Nathaniel, but that's as far as I'm going."

"Why?"

Alicia made up her mind not to talk about it anymore. She picked up her soup. "It's cold now. Can you ask Harrison to heat it up, please?"

Lauren took the bowl. "Sure. You're off the hook for now."

"Thank you. How about we watch *Emma?*" Alicia asked, hoping to quickly change the subject.

"You know she's not going to let us say another word." Gabby got up. "I'll get the DVD from downstairs."

"I'll heat up your soup and get some popcorn for the movie." Lauren headed for the door.

"Thank you." Alicia smiled.

"I hope you know this conversation isn't over."

"Believe me, I know." Alicia nodded.

"We'll be back." Gabby grinned as she and Lauren left the room.

Alicia knew she'd only bought herself a little more time. She had to do something for Nathaniel. After all, he had saved her life, and just being nicer didn't seem like enough. *What do you get for the man who saved your life? I don't think Hallmark makes a "thank you for saving my life" card. I have to do something personal,* how personal she didn't know.

CHAPTER 9

A couple of hours later after Lauren and Gabby left, Alicia felt a little restless lying in bed. "Oh," she sighed as she attempted to find a comfortable position. *This isn't going to work. I have to do something.* She flung the covers back and got out of bed. Alicia put on a pair of jeans and shirt and went downstairs.

Harrison was at the table reading the paper. "What are you doing out of bed?"

"I'm fine, Harrison."

"You nearly killed yourself this morning."

"Believe me, I know, but it's over with. Can we please move on?" she begged.

"I hope you learned a lesson."

"Yes. I'll never leave the house again without my keys."

Harrison rolled his eyes. "You are so stubborn."

"I know that, and so do you."

"Did you enjoy the movie with the girls?"

"Yes. *Emma* is one of my favorite movies, even though I've seen it a hundred times or more."

"I know. Are you hungry for something more than soup now?"

"Yes, but I thought I'd come down and make dinner."

"Are you sure you feel up to cooking?"

"You know I always have energy to entertain."

Harrison was perplexed. "What do you mean, entertain?"

"I thought that maybe you would invite Nathaniel to join us. He did save my life today."

He was dumbfounded. "You want to invite Nate to dinner?"

"Sure." She went over to the refrigerator. "Do we have lamb chops?"

"I think so."

"Good. We can have lamb chops with a lemon-basil sauce, Mesclun salad and . . ." She put her hand on her hip. "Do we still have the pound cake I made?"

"Yes. I don't know how much is left." He went over to the counter and lifted the cake dome. "It's not too bad."

Alicia looked over. "That's plenty. I have lemon curd and raspberries to make individual trifles. All I have to do is make whipped cream to top it."

"Sounds like a plan to me. What do you need to me to do?"

"I need you to go next door and invite Nathaniel."

"Why don't you just call him yourself?"

"Do we have his phone number?"

Harrison went over to the counter drawer and leafed through her phone book. "Here it is."

He took the phone off the base and dialed. "Here you go."

"No, you talk."

"Hello?"

Alicia reluctantly took the phone. "Hello, Nathaniel. It's Alicia."

"Hello, Alicia. How are you feeling?"

"I'm good, thanks."

"Glad to hear it."

"Umm, the reason I'm calling is to invite you to dinner tonight to thank you. Uh, I'll understand if you already have plans . . ."

"I'd love to. Thank you."

"You would?" She seemed genuinely surprised.

"Yes. What time should I be there?"

She looked at the clock. "Dinner will be ready in an hour. Is that all right?"

"Sure. I'm looking forward to it."

"Okay. We'll see you then."

"Okay." He hung up.

Alicia stood with the phone in her hand. Harrison laughed as he took it away from her.

"You look nervous."

"I'm not nervous." She began to gather the ingredients. A few things rolled on the floor.

"Right." He was tickled.

"Just help me."

"Yes, ma'am."

While Alicia cooked the lamb chops and made the sauce, Harrison tossed the salad, then set the table. As he walked between the kitchen and dining room he watched Alicia methodically put a lovely, sumptuous and even sexy meal together.

"Harrison!" she called.

"Yes?" He quickly went back into the kitchen.

Alicia balanced three desserts in her hands. "Would you please hold the fridge open for me so I can put these in to chill?"

"Sure." He held the door while she put them in.

"Thank you."

He looked at the clock. "I think you'd better go change."

"Oh yes." She took her apron off. "I'll be back in ten."

"Take your time," he said as she walked out. "Believe me, he thinks you're worth the wait."

"You just had to say it, didn't you?"

"Would you expect any less from me?" He chuckled.

Once upstairs in her room Alicia stood in front of her closet. "Oh, my God, I have Lauren's disease. What am I going to wear?" She sat on the edge of her bed. *What's wrong with me? It's not a date and even if it were a date he's already seen me in my bra.* She hung her head. *I can't believe I'm letting this drive me nuts.* She stared into her closet. "There it is." She got up.

When the doorbell rang, Harrison answered it.

"Hi, Nate, come on in."

"Thanks." He stepped in carrying a bottle of wine. "I wasn't sure what was on the menu, but I brought Cabernet Sauvignon." He showed it to Harrison.

"This will go nicely with the lamb chops you're having."

"You're not having dinner with us?" Alicia asked as she descended the stairs.

Both men were speechless as Alicia descended the stairs in a cotton short-sleeved dress that showed off a little cleavage and her shapely legs.

"No, Edie Buckley asked me to be a fourth at bridge tonight."

"Why didn't you mention this to me earlier?" She walked over.

"I guess in all the excitement of the morning it slipped my mind." He picked his keys up. "I think you're in good hands here." He kissed her cheek. "Enjoy. Have a good night, Nate."

"You too, Harry," Nathaniel grinned.

Harrison walked out.

"You look lovely."

"Thank you."

"It smells great in here."

"I hope you're hungry."

"I brought my appetite." He hesitated. "I wasn't sure what wine to bring but I settled on Cabernet Sauvignon. Harrison said we're having lamb chops."

Alicia nervously combed through her hair with her fingers. "Yes, Cabernet Sauvignon goes nicely with lamb. Good choice." She paused. "I guess we should go in."

He stepped out of her way. "After you."

Alicia and Nathaniel were greeted by a very romantic table setting complete with candles and mood lighting.

I'm going to kill Harrison, Alicia thought.

Nathaniel looked quite pleased. "This looks terrific."

"It does."

"Allow me, please." He held her chair out.

"Thank you." She sat down.

Nathaniel spied the wine opener on the table. "Shall I?"

"Please do."

He opened the wine and poured two glasses before taking a seat.

Alicia raised her glass. "Here's to my rescuer. Thank you."

"I'm glad I was there."

Once they toasted, Alicia timidly sipped her wine. Nathaniel found her nervousness cute. She was usually a pretty cool customer.

He looked at his plate. "This looks amazing. How is this prepared?"

"I seasoned and pan cooked the lamb chops, then I made the lemon basil sauce to finish. I was going to make a summer vegetable like asparagus, but then I thought you would appreciate a nice light salad."

"I'm a bachelor, Alicia, I appreciate any meals that don't come in a box or bag."

She laughed. "Then dig in."

"I will." He cut into a lamb chop and took a bite. "Oh, this is amazing."

Alicia was tickled as she prided herself on her ability to prepare lamb chops that were moist and cooked perfectly instead of overcooked and dry. "I'm glad you like it."

He took a few more bites. "You know, Alicia, I've always wanted to know what inspired you to be the domestic diva you are. I know you can cook, but you've taken it to another level."

She put her napkin down. "No one has asked me that in a long time." She pondered a moment. "I wish I could say it was some glorious family tradition, but it was necessity. My parents worked full time and they really didn't have the time to make meals for my younger sister and me. As the oldest I pitched in to cook, and that's when I realized I liked to cook. So I started experimenting with new recipes and trying them out on my family . . ." She trailed off. "The rest is history."

"Somehow I think there is more to it than that."

"There was more to it. Cooking was a way for me to express my creativity and show love to the people I cared about. I didn't come from one of those touchy-feely and share-your-emotions families. My mother worked in the junior high cafeteria and my father was a math teacher. They had to work hard for my sister and me to have a better life. Cooking was the least I could do to repay them."

"You're a good daughter."

"I try to be. Now that I've got the show, my books and the magazine, it feels good to do things for my parents." She started to laugh.

"What's so funny?"

"I was just thinking about my parents. They always wanted a Winnebago, and my sister and I went in together and got them one for their forty-eighth anniversary. Now they're off to see the real America, or as my sister says, they're off terrorizing the countryside." She let out a hearty laugh.

Nathaniel was tickled to see her so unguarded. "Your parents sound like fun."

"They are fun. We had a GPS installed, but somehow I know they're still arguing over who can read a map better."

He laughed.

Alicia sipped her wine. "This is good. I'm glad you brought it."

"Me, too."

Alicia put her glass down. "There's something I want to say, but I'm afraid you'll take it the wrong way."

"Go ahead and say it. I'm a big boy."

"I'm surprised you were available for dinner tonight. You usually have . . . company."

Nathaniel laughed. "That's your polite way of saying I have a lot of women traipsing in and out of my place, isn't it?"

"Yes. Emily Post covers a lot of situations, but this isn't in any of her books."

"Maybe she should add a chapter. I bet she'd sell more books."

"I bet you're right."

"Anyway, to answer your question, even I need a little down time. Did that answer your question?"

"Yes. Thank you for not getting offended."

"It's not a problem, Alicia. I don't offend easily."

"That's good to know." She took another sip of wine. "I'll change the subject a little, Nathaniel. Why did you go into medicine? Like my mother says, your family has been walking in high cotton for some time."

"Well, I was never interested in the moneymaking end of the family wealth. I wanted to help people, and I really liked medicine."

"I see. So why do you practice in Scarsdale?"

"Socialites need good doctors, too," he quipped.

"Somehow I don't believe that's the reason."

"I'll bite. What do you think my reasons are?"

"I suspect it has something to do with all those exotic photos and keepsakes you have in your house."

"Interesting theory . . ."

"I've traveled enough to know the difference between an African souvenir and a handmade gift."

"And I thought you were too out of it to notice anything this morning."

"I couldn't help but notice. Am I on the right track?"

"You're very perceptive."

"So while everyone here thinks you're off on another wild extended holiday, you're really on a mission."

"I work with Doctors Without Borders in Africa. The number of AIDS cases in Africa is astounding, and the fact is most of those numbers don't include the countless villages where nearly all the women and children have AIDS. They are the poorest people, with no access to any of the drugs that can help prolong their lives."

Alicia was moved by his sincerity. "Wow."

"The trade-off for me is I spend time here treating migraines, stomach ailments and allergies, so I can make a difference with my time and money to help those who really need it."

"You know what really impresses me is that you don't just write a check at a charity luncheon. You give of yourself. That's truly wonderful."

"Thanks." He smiled. "Don't spread it around. It might ruin my hard-won reputation."

"Your secret is safe with me." She finished her glass of wine.

In the course of an hour Alicia went from thinking of Nathaniel as a doctor/playboy to a doctor with a conscience. It appeared she'd found more than just a rescuer in him; he was a real unsung hero, much like her Kurt.

After dinner Alicia and Nathaniel retired to the living room for dessert and coffee.

Seated comfortably on the sofa, Nathaniel licked his spoon like a little boy. "I'm telling you, Alicia, you spoiled me tonight."

"My pleasure."

He put the dish down and leaned closer to Alicia. "There's something else I've always wanted to know."

"I'm listening."

"I always see Lauren and Gabby here. You three are like the three amigos. You guys have been friends a long time."

"Yes. We met at Miss Porter's Boarding School in Connecticut."

"I've heard of that place."

"It's an *expensive* girl's boarding school. Lauren's from Bayside and I'm from Amityville. Our parents couldn't afford to send us there. We both went on scholarships. Like you, Gabby's family had money, so she had no problem getting in." She sighed. "Anyway, we were three scared girls away from home for the first time and we just bonded."

"You were lucky."

"I couldn't have ordered better friends." She started to snicker.

"What's so funny?"

"I was just remembering. Gabby told her parents she was bringing two friends from school home for break. The look on her mother's face when she saw us . . ."

"A real 'guess who's coming to dinner' moment, huh?"

"Oh, God yes. And then we were fat, too. I thought Mrs. Blanchard would die on the spot."

Nathaniel burst out laughing. "I can imagine. How was her dad?"

"Mr. B was cool. He would have the cook secretly bring us ice cream after Mrs. Blanchard gave us fruit and cottage cheese for dessert."

He made a face. "Yuck, cottage cheese."

"No kidding."

"Tell me," he leaned forward, "what kind of shenanigans did you girls get into at boarding school?"

"I forgot girls' boarding schools are the stuff young men's dreams are made of."

"I have to admit it crossed my mind."

"Well, I hate to disappoint you, but we weren't a part of the 'in' girls who went on dates, spent hours doing their hair, smoked pot or snuck boys up to their rooms. We were straight A students. Our only crime was being big in a sea of skinny and mostly blonde girls. Gabby, though, had the blonde thing covered."

"You survived."

"Yes, we did." Alicia had a far-off look in her eyes. "It would have been nice, though, if someone had asked us out, even once."

"It was their loss." Nathaniel took a chance and got closer to Alicia. "I bet you were a beautiful girl."

Before she could utter a word he kissed her gently. "And you're a beautiful woman." They kissed again, and though the first kiss took Alicia by surprise, she kissed him back the second time. The kiss intensified as they wrapped their arms around each other.

Nathaniel struggled to keep his hands still. He longed to explore the curves of her body and feel her soft skin under his touch, but he held back. Alicia tingled from head to toe. It was a rush she hadn't felt since Kurt. She wanted more and it scared her.

She pulled away. "Oh." She pulled at her dress nervously.

"Alicia, I don't want to push, but I want to spend more time getting to know you, and I hope you want to know more about me."

"I do. It's been a long time."

"I understand. You're a widow."

"Yes, and I haven't gone out with a man for coffee, let alone a date."

"I totally get that."

"Do you really? I need to do it at my own pace. Can you live with that?"

"Yes." He stood up and took her by the hand. "As long as it takes."

"Thank you." She got up.

"It's getting late. I should let you get some rest."

"Okay."

She walked him to the door.

"How about dinner on Friday night?"

She laughed. "You don't waste any time, do you?"

"Not when something's important to me."

"Dinner would be nice."

"Great. I know I only live next door but I'll pick you up at seven. Is that okay?"

"Sounds good."

"Great." He kissed her hand.

Alicia's stomach filled with butterflies as Nathaniel leaned in for another kiss. They were on fire the minute their lips touched again, so enraptured they didn't notice a tickled Harrison had come in.

Harrison cleared his throat and the bubble burst.

"Oh, hi, Harry." Nathaniel smiled.

"How long have you been standing there, Harrison?"

"Long enough." He chuckled.

Nathaniel turned to Alicia. "On that note, thank you for dinner and I will see you Friday night."

"You're welcome. I'll see you then."

He kissed her on the cheek. "Good night, Alicia. Sweet dreams."

"Good night, Nathaniel."

"Check you later, Harry." He patted him on the back.

"Okay, Nate."

Nathaniel walked off with a little pep in his step. As Harrison closed the door, Alicia tried to make a clean getaway. She made it up four steps.

"Oh no, you don't, young lady. You're not getting away that easy."

Alicia stopped.

"I know we said you should be nicer to Nate, but I didn't know you'd be that nice," he teased.

"I don't know what happened. We had a nice time at dinner."

"Obviously." He winked.

"Don't do that, Harrison. I actually feel kind of guilty." She sat down on the staircase.

"Why? You didn't do anything wrong. I was just teasing you."

"I know, but I haven't kissed anyone like that since Kurt."

He walked over and took her hand. "It's okay, Alicia. You haven't cheated on your husband."

"Why does it feel like I did?"

"That's only natural, Alicia. You feel like that because you're getting on with your life, which is something Kurt would have wanted you to do."

"My head says the same thing, but my heart is another matter altogether."

"Give it a chance with Nate. Are you going out with him?"

"He asked me out to dinner on Friday night."

"Did you say yes?"

She nodded.

"Good." He helped her up. "Go out, have a good time and just enjoy yourself. If today has proven anything, it's that life can change in an instant. You need to live in the now."

"I know you're right." She yawned.

"Gabby and Lauren will be thrilled."

"It's just a date, Harrison. I didn't split the atom." She began to climb the stairs.

"You're going on a date for the first time in how many years?"

"I'm afraid to count."

"As far as we're concerned, this ranks right up there with solving global warming."

"You're hilarious, Harrison," Alicia said wryly.

"I've got a million of 'em."

⁊

Just before she went to sleep, Alicia sat on the edge of her bed and stared at the photo she kept of Kurt in her night table. *Nathaniel's the kind of guy you would have a beer with, I think.* Her fingers lightly outlined his image. *Oh, my God, Kurt. I kissed him. What would you think about that?*

Harrison saw her through a crack in the door. "Alicia?" he knocked.

She put the photo back in the drawer and slipped into bed. "Come on in, Harrison."

He walked in. "I just wanted to see if you needed anything before I went to bed."

"I'm fine, Harrison. Thank you."

"Okay." He paused. "I saw you were saying good night to Kurt."

"I don't do it every night like I used to, but I wanted to see his face before I went to sleep."

"I understand."

"Harrison, do you really think Kurt would be okay with my going out? Give me your honest opinion."

He smiled warmly. "Alicia, I already told you I'm sure of it."

"I know you did, but I still feel weird."

"It's only natural you'd feel weird. Kurt was the first and only man you ever loved."

"I thought we'd be together forever."

"You're still together. He's right there in your heart, just like Martha's in mine."

Alicia smiled. "Oh, my God. I kissed Nathaniel Becker." She shook her head. "What was that about?"

"If I had to guess, I'd say you were attracted to him."

"I don't understand."

"What's to understand, Alicia? You like him. You really like him." He did his best Sally Field impersonation.

Alicia threw a pillow at him. "Hey! You're a regular comedian tonight, aren't you?"

He picked the pillow up. "All kidding aside, Alicia, you're going on a date, that's all. Whatever happens after that, you'll deal with it. For now, take it one day at a time."

"You're right. I should relax." She snuggled under the covers.

"Now get some rest."

"Good night, Harrison."

"Good night, dear."

CHAPTER 10

Although Ken had returned his apartment key, Lauren decided she was better off working from her office in case Ken rang the doorbell with his latest conquest. Moreover, she wanted an excuse to wear the new cream-colored "non-Hillary" pantsuit she'd bought from Lord and Taylor. She possessed an extensive wardrobe and although In the Mix Productions had a dress-down policy for the summer to give people a break, she rarely exercised her right to dress down. She was, however, exercising her right to be on the phone.

"So you're telling me she and Nate are going out?" She grinned like a Cheshire cat.

"You heard it here first," Harrison said.

Lauren laughed. "Will wonders never cease?"

"Not if Nate has his way."

"He is into her. It's about time she noticed." Lauren tapped the desk.

"Amen to that, sister."

"Where is Alicia anyway? I was sure I'd hear her stirring by now."

"Believe it or not she's still in bed. I think yesterday's events caught up with her."

"Good. She needs the rest." Lauren looked at her watch. "Listen, Harrison, I've got a stack of paperwork to get through. I'll give her a call later so I can tease her."

"I know you will."

"I'll talk to you later."

"Okay, Lauren."

Lauren hung up the phone and spun around in her chair. "Alicia's going on a date with Dr. Nate." She laughed. "Heck, it even rhymes."

"Knock, knock."

She looked up. It was Ken's agent, Patrick. "Hey, Patrick, what brings you by this neck of the woods?"

The short, silver-haired man smiled wide with his baby blues. Lauren knew he wanted something.

"Do you have a few minutes?"

"Have a seat." She motioned for him to sit and braced herself. "What's up, Patrick?"

"Ken called me about the email the network sent you."

"I forwarded it to you. Didn't you get it?"

"Yes."

"I thought it was pretty self explanatory."

"You're right, it was."

"Then why are you here?"

"Ken asked me to try to convince you to work with me on it."

"Why? You're more than capable of dealing with the powers that be."

"He's used to having you on it as well."

"And what do you think?"

"I think he's the client. I'm just following instructions."

Lauren shook her head in disbelief. "He's already a field commentator on the highest rated NFL show on television, and now they've asked him to cover the training camps this summer. It's all good. What more does he want?"

Patrick just looked at her.

A light went off in her head. "He wants to be one of the guys behind the desk, doesn't he?"

"He is a football great."

"Those guys paid their dues to get where they are. They didn't have the advantage of being married to a network insider."

"I get it, but you know how Ken is when he has something on his mind."

"Enough said. You can tell him you asked and I said no. If he wants it, he's going to have to wait and work like they did."

"He's not going to be happy."

"It's not my job to worry about Ken's happiness anymore. He's a big boy and he can take care of himself."

"Everything else aside, Lauren, I am sorry about the divorce. I know Ken ruined a good thing."

"I appreciate your saying that, Patrick." She sighed. "Life goes on."

He got up. "Is it okay if I give you a hug good-bye?"

"Sure." She stood up and they hugged.

"You take care of yourself, Lauren."

"You too, Patrick."

When he left her office, Lauren turned her chair to face the window. *It's hard for me to swallow that for the*

*second time in a row I picked a man who was more inter-
ested in what I could do for him than in me.* She sighed
aloud. *I paid my dues. Mitchell thought he was going to ride
my coattails to go from production assistant to executive producer, and when that didn't happen he was out the door.
Ken said he wasn't interested in playing the game with the
network.* She huffed. *That was a joke.*

Her phone rang.

"Lauren Jules-Jones," she answered, still in a huff.

"Whoa! Who put a bee in your bonnet?" Gabby
asked jokingly.

"Sorry. Patrick was here."

"Ken's agent was there? What did he want?"

"He was doing Ken's bidding." She shrugged it off.
"It's not worth talking about. Anyway you're calling
about the big news, I bet."

"Yes. Alicia's going on a date."

"Can you believe it?"

"I think something must have happened in that
pool."

"As bad as it was, it was sort of romantic. I mean, she
fell in the pool and he rushed over and pulled her to
safety."

"And he gave her mouth to mouth."

"Alicia doesn't remember any of it."

"I bet you he does."

"Have you talked to her yet?" Lauren asked.

"I called earlier, but Harrison said she was still in bed."

"Oh, that doesn't sound like her at all. You know
Alicia gets up with the worms."

"I know. I bet after yesterday Harrison has her on lockdown."

Lauren laughed. "You know she's going nuts."

"God knows I love her, but she's a royal pain in the butt if you try to hold her down."

"Let's hope we don't wind up with two people in recovery."

⁂

"You know I'm the person who signs your check," Alicia fumed.

"I know." Harrison put a tray of tea on the table.

"How am I supposed to stay on top of things if I'm not in my office?"

After the pool incident Harrison had been keeping a more watchful eye than usual, so instead of being in her office, Alicia was exiled to the family room.

"You have your fan mail to keep you busy," Harrison said, nodding towards the bag of letters next to her.

"What about my email?"

"You have a staff to help you with it. Why don't you let them do their job?"

Alicia shot him a dirty look as she opened a letter.

"Was that so hard?"

She opened the letter.

"Who's it from?" Harrison asked as he sat down.

"It's from Nadia Duncan, who watches on WABC TV in New York. Nadia says she enjoys all of the cooking, decorating and entertaining ideas, but she wants to know if I'll ever expand to include gardening tips."

"She obviously doesn't know your background." He laughed.

"That's true. I'd much rather read *The Good Earth* than put my hands in it. Kurt was the garden lover." She paused a moment. "He would spend weeks, even months, creating just the right soil mixtures for every tree, flower and potted plant we had. Whenever I wanted to know where he was, I'd just follow the dirt trail."

Harrison smiled.

She pondered a moment. "You know, we do give gardening tips in the magazine. Maybe I should think about adding a 'green' corner."

"That's not a bad idea."

"I'll talk to Lauren about it."

"See? It's not so bad going through actual mail for a change."

"You might have a point," she admitted grudgingly.

"Mind if I write that down?" he joked.

"I'm not that bad."

He got up and kissed her on the forehead. "No, you're not that bad at all."

The doorbell rang.

"Are you expecting anyone today?" Harrison asked.

"No. Must be a delivery or something."

"I'll be right back."

"Okay." Alicia went back to sorting through the bag of letters. "I thought they said letter writing was dead." She looked at all three bags.

"Look who I found."

Kurt Jr. rushed over to the sofa and hugged her. "I heard what happened yesterday in the pool. I would have been out here yesterday, but we were working way out east and I had no reception."

"I understand. I'm fine, sweetie." She patted his back.

"Are you sure, Mom?" His eyes seemed to fill with tears. "I'm so sorry I wasn't here yesterday."

"Oh, sweetie, if you cry I will fall to pieces right here."

He wiped his eyes. "I know, Mom. It's just the thought of losing you . . ."

She caressed his cheek. "I'm not going anywhere. You see I'm still in one piece."

"Thanks to Nathaniel Becker," Harrison added.

"I have to be sure to thank him, too. I'm sure you thanked him."

"Sure," Alicia said weakly.

"Mom, the man saved your life. Surely that rates a thank you."

Alicia looked over at Harrison, who looked at the wall.

"What's going on here? What's with the looks?"

Alicia knew she needed to bite the bullet and tell him about the date, but she was hesitant.

"I'll leave you two alone for a while. I'll be in the kitchen if anyone needs me." Harrison left.

"What is it, Mom? Are you really okay?"

"Well . . ." she began.

"Come on, you're killing me, Mom."

"I invited Nathaniel to dinner last night to thank him."

"Oh, that was nice."

"I thought it was the least I could do, but then . . ."

"Then what?"

"Nathaniel asked me out to dinner Friday night and I agreed." She braced herself.

Kurt Jr. didn't say a word.

"I realize this is sudden, so if you're not comfortable I won't go."

"Why in the world would you think that, Mom?"

"It's one thing to say you want me to date, but it's something different when it happens."

Kurt smiled. "I've been the one telling you that you needed to date."

"But you and your dad were so close."

"Mom, I love Dad and I miss him every day, but I want you to be happy and live your life. I think it's great that you're going out on a date."

Alicia felt a tear roll down her face. "Thank you." She kissed his forehead.

"I can't say I'm surprised it's Nate."

"Is that right?"

"Yeah, Mom. It's kind of like elementary school. Guys pick on the girls they like, and Nate never seemed to miss an opportunity to get under your skin."

She laughed. "So you mean even though they go from recess to recessive hairlines guys still use playground tactics? That's funny."

"It works."

"Apparently."

Kurt Jr. leaned back on the sofa. "So how long has it been since you've been on an actual date, Mom?"

"Ronald Reagan was president."

"Wow."

"Hey!" She playfully hit him on the shoulder. "It's not like I said Lincoln."

"Okay, Mom." He rubbed his shoulder.

Harrison walked back in. "Everything okay in here?"

"Yes, Mr. H. Mom's going out with Nate."

"I know. Will wonders never cease?"

"You think Nate knows what he's in for?"

"Hey!" Alicia protested.

"I'm just teasing, Mom."

"Kurt, I made your Mom's sour cream coffee cake. Can I interest you?"

He jumped up. "You don't have to ask me twice." He turned to Alicia. "Are you coming, Mom?"

"You go ahead for now. I'm going to go through a few more letters and then I'll join you."

"In case you're thinking about it, I locked your office door."

"Okay, warden."

"Very funny, Alicia," Harrison said as he turned to leave.

As Alicia sorted the letters she listened to Harrison and Kurt Jr. chat in the kitchen, and for a moment she remembered the sounds of him and his dad from the house in Bronxville. Kurt had had an infectious laugh that filled whatever room he was in and Kurt Jr. sounded

189

just like him. Deep down Alicia knew that a man who loved life as much as Kurt did would want her to get on with the business of living.

⁓

After she'd spent the day supervising new installations and working with the event planner for the upcoming exhibit, Gabby returned to her office. She still looked pulled together in a simple yet classic black sheath dress with a soft yellow jacket. She knew the outfit would make a nice transition from day to evening for her date with Nigel.

"I have to remember to ask Victor about the lighting crew," Gabby mumbled as she jotted her thought down.

Robin walked in. "Listen, I know it's the end of the day but I need a little caffeine. Do you mind if I go on a Starbucks run?"

"Sure, go ahead."

"Do you want anything?"

"No, I'm going to dinner in a little while."

"Okay. I'll be back in a flash." She turned and left the office.

Gabby sat down and wrote her notes.

There was a knock at the door.

"Yes?" She looked up and saw Terrence Talbot. Tall, slim and blond, he was a tanner version of her ex-husband Bill.

"Hi, Gabby. It seems your assistant stepped away from her desk, so I took a chance."

"She went on a Starbucks run. How are you, Terrence?"

"I'm good, thanks. I was in the neighborhood on business and thought I'd stop by and say hello."

"That was nice of you. Come on in and have a seat." She motioned. *I'm going to kill my mother.*

"I ran into your mother a couple of weeks ago at the club."

"I know, she mentioned that at tea last Sunday."

"Oh, she did? I told her to tell you hello, but she said I should do it in person."

"That's my mother."

"So how have you been? I haven't seen you around the club in forever."

"The gallery keeps me busy."

"I noticed. How are the kids?"

"They're great, thanks. Ian's bouncing between the city and the Hamptons, and Lizzie's in Europe."

"They sure grow up fast."

"True. How are you?"

"I can't complain. I did go out west on business for a while. The weather was great but I still caught a cold . . ."

Terrence continued to drone on. Gabby tuned him out but nodded as if she was paying attention. *This is why he's been divorced six times. His ex-wives wanted to avoid death by boredom. He's the dullest man I know, and naturally he's the one my mother sends my way.*

"Gabby?"

"Oh, I'm sorry. Say that again."

"I asked if you were free to join me for a drink this evening."

"I'm sorry, I have plans this evening."

"I see. Perhaps another time."

"Perhaps."

He got up to leave. "It was good seeing you, Gabby."

"You too, Terrence," she lied.

Gabby waited a minute before she picked up the phone.

"Good afternoon, Blanchard residence."

"Hi, Ms. Cummings, it's Gabby. Is my mother around?"

"I'll check. Hold please."

"No problem." Gabby tapped her fingers on the desk. Her mother picked the phone up. "Hello?"

"Hello, Mother."

"Hello, Gabby. How are you?"

"I'm fine, Mother. How are you?"

"I'm good, dear."

"That's good to hear." She paused to take a breath. "Well, Mother, you will never guess who just dropped by the gallery. Terrence Talbot."

"Is that right? I guess he had business in the area."

"Business you sent him on."

"What do you mean?" She made an attempt to sound innocent.

"Come on, Mother. You were talking about him on Sunday and suddenly he shows up at the gallery in the middle of the week."

"Can I help it if great minds think alike?"

"Mother, Terrence Talbot is the dullest man on two legs. Haven't you ever noticed how women tend to scatter when he walks into a room?"

"That's what's wrong with you young people. You put too much emphasis on superfluous things."

"I don't think wanting to be with someone who is intellectually stimulating is superfluous."

"Gabrielle, you're getting older and not thinner. You can't continue to be so choosy. Do you want to end up alone?"

Bunny's words cut her. "Is that what you think, Mother? That I'm an old, fat divorcee who should be happy for any attention thrown my way?"

"I didn't say that."

"But that's what you meant."

"I meant no such thing."

"Well, Mother, despite your pronouncement I have plans with someone this evening, and it's not gallery-related. It's a date."

"I see."

"In fact, he'll be here in a little while and I need to freshen up. I'll talk to you later, Mother."

"Who is this fellow? Do we know him?"

"Give my love to Daddy. I'll be there this weekend to see him. Love you, Mother." She hung up and quickly left her office.

"I'll be in the ladies' room."

"Okay," Robin said as she sipped her coffee.

Gabby rushed to the ladies' room and went straight for the mirror. She studied her reflection, taking note of the fine lines on her face. *Am I kidding myself? I'm not a spring chicken and winter's coming.* She sighed. *Why do I let my mother do this to me? I just spent an amazing night with a man who made me feel like Botticelli's Venus.* She chuckled, stepped back and checked her outfit. She turned around to check out the rear view. "Not bad." She wiggled and then walked out, straight into Nigel.

"Hey, fancy meeting you like this." He smiled.

"Hi. I didn't expect you until later."

"I snuck out a little early today. I couldn't wait to see you." He put his arms around her.

Gabby felt herself turn into jelly. "I'm glad you did."

Soon they were locked in a sexy embrace.

"Hmm mm." Robin cleared her throat.

"Oh, Robin," Gabby was a little embarrassed. "You remember Nigel Clark."

"Yes."

"Nice to see you again." He shook her hand.

"You, too."

"Do you need something from me?"

"Oh yes, I almost forgot. Is there anything else you need me to do before we lock up tonight?"

"You know, I did want to talk to you for a minute. Do you mind, Nigel?"

"Not at all. I'll wait for you out here."

"I'll only be a minute." Gabby and Robin went into her office.

"What's the matter, Gabby?"

"I just wanted to explain about Nigel and me . . ."

She cut her off. "Gabby, it's none of my business."

"You work here, and he is a part of the new artist exhibition."

"Relax, Gabby, I know he didn't get a spot in the show because of your relationship."

"I didn't want you to have the wrong idea."

"It didn't even cross my mind. Do you know what I thought?"

"What?"

"You go, girl!" She chuckled. "He's a cutie."

"He certainly is." She blushed.

"Now go and have a good time tonight."

"I will. Thanks." She walked back out.

"Is everything okay?" he asked.

"Yes." Gabby grinned. "I'm ready when you are."

"Have a good night, you two." Robin waved.

"We will." Nigel winked.

A short while later Gabby and Nigel arrived at Restaurant Daniel, a very classy yet warm restaurant with an earthy appeal. Since it was a winner of the *New York Times* coveted five-star rating, Gabby was shocked Nigel was able to get a reservation. It was usually booked up at least a month or more in advance.

"Are you surprised?" He rubbed her hand.

"Yes, pleasantly surprised. How on earth did you get a reservation so soon?"

"Suffice it to say that being an investment banker has privileges that go far beyond money." He raised his eyebrow.

"This is very cool."

While they waited for the maître d', Gabby noticed Babette Henderson approaching. "Oh great," she groaned.

"What's wrong?"

"Do you see the brunette heading our way?"

"Yes."

"That's Babette Henderson. Her mother Faye and my mother have been friends forever."

"Do you know her from your boarding school days?"

"No, it's more like my short-lived debutante days."

The slim, petite Babette came closer. "Gabby, I thought that was you."

She went in for the European air kiss. "It's good to see you, Babette. Are you here with your mother?"

"No, Mother's in Monaco. I'm here with Ryan Fredericks. You remember him, don't you? He was on the polo team with Bill."

"Yes." She nodded.

She looked at Nigel. "Aren't you going to introduce us?" Babette asked eagerly.

"Oh, where are my manners. Babette, meet Nigel Clark."

The two shook hands.

"It's a pleasure to meet you, Ms. Henderson."

"Please call me Babette." She grinned.

They stepped up to the maître d'. "Name please."

"Nigel Clark."

He checked the book. "Yes, sir. Your table will be ready momentarily."

"Thank you."

"That gives us a little time to powder our noses." Babette smiled.

"Sure."

"I'll only be a minute," Gabby said.

"I'll be here." He smiled.

Gabby and Babette went to the ladies' room. Gabby wondered what Babette wanted and didn't waste time asking. "So what's going on, Babette?"

"I was going to ask you the same thing. The last time I saw your mother she mentioned something about Terrence Talbot."

"I'm not seeing Terrence, I can assure you."

"Good. If there was anyone who missed his calling as an anesthesiologist it was him. The man is mind-numbing."

Gabby snickered. "If I didn't know any better I'd say you were talking from experience."

Babette had been through one of the more contentious society divorces several years back. Her hand-picked husband Trip Collins was a philanderer, and the last straw came when he bedded one of their daughter's friends.

Babette dabbed her face with powder. "I made the mistake of dating him when he was in between wife number five and six." She closed her compact. "It was just after Trip and I divorced and I had something to prove."

"I see." Gabby was a little taken aback by her candor.

"If you think talking to him is like watching paint dry, you're lucky that's all you know."

"Wow." Gabby retouched her lipstick.

"So Nigel, he's quite a looker."

"Yes."

"Good for you."

"Thanks." She paused. "So you and Ryan are together?"

"No. We're just friends having a nice night out. Frankly, I think I'm Ryan's beard, only he doesn't know it or hasn't admitted it to himself yet."

"Bill always thought he swung both ways."

"He did? I'm surprised he never said anything."

"As long as he could ride a horse and play polo, Bill could have cared less if he swung sideways."

Babette laughed. "I guess we'd better get you back to your date."

They walked out of the ladies' room to a waiting Nigel.

"You two enjoy your dinner. It was nice meeting you, Nigel. I hope I see you again." She shook his hand.

"Thank you. I think that would be nice."

Babette walked back to her table.

"I can show you to your table now," the maître d' said.

"Thank you."

They followed him to a table, where he seated Gabby. "The waiter will be over to take your drink order."

"Thank you." Gabby smiled at him.

"So are you going to tell me?"

"Tell you what?" Gabby said coyly.

"What went on in the ladies' room?"

"Nothing, just a little girl talk, that's all."

"Are you sure? She is from your world and I thought she might have said something."

"She did say something."

"What?"

"Basically it was the equivalent of go for it." She chuckled.

"Is that right?"

"Yes. She thinks you're cute."

"She does?"

"Yes, and she's right."

"Well, your opinion is the only one that counts with me."

"Glad to hear it."

"You're not worried she's going to run off and tell your mother or her mother?"

"No. We've both been burned by the society setup, so it's live and let live."

Nigel raised his water glass. "Here's to that philosophy."

She raised her glass to toast. "Cheers."

❧

On the other side of town, exhausted and still a bit agitated, Lauren left her office and met Randy at the restaurant. Together they went shopping for the ingredients to make shrimp and chicken *paella*. Unlike Alicia, Lauren was not the domestic type. Shopping for her consisted of visits to various department stores and boutiques. She barely knew what the inside of Cristedes looked like, let alone the various food shops of Chelsea. However, Randy made shopping fun as he juggled bell peppers in the produce aisle and playfully chased her with prawns at the local fishmonger's. His levity lifted her mood.

Once they arrived at his apartment, Lauren relaxed with a glass of wine while Randy got dinner underway. Lauren toured his spacious two-bedroom apartment with its oak floors, custom-designed bathroom and gourmet kitchen with all stainless steel appliances. Randy's apartment was impressive, and so was the view.

"I love your place. You've got a great view."

"Thanks," he called from the kitchen. "I like it here."

Lauren looked down to the street at all the couples walking by. "The neighborhood is colorful."

He laughed. "It certainly keeps things interesting."

She walked to the kitchen. "I have to ask."

"You want to know why a straight guy would live down here."

"Now that you said it out loud, I feel bad for thinking it."

"That's okay. You're not the first to wonder." He chopped up the bell peppers. "I like it here. The people are nice, they look out for you and if I ever run out of an ingredient I have a better than 95 percent shot that someone in the building has it."

She couldn't help but laugh. She took a whiff. "Oh wow, that smells amazing. Can I help you with anything?"

"As a matter of fact, if you would, please stir this while I add the other ingredients."

"Sure." She took the spoon.

Randy added the rice, shrimp, bell peppers, roasted red bell peppers, and olives. "Now you just keep stirring."

"Okay."

Randy poured a glass of wine.

Lauren's arm got tired. "How long am I supposed to stir?"

"Twenty-five minutes."

"What?"

He started laughing. "You can stop stirring." He adjusted the flame on the stove. "I just have to keep an eye on it."

"Good. I thought my arm was going to fall off."

"I'm sorry." He kissed her shoulder. "Does that help?"

"A little," she said coyly.

"Okay." When he lightly kissed her on her neck, Lauren felt her knees buckle a little. "How was that?"

"That was a little better."

He caressed her cheek, then lightly touched her lips with his. A shiver went down her spine. Soon the two of them were pressed together against the counter, kissing fervently. Clothes were beginning to be peeled off when Lauren stopped suddenly.

"We can't do this."

"Why?"

"You're cooking dinner, and even though I don't cook, I know you have to watch rice."

He went to the stove, turned off the burner and covered the pot.

"What are you doing? The rice can't be done already."

"It isn't. The heat from the pot will continue to cook the rice. This way the rice will be perfect and the shrimp won't be overcooked. Now." He went back and put his arms around her. "Where were we?"

"Right about here." She put her arms around him.

As they kissed, Randy unbuttoned her blouse and she pulled his shirt off. She kissed his chest, shoulders and neck with great deliberateness. "Oh, Lauren," he moaned softly. He picked her up.

"Oh, my." She was a little astounded. She'd never been picked up, and she liked it.

He carried her to the bedroom and laid her on the bed. Randy slowly removed her skirt. He stopped to admire the way her curves looked in her lingerie. "Oh, baby, you're beautiful, but you're even more beautiful without this."

He unhooked her bra. "Oh, baby." He softly ran his lips over her breasts and between them. The feel of his breath on her skin titillated her and she wanted more. Emboldened, she rolled over on top of him and threw her lingerie aside. She kissed him passionately while her hands explored his body. Unable to contain himself, he pulled her to him and their bodies began to move in sync until sweet release came.

Wrapped in a sheet, Lauren had a picnic *paella* dinner with Randy in his living room.

"This is so good." Lauren savored another forkful.

"Thanks."

"I love the crusty bottom. It's my favorite part."

"Mine, too."

"I meant to tell you earlier that I loved the table setting you did in the dining room. I didn't realize your talents extended to table linens, china and glassware."

He sipped his wine. "I have a confession to make. I didn't set the table."

"You didn't?"

"No. I asked my neighbors Adam and Preston to help me out. They have an interior design firm. In fact, they did my apartment."

"Really?"

"Yes. Before them I had a typical bachelor's apartment with no real furniture. Once they saw my place, they did a Queer Eye for the Design-Challenged Guy and the rest is history."

"They did a great job. I like their design aesthetic."

"I do, too." He drank a little more wine. "I told them I had a special lady coming for dinner, and I wanted to set the mood with a romantic table setting."

She smiled warmly. "You did that for me?"

"Yes."

As she leaned over to kiss him, the sheet slid down, revealing her breasts. "Oops." She started to pull it up. Randy stopped her.

"Leave it. I think the view is spectacular."

They kissed.

"How about we have dessert?"

"Sounds good to me," she said breathlessly.

They went back to the bedroom where they put the cherry on the evening, several times.

✍

Nestled away on East End Avenue near Carl Schurz Park, Gabby and Nigel enjoyed a glass of wine in his apartment.

"I like your place." She looked around. "You know, you really don't live all that far from me."

"Yorkville is nice. It's on the Upper East Side, but it's certainly not Park Avenue."

"Oh, people put too much into that whole zip code thing here in the city."

"You're right about that."

"What made you move here?" she asked as she sipped her wine.

"I like the area. It's quiet and no one really bothers you."

"It's a sanctuary."

"Yes, it is. I spend my whole day with people who are stressed out over keeping their status, especially my fellow bankers. I don't need it. I leave my job at the office."

Gabby was pleased. "That's refreshing."

"I guess you know something about driven people."

"Oh, yes. My father was driven when it came to work, too, but it didn't have anything to do with status."

"No?"

"No. I think it was about proving himself to my grandfather." She sighed. "My father was born into third-generation wealth, so his status was secure. But he never liked the idea of the idle rich. He was never one to hang out at the country club or even the University Club of New York. My dad loved the art of the deal before

Donald Trump even had one hair on his head for that great cowlick of his."

Nigel laughed.

"It's true. He wanted to be a great businessman, and the fact that he added to the family fortune was just the icing on the cake."

"Your dad sounds like a great guy."

"He is. I adore him. He always made me feel like his special little girl, and he still does." She looked down. "He had a stroke a few years back and now he doesn't get around like he used to."

"I'm sorry to hear that."

"Thanks. But rehab has really helped him. Even though his voice is soft, he can talk. He just can't travel all that much and I know that kills him because he loved traveling, and he really loved the roaming the city."

"So your parents are still here in the city."

"Oh yes, there's no way Bunny is giving up the Park Avenue address."

"Bunny?"

"Bunny's my mother and she was, I mean, is the complete opposite of my father. She's all about status."

"Does she come from money?"

"Yes. She was raised in the finest homes and had the best education to land a husband. I will say, though, that she and my father are a rarity in their circles. They were an actual love match and they still are."

"They're a couple of lovebirds, huh?"

"Yes. She loves my dad more than anything. It's one of the few things we agree on." She sipped her wine.

"Do I detect mother-daughter issues raising their ugly head?"

"A few, but I don't want to turn this lovely evening into a therapy session."

"You won't. Nothing can ruin this evening. I'm having a great time." He kissed her.

"Me, too," she sighed.

"You know, both my parents were like your dad when I was growing up, but they came from poor backgrounds and they had a lot to prove in order to be successful."

"I can imagine, but look how wonderfully you turned out."

"My folks were determined that I'd be more than a little better off than them. My father worked at one of the big defense companies on the Island. He started at the bottom and worked around the clock. He became a part of management within five years and never missed more than a week of work in twenty-five years. My mother was a surgical nurse and she worked more shifts at the hospital than most doctors. I used to ask her why she didn't become a doctor. She was certainly smarter than most of the physicians she worked with."

"What did she say?"

"She told me that back then the only career options for black women were teacher, social worker and nurse. She chose nursing and didn't look back."

"Sometimes you forget about the bad old days."

"My parents never let me forget. They wanted me to strive for the platinum ring, and now that I'm a parent I feel the same way for my son."

"Is he interested in numbers or art?"

"So far, video games seem to be his number one interest, but I've seen his sketching pad when he stays with me. He's talented."

"They say the apple doesn't fall far from the tree."

Nigel noticed how the light framed her face and made her blonde hair sparkle. He leaned in to kiss her. Gabby allowed herself to melt into his arms. He was so strong, yet his delicate artist's touch made her feel priceless. He unzipped her dress so it draped around her shoulders. He slowly planted light kisses along her shoulders and up her neck. He reached down and pulled her dress down around her arms. Gabby felt herself letting go before she suddenly she became self-conscious.

"What's wrong, baby? Am I moving too fast?"

"No." Gabby heard her mother's words ring through her head.

"What's the matter?"

"I said I wasn't going to bring up mother-daughter issues, but today my mother reminded me I was old and fat."

"Oh, honey."

"I thought I shook it off, but here it is raising its ugly head." She hung her head.

He lifted her face towards him. "You are the sexiest woman I've met in a long time."

She blushed like a schoolgirl.

"As an artist I pride myself on recognizing beauty and you, my dear, are a work of art. Stand up for me."

When she stood her dress fell to the floor.

"Look at you. You have the curves and lines artists dream about." He outlined her body with his finger. He stopped at her waist. Kissing her, he skillfully removed her panties, then got up and quickly removed his own clothing. The passion built so fast they found themselves against the wall of his living room. Gabby felt as if the sheer force of their lovemaking might push them through the wall that held them. Gabby wanted to grab hold of something when Nigel grabbed her hands and lifted them over her head so the passion seemed to flow through to her fingertips.

CHAPTER 11

Before Alicia knew it, Friday arrived. Anticipation of her date with Nathaniel was high for everyone except her. Alicia was scared. The woman who took on the big magazine boys and Wall Street was scared of a first date.

To keep her mind off the evening ahead, Alicia spent the afternoon in her office, where she checked her email and sorted through papers and files. Any other time Harrison would have gotten after her about working too much, but he knew she had a lot of nervous energy to work off and it was best to stay out of her way.

Harrison knocked on the door as she rifled through papers. "Yes?" She didn't look up.

"Ron Wilder is here to see you."

"Ron is here?" She looked puzzled.

"Yes. He says he has some papers that Barbara needs you to sign."

"Oh, okay. Send him in."

"Okay." Harrison disappeared.

Barbara didn't say anything about papers in her email. Maybe something came up, Alicia thought.

Ron entered the room with a folder. "Hi, Alicia. I'm sorry to disturb you this afternoon."

"That's not a problem." Alicia smiled.

He walked over to her desk and stood close to her as he put the folder in front of her. "Here you go."

"Thank you." She opened the folder and read the documents. "This doesn't look too pressing, but I guess that's our Barbara, always on top of things." Alicia signed the document. When she turned to hand it to Ron he leaned over and kissed her so hard she nearly fell over in the chair.

"Ron!" She stood up.

"I'm sorry, Alicia. I've wanted to do that for so long."

"Oh, my God," she said, still stunned.

"You're a beautiful woman, Alicia. I didn't want to press you because you're a widow and all, but I really like you."

"I don't know what to say."

"Just say you'll give me a chance."

Alicia looked away. "Ron, you're a nice guy and I like you but . . ."

"You don't like me in that way, right?"

"I'm sorry. I had no idea you felt this way."

Dejected, he looked down at his shoes. "I understand." He picked up the folder. "I'll let myself out."

"Please, Ron. I'm really sorry."

"So am I." He rushed out.

Alicia flopped in her chair. "I can't believe it."

Harrison walked back in. "Ron just rushed past me like a bat out of hell. What happened?"

"You wouldn't believe me if I told you."

"He made a pass at you."

"How did you know?"

Harrison snickered. "You know, Alicia, for such a smart woman you really don't see what's in front of you."

"What does that mean?"

"Ron Wilder has had a crush on you for years now. In fact, whenever I would lose track of you at one of your big office parties, all I had to do was find Ron and you would be in the vicinity."

"How could I be so blind?"

"Don't beat yourself up about it. I'm sure he'll get over it."

"I hope so. He really is one the best editors I have."

"Well, my dear, you need to put that on the shelf for now. You've got a date in a few hours."

"How am I going to have a good time with this on my mind?"

"Something tells me Nathaniel will take your mind off your troubles."

"Oh, boy." Alicia buried her face in her hands.

Harrison rubbed her back. "It's just a date, Alicia, not a firing squad."

For the remainder of the afternoon Alicia didn't know whether to be relieved or freaked out. Luckily for her, Lauren and Gabby drove up from the city to help her. The three of them examined Alicia's closet.

"Do you have anything without sleeves, Alicia?" Lauren searched through the rack.

"Yes. You're in my early spring section. Go two racks over. That's where summer is." Alicia sat down in her robe.

Lauren thumbed through the racks. "This isn't much better, woman." She looked disappointed.

"Oh, who asked you?" Alicia was perturbed.

"Okay, ladies, let's not get anything started. I think Alicia's nervous enough."

"You're right, Gabby. I'm sorry, Alicia."

"So am I. I didn't mean to snap at you." She looked at her closet. "My wardrobe hasn't had to be date-ready since Joan Collins rocked shoulder pads on *Dynasty.*"

"Oh, boy," Gabby sighed.

"Well, it's too late to go shopping. He'll be here in an hour." Alicia looked at the clock.

"Hold on a second. I'll be right back." Lauren left.

"Where's she going?"

Gabby shrugged her shoulders. "It beats me."

"So Gabby, you're looking well. How's everything going with Nigel?"

A big grin came over her face.

"You don't have to say a word. Your face says it all."

"It's that obvious?"

"Yes, it is. You look really happy."

"I am happy. At my age I didn't think it was possible to meet a dashing man who'd sweep me off my feet."

"From the look on your face I'd say he's swept you off your feet quite a few times already." She winked.

"Ms. Archer, I'm surprised at you."

"Come on, it's true, isn't it?"

"Yes."

"You lucky girl."

"Your turn is coming, you know."

Alicia's body filled with dread. "Don't say that. I can only handle one thing at a time, and right now dinner is as much as I'd like to think about."

"I understand. But are you saying that you haven't kissed Nathaniel?"

Alicia got up and went to the racks. "Maybe there's something in here."

"Oh, my God, you did kiss him," Gabby said excitedly.

"So what if we did kiss? It was only once or twice."

"How was it?"

"It was nice." Alicia downplayed it.

"If you're answering like that, he must have blown your espadrilles off."

"Almost," she sheepishly admitted.

Gabby laughed and clapped.

Lauren came in with a garment bag. "What's going on here?" She hung the bag up.

"Alicia and Nathaniel kissed the other night."

"Get out of here! Oh, you little tart, you," she teased.

"You're another one who's beaming with the glow of new romance and great sex around here, Lauren."

"I cannot tell a lie." She smiled.

"The Austen Aristocrats are getting their grooves on," Gabby joked.

"Speak for yourselves. I'm just going on a date, and from the looks of things there won't be any grooving for me, unless of course Nathaniel's into the whole schoolmarm/domestic doyenne look. Maybe I can do a cooking segment instead."

"That's where you're wrong, Alicia." Lauren unzipped the bag and pulled out a little black dress. "What do you think?"

"I love it," Gabby said enthusiastically.

Alicia got up to take a closer look. "It's very nice. Is this from your private collection?"

"No. I ordered it from IGIGI for you."

"You did? When?"

"I called Yuliya, the designer and creator of IGIGI, and I told her I needed a sexy little black dress in a size 16 as soon as possible. She was able to make it happen."

"You must have some serious special shopper points." Gabby shook her head.

"I got it, didn't I?"

"Do you like it, Alicia?" Gabby asked.

"It's perfect and gorgeous. You know how much I love anything easy to wear."

"Good. Now let's get you ready, my dear."

Alicia's cell phone rang.

"Don't you dare answer it," Lauren warned.

Alicia ignored her and picked it up. "It could be important." She pressed the talk button. "Alicia Archer."

"Alicia?" Barbara stood at the layout desk.

"Hey, Barbara. What's going on?"

"I guess you haven't heard."

"Heard what?"

"Ron Wilder took a sudden leave of absence. The whole office is talking about it. You saw him this afternoon. Did he say anything to you?"

Alicia's shoulders shrank. "No."

"I thought I'd let you know."

"Are you okay, Barbara?"

"Why wouldn't I be, Alicia? You're the only one who thought he liked me."

"I guess Leslie will fill in for him. Did he say how long he'd be gone?"

"No. No one knows." She paused. "Listen, I need to get back to work. I'll let you know if I hear anything. Talk to you soon."

"Okay." She closed her phone.

"What's wrong, Alicia?" Gabby asked.

"That was Barbara Folsom. She just told me Ron took a leave of absence."

"Really?" Lauren was shocked. "When's the last time you spoke to him?"

"He was here this afternoon with some papers for me to sign."

"Oh really?" Lauren was suspicious.

"Can you just help me get dressed, please?"

"Oh no, something happened here. You might as well spill it, sister. Otherwise you're going on your date naked." She paused. "Although I don't think Nate would mind that at all."

Alicia vacillated.

"Well?" Lauren had her hand on her hips.

"He kissed me. There, I said it. Can I just get dressed now?"

"What did you do?" Gabby said inquisitively.

"I certainly didn't kiss him back, if that's what you mean. I told him he was a nice guy."

"Ouch. No wonder he took a leave of absence."

"I wasn't mean about it, Lauren."

"You could have been as sweet as pie, but rejection is rejection."

"I feel bad enough, Lauren."

"He's a big boy. He'll get over it," Gabby said reassuringly.

"Gabby's right, and now we need time to get you ready."

Gabby and Lauren helped Alicia with her hair, makeup and accessories. They even managed to find a black pair of pumps with the perfect balance of comfort and sexiness. Forty-five minutes later Alicia was date ready.

They stood in front of the mirror.

"You look good, Alicia."

"Thanks, Gabby."

"Let me do this." Lauren went for the bra straps.

"Hey," Alicia protested. "The girls are as far up as my bra will take them. Who do you think you are? My mother? My mother's the only one who tries to get my boobs as close to sitting on my shoulders as possible."

They laughed.

"I pay top dollar to keep the girls where they're supposed to be." Alicia turned to see the side view.

"You look good," Lauren agreed.

The doorbell rang.

"He's here," Gabby said excitedly.

Alicia took a deep breath. "Here we go." She walked towards the door, Lauren and Gabby on her heels.

"Do you have your camera?" Lauren asked.

"I have the camera in my cell."

Alicia turned around. "It's a first date, not the prom." She took a deep breath and walked down the hall to the top of the stairs.

"Here she is." Harrison looked up.

Though usually dressed in khakis and polo shirts, Nathaniel wore a crisp pair of black slacks, a blue Oxford shirt with a tie and a sports jacket. He stared as Alicia descended the staircase, unable to take his eyes off her. Lauren and Gabby were behind her like two proud mothers.

Nathaniel extended his hand to help her down the last step.

"Thank you." She smiled.

"You look fantastic."

"Thank you. So do you."

He put his arm out. "Shall we?"

She took his arm. "Yes."

"I'll have her home at a decent hour," he grinned.

"Have a good time, you two." Harrison grabbed the door.

"Call us tomorrow, Alicia," Lauren called after her.

"Okay."

They walked out and into the summer evening air. Nathaniel opened the door of his Jaguar XJ. "Your chariot awaits, my lady."

Alicia looked at him. "My chariot awaits?"

"I know that was corny, but how else am I supposed to act in front of a beautiful woman?"

"Nice recovery." She was impressed.

"I try." He closed the door and got in. A minute later they were on their way to dinner.

"Can I ask where we're going?"

"It's a surprise. I think you'll like it."

"Okay, I'll take your word for it." She crossed her legs.

Nathaniel found it hard not to look. Her legs looked so smooth and soft, it distracted him, and the car veered a little.

"Hey!"

"Whoa!" He quickly corrected it. "Sorry about that."

"It's okay." Alicia was secretly tickled. *I guess my legs look better than I thought.* She smiled slightly.

He took a deep whiff. "What perfume are you wearing?"

"Oh, is it too much?"

"No, not at all. It smells great."

"Thank you. It's Ange ou Demon by Givenchy. My father gave it to me for Christmas."

"It's very nice." Nathaniel felt that he'd soon need to cross his legs for an entirely different reason than Alicia so he sped up.

"Hungry?"

"Starving. We can't get there soon enough."

Less than a half hour later they arrived at the Ritz Carlton Westchester. Nathaniel pulled up and the valet helped Alicia out of the car.

Nathaniel walked over and took her arm. "Thanks, man. I'll take it from here."

"I'm impressed, Nathaniel. I've wanted to try 42 for a while now."

"You've never been here?"

"No."

"Well then, my dear, you are in for a treat."

They got in the elevator and two minutes later they were at 42. The restaurant offered spectacular views of Long Island Sound all the way to Manhattan. The minute the maître d' saw Alicia, the staff went on high alert. As Alicia walked in and saw the majestic view she forgot all about her trouble with Ron.

"Good evening. I have a reservation under the name Becker."

He checked the book. "Yes, Dr. Becker. Your table is ready." He turned to Alicia. "*Mademoiselle* Archer, it is a pleasure and honor to have you here this evening." He kissed her hand.

Alicia was surprised. "Thank you."

"Please follow me."

He led them to an intimate table for two near the window and away from the crowd. Once Alicia entered the restaurant, however, there wasn't much chance they'd go unnoticed for the night.

The maître d' held Alicia's seat. "Here you go."

She sat down. "Thank you again."

"No problem."

Nathaniel was a little bothered by the way he fawned over his date.

"I will send your waiter over right away, Dr. Becker."

"I appreciate that."

As he walked away, Alicia couldn't help but laugh.

"What's so funny?"

"You are. You should have seen your face when he held my chair." She chuckled.

"That's my job. You're my date."

"I'm sure he knows that."

"Well, let's make sure he does." He picked up the wine menu. "Hmm. Are you in the mood for sparkling wine or champagne?"

She shrugged. "You pick."

"Okay." He studied the list.

The waiter walked over. "Good evening. May I get you something to drink?"

"Yes. We'll have the Perrier-Jouet Fleur de Champagne Brut 1999."

"Very good, sir. Glass or bottle?"

"Glass. I want to keep a clear head tonight."

"Thank you." The waiter left.

Nathaniel casually looked at all the people staring their way. "It seems you have some fans here."

"Maybe," she answered nonchalantly.

"There is no maybe about it, Alicia. The place started to buzz the minute you walked in. Let's face it, you're a celebrity."

"Oh, please, I'm a celebrity in the world of domesticity." She sipped her water.

"Excuse me?" A man tapped her shoulder.

"Yes?"

"Aren't you Alicia Archer, the host of *Everyday Elegance*?"

"Yes."

He waved at a woman seated at a center table. She immediately got up. "My wife just loves you."

"Oh, thank you."

"Oh my God, it is you! I'm Margaret and this is my husband Lionel. I watch your show every day."

"That's so nice. Thank you so much."

"I tried your recipe for no-bake lemon pie and it came out perfectly."

"Oh, good."

The waiter returned with the champagne. "Pardon me," he said as he placed the glasses on the table.

"I'm having dinner with this gentleman this evening." She tried to back out of the conversation gracefully.

"Oh, we're sorry. Margie, she's on a date. We should go back to our table."

His wife turned to Nathaniel. "I'm sorry, but do you mind if we get a quick picture?" She went back to Alicia. "No one will believe us."

Nathaniel restrained his laughter.

"Sure, but then we'd really like to order dinner."

"Thank you." Margaret hit her husband's arm. "Lionel, get the cell phone."

She pulled another chair up and sat. "Okay, honey, take the picture."

"Okay." He snapped the photo.

"Now can you take a picture of the three of us, please?" she held the phone in front of Nathaniel.

"Sure." Nathaniel took the phone and snapped the photo. The grateful couple hugged Alicia profusely before they went back to their table.

Nathaniel covered his mouth. "Now what were you saying about not being a celebrity?"

"Go ahead and laugh," she chuckled.

"This date has gotten off to an auspicious start." Nathaniel smiled.

They managed to get through the rest of their evening without further interruption. A couple of hours later they were seated on a park bench in Saxon Woods Park with coconut tiramisu to go and two spoons.

"Cheers!" They toasted with their raised spoons.

"After you," Nathaniel said.

"Thank you." She closed her eyes and savored the taste.

"So you like it?"

"Yes, it's very good."

He tried a spoonful. "Oh yes, that is nice."

She looked around. "I'm glad we came to the park for dessert. It's so relaxing here."

"I'll say. You caused quite a stir at the restaurant."

"I guess I did."

"I'm pretty sure the head chef, owner and pastry chef don't make it a habit to pull up a chair with their patrons."

"I'm sorry about that." She was embarrassed by the attention.

"Don't be. It's nice to know what life in the fast lane is like."

"Life in the fast lane?"

"Let me rephrase that, life under the celebrity spotlight."

"That's a little better. Not much, but better overall."

They ate quietly for a few minutes.

"Alicia, there's something I want to ask you."

"Okay."

"It's about your husband."

"I see." She paused. "I haven't been on a date since the eighties, but I do seem to remember something about it being bad form to talk about previous relationships on a first date. At least that's what all the magazines and books say."

"Usually I'd agree. But in your case it's different. You're a . . ." He hesitated. "Um . . ."

Alicia decided to put him out of his misery. "I'm a widow. It's okay, Nathaniel. You can say it."

He laughed nervously.

"What about Kurt?"

"How did you two meet?"

"We met in college."

"Was it love at first sight?"

Alicia laughed. "Hardly. I was an economics major from Long Island and he was an environmental science major from California. Kurt organized recycling programs for old exam papers and textbooks. He put student carpools together to reduce carbon emissions and planted God knows how many trees and plants to beautify the world and clean the air."

"He was ahead of his time."

"I know. Kurt had no use for capitalistic econs, as he called us. I minored in creative writing, so I wasn't all bad, but still we argued and debated every time we saw each other."

"Sounds like a love match to me."

"Well, we were the last two people to figure it out. We officially began dating in our senior year and we got married a year after graduation."

"Then along came Kurt Jr."

"Yes, and we had our family."

"You and Kurt didn't want more children?"

"It would have been nice, but I was lucky to get pregnant with Kurt Jr. I developed some problems afterwards and after going around in circles with the doctors, I had a hysterectomy."

"I'm sorry."

"It's okay. We were happy to make three our magic number." Alicia looked far off.

"You still miss him a lot."

"I do." She nodded. "He was a wonderful, kind and giving man. He was so full of energy and life it was infectious. You couldn't help but have a good time if Kurt was there. When they told us he had pancreatic cancer, he did his best to keep his spirits up. It just seemed to take him so fast."

"It's an awful disease."

"That's why I started the Kurt Archer Memorial Fund, so we could raise money for more research into all cancers and to fund environmental projects to benefit the earth. It's what he would have wanted."

"I bet you he's proud of you."

"I hope so." She looked up. "Now it's my turn to ask a question."

"Shoot."

"Do you have any lost loves, or maybe one that got away?"

"Yes, I do."

"Really? I didn't think any woman could resist you."

"Oh yes, it happened."

Alicia sat back to listen. "I'm intrigued."

"I knew the minute I laid eyes on her she was something special. I was smitten."

"It's hard to think of you as being smitten."

"Why?"

"I've seen gorgeous women fawn all over you and you're a pretty cool customer. Otherwise they wouldn't try so hard."

He shrugged his shoulders. "They may have been gorgeous, but they were mostly lightweights. This woman was the total package. She was intelligent, beautiful and sexy as all hell."

"She sounds perfect for you. What happened?"

"She wouldn't give me the time of day. I mean, she was polite and all, but I could never break through. So I developed a strategy."

"What was your strategy?" She was intrigued.

"I noticed that my nice guy thing wasn't working, but when I teased her, I got a reaction and at least that was something."

"And that was enough for you?"

"It had to be at the time. Now I think it's changed."

Alicia looked confused. "I thought you said she got away."

"I thought she did but then she invited me to dinner." He took her hand in his. "And I have no intention of blowing it."

"You were talking about me?" Alicia felt more than a little naïve.

"Yes. You blew me away the minute I saw you."

"Don't do this, I cry at the drop of a hat."

"A tough girl like you?" He caressed her hand.

"I'm a sap for romance."

"Don't tell anyone, but so am I." He grinned.

Off in the distance someone had Jason Mraz's "I'm Yours" playing on the radio.

He stood up. "May I have this dance?"

"What?"

"Come on, let's dance."

Alicia put aside her shyness, rose and they began to dance. They did a little two-step and he twirled her around the lawn.

"I'm yours," he sang into her ear.

She put her head on his shoulder and they rocked back and forth for the rest of the song. Once it trailed off he lifted her face up. "It's true. I'm yours." He gazed into her eyes. They kissed tenderly under the tree as the summer breeze whispered romance.

A little while later they kissed good night on her front step.

"I'll call you tomorrow."

"Is that still three days from now in guy talk?" She smiled.

"I'll call you tomorrow." He kissed her again.

"Okay. Good night." She turned the knob.

"Good night, baby. Sweet dreams." He winked.

Alicia opened the door and stepped inside. *Nathaniel Becker was smitten with me.* She smiled to herself.

"I take it you had a good time." Harrison had a glass of milk in his hand.

"Did you wait up for me?"

"Actually, I came down to get a glass of milk."

"Oh, sure," she said suspiciously. "A bomb couldn't wake you once you're asleep. Admit it, you stayed up."

"So what if I did? I wanted to find out if you had a good time, and judging by your expression, I'd say you had a great time."

Alicia put her bag down on the table. "I did."

"That's good to hear." He looked at the clock. "It's late. You can tell me all about it in the morning."

"Okay." She began to ascend the staircase.

Harrison peeked out the window. Nathaniel was getting in his car with a big grin plastered across his face. "I take it there will be another date?"

"I think so."

"If the goofy look on Nate's face is any indication, I'd say there will be many more dates in your future."

CHAPTER 12

On Saturday Bunny called to say that she and Mr. Blanchard were out at their country estate in the Hamptons, so Gabby's quick visit would be more of an all-day event. Naturally Gabby called for reinforcements. By ten a.m. Lauren and Alicia were in the back of a limo for what they thought would be a leisurely day of spas, shopping and lunch.

"I want it on the record I was lured here under false pretenses." Lauren folded her arms.

"I second that." Alicia raised her hand.

"You said it was going to be a girls' day in the Hamptons." Lauren huffed.

"It is a girls' day. We're together and we always have a good time."

"You left out the part about going to your parents' place for tea." Alicia added.

"I know. I thought my parents were going to be in the city this weekend, and I promised my dad that I'd see him today."

Lauren and Alicia looked at each other. Although Bunny made them feel tolerated, Gabby's dad had always made them feel welcome from the moment they'd walked through the door thirty-two years ago.

"You don't play fair. You know we love your dad." Lauren unfolded her arms.

"Am I forgiven?"

"Is she?" Alicia asked Lauren.

"Oh, all right. At least we're dressed for it." She pointed to the Yacht Club wrap dress she wore. "By the way, Alicia, I love that black and white number you have on."

"Thanks." She smiled. "You're not the only one who shops online. This is the Kiyonna Manhattan dress."

"Nice."

Gabby looked at her blue T-back sundress. "I think I'm the underdressed one here."

Lauren dismissed her assessment. "Of course you're not underdressed."

"Thanks. And if I haven't said it before, you guys are great for not jumping out of the car once you knew where we were heading."

"Don't think it hasn't crossed my mind. But I like this dress too much to ruin it," Alicia said jokingly.

They laughed.

"Seriously, you two are the best friends anyone could ask for."

"Not so fast. I think we deserve a trip to Levain Bakery for one of those chocolate chip walnut cookies for dessert. Because you know not only are we going to have those little grass-filled tea sandwiches, but to add insult to injury, we're going to top it off with cottage cheese and fruit for dessert. "

"It's watercress, Lauren. I promise you we're not having weeds." Alicia laughed.

"You could have fooled me."

"Come on, Lauren, maybe it won't be that bad."

"You think so, Alicia?"

"We might have a yogurt parfait with fruit and granola, right, Gabby?"

"Right. Mother did say Cook has expanded her repertoire."

"Maybe yogurt and fruit might not be so bad after all," Lauren relented.

"Oh, my God, you are having good sex, aren't you? You just turned down chocolate." Alicia was amazed.

Gabby laughed. "She's got you there."

"Can I help it if I'm happy and I know it?" She winked.

"Is that a no for Levain Bakery?" Gabby asked.

"I reserve the right to revisit this, depending upon how good the granola is."

"Deal."

Alicia looked out the window. It was bumper-to-bumper. "Oh, great, we're stuck in Saturday morning Hamptons traffic."

"At least you're not driving," Gabby noted.

"True. However, it does give us the chance to hear about your date, Alicia."

"Lauren, I already told you. I had a good time."

"You went on your first date in twenty-three years and you think we're going to settle for the *Cliff's Notes* version?" Lauren scoffed.

"Oh, for heaven's sake, you two," Alicia sighed.

"You've got nowhere to run." Gabby smiled.

"Uncle."

"It's about time." Lauren clapped. "You had dinner at 42. Now that's a recipe for romance if I've ever heard one."

Alicia laughed.

"What's so funny?" Gabby asked.

"It's definitely a romantic place, but I wouldn't say we had a romantic evening there."

"What do you mean?" Lauren was confused. "I thought you said you had a good time."

"I have two words for you, *fanaticus interruptus.*"

"You're kidding?"

"I'm not kidding, Gabby. The overall interruption didn't last too long, but when people start taking pictures of you with their cell phones, it sort of takes the wind out of the sails."

"How did Nate take it?" Lauren asked.

"He was a good sport."

Gabby shook her head. "I'm telling you, people are something else. You were in a sexy black dress with a good-looking man at a romantic restaurant with a view and somehow people still managed to mistake it for a Kmart appearance."

"Yes. It was like they announced, 'Attention, all diners. Alicia Archer's in kitchenware with her new table collection.' "

They laughed.

"What can I say? It's the price of fame." Alicia shrugged.

"I certainly hope you had a chance to make up for it later," Lauren said.

"We did." She smiled like a schoolgirl.

"Oh really?" Gabby's ears perked up.

"Not that kind of making up. We got dessert to go and drove over to Saxon Woods Park."

"What did you get?"

"Tiramisu."

"Oh, that was romantic." Gabby giggled.

"We shared dessert, talked and then we danced."

"You danced?"

"Yes, Lauren, I danced. It's not like I don't know how."

"I didn't say that. I know you can dance."

"Did you kiss?" Gabby asked coyly.

"What? Are we fourteen again?"

"No, but every girl wants to talk about the kiss. So?"

"Yes, and that's how we ended the evening."

"That's sweet," Gabby said dreamily.

"I take it you're going out again?"

"I think so. He said he'd call me today."

"I'm so happy for you."

"Thanks, Gabby, but all I did was go out on one date."

"Still, it's a start."

"Okay, now that we're all caught up with Alicia, how are things going with Nigel?"

"Good."

"Oh, you'd better do better than that, Gabby. After all, he's the reason we're going to Long Island's version of *Brideshead Revisited*," Alicia said.

"You'd better spill the beans. What's going on?"

"I have two words for you, Terrence Talbot."

"No," Alicia groaned. "She tried to set you up with him?"

"Yes. She made sure he just happened to be in the area around the gallery."

"Who's Terrence Talbot?"

"He's the paint prince. His company manufactures the residential and commercial paints you see in the big home improvement stores."

"How do you know him, Alicia?"

"I met him at a couple of charity events. He talked to me about the process they use to make different shades of white paint for at least half an hour. Frankly, it would have been more scintillating to watch paint dry."

"Oh, he's that bad?" Lauren winced. "Bunny sent him your way, Gabby?"

"It figures," Alicia added.

"I know and when I told her no thanks, she reminded me that I can't be choosy, since I'm not getting any younger or thinner."

"Ouch, no wonder you wanted us to come today," Lauren said.

"And I kind of told her I was seeing someone."

"You kind of told her? What does that mean?" Alicia asked.

"I told her I had a date and didn't need Terrence."

"Now she's going to be after you to find out who it is and you're not ready to tell her about Nigel."

"No, I'm not. Do you think that's bad? I'm not ashamed of him."

"No one thinks you're ashamed of him, Gabby. Tell her about him when you're ready."

Alicia looked out the window. "We're getting closer."

"I called Ian and told him I'd be here for a little while today. He's out here every weekend. He might drop by."

"He's twenty-two years old. The last thing he wants to do in the Hamptons is come to his grandparents' place for tea," Alicia laughed.

"She has a point," Lauren added.

Gabby nodded. "I think I'm really building something special with Nigel and I want to enjoy it for a while before . . ."

"You put him through all of this." Lauren pointed to the house as they drove onto the estate.

"Yes. Will you help me?"

"Of course we will, but eventually you're going to have to stand up to your mother."

"I know, Alicia, but as long as I have my best friends and fellow Aristocrats, I'll be okay." *I hope.*

⌘

Situated on a little over one-and-a-half acres in East Hampton a block from the ocean, the Blanchard family's historical 6,000-square-foot three-story mansion was a sight to behold. Originally built in the early 1900s, it had been in the family for decades and undergone several transformations to update its style.

As they got closer to the door, they saw Mary waiting at the entrance for them. A pleasantly plump woman,

Mary Cummings had been the house manager for the Blanchards since Gabby was ten. Although graying, she still had the same spark in her brown eyes and the temperament to work with Bunny's exacting standards.

The driver got out.

"Here we go, ladies," Gabby said.

They stepped out of the car.

Mary walked over. "Hello, girls. It's good to see you."

Alicia hugged her. "How are you, Ms. Cummings?"

"I'm doing well, young lady. You look good."

"So do you."

Lauren hugged her next. "It's been a while."

"I know."

Mary turned to Gabby. "Hello, my girl." She grinned as she hugged her.

Gabby had been close to Mary growing up. Whenever her mother would chide her for her eating habits, Mary was there to reassure her that she was pretty, no matter what size she was. Plump all her life, she shared a kinship with her young charge and Gabby was grateful.

"Hi, Ms. Cummings." She smiled widely.

"Now there's the smile I love so much. Come on in, girls."

While the house looked stately from the outside, it was cozy. The Fifth Avenue townhouse didn't have the same warmth with its marble and granite entryway. The entry here was wood leading up the stairs to a bay window that overlooked the immense backyard.

"Your mother and father are in the great room."

"Thanks, Ms. Cummings."

"I'll be there in a minute to help serve the tea." She went off to the kitchen.

When they walked in, they saw Mr. Blanchard.

"Daddy."

"Hey, sweetheart, how's my girl?" he said softly.

"I'm good, Daddy." She threw her arms around him.

When Gabby was a little girl she thought her father was the smartest, strongest and most handsome man in the world. At well over six feet, four inches with sandy blond hair and blue eyes, he fit the bill for many years until the stroke. Even though he could no longer scoop her up in his arms, in Gabby's mind's eye every hug lifted her ten feet off the ground.

"I brought two other people to see you, Daddy."

"Hi, Mr. B, it's good to see you." Alicia kissed him on the cheek.

"Indeed it is, Mr. B. How are you?" Lauren added as she kissed his cheek.

"I'm surrounded by lovely ladies. What more could I ask for?"

"Richard, I have the blanket for your legs." Bunny entered the room.

"Hello, Mother." Gabby went over and hugged her mother.

"Hello, dear. I didn't hear you come in. Your dad wanted a blanket for his legs." Carefully and lovingly she placed the blanket over him. "Is that good, honey?"

"Yes. Thank you, my love," he said softly.

"You're welcome." She kissed his forehead and then turned to Lauren and Alicia, who were on their feet.

Alicia spoke first. "Hello, Mrs. Blanchard. You look well."

"Hello, Mrs. Blanchard, I second that."

"Thank you, Alicia and Lauren. Please sit down and be comfortable."

They sat back down.

"I am so glad you could make it here today. I know what a nightmare traffic is."

"We got caught in a little traffic snarl, but it wasn't too bad, Mother."

"The Hamptons aren't what they used to be. Years ago it was a nice getaway from the heat of the city, and now with everyone descending on the beaches, it looks more like Coney Island."

"I could go for a Coney Island hot dog." Mr. Blanchard smiled longingly.

"I'll have to get a couple for you, Daddy."

"You'll do no such thing. He has to watch his diet."

"Okay, Mother." Gabby winked at her father. She'd sneak one to him.

"Alicia and Lauren, Gabby tells us your show is doing quite well. Congratulations," Mrs. Blanchard said.

"Thank you. I'm very happy with it." Alicia smiled.

"And since you're the producer, Lauren, I'm sure you have a lot to do with its success."

"I think we make a good team."

"I always said teamwork was important," Mr. Blanchard piped up.

"You're right about that, Mr. B," Lauren said.

Just then Mary came in with the tea service, followed by two maids with the additional refreshments. As they set up the table, all three were shocked to see the tea sandwiches had been replaced by mini quiches, canapés, mini focaccia with olive tapenade, real fruit tarts, scones and madeleines.

"Well, Alicia, Cook is quite anxious for your comments. She got the recipes from your show."

"I'm flattered." Alicia beamed.

"So please help yourselves and Mary will serve the tea," Bunny said graciously as she got up to make a small plate for Mr. B.

Gabby, Alicia and Lauren tentatively made their way over to the buffet table.

Lauren leaned over Alicia's shoulder. "Are we in the right place?" she whispered.

"It looks like my parents' place, but there's something going on here." Gabby was leery.

The doorbell rang.

"Ladies, I think we just fell down a rabbit hole," Alicia whispered as she picked up a plate.

Gabby was filled with dread. She hoped it was Ian and Emily.

Terrence Talbot walked in. "I hope I'm not late for tea," he announced.

Alicia turned to Gabby. "I think I see a stop at the Levain Bakery and a big chocolate chip cookie in your future."

Gabby looked at Terrence, who was all prepped out in chinos and a polo shirt. "I think I see two chocolate chip cookies."

❧

Gabby, Lauren and Alicia looked as if they'd been given detention after they'd sat through an hour of Terrence's discussion on color mixing and the difference in how flat, semi-gloss and high-gloss paints were manufactured. Fortunately, Mr. B fell asleep less than ten minutes after Terrence began his lecture, but he was the only one allowed to nod off. Bunny, on the other hand, kept the conversation afloat as she tried to entice Gabby to talk.

"Gabby, didn't you just have painters at your place?"

"Yes, Mother. I had my office re-painted." She sipped her tea.

"Did they use my paint? A lot of professional painters prefer ours."

"I can't say I checked what brand of paint they used. I just wanted them to use the colors I requested."

Lauren nearly gagged on her lemonade.

"Oh my, are you all right, Lauren?"

Lauren cleared her throat. "I'm fine, Mrs. Blanchard. I think it just went down the wrong way."

Alicia covered her mouth to keep from laughing.

Mrs. Blanchard got up. "How would you girls like to go outside and get some air? The gardens are so pretty, and you can relax a little by the pool."

Lauren and Alicia practically leaped from their seats at the mere mention of an escape.

"That sounds good, Mother." Gabby started to get up.

Her mother stopped her. "No, Gabby. You stay here with your dad and Terrence. I'll take the girls."

Gabby reluctantly sat back.

"You can join us in a little while." Lauren gave her a halfhearted smile as she and Alicia followed Bunny out of the room.

Terrence got up and sat next to Gabby. "Alone at last."

Gabby's skin crawled. "We're not exactly alone." She looked over at her father.

"I know, but your dad is fast asleep."

"Gabby?" Mr. B said softly.

"Yes, Daddy?"

Mr. B yawned. "You're still here. Can you wheel your old dad to the sunroom?"

Gabby leaped at the chance to escape. "Sure, Daddy." She quickly got behind his wheelchair. "If you'll excuse us, Terrence."

"Sure. Can I help?"

"No, thank you, young man. You stay and enjoy one of those desserts. Bunny will be along soon to keep you company."

"Yes, sir."

Gabby wheeled her father out of the great room.

"Thanks, Daddy. You saved me again." She stopped to kiss his cheek.

"Don't mention it, sweetie. You know it was a little bit of self preservation, too."

"What do you mean, Daddy?"

"The man was boring enough to put me to sleep. If I'd listened any longer, he might have induced a coma."

Gabby laughed.

✑

Bunny gave Lauren and Alicia a short tour of the gardens before one of the staff came out to get her for a telephone call. In the meantime Lauren and Alicia sat under an umbrella by the pool.

"When you said that watching paint dry was more scintillating than a conversation with Terrence Talbot, I thought you were kidding."

"I told you. Obviously the man is in love with the sound of his own voice. Otherwise he would have shot himself a long time ago."

"I'm surprised someone else hasn't beaten him to it. Has he ever been married?"

"Terrence Talbot has been married six times."

Lauren's face fell. "Get out of here. He convinced six different women to marry him?"

"It's more like his bank account convinced them."

"He's paying alimony to six women?"

"I think they each got lump sum settlements, which I'm sure is more like workman's compensation, since they'll never get the time back they wasted listening to the finer points of custom paint colorization."

As Lauren cracked up, her custom tone on her cell let her know she'd received a text. She read it and rolled her eyes.

"That doesn't look like good news. Who was it?"

"Ken."

"What's he texting you for?"

"He wants to try to become a desk commentator for *NFL Weekly*."

"And what does he expect you to do for him? He has an agent."

"I told him that, but it hasn't stopped him from trying to get me on board."

"He's got some nerve."

"Tell me about it. He even sent Patrick to my office to plead his case."

"I know you told him no way."

"I did. He understood, but Ken's another story."

"He's used to getting his way."

Alicia's cell phone rang. "Excuse me."

"Sure."

"Hello?"

Nathaniel was in his backyard. "Hello, Alicia, how are you?"

She grinned. "I'm good, Nathaniel, how are you?"

"I would be better if I were in the Hamptons with you."

"That's sweet of you to say. It was a last-minute thing."

"I know. Harrison told me you're on the Blanchard estate."

"Indeed I am."

"Are you staying overnight?"

"Oh no, we're heading back this afternoon."

Nathaniel laughed. "You answered that fast."

Alicia laughed. "I know. It's not like I'm trapped in some hell hole in Tijuana."

"Gabby is," Lauren interjected.

"Lauren is with you, too?"

"Yes. She and I are out by the pool."

"Where's Gabby?"

"Poor thing is trapped with the dullest man alive."

"That's kind of harsh. Who is it?"

"Terrence Talbot. Do you know him?"

"The paint prince and I went to the same boarding school. And you're right, he is the dullest man alive." He paused. "So are you doing anything tonight?"

"No."

"I thought that maybe you could help me sharpen my culinary skills. I bought your latest cookbook, and I got the stuff to make short ribs, potatoes with butter and thyme and sautéed spinach."

Alicia was touched. "Well, I think that's fair."

"Do you think that makes it a date?"

"Yes. What time?"

"Maybe around seven."

"Okay."

"I'll see you then. I can't wait."

"Neither can I."

"Bye, honey."

"Bye." She closed her phone.

Lauren grinned.

"What?"

"Look at you. It seems Gabby and I aren't the only ones with a glow," she teased.

"Maybe so, but my glow is strictly vertical."

"I know it's been a while for you, Alicia, but you can get this glow horizontally, too. Hell, you can get it sideways and even upside down."

"Are you trying to scare me? I'm nowhere near ready to get naked and assume the positions."

"I'm only teasing, Alicia. I'm only teasing. Besides, you'll know when you're ready to make that step. In the meantime I'm pretty sure Nate is fine with your schedule."

"He told me we'd go as slowly as I need to."

"See? So what are you two doing tonight?"

"We're cooking at his place. He wants to make something from my cookbook."

"Oh, that's precious."

"I know. It's not exactly dinner with a five-star chef, but it's good."

"It is nice to be with a man who can cook."

"I bet. Are you doing anything together this weekend?"

"It's crazy with the restaurant today, but he did take Sunday off for us."

"Nice."

Lauren looked back at the house. "Do you think Gabby was able to escape?"

"With Mr. B in there I'm sure she was able to get away from Terrence. However, Bunny is another story."

❧

Though she appeared calm and pleasant, a highly annoyed Bunny walked into the sunroom with Terrence.

"Excuse me. Terrence has to take his leave."

"Oh really?" Gabby tried to disguise her relief.

"Yes, there's an emergency at the company I need to handle," Terrence said.

"There's a paint emergency?" Mr. B. appeared perplexed.

"It's a transportation issue and I've got to get down there to see what's happening with the trucks." He turned to Bunny. "Thanks so much for inviting me."

"You're welcome. We have to do it again."

When he walked over to Gabby, he looked like a man who wanted to plant a kiss on her, so she quickly extended her hand to shake his and thus headed him off at the pass. "It was nice seeing you, Terrence."

He was obviously dejected, but he went with it and shook her hand.

"It was nice seeing you, too, Gabby."

Mr. B. spoke up. "Drive carefully now."

"I will, sir. Thank you." He turned to Gabby. "Maybe we can get together sometime soon."

"That would be nice," her mother answered for her.

"If you'd say my goodbye to Alicia and Lauren, I'd appreciate it."

"Consider it done." Gabby smiled.

Bunny waited to see if Gabby would make a move towards Terrence. She didn't. "I'll walk you to the door, Terrence." Bunny and Terrence left.

"You know she's going to let me have it when she gets back here, right, Daddy?"

"She's your mother, but you are entitled to be your own woman. Don't forget that."

"I won't, Daddy."

"Gabrielle Blanchard, what were you doing in here while we had a guest?"

"Daddy wanted to be moved to the sunroom. And we had guests, Mother, plural. Or did you forget about Lauren and Alicia?"

"Of course not."

"I asked her to bring me here and keep me company, Bunny."

"You left Terrence by himself. Have you no manners?"

Gabby was equally vexed. "Of course I have manners, Mother, and I really came out here to be with Daddy, and not to be blindsided with a setup."

"What if I tried to set you up? Terrence is a good catch."

"But I told you I was seeing someone and still you couldn't resist."

"How serious could it be if you won't even tell me who this man is?"

"It's serious enough that I want to keep it to myself," she huffed.

"Oh, good Lord, it's another artist. Hasn't this family had enough of those people?"

"Bunny, don't do it," Mr. B warned.

Gabby rolled her eyes. She knew who her mother was talking about. Her older brother Dick had married Elena Green, an artist who grew up on the South Side of Chicago. Yet despite the fact that Elena studied art in Europe and was a well-known and respected sculptor, Bunny could never get over the fact that her eldest son had looked outside the proper society girls and married someone who was barely middle class. It was one of the attributes Gabby disliked the most about her mother.

"You know, Mother, Dick and Elena have been happily married for twenty-eight years, which is more than I can say for some of the women you wanted him to marry who are now bucking to be the next Liz Taylor."

"That's not true. Joan Webber has only been married once and now she's single."

Gabby couldn't believe her ears. "Joan Webber came out, Mother."

"What do you mean she 'came out'?"

"I don't mean as a debutante. She came out of the closet. That's why she got divorced. She's a lesbian."

"Oh you're just saying that."

"No, Bunny, even I know about that," Mr. B added.

"But that's not even the point, Mother. You don't trust us to make the right decisions for our own lives. I did it your way once and it didn't work out. Now I want to choose someone I want to be with based on how I feel and not how it looks to other people."

"We don't live in a bubble, Gabby. Our choices matter."

"That's where you and I differ, Mother. I think happiness matters."

"So you are with an artist."

"What if he is an artist? What does that have to do with anything?"

"You have a gallery. He could be using you to get ahead."

Gabby laughed. "He doesn't need me to get ahead. He's talented enough to make it himself."

"Sometimes you are so naïve," Bunny huffed.

Gabby had had enough and stood up. "It's getting late and the girls have plans. We'd better be heading back before the mass exodus begins. If you'll excuse me." She left the room.

"You just can't stop yourself, can you, Bunny?" Mr. B said as he shook his head.

"Richard, you know I only want the best for our daughter."

"Then leave her alone and stand by her choices and decisions. We've been over this time and again. Stop with the parade of mind-numbing suitors."

Bunny laughed. "You think they're mind-numbing, Richard?"

"This last one talked to us about paint for nearly an hour. What do you think?"

A smile washed over her face. "And how do you know that? You fell asleep less than ten minutes in."

"Correction, my love, I closed my eyes. His tone was so monotonous it was like trying to fall asleep when the emergency broadcast system is on."

She laughed and then kissed him. "You were never boring, my love, and you're still filled with surprises."

"Thank you. Now do us both a favor and let our daughter run her own love life. She might be our baby, but she's forty-six years old."

Just then Gabby returned with Lauren and Alicia.

"The driver brought the car around. We're heading back to the city."

"All right, dear," Bunny answered.

Lauren and Alicia went in and kissed Mr. B.

"You take care of yourself, Mr. B," Alicia said cheerfully.

"We'll come by and visit you in the city next time," Lauren added.

"I look forward to it."

"Okay, Daddy. You be sure to do everything the doctor tells you." She fixed his collar. "I'll bring you that hot dog," she whispered before she kissed him. "Love you, Daddy."

He smiled. "Love you, too, princess."

"Thank you for having us, Mrs. Blanchard. It was lovely and please tell Cook she hit one out of the park with her menu." Alicia shook Bunny's hand.

"Thank you so much. I'm sure that will mean a lot to her."

"It's been a pleasure, Mrs. Blanchard. Thanks for inviting me." Lauren shook her hand as well.

"Thank you for coming."

Gabby hugged her mother. "I guess I'll see you in the city next week. You are coming back in on Monday, right?"

"Yes, so we'll have tea next Sunday."

"Okay."

They left and headed back for the city and Scarsdale, but not before they stopped and got three big chocolate chip cookies from Levain Bakery. Although Gabby was the one who needed it, Lauren and Alicia had one to express solidarity. Or so they pretended.

CHAPTER 13

When Gabby got home she stripped down to the bare essentials, a comfortable sundress and flip-flops. She went out onto the terrace with a glass of wine and a copy of *American Art Review*.

"Ms. Blanchard, do you need anything before I go?"

"No, Rosie, I'm good. You go on and have a good evening."

"Okay, ma'am. Good night."

"Good night, Rosie."

Gabby sipped her wine and flipped through the pages in an effort to put the day behind her. *When will I learn? I should know better when it comes to my mother.* She sighed aloud.

"Was it that bad of a day?"

She turned around. "Nigel."

"Rosie let me in on her way out. I hope that was okay."

"Of course."

"So was it that bad of a day?"

She went over and put her arms around him. "Not anymore."

Gabby and Nigel kissed with a real sense of urgency, and they barely made it inside before their clothes came off. Soon their nude bodies were on the floor with only a Persian rug between them and the hardwood.

"Oh, I missed you," Gabby whispered.

"I missed you."

Gabby's senses were on edge for his touch on her body and he didn't disappoint. He covered her with kisses from her head down to each one of her toes. She rolled over on top of him to return the favor. Slowly her lips and tongue explored his hard body. He tensed up as she raised the stakes near his navel.

"Oh," he moaned.

The sound of his pleasure delighted her.

Soon he couldn't take anymore and he pulled her close to him. "I want you now." A moment later they climbed the heights of pleasure and held on tightly to one another as they reached the peak of complete pleasure.

A little sleepy but satisfied, Gabby opened her eyes to see Nigel looking at his cell phone intensely.

"Nigel? Is everything okay?"

"Sure." He tried to downplay it.

She sat up. "It doesn't look that way to me. Do you want to talk about it?"

"It's nothing. I got a text from my son's mother, that's all."

"Is something wrong?"

He sighed. "The tuition at my son's school for the fall is coming due."

"Oh, I know about that. I assume you split the cost."

"No. I pay the full tuition for the Lake Forest Academy."

"I didn't know he went there. Isn't it one of the most expensive private schools in Chicago?"

"It's *the* most expensive school in Chicago." He looked troubled.

Gabby decided she'd tread lightly. "I don't mean to pry, and you can tell me to mind my business, but are you having trouble with the tuition?"

"No," he said abruptly.

"You know I'd be happy to help you out if you need it."

His pride in jeopardy, he got up and grabbed his pants. "I don't need your money."

"I didn't say you did."

"That's not what it sounded like to me," he said as he quickly pulled his pants up.

"Nigel . . ."

"No." He put his hand up. "I don't want to talk about it." He put his shirt on and grabbed his shoes. "I'll call you later."

Before Gabby could get a word out, he walked out of the living room and out of the house. She lay back on the floor. "I feel like I've been in a hit and run. What did I say?" She asked aloud as she sat up to get the phone. When she got Alicia's answering machine, she called Lauren.

"Hello?"

"Hi, Lauren."

"Hey, Gabby, how's it going?"

"It was going well."

Lauren sipped her drink. "I don't like the sound of that."

"Nigel was here and we had a great time together, you know . . ."

"Yes, Gabby, we're not ten. You were doing the horizontal hula. More power to you, girl."

"Afterwards I noticed he looked a little pensive, so I asked what was wrong. He told me his son's tuition was due."

"It's about that time of year. Where does his son go to school?"

"The Lake Forest Academy in Chicago."

"Ouch! I don't even have children and I know that's the most expensive school in Chicago."

"I know. I offered to help if he was having a problem."

"No, you didn't," Lauren groaned.

"Was I wrong?"

"I'm pretty sure he didn't tell you about it so you could give him money."

"I thought it was a nice thing to do."

"It was nice, but he's probably got his pride. Have you talked to him about his son?"

"We've talked about him a little but never in detail."

"It sounds like you should have a conversation."

"He said that he and his ex have a good relationship. He even gets along with her husband."

"If he looked upset about tuition, I'm pretty sure it's not exactly *A Very Brady Christmas.*"

"You could have a point. What should I do?"

"Ask him about it. You don't have to accuse him of lying about anything, but you need to know what you're getting into."

"Oh, brother."

"Just talk to him."

"I'll give him some time to cool down. I'll call him tomorrow."

"Good plan."

"Thanks. So what are you doing tonight?"

"Randy's coming over after work."

"A little late night rendezvous. Nice."

"I think so, too."

"By the way, have you spoken to Alicia? I tried to call her but I got her voice mail."

"I think she's having dinner with Nate tonight."

"Good. It's nice to know she's getting out."

"I know." Lauren took another sip. "Are you okay now?"

"Yes. Thanks for listening." She looked at the clock. "Well, I'm going to take a bath and relax tonight."

"That sounds like a plan. I'll talk to you later."

"Okay. Have a good night."

❦

That evening Nathaniel proved to be a quick study in the kitchen. Alicia watched as he stirred the fennel, celery, carrots, onions and leeks in the pot. She added the garlic and then the Cote du Rhone wine. While the pot came to a boil, she and Nathaniel partook in a glass of the wine.

"This is nice," he said as he sipped his wine. "If I knew cooking was this much fun, I would have gotten into it years ago."

Alicia laughed, then added the salt and pepper.

Nathaniel held up the thyme sprigs, rosemary and twine. "What am I supposed to do with this?"

"You're going to make a bouquet garni of sorts."

"A what?"

"You're going to tie the herbs together and add them to the pot."

"Okay. Can you help me with that one?"

"Sure." Alicia gathered the herbs together and then took the twine to wrap them. She found it a little difficult to tie the twine. "Damn!" She was frustrated.

"What's the matter?" Nathaniel looked concerned.

"I sometimes have problems doing small things like this. In the studio I have someone who acts as my sous chef and preps everything."

"No worries, sweetie, I'll tie it."

He tied the twine. "Don't we make a good team? Maybe I can be your sous chef."

Alicia smiled.

"Now that's what I want to see." He leaned over and kissed her.

His sweetness unsettled her a little. "Now you get the ribs and I'll pour the stock."

"Yes, chef."

They finished the short ribs together and Nathaniel put the pan in the oven. The potatoes were already going, and there was nothing left to do but sit and enjoy one another's company.

"How about we go in the living room where it's cooler?"

"Okay."

They retired to the living room and sat on the love seat.

"How was the rest of the day in the Hamptons?"

"Not bad. Lauren and I stayed outside and out of the line of fire."

"I take it the drive-by fix-up didn't go over well."

"No. Gabby has met someone and she seems to be really happy with him."

"Does her mother know that?"

"Probably, but Bunny is Bunny. Her will be done."

Nathaniel chuckled. "What about your parents? What are they like?"

"Walter and Loretta Carlson are actually pretty cool parents."

"They never got involved with your love life?"

"For a long time I didn't have a love life for them to be worried about. I certainly didn't date as a teenager. If anything, they were more worried I was too obsessed with Jane Austen."

"You're a big Austen fan?"

"Oh, yes, I fell in love with her books a long time ago. I love that sexy pre-Victorian/Victorian way of romance."

"I've never heard it described as sexy."

"When you think about it, the stories are filled with sexual tension under the guise of manners. The long looks across the room between Emma and Mr. Knightley. The heated yet polite exchanges between Elizabeth Bennett and Mr. Darcy." Alicia closed her eyes and sighed.

"I have to re-read those books. Do you like any other authors?"

"I love Edith Wharton's *Age of Innocence.*"

"You consider that a hot book, too?" he asked, surprised.

"Yes. The chapter when Newland Archer slowly unbuttons Countess Olenska's gloves to kiss her hand is one of the sexiest things I've ever read. It's essentially the prelude to adultery, but you totally get caught up in the romance of it."

"I take it you loved the movie."

"Yes." She smiled. "I never thought of Daniel Day Lewis as a sex symbol, but after that movie he moved to the head of the class."

"I'm going to put that book and movie on my list, too."

Alicia laughed. "Let me know what you think afterwards. I'll be interested to hear a man's perspective."

"I will. Did Kurt enjoy your pantheon of authors?"

"I wouldn't say he enjoyed them per se, but he was cool with my Austen Aristocrats meetings."

"Your what?"

"It's the club Lauren, Gabby and I started back in high school. We're all Austen fans and that's how we spent our Friday nights back then. Only we had so much fun, we kept it up."

"You still meet?"

"Yes." She sipped her wine.

He grinned.

"I don't know if that's a bemused look or what."

He took her wine glass and put it on the table next to his. "It's a 'you're so cute I just have to kiss you' look."

At first their lips touched lightly and then grew more sensual. Degree by degree their temperatures rose. However, the temperature weren't the only thing on the rise as Nathaniel pulled away suddenly and jumped to his feet. "Shouldn't I check the oven now?"

Alicia was a little thrown, but she recovered. "Sure."

Nathaniel rushed into the kitchen and opened the freezer. He grabbed a bag of frozen peas and put it on the front of his pants.

"Is everything okay in there?" Alicia called.

"It's fine. You just relax, I have everything under control."

"Okay!"

A minute later Nathaniel put the peas back in the freezer and checked the oven. "The ribs look good. How much longer do you think?"

Alicia entered the kitchen. "Let me look." He moved slightly so she could get in front of him. When she bent forward, her rear brushed against him. As Nathaniel crossed his legs, a mischievous grin came over Alicia's face. *Nice to know I've still got it.* She checked the ribs. "I think we're done."

"Wonderful. I'll take them out and dinner will be served."

Alicia and Nathaniel enjoyed a wonderful dinner together before he walked her back to her place. When they kissed good night, the same passion that overcame them on the love seat returned. Nathaniel ran his hands down her back and lightly traced his fingers around her hips and back up to her neck. Her red hair felt like silk between his fingers and her perfume permeated his senses. He wanted her as he'd never wanted a woman before, but he knew it would take time.

"Thank you for dinner."

"Thank you for being such a good teacher." He kissed her again. "I'll call you tomorrow."

"Okay." She smiled and went inside.

Nathaniel waited for the door to lock and then he hurried back to his place. Although as a doctor he knew cold showers didn't really work, he needed to do something until Alicia felt ready to be with him.

∽

When Lauren opened her door at eleven p.m. she found a tired yet still incredibly sexy Randy at her door.

"Hey, baby." She kissed him.

"I really needed that."

"Well, then, please take a load off and I'll be right back."

Randy sat down. "Did you have a good time in the Hamptons?"

"That depends on how you define a good time."

"That sounds ominous." He lay back on the sofa.

"Have you heard the term 'ambush makeover?' "

"Yes."

"Gabby's mother turned it into an ambush setup."

"Oh, I guess it didn't go over well."

"That would be an understatement."

"Poor girl. Is she okay now?"

"Yes."

"I'm glad to hear it."

Lauren returned with a tray with two glasses and a pitcher of cosmopolitans.

"I might not be able to cook, but I make a great cosmopolitan."

He smiled wide. "Ah, that sounds like just the ticket, although alcohol has been known to get you into trouble."

She put the tray down and sat next to him. "I don't think it got me into trouble at all. As a matter of fact, I believe it got me out of trouble."

"Is that right?"

"Yes."

"All kidding aside, have you heard from Ken again?"

Lauren told him about Ken's quest for the network and how he tried to get her to do his bidding.

"He texted me today and I ignored him."

"Do you think that was wise? He'll only keep it up."

"Randy, I've been very clear that I have no intention of helping him. He's gotten as far as he will on my back. I'm not carrying him anymore."

"Are you sure you can live with that?"

"Yes. I'm very sure." She took her robe off and revealed her sexy black babydoll.

"Oh, my." Despite his exhaustion he was aroused.

"Do you like it?"

"Yes," he said emphatically.

She raised the pitcher to pour. He stopped her. "I thought you wanted to relax," she said.

"I'll relax later. Come here." He pulled her to him.

There was no need for the cosmopolitans.

❧

Monday couldn't come quickly enough for Gabby; she needed to find respite from her thoughts. She hadn't heard one peep out of Nigel since Saturday, and it bothered her to no end.

Robin knocked on the door. "Gabby?"

She looked up from her computer. "Hey, Robin. What's up?"

"I was going to go on a coffee run. Do you want anything?"

"Sure." She rubbed her eyes. "I'll take my usual."

"Okay. A grande decaf latte it is. One of the interns is going to cover the phones for me."

"Not a problem. Thanks, Robin."

"You're welcome. I'll be right back."

Gabby went back to her computer. There was another knock. Without looking up, Gabby reached for her purse. "You forgot to get the money for my latte."

"Gabby."

She looked up. It was Nigel. "Hi." She looked at her computer's clock. "I'm surprised to see you. Isn't this the middle of your work day?"

"It is, but I couldn't get any work done, so I decided to come over here."

"Are you here for advice on the market? I do watch CNBC."

He laughed. "Do you have a few minutes or so?"

"I do. Have a seat."

He sat down. "Listen, I came over to apologize for the way I behaved the other night. I shouldn't have flown off the handle like that."

"It was completely out of left field."

"I know. I haven't been totally honest with you about my situation with my son's mother."

"I see."

He took a deep breath. "I used to have a good relationship with her, but that changed when I found out she used the child support and school tuition money to pay her bills. So I went to court and now I pay his tuition directly. Ever since then she's made it impossible for me to see, speak or spend time with Nigel Jr."

"Why didn't you tell me?"

"I was embarrassed."

"Why would you feel like that?"

"I'm essentially a forty-something man who's going through baby mamma drama."

"So you have baggage from a previous relationship. Who doesn't?"

"You didn't sign up for this, Gabby. If you want to rethink this whole relationship I'll understand."

"Why would I do that? I want to be with you. I'm ready to take the ups and the downs."

"Are you sure? Deidre can be a force unto herself."

"As long as we're together I can handle anything."

Just then Robin appeared in the doorway. "Oh, I can come back."

"Come in, Robin, it's okay." Gabby waved her in.

"Hi. Nigel. How are you?" She asked as she put Gabby's Starbucks on her desk.

"I'm fine. How are you?"

"I can't complain."

Gabby held out her money. "Here you go."

Robin walked away without taking it. "Your money is no good here. It was good seeing you, Nigel."

"You, too."

"So are we okay now?" Gabby asked.

"Yes." He looked at his watch. "I'd better get back to my office." He got up and walked around the desk, leaned in and kissed her. "I'll talk to you later."

"Okay."

Gabby sipped her latte as she watched him leave her office. *Baby mamma drama with a teenager can't be easy.* She picked up the phone.

"Hello?"

"Alicia?"

"Yes, Gabby, it's me."

"It must be a Freudian slip. I meant to call Lauren."

"Well, thanks a lot." She tried to sound offended.

"You know what I mean. Of course I always want to talk to you, too."

"That's better. You made me sound like a miserable stepchild."

"Sorry."

"What's up?"

"I guess you could say I had a little spat this weekend with Nigel, but it's resolved now."

"What was the little spat about?"

"He's got some issues with his ex and their son."

"Ex and the city. There's nothing too unusual about that these days."

"When we first met he told me everything was fine, even peachy. Honestly, it sounded like they were Bruce, Demi and Ashton reincarnated."

"They're a freak of nature. No one is like that in real life," Alicia scoffed.

"It is pretty freaky, isn't it?"

"I think he didn't want to risk scaring you off, but he should have been honest with you."

"It's not like he's a Willoughby."

"The eighteenth-century version of Mr. Love 'em and Leave 'em? I should think not. But . . ."

"I told you we resolved things."

"I won't push my luck."

"Good." She paused. "Listen, I have to get back to work. We have a couple of new pieces coming today."

"Okay. I'll talk to you later."

"Sure. Wait. Before I go, how was dinner with Nate the other night?"

"It was nice. We had a good time."

"I'm glad to hear it." Gabby smiled.

"I bet you are. I can hear you grinning. I'll catch you later, Gabby. Bye."

"Bye."

Starbucks in hand, Gabby left her office.

CHAPTER 14

Over the next few weeks of the summer the temperatures weren't the only things hot. Alicia, Gabby and Lauren spent more time with the new men in their lives. While Randy and Nigel may have steamed up the nights with Gabby and Lauren, Nathaniel's evenings ended quite differently. As the kisses between him and Alicia got hotter, his cold showers got longer. Nathaniel thought he was in danger of getting frostbite in very inopportune places, but Alicia was worth an icicle or two.

A week before Gabby's big new artist exhibit, the Austen Aristocrats gathered for a long overdue afternoon meeting at Alicia's place. The three of them stretched out in Alicia's family room with their books.

Harrison brought in a tray of lemonade and cookies. "Here you go, ladies." He set it down on the table.

"Thanks, Harrison." Alicia smiled.

"You're welcome." He looked around. "I see you mean to catch up on old business today."

"Oh yes, we've all been a little distracted of late," Lauren said.

"That's putting it mildly." Gabby poured a glass of lemonade.

"Now that's not a bad thing, girls. While I love to see you together, it's nice that you have other interests." He winked.

"True, Jane did have to dream these stories up," Lauren said sweetly.

"Oh, and it's nice to have the real thing." Gabby grinned.

"You're awfully quiet, Alicia. Don't you agree?"

"Oh, sure, the real thing is better any day." She seemed distracted.

"Well, I think I will leave you ladies to your meeting. Call me if you need anything."

He left and closed the door.

Gabby piped up. "Okay, Alicia, I know you have something on your mind and it has to do with me."

"Oh, for heaven's sake. You were the one who told me he wasn't honest about the issues he's having with his ex over his son."

"Yes, but I also told you we've talked and everything has been fine."

"Are you sure you know everything?" Lauren asked.

"I do. I know he's a good father."

"I don't doubt he's a good father, but you're stepping into tricky territory."

"How so?"

Alicia sighed loudly. "Let's just drop it. She's gone Pollyanna on us. We've said our peace."

"Thank you."

"Let's change the subject," Lauren said.

"Fine. Are you ready for the exhibit, Gabby?" Alicia asked.

"Almost. It will be nice having a good-looking man like Nigel on my arm for the event."

"I can't wait to meet him. Can you, Alicia?"

"Despite what you might think, I'm looking forward to it, too." Alicia looked distracted.

"Okay, what's up with you?" Lauren asked.

"Nothing. I have a few things on my mind, that's all."

"No, it's more than that." Gabby wasn't convinced.

"Is everything okay with you and Nate?"

"Yes, everything is wonderful between us. We went to dinner in the city last night."

"Oh, that was nice," Gabby said.

"It was nice."

"But?"

Alicia sighed. "I'm afraid Nathaniel's going to get tired of me."

Lauren was taken aback. "Why on earth would you say that? It's obvious the man is crazy about you."

"I know, but we haven't . . ."

"You haven't what?" Gabby asked.

"You know . . ."

"You haven't taken the lid off the cookie jar?"

Alicia couldn't help but laugh. "I hadn't thought of using that expression, Lauren, but no, I haven't taken the lid off."

"Has he said something to you about it?"

"No, he hasn't said a word."

"Well, he knows you've been a widow for a long time and you wouldn't just hop into bed."

"I know, Lauren, but he is a man. How much longer can he hold out?"

Lauren tried to reassure her. "He cares about you, he'll wait as long as it takes. Somehow I don't think that's the whole story, is it, Alicia? There's something else bothering you."

"Yes. It's not just that I haven't had sex since Kurt died." She hesitated a minute. "I haven't had sex since I was diagnosed either. I don't know if I'll be different."

"Have you asked the neurologist about it?"

"Yes. He said a lot of patients have normal, sexually fulfilling sex lives with a healthy libido."

"That answers your question. You don't have anything to worry about." Gabby smiled.

"But how do I know I'm one of them?"

"I don't want to sound like a Nike commercial, but you have to just do it. That's the only way you'll know for sure."

"Oh, God," she groaned.

"Hey, at least Nate's a doctor. If anyone should understand, it's him."

"Have you talked to him about it?" Lauren asked.

"Don't be silly. Of course I haven't. I mean, how would I bring it up?"

"I guess that would be awkward."

"You think?"

"Listen to you, you're getting all worked up about it for no reason. When the time is right, you'll know it and you might not need to say a word," Gabby said.

Alicia thought about it for a minute. "True."

"And if there is any issue, you can deal with it together," Gabby said as she hugged her.

"You'll know when the time is right," Lauren assured her.

Alicia wondered if the right time was closer than she thought.

❧

A couple of hours after the meeting broke up and the girls went back to the city, Alicia was quietly reading in the living room when Harrison popped in.

"Okay, I'm heading out for a while. Do you need anything?"

"No, I'm good." She turned and looked at him all spiffed up. "You look good."

"Thanks. I'm meeting some friends I made from the MS caregivers group."

"I think it's great you keep in touch."

"You can't go through something like that and just cut it off. We went through some real ups and downs together. Like you, they helped me through a lot."

"You know I'd do it again in a minute."

"I know." He walked over and kissed her on the forehead. "You stay cool and I'll see you later. You promise you'll be a good girl?"

"I promise."

"Good." He kissed her forehead again. "See you later."

"Have a good time," she called after him.

Alicia continued reading for a little while. "What am I doing?" She closed her book, got up, and went over to the mirror. *Maybe it's time to take the lid off the cookie jar.* She fluffed her hair and let out a deep breath. "Here I go."

Alicia walked out of the house and over to Nathaniel's place. As she got closer, she noticed a brunette at the door with Nathaniel. The brunette wore a trench coat and heels. That was all Alicia had to see. Just as she turned on her heel, Nathaniel saw her.

"Alicia!" He closed the door and walked past the brunette.

"I'm sorry to have disturbed you," she huffed.

"It's not what you think!" He ran after her and grabbed her arm. "Wait."

"She's wearing a trench coat and heels in 90-degree weather. I don't have to be a psychic to know she's not wearing anything else."

"I didn't know she was coming and I didn't let her in."

"Oh, is that right? You turned down a package like that? She was practically gift wrapped."

"That's right!"

"Why? Why would you turn her down?"

"I'm in love with you, Alicia. I don't know if you noticed, but I am over the moon, crazy in love with you," he blurted out.

Alicia stood there, stunned to hear the words.

"Come on, let's get out of this heat. This isn't good for you." He walked her back to her place. Alicia still hadn't said a word by the time they were inside.

Suddenly she said, "You're in love with me?"

"Yes."

"I thought that since we haven't been together . . ."

"That I'd jump at the chance to have sex with just anyone."

"I'm ashamed to admit it, but that's what I thought. I've lived next door to you for a while, Nathaniel, and I've seen women throw themselves at you."

"That's in the past for me, Alicia. You're the only woman I want."

"Even though we haven't been together in that way?"

"Yes. I don't care how long it takes and how many cold showers are in my future. You're worth the wait."

With those words Alicia came closer and they kissed. She began to unbutton his shirt, but he stopped her.

"We don't have to do anything, you know."

"I know." She continued to unbutton.

"Are you sure?"

"I'm sure." She took him by the hand and led him upstairs to her bedroom. Nathaniel took his shirt off and slowly they undressed each other. As he stood before her nude, Nathaniel looked like a Greek God, chiseled, smooth and as hard as granite. Alicia sat down and while he kissed her, he removed her bra. His eyes widened when he saw her beautiful breasts. Alicia's body tensed as he lightly caressed and kissed them. He kissed her neck. "We'll go as slow as you want," he whispered. Alicia lay back on the bed, and he continued to kiss her body all over. When he reached her navel, he gently pulled her lacy panties off. Without thinking Alicia put her arms over her body, but Nathaniel kissed them and put them to the side.

As his hard body hovered over her, her senses overwhelmed her. They kissed and soon their bodies intertwined and their heart beats in syncopation. Alicia held on to him as she experienced pleasure like she hadn't in years.

A little while later Nathaniel awoke and found Alicia's back was to him.

"Hey sweetheart." He kissed her shoulder, then paused when he heard her quietly weeping. "Hey, what's wrong, honey?"

She rolled toward him, eyes filled with tears.

"Oh, honey, are you okay?" He wiped her tears.

"You're going to think I'm crazy."

"No, I won't."

"I feel like I betrayed Kurt."

"It's not crazy at all."

"Of course it is, we just made love."

"No, it isn't. You still love him and I understand that."

"You do?"

"Yes. It's one of the things that made it so easy to fall in love with you. I don't ever expect you to stop loving Kurt just because he's not here anymore. He's in your heart."

Alicia sniffled. "You're really wonderful. I love you."

The words lifted Nathaniel ten feet off the ground. "You have no idea how happy it makes me to hear you say those words."

"I mean them."

"I know you do, and that's what makes it all the more special to me."

He kissed her and then he proved just how special it was to him several times that afternoon.

∾

Lauren stopped at one of her favorite organic bath shops on her way home. As she perused the aromatherapy oils, her cell phone rang.

"Lauren Jules-Jones."

"Hi, Lauren."

"Hey, Joe, how's my favorite attorney?"

"I'm not bad, but this isn't a social call."

Lauren stopped in her tracks. "I'm in a boutique. Should I leave?"

"I think that's a good idea."

Lauren walked outside. "Okay, I'm outside."

"I got a call from Ken's lawyer today and it looks like he wants his equity out of the apartment."

"What? That wasn't a part of the deal we agreed to."

"I know, and you waived spousal support, too, so I don't know what's going on."

"I think I do." She seethed.

"Do you want to let me in on it?"

"I know you're my attorney, but the less you know the better, at least for now."

"I don't like the sound of that."

"I'm not going to kill him, if that's what you're worried about. I'd like to kill him, but he's not worth it."

"That's comforting to hear, but I still want to know what this is about."

"It's a power play. He wants me to do something for him and I refused to help him."

"Is it something illegal?"

"No. This is about his ego more than anything else," Lauren said as she got into a waiting car.

"This is about his ego?" Joe was confused.

"He wants me to help him get on a sports show."

"He's already an on-field correspondent for *NFL Weekly*."

"He wants to be a desk commentator and analyst. Hold on a second, Joe."

"Okay."

"Tony, I need to go to the studio."

"No problem, Ms. Jones," he answered.

Lauren went back to her call. "Thanks for holding."

Joe continued. "So what you're telling me is he wanted you to help him with that."

"Yes."

"I know he and his lawyer might think this is a negotiation tactic, but this smacks of blackmail."

"That's why I'm heading for the studio now. I know he's covering for the weekend sports guy, and I want to talk to him about this face to face."

"Wait a minute, Lauren, I don't think that's a good idea. You should let me handle this."

"I will let you handle it, but first I want to try it my way."

"Fine, I know I can't stop you. Please let me know what happens."

"I will. I'll talk to you later." She closed her phone.

Less than fifteen minutes later she was in the studio and headed for the hair and makeup area, where she knew he'd be getting made up for the broadcast. He was in the chair when she walked in.

"Hello, Lauren, how are you?" the makeup artist asked.

"I'm good, Kelly. How are you?"

"Not bad." She continued working.

"What brings you by, Lauren?" Ken asked.

"Kelly, could you give us a minute?"

"Sure." She walked out.

"You know perfectly well why I'm here. I got a call from my lawyer that you want to renege on our agreement."

"I gave it some thought and I decided that I put as much into that apartment as you, so why shouldn't I get my fair share?"

"I waived spousal support, Ken. This was supposed to be a non-starter."

"It's easy enough to solve. All you have to do is buy me out."

"I don't have that kind of money just lying around."

"Then we can sell the apartment and split the proceeds."

"And where am I supposed to live with that money in New York City? Besides, I love that apartment. You can't do this to me," she fumed.

"That's for the lawyers and judges to decide unless . . ."

"Unless what?"

"You help me with the network."

Lauren was enraged. "Are you blackmailing me?"

"I wouldn't call it blackmail. It's a negotiating tactic."

"You're a real son of a bitch."

"Maybe I am, but I want to be a desk commentator, and I deserve it."

"I don't produce *NFL Weekly* and don't have a say in who they hire."

"But you know the people who do."

"And if I don't?"

"Then the lawyers will sort it out and who knows how long that will take," he said smugly.

"You're willing to drag this divorce out."

"It's up to you."

"You're a real piece of work, Ken. God doesn't like ugly."

"I'll worry about God after I'm behind the desk."

When Lauren looked at Ken, she no longer saw a former football great but a thug in a suit willing to do anything to get his way. It seemed poetic that in his former life he had literally knocked people over for a living.

Lauren stormed out of the makeup room. *How could I have been completely taken in by the likes of Ken Jones? Alicia always said there was something about him she just didn't trust, and now I see how right she was.* When she got outside Tony opened the car door and she got in.

"Where to now, Ms. Jones?"

"Home, please."

Lauren's head pounded as she realized her options were untenable at best. When she got home she put her key in the door and went in. She looked around at the place she'd called home.

"Hey, baby."

She was startled, then relieved, when she saw Randy. "Hi."

"I hope you don't mind. I convinced the building manager to let me in."

"Of course I don't mind, but how did you convince George? He's a pretty tough customer."

"I leap-frogged him to the top of our reservation list. Turns out he and his wife love tapas."

"I see. What smells so good?"

"I'm whipping up a little something for us."

Suddenly Lauren was overcome with emotion and she began to cry.

Randy went over and held her in his arms. "Oh, baby, what's wrong?" Dinner was on hold.

For the first time in a long time Lauren folded in on herself. She didn't need Randy to say anything. His arms were enough to comfort her.

A little while later Randy and Lauren were on the sofa. She was calmer.

"Do you feel better now?"

"I do."

"Do you want to talk about it?"

"I don't think this is something talking can help."

"Why don't you let me decide, okay?"

She wiped her eyes. "I might be forced to sell my apartment."

"What? Why?"

"Ken."

"What about him? I though he agreed you'd keep the apartment."

"He changed his mind."

"Does this have something to do with the show you told me about?"

She nodded. "I can keep the apartment free and clear if I talk to the network about him being a commentator on the show."

"That's blackmail, Lauren." Randy was steamed.

"I don't want to do it, so either I have to buy him out, which I can't afford to do, or sell the place and split the proceeds, which I don't want to do."

"Did you tell your lawyer?"

"Yes. He said it sounded like blackmail, too."

"Then let him handle it."

"Listen, Randy, this isn't my first time at the rodeo. I've been through two divorces and I know that I can't allege blackmail without proof. It will be a case of his word against mine. If I tell a judge he's trying to blackmail me, he can simply say he reconsidered his earlier position and wants to negotiate."

"Oh, that's slick," Randy said, disgusted.

"The bottom line is it will drag this divorce out and I want to put a period at the end of this sentence and close the book on Ken Jones."

"Let me help you buy him out."

Lauren was floored. "What?"

"I'll help you buy him out."

"You'd do that for me?"

"Yes." He paused. "I know we haven't been seeing each other for very long, but we're not kids anymore, and I for one know myself and my feelings."

"What are you saying?"

"I love you, Lauren." He let out a deep breath. "There, I said and I mean it."

Lauren's heart skipped a beat. "Oh, Randy."

"You don't have to say it back to me. I just thought you should know."

Lauren climbed into his lap and put her arms around him. She looked into his eyes and saw everything she'd been looking for in a man. "Oh, God, Randy, I love you, too."

He pulled her to him in a passionate embrace fueled by the urgency of newly professed love. All the day's worries disappeared as their clothes came off. Nude, they stood face to face. "You're gorgeous," he whispered and he began to plant butterfly kisses up and down her body. Lauren's knees buckled as her body craved for more. Randy lifted her, took her to the bedroom and laid her on the bed. Lauren's hands explored his body, her light touch making him quiver. A moment later they were wrapped together as their bodies moved in harmony.

Later Lauren lay in Randy's arms after he drifted off. *As angry as I am with Ken I have him to thank for meeting a real man like Randy. And best of all, he loves me.* She smiled. She now knew that she could face anything Ken threw her way. Randy had her back and whether she kept her apartment or not, she'd always be home with the man she loved.

❦

Alicia sat in the backyard under the stars and listened to the warm summer breeze whispering through the trees.

"Do you mind if I join you?"

"Don't be silly, Harrison. Have a seat."

"Thanks." He stretched out on the chaise lounge next to her.

"How was your visit today?"

"It was good to catch up with everyone. Even though it was a little weird since I didn't have Martha to talk about, there were other widows and widowers there so that made it easier."

"That was good."

"Some of them have even moved into new relationships. Heck, there are even a few engagements in the bunch."

"Wow."

"That's the thing about spouses who were also care-givers. Even when their beloved is gone they still have a lot of love and caring to give. But sometimes it takes them a while to realize they're allowed to move on and give that love to someone else without feeling guilty."

A tear rolled down her cheek. "You always know what to say, don't you?"

He wiped the tear with his finger. "Dear girl, it's written all over your face. You're in love."

"I didn't know this was going to happen."

"That's what makes love so wonderful. It's unpredictable."

"I'm happy and sad at the same time, if that makes any sense."

"It makes sense to me. Falling in love with Nate and showing him how much you love him doesn't mean you didn't love Kurt. It just means you made a little more room in your heart for both of them." He kissed her forehead.

"Thank you, Harrison. I love how we can have 'the talk' without . . ."

"You having to say a word," he finished.

"Right." She looked down at her Blackberry.

"What's with the PDA on such a relaxing evening?"

"My kitchenware line launch with Macy's is this week. I've got five store events and Viola just emailed me the schedule."

"Are you sure you can handle so many things this week? You do have Gabby's new artist exhibit on Friday."

"I have a couple of days to rest in between the last store event and the exhibit. I should be fine."

"I hope you're right."

"Haven't I been a good girl this summer?"

"Relatively."

"Still, that's an improvement, and after this I'm not doing anything else but getting ready for the new season."

"If you say so." He sounded unsure.

"Quit worrying. I'll be okay."

❧

With the new artist exhibit less than a week away Gabby pulled out all the stops out at the gallery. It promised to be a well-attended and well-covered event, which was what Gabby strove for as she worked around the clock except for the Austen Aristocrats meeting earlier that day.

She was on her third cup of decaf when the phone rang.

"Hello?"

"Mom?"

"Hi, Lizzie, how are you, honey?"

"I'm good."

"Where are you now?"

"Paris."

"Oh, that's wonderful. Are you having a good time?"

"I'm having a great time." She sounded enthused.

"Good." She paused. "It sounds quiet. Where are your friends?"

"They're still partying the night away, but I'm pooped. Besides, this will give me a chance to get some sleep before the snorers return."

Gabby laughed.

"I also wanted to call you because I knew you'd be up worrying over the new artist exhibit on Friday. How are you holding up?"

"It's the usual level of insanity."

"Is Victor throwing fits?"

"He's more reliable than Old Faithful."

Lizzie laughed. "But he's the best at what he does."

"That he is, my dear, and that's why we put up with it."

Lizzie yawned. "Sorry about that, Mom. I'd better hit the sack."

"All right, sweetie. Thanks for calling."

"Love you, Mom."

"Love you, too."

Lauren looked at the clock. *Wow, I didn't realize how late it was. I'd better get some rest too.* She shut her laptop down. Just as she was about to head upstairs she checked her voice mail. There were no new messages. *I guess Nigel was busy today. I'll give him a call tomorrow before Mother comes for tea.* She shut off the lights and headed up the stairs.

CHAPTER 15

Alicia awoke to the smell of coffee and flowers the next morning. As she opened her eyes, it looked like the FTD elves has been busy.

"Good morning." Nathaniel held a breakfast tray.

"Good morning. What's all this?" She sat up.

"It's breakfast in bed."

"I can see that. Where did all the flowers come from?"

"It pays to make a few house calls on a florist."

She looked around. "I'd say you're right. It looks like he cleaned out the shop." She sat up. "So what do you have there?"

He put on the tray on the night table. "I have orange juice, strawberries, whole-wheat toast and coffee."

"Very nice, but I must look a fright."

"No, you're perfect." He kissed her neck.

She giggled. "Thank you. That tickles."

He continued to kiss her neck.

"Oh, that feels nice." She paused. "But you know Harrison's home."

"Harrison left after he helped me get the flowers into your room while you were asleep."

She looked at the clock. "You had to get up pretty early then. It's only seven-thirty a.m."

"I know. Now it's just you, me and the flowers." He winked as he leaned in to kiss her. Alicia was hypnotized by spark in his blue eyes, and when they kissed, the energy between them was electric. Alicia ran her fingers through his dark, wavy hair as she pulled him closer. Breakfast long forgotten, Nathaniel undressed and climbed into bed with her. A minute later Alicia's nightgown was on the floor.

A little while later Alicia and Nathaniel enjoyed the morning peace in each other's arms.

"Do you want to have breakfast?" he asked.

"No, I'm fine." She sighed. "I wish it could be like this all week."

"It could if you want it to."

"That's a very nice thought, Nathaniel, but I'm on duty this week."

"What do you mean, you're on duty? Is your hiatus over?

"No. My housewares line launches at Macy's this week."

"Wow, that's a big deal."

"It's been in the works forever and now it's here. I have five in-store events starting tomorrow and ending on Wednesday."

"Are they in New York?"

"Yes. I've got two on Long Island, two in Westchester and the last one in Herald Square."

"It sounds like a lot for you to do in a short time. Are you sure you can handle it?"

"Now you sound like Harrison."

"He's right to ask. You do have a lot on your plate this week."

"I'll be fine. I'll let you in on a little secret." She motioned him to come closer. "My boyfriend's a doctor. He'll take good care of me." She smiled.

"This isn't Monopoly, Alicia. Having a doctor boyfriend doesn't mean you have a get-out-of-jail-free card."

"Doesn't it?" she teased.

"Your health isn't a game, Alicia. It's time you start taking it seriously."

༺ঞ༻

Lauren sat on the balcony of her apartment and took in the view of Manhattan in all its Upper East Side glory. She'd come a long way from the one bedroom she'd shared with her Grandma Lee in Bayside. *I earned my way here just like Grandma said I could. She knew I had the ambition to make it here. She also warned me that men would see my determination and the good ones would help with the drive, but the bad ones would be content to go for the ride. And what did I do? I picked three hitchhikers in a row.* She sighed.

"Here you go, baby." Randy handed her a cup of coffee.

"Thanks." She took a whiff and then sipped.

Randy looked at the view. "You really have some view from up here."

"I know. It's one of the reasons I was so keen on this place. It felt like a little piece of Shangri-La up above the world." She sighed.

"Do you want to talk about it?"

"I was just thinking about my life in Bayside with my Grandma Lee. She was the one who raised me."

"If you don't mind my asking, what happened to your parents?"

"I don't mind. My father died in a car accident before I was born and Caroline, my mother, couldn't handle life as a single parent, so she gave my grandmother custody."

"I'm sorry."

"Don't be, I got the best part of the deal. Grandma Lee gave me all the love, attention and support I needed. We may not have had much materially, but we were wealthy in ways that counted."

"You know, that says a lot. I know people who grew up with both parents who never felt like you. You're lucky."

"I know." She sipped her coffee. "I remember how proud she was when I graduated from Dartmouth. I thought they were going to have to tie her to the ground. She was very sick by then, but nothing was going to keep her from being there." Lauren choked up. "She died two months later."

"I'm sorry." Randy rubbed her hand.

"I never realized how much I depended on her love and support. She was the only family I had. I did have Alicia and Gabby, but when they got married and started their own families, I felt like the odd man out."

"I'm sure they didn't exclude you."

"Oh no, they made me feel like a part of their families. But I wanted my own family. That's when the trouble started."

"What do you mean?"

"My unfortunate marriage choices in my search to have my own family, or at least someone who I thought would always be there to love me."

"Everyone makes mistakes in love, sweetheart."

"Yes, but in baseball terms I struck out three times."

"That's okay, Lauren. Even baseball players get up to bat more than three times in a game. You are by no means out of it, if I say so myself." He kissed her hand.

She smiled warmly. "I'm not?"

"Not at all." He stood up and pulled her to him. "I love you and you're stuck with me."

She wrapped her arms around his shoulders. "Are you sure? Even with this Ken thing hanging over me?"

"Yes. I can help you with the money for this place."

"I love you, but I want to do this myself."

"Are you sure?"

"Yes."

He kissed her. "Now let's stand here while you survey your kingdom like the queen you are."

Lauren laughed. "All hail the queen!" In that moment she realized she didn't need the apartment or the view, but she would fight for it. She wasn't sure how at the moment, but she'd find a way to sack Ken at his own game.

❧

It was early Sunday afternoon and Gabby had Bunny over for high tea early again. With so much work to do for the upcoming week, every moment counted and Gabby had to get back to business sooner rather than later. This afternoon's high tea was more traditional with the proper "grass" and cucumber sandwiches followed by scones and crumpets.

As usual, poor Rosie had her maid's uniform on. She looked incredibly uncomfortable as she stood by on the ready to clear dishes as soon as Bunny put one down.

"You know, I ran into Terrence and he told me he was coming to the exhibit Friday."

Gabby tried not to roll her eyes. "A lot of people come to the exhibit, Mother."

She shook her head. "I don't understand why you won't give him a chance."

"You're kidding, right, Mother? Were you not there when he talked about paint for nearly an hour solid?"

Before Bunny could stop herself, she let out a guffaw. "I suppose watching paint dry would have been more interesting." She quickly covered her mouth.

Gabby fell out laughing. "You're right about that, Mother." For the first time Gabby saw a side of her mother she hadn't seen in years.

The doorbell rang and Rosie went to answer it.

"Were you expecting anyone else today?"

"No."

A few moments later Rosie returned, followed by Nigel, who had a huge bouquet of flowers in his hands. Gabby's heart leaped the moment she saw him.

"Oh, how lovely, someone sent you flowers today." Bunny smiled.

"Hi." Nigel smiled.

"Hi."

"Do you have something for the young man? Rosie, would you please get Ms. Blanchard's purse?"

Rosie looked confused.

Gabby got up and took the flowers from Nigel. "Mother, he's not a delivery man. This is Nigel Clark. He's one of the artists exhibiting this Friday."

"I see," she said.

"Nigel, this is my mother, Mrs. Bunny Blanchard."

"It's a pleasure to meet you, Mrs. Blanchard." He put his hand out.

"Likewise," she said politely.

Gabby figured it was as good a time as ever to bite the bullet. "Mother, Nigel is also the man I've been dating."

Bunny looked as if she were about to choke on her crumpet. "I see."

Gabby turned to Nigel. "Thank you for the flowers."

"You're welcome. You've been working so hard I thought you deserved something beautiful."

"That was so thoughtful of you."

"Gabby, aren't you going to invite him to sit down?"

Gabby was taken a bit off balance by her mother's question. "Oh yes, please sit down and join us."

"Are you sure? I don't want to intrude."

"It's no trouble at all. Rosie, will you please pour Mr. Clark some tea."

Nigel waited until Gabby was seated and then he sat. Rosie served him the tea.

"Thank you, Rosie."

"You're welcome, sir."

"So Mr. Clark . . ."

"Please call me Nigel."

"All right then, Nigel. Tell me a little about yourself. How long have you been an artist?"

"According to my parents, I picked up a paintbrush when I was about three."

"So you got started early."

"I'd say so."

Gabby nervously sat in between them and waited for her mother to lower the boom.

"Is this your first show?"

"As a matter of fact it is. Although art is my passion, I do it more as a hobby."

"Mother, Nigel's an investment banker," Gabby interjected.

Bunny looked surprised. "Really? Where?"

"Mother!"

"It's just a question, dear."

"I'm a partner at Longford and Lowe."

"My husband went to school with Peter Longford."

"Is that right? Mr. Longford is a great guy. He mentored me when I joined the firm." He smiled.

"That sounds like Peter." Bunny nodded.

So far so good, Gabby thought.

"Are you a native New Yorker?"

"Yes, I'm from Long Island."

"One of Gabby's best friends, Alicia, is from Long Island, too."

"She's from Amityville," Gabby interrupted.

"Is that close to where you lived?"

"It's not too far." Nigel looked at the clock. "I really hate to cut this short, but I'm meeting a client for a late lunch."

"On a Sunday?" Bunny asked.

"Yes. He's an orthodontist and his only day off is today."

"That's a mark of dedication." Bunny smiled.

"Thank you." He got up. "It was a pleasure meeting you, Ms. Blanchard." He shook her hand.

"Same here, Nigel."

"I guess I'll see you at the exhibit on Friday evening."

"Indeed."

Gabby got up. "I'll walk you to the door."

Once they got to the door, Gabby planted a big kiss on Nigel.

"Wow. What was that for?"

"For being you and for being a good sport while my mother drilled you."

"I wouldn't say she was drilling me. She was curious, that's all."

"Okay, you may have a point there. Anyway, thank you for the flowers. They are gorgeous."

"You're welcome." He kissed her. "You know, I came over here to tell you about something."

"What?"

"I kind of got derailed by your mother."

"Mother does tend to do that."

He looked at his watch. "I'm really running late. I'll talk to you about it later."

"Is it important?"

"It'll keep until later. Now I'd better get going."

"Okay, baby." She waved as she watched him walk off. *Okay, time to face the firing squad. I wonder if it's proper to use my napkin as a blindfold?*

When she got back upstairs Bunny was on her second scone. "These are really delicious, Gabby. What bakery did you go to?"

"I didn't go to any bakery. Rosie made them. It's one of Alicia's newest recipes." She sat back down.

"Is it in one of her cookbooks?"

"Not yet. I can make a copy for you to give to Cook if you'd like."

"Oh, good. Thank you." She sipped her tea.

"Okay, Mother."

"Okay what, dear?"

"I know you have something to say about Nigel."

"He's seems like a nice young man. He's certainly handsome."

Gabby was flabbergasted. "That's it? That's all you have to say?"

"Your father and I had a talk and he basically told me to lighten up. So that's what I'm doing. It's your life."

I have to smuggle two Coney Island hot dogs for Daddy now, she thought, smiling.

"I do have one observation."

"I knew it was too good to be true."

"Hear me out, young lady. Do you think it's wise to have his painting in this exhibit? You are seeing him."

"I thought about that, Mother. We started dating after he made it into the show, not before."

"That may well be, but it sounds like you're splitting hairs. I may not be in the art world, but I've been around long enough to know that people won't look at it that way. Especially artists who didn't make the cut."

"Honestly, Mother, his talent speaks for itself."

"I'm sure it does. Nevertheless, tongues will wag when they see you together."

"Let them wag." Gabby was agitated. "What does it matter as long as it's a great show with really deserving artists?"

"It depends on how people define 'deserving.' Obviously he's not hurting for money and his art is a hobby. Aren't you the one who told me how many artists are all about their work and not much else?"

"Yes. Still, am I supposed to deny a very talented artist a chance to showcase his work because he's not a starving artist? Fifteen out of the sixteen meet the starving criteria. I think I'm okay."

"It's the Sixteen to Watch exhibit now?"

"Yes."

"I see."

"What's with that tone?"

"Gabby, I've said all I'm going to say on the matter. It's your gallery, just like it's your life."

"Thank you."

On the one hand Gabby was pleased that her mother didn't rake Nigel over the coals. However, her words about the exhibit rang in her head.

CHAPTER 16

By Wednesday Alicia was exhausted after events from Westchester to Long Island. However, the biggest of the launch events was at Herald Square. Crowds had gathered early for her presentation of the new line. Store executives, as well as board members of Archer Omnimedia, were there as Alicia worked the press, took photos and met shoppers. Gabby and Lauren mingled with shoppers in Macy's giant housewares department.

Lauren picked up a food mill from the Alicia Archer Collection. "What's this?"

"It's a food mill."

"It's a what?"

"It's a food mill. It's a predecessor to the blender."

"How does it work?"

Gabby laughed. "You have to turn it manually."

"Why in the world wouldn't you just use a blender?"

"A food mill lets you control the texture, as opposed to a blender, where you're at the mercy of the blade."

Lauren looked confused.

"It's a good thing you're dating a chef."

"Ha, ha, very funny." She put the box down.

Gabby noticed a young redhead near Alicia. "Lauren, is that Taylor?"

Lauren glanced over. "Oh yes, that's her."

"What is she doing here?"

"I guess she's here as the managing editor of the magazine."

"Why? It looks like the PR team has it covered."

Lauren noticed Taylor as she chatted up three men in business suits. "Is that . . ."

"What?"

"I see it now. She's here to cover the male board members, Wasser, Flaherty and Maine."

At 55 years old, bald, and slightly pudgy, Howard Wasser was the oldest of the trio and his eyes had the tendency to roam over a woman's form when he spoke to her. Next to him was tall, nerdy and white-haired 54-year-old Timothy Flaherty, who after being married for 25 years, was determined to make up for lost "prowl" time. Then there was 52-year-old Edward Maine. A relatively short man with a slight build, he reminded Alicia of Ralph Furley of *Three's Company* in both looks and lack of skills when it came to women.

Lauren and Gabby watched as the men lapped up Taylor's attention.

"You know what's worse than seeing a midlife crisis up close?" Lauren asked.

"What?"

"Watching three midlife crises."

Lauren and Gabby laughed.

"What did I miss?"

"Nate," Lauren said, surprised.

"Alicia didn't tell us you were coming."

"She didn't know." He looked over as Alicia posed for another photo op.

"She'll be glad you came," Lauren said.

"How long has she been at this? I half expected it to be over by now."

Gabby looked at her watch. "Three hours and counting."

Nathaniel grew concerned. "That's a long time to be at this. Not to mention this is her fifth appearance, isn't it?"

"Yes," Gabby nodded.

All three watched as Alicia excused herself to get a bottle of water. Her legs gave slightly when she finished drinking.

"Oh, she's had enough," Nathaniel said as he made his way over to her. Gabby and Lauren followed. Alicia's publicist, Viola Sherwood, did her best to keep the crowd at a distance while she composed herself.

"She needs a little air, folks. Let's give her a minute."

"Is she all right?" a reporter asked.

"She's fine. It's been a long day." Viola smiled.

Lauren walked over to Viola. "Hi, Viola. I see they're keeping you busy."

Originally a business professor, Viola Sherwood embarked on a new career in public relations after she retired. A strategic marketing wizard, she was the head of PR for Archer Omnimedia and rarely had to leave her office. However, the launch of the Alicia Archer Collection was just the sort of event to get her out of the office. Although she was sixty years old, she barely looked a day over fifty.

"You've got that right, Lauren. How are you?"

"I'm good, thanks."

Nathaniel went over to Alicia. "Are you okay?"

"Nathaniel, I didn't know you were coming today."

"I wanted to surprise you." He paused. "Look at me, please." He studied her eyes.

"Are you examining me?"

"Well, I don't have my stethoscope with me but . . ."

She interrupted. "People will notice." She looked around.

"Let him look at you, Alicia. No one will know anything," Gabby reassured her.

"Fine."

"Your eyes are a little red and I'm sure you're feeling a little overheated with the crowd."

"I am a little warm."

"They tell me you've been at this for more than three hours today. I think you can call it a day, can't you?"

Alicia noticed Taylor lurking nearby. "I'll call it a wrap, but let's play it cool. The hyena and the Three Stooges are circling."

"Who's circling?"

"Taylor Dawes, the managing editor of the magazine, and three of the board members, Howard Wasser, Timothy Flaherty and Edward Maine," Gabby elaborated.

"What about them?"

"Alicia's convinced Taylor is angling to get her job."

"You know I'm right here. I can speak for myself. However, I'd prefer not to talk about it right now. Okay?"

"Okay." Gabby backed off.

"Viola."

"Yes?" She walked over.

"I think I'm ready to call it a day."

"Not a problem." Viola went up to the microphone. "Ladies and gentlemen, we'd like to thank you for coming out this afternoon. Let's give a big hand to Alicia Archer."

The crowd clapped as Alicia waved.

Lauren walked over. "Okay, it looks like you're in the clear to head home and get some rest."

"Amen," Gabby agreed.

"I thought we'd go to lunch."

"We can have lunch together anytime. Besides, we're going to be together for Gabby's big night on Friday."

"That's true."

"So can I drive you home?" Nathaniel asked.

"You drove down from Scarsdale?" Alicia asked, surprised.

"Sure. It wasn't a problem."

"I have to call and cancel my car service."

"Don't worry about it. I know your driver, I'll call him," Lauren offered.

"Thanks." She got up.

Taylor walked over. "Great event, Alicia."

"Thanks."

"Are you leaving already?"

"Yes. It's been a long day already."

"Are you feeling okay?"

"I'm just a little tired." Alicia was getting annoyed. "So if you'll excuse me . . ."

"Sure. I'll talk to you soon." She walked away.

"Okay."

"Oh," Alicia groaned.

"All right, Alicia, just breathe," Lauren said, smiling.

Nathaniel kissed her cheek. "I'm parked not too far from here. I'm going to run and get the car. Can you meet me out front near the men's store entrance?"

"Sure. We'll get her there."

"Thanks, Gabby." Nathaniel made a dash for the escalator.

Two security people walked Alicia, Gabby and Lauren to the elevator and through the store. They waited in front with them.

"So, Alicia, before Nathaniel gets here with the car, is there anything you want to tell us?" Lauren asked.

"Like what?"

"I don't know, maybe something about a cookie jar?"

Alicia made a face.

"Oh, my goodness, did I hear a lid pop?" Lauren asked, smiling.

"What makes you think that?"

"Perhaps the fact he drove down here in the middle of the afternoon at the height of New York City traffic."

"Why wouldn't he do that anyway?" Alicia asked facetiously.

"Maybe he would, but you're positively glowing and I know you're not pregnant, so there can only be one other reason."

"Come on, Alicia, spill. We told you."

"Yes. The lid came off. Are you happy now?"

Lauren and Gabby practically squealed.

"The question is, are you happy now?" Gabby laughed.

"Yes. I'm very happy."

Nathaniel pulled up to the curb. One of the security guards opened the door for Alicia.

"Thank you," Lauren said as she and Gabby helped Alicia to the car. When Alicia got in, Nathaniel did her seat belt for her.

Lauren and Gabby looked at one another. "That's so cute," Lauren said.

"Oh, cut it out," Alicia scoffed.

"You get home safe."

"We will," Nathaniel answered.

"I'll call both of you later." Alicia waved.

"Okay," Lauren said as she and Gabby watched them pull off, "how about we grab a little lunch?"

"That sounds like a plan to me."

❧

Many of the restaurants were crowded, so Lauren and Gabby opted to dine al fresco close to their stomping grounds on the Upper East Side. After they stopped for a salad from Agata and Valentina, a gourmet food store, they grabbed a bench at Carl Schurz Park and lunched while they watched the boats go by.

Gabby took a deep breath. "It's such a beautiful day. I'm glad we decided to eat here instead of a restaurant. I could use a break from the hustle and bustle, especially this week."

"I understand, but your exhibit is one of the social highlights of the season and a chance for me to put on couture." Lauren grinned.

"Ah, I take it you've got something special up your sleeve."

"You'll see." She winked. "How are things progressing now that you're in the final stretch?"

"Overall, it's going well. Victor is his usual super-high-strung self."

"He's such a perfectionist but he gets the job done every year."

"Is Nigel excited?"

"Yes." She smiled. "He's like an expectant father." Gabby looked off at the bridge in the distance.

"What's the matter, Gabby?"

"I was just thinking about something my mother said to me the other day."

"What did she say?"

"Well, it was after she met Nigel."

"Hold the phone. Back up. Bunny met Nigel?"

"He came over to bring me a bouquet of flowers while Mother and I were having tea."

"How did that go over?"

"It wasn't so bad after I told her he wasn't a delivery guy."

Lauren laughed. "I'm sorry, but that totally sounds like Bunny."

"I know."

"So what happened? Did she give him the third degree?"

"No. She had a nice conversation with him."

"Really?" Lauren was shocked.

"Yes. She surprised me, too. It was a nice visit until he had to meet a client for an appointment."

"Have you spoken to him since he met Bunny?"

"No. He's out of town for a conference until tomorrow, I think."

"Tell me, did Bunny let loose after he left?"

"Yes and no."

"What do you mean?"

"She didn't have anything to say about him being African American, but she did make a comment about his being in the exhibit. She thinks it's a conflict of interest."

"Hmm."

"Do you agree with her?"

"Gabby, far be it from me to tell you how to choose artists for your gallery."

"You think I put him in because of our personal relationship?"

"No, I know you choose artists based on talent."

"But . . ."

"Bunny may have a point. Whether you picked him before or after you started dating won't matter to some people."

"By people, you mean other artists and the gallery's patrons."

"Maybe." She shook her head. "You know what, don't listen to me. I'm the last person who should offer you any advice on this stuff."

"Why would you say that? Is something going on?"

"You know that saying, no good deed goes unpunished?"

"Yes."

"It's truer than you know."

"What happened?"

"You remember when I told you that Ken's agent Patrick paid me a visit?"

"Yes. You told me it wasn't worth talking about."

"I didn't think it was at the time."

"Now you're making me nervous."

"Ken wanted me to help him get on as a desk commentator for *NFL Weekly*. I told him and Patrick no, I couldn't help him."

"Why would he think you would help him? You're getting divorced. Besides, didn't you call in a favor to get him an audition to be a field reporter?"

"Yes." She sighed. "Ken has decided that I can do more for him."

"What?"

"He said that either I help him get the job, or I have to buy him out of the apartment, or sell it and split the proceeds."

"Wait a minute, he can't do that. You have a signed agreement."

"He's already done it. His lawyer called my lawyer and said he'd had a change of heart."

"Oh, my God, he's a real louse."

"I know."

"What are you going to do?"

"I'm not sure yet. What I can tell you is the giant slalom will be a main event in hell before I help Ken Jones get behind the desk at *NFL Weekly*."

"If it's a matter of money, you know I can help you."

Lauren smiled. "I know and I really appreciate it, Gabby, but I'm going to tell you the same thing I said to Randy. I will figure this out."

"Randy offered to help?"

"Yes. He's been a real sweetheart through this whole thing." She chuckled. "It's so funny that Ken is the reason I met him in the first place."

"That's irony for you."

"That's love for you."

"Love? Did you say love?"

"Yes. Randy said he loves me."

"And what did you say?"

"I told him I love him, too."

"Oh, I'm so happy for you." Gabby hugged her.

"Thanks. Speaking of love . . ."

"Yes?"

"What about you and Nigel? Any declarations you want to share with the class?"

"No." Gabby felt a little embarrassed.

"Come on, you can talk to me."

"He hasn't made any proclamations."

"How do you feel? Do you love him?"

"Yes, I think I do."

"Then what's wrong with your tongue? Why can't you go first?"

"Because he's the guy. He's supposed to say it first."

"Gabby, it's one thing to love Jane Austen's novels, but it's another to live them. There's no rule you can't say it first."

"Did you say it to Randy first?"

"We're not talking about me."

"See?"

"I don't count anyway. I was drunk and slept with him the first night we met, so I get an exemption."

They laughed.

"Seriously, Gabby, when it comes to matters of the heart, there are no rules." She sipped her water. "Look at Alicia and Nate."

"Alicia was the only one who didn't see it coming."

"Speaking of Alicia, I wonder how she and Nathaniel are doing this afternoon."

"If we know Alicia, and we do, she's probably giving him a hard time about resting."

"You're right. Still, I think Nathaniel is just the man for the job. He can hold his own."

"More power to him. That is one stubborn woman," Gabby said.

"Between him and Harrison, I think they just might have her cornered." Lauren smiled.

❧

Arms folded in bed, Alicia looked like a prisoner in her own bedroom.

"You can pout all you want. You're staying put until Friday," Harrison said as he placed a lunch tray on the night table.

"This isn't fair," she protested.

"It's for your own good," Nathaniel said, walking in. "You can get out of bed if we go see the doctor covering for Dr. Stuart."

"No. I only see Dr. Stuart."

"I told you she wouldn't budge."

Nathaniel sat down on the bed. "Why? He's a professional and he's held to the same doctor/patient confidentiality as any other doctor."

"You don't understand."

"Try me."

"I'll be in the kitchen if you need me," Harrison said as he left the room.

"I don't want to take the chance. What if someone sees me going into his office? At least with Dr. Stuart I can go early in the morning before he sees any other patients and get on with my day."

Nathaniel shook his head. "We don't live in the Dark Ages."

"Oh, you don't think so?"

"No."

"Let me tell you, speaking as a full-figured African-American woman, I know it still exists." She let out a heavy sigh.

"You never struck me as someone who worried about size."

"That's because I don't worry about it. Other people do." She paused. "I was lucky enough to be raised by parents who always told me I was beautiful. I will admit it was a little hard to be full-figured at Miss Porter's

Boarding School, since most of the girls there would have given up a limb before they gained an ounce."

"I know the type well." He shook his head.

"Thankfully I had Lauren, Gabby and the Austen Aristocrats, which made it easier for me. I also had a husband who loved me. All of me."

"I don't know many people who can say that."

"Neither do I. Kurt always said I should have been more than just a lifestyle editor, because not only did I love it, I lived it. I looked forward to planning menus, going grocery shopping and entertaining friends and family. Nothing gave me greater pleasure than making a home for him and Kurt Jr." Her voice caught and she took a moment to catch her breath.

Nathaniel rubbed her hand.

She wiped her eyes. "They were the most wonderful days of my life. After I lost him, I felt like a rudderless boat, just floating there. I didn't know what to do and that's when I decided the best thing I could do was share it with others. I would show people through something as simple as cooking how they could turn their house into the kind of home I had with him. It gave me a purpose and direction."

"So off you went."

"With a vengeance. I had a vision of a lifestyle brand from the moment I wrote my first cookbook. As a magazine editor it didn't take much for me to find a publisher, but getting a cooking show was a lot harder. When Lauren pitched me to her production company, they weren't sure because I didn't fit the mold. I wasn't the typical young, perky or thin host viewers were used to seeing. They didn't think I would do well with the target demographic, but I knew I was the real thing and I proved it with one hell of a demo. We were green lighted for only eight episodes and the response to this full-figured woman was beyond what they expected. A year after my first season, I was syndicated. Now, you'd think it would be easy for me to find investors and launch a magazine, but it wasn't. I had to court a lot of people."

"People like the Three Stooges?"

"Yes," she groaned. "Still, I put up a good deal of my own money for Archer Omnimedia."

"You made it happen."

"I had to. And when the time came, people told me I couldn't take my company public. I did and disproved all the naysayers. Still, I've had to prove I belong as the chief executive of the company *I* started. What man has to do that?"

"I get it. I also get that this is as much about Kurt as it is about you."

"Does that bother you?"

"Of course it doesn't bother me. What bothers me is at the end of the day, you have to take care of yourself and although I wasn't fortunate enough to meet Kurt, I'm pretty sure he'd agree with me."

"He thought I was a workaholic, so you're probably right."

"See. Of course, if you let people know about the MS, you'll relieve some of the stress of keeping this secret."

His words fell on deaf ears. "You know what, Nathaniel, I'm a grown-up. I don't need you to tell me what to do."

"I wasn't trying to tell you what to do. I just think you need to slow it down. You can't do everything."

"What is that supposed to mean? I can't do everything because I have MS, right?"

"Don't put words in my mouth."

"That's what you meant. You know, I'm not in the market for an owner."

"What?"

"You heard me."

"You don't mean that."

"Of course I do."

Nathaniel picked up his jacket. "I'm going to leave before I say something I regret."

"You do that."

Nathaniel rushed past Harrison. A few seconds later the door slammed.

"What happened up here? I leave you for a little while and all hell breaks loose."

Alicia wiped her eyes. "Nothing."

"Those red eyes don't say nothing to me." He sat on her bed. "Talk to me."

"Nathaniel tried to tell me what to do, and you know how much I hate that."

"He was doing nothing of the sort. He cares about you."

Alicia looked away.

"You goaded him into a fight so you could send him away, didn't you?"

"I'm sick, Harrison. I've never thought of myself as a sick person before today. How can I burden someone with this? Nathaniel has had his choice of young, healthy women. Why would he choose to be with a woman he knows is sick?"

"He loves you, Alicia. You're not a burden to him."

"Maybe I'm not one today, but what about tomorrow, next week or next year? Does a healthy man really want to be saddled with a woman with a chronic disease?"

"Nate came into this with his eyes open. Don't forget he's the one who rescued you from the pool."

"I know. But it's one thing to be a one-time hero. It's another thing to carry the princess around on your back all day. I care about him too much to do that to him."

"Bull. You're just afraid of what you're feeling."

"I'm not changing my mind. I can't do this to him. He's better off."

"What about Gabby's event?"

"I suppose we'll go together, but that will be it."

Harrison shook his head in disgust. "You know, my dear, I love you like a daughter and sometimes I'd like to put you over my knee."

"I'm sorry, Harrison." She flashed him a look with her sad brown eyes.

"That's not fair."

"I have to do something."

"Well, if you have to do anything, it's take a nap. Can you do that for me?" Harrison got up.

"Okay."

When Harrison closed the door, a flood of silent tears streamed down Alicia's face. She did love Nathaniel but she couldn't stand the thought of being the albatross around his neck. She knew it would hurt for a while but she felt it was best to let him go without guilt.

∽

With Randy busy at the restaurant, Lauren went back to her apartment to relax for the rest of the afternoon. After she put her keys down, she checked her messages as she got out of her clothes.

You have two new messages.

"Lauren, it's Ken. Football season is coming up quickly and I haven't heard from you. Give me a call."

Lauren shrugged it off. "I'm not calling him."

The second message played.

"Lauren, you know I'm serious. If you're serious about staying in that apartment, you'll do what I asked you to do."

"He's got some nerve," she huffed as she went into her closet.

The phone rang.

Lauren walked out and checked the caller ID just in case it was Ken. It wasn't. It was the restaurant.

"Hello?"

"Hey, honey, how are you?"

"I'm good, thanks. How's it going there?"

"It's chaos as usual, but I do have some news to share."

313

"Cool. Can I assume it's good news?"

"It's very good news. The *New York Times* is doing a feature on the restaurant."

"Oh, that's great news."

"Thanks. I'm really excited."

"You should be. It's not easy to get in the pages of the *Times.*"

"I know. So how was Alicia's launch?"

"It was great. A lot of people turned out for it."

"That's good. Maybe one day I'll have my own line of kitchenware."

"Don't be surprised if it happens. All it takes is a lot of determination and hard work."

"And you have to know the right people."

"That's true, too."

"You know, I'm really looking forward to Friday night."

"So am I."

"Not only will I finally meet Alicia and Gabby, I'm going to have the most beautiful woman in the room on my arm."

"Aww, that's sweet of you to say." Her voice faded.

"Okay, what's on your mind?"

"Nothing. Don't worry, I'm fine."

"I'm not buying that for a minute. I know it has to do with Ken."

She let out a heavy sigh. "He called."

"Did you speak to him? What does he want now?"

"No, I wasn't here. He left a message about the same thing."

"Lauren, I know you want to handle this yourself, but the NFL season is fast approaching. He's only going to ramp it up."

"I know. He left two messages today."

"Have you thought any more about my offer? I'm serious."

"I know you are, and I really appreciate it."

"But you're not going to take me up on it, are you?"

"Probably not."

"What if I make it a loan?"

"I still wouldn't do it. Listen, sweetie, you don't know how much it means to me that you offered."

"Okay, I won't pressure you. But I'm not taking it off the table."

"If you insist," she laughed.

"I insist. Listen, sweetheart, I've got to run but I will see you Friday night."

"Okay."

"I love you."

"Love you, too." She hung up.

Lauren stretched out on her bed. She knew Randy was right. With the NFL season fast approaching, the situation with Ken would get worse before it got better, and if she thought he was a pain in the butt before, he'd be a royal pain the longer she made him wait.

"That's it," she said aloud, smiling. *I love you Randy. You just gave me what I need to get this handled.* She picked up the phone. *Now I'll call Joe.*

With Rosie gone for the day and the big exhibit around the corner, Gabby decompressed with a cup of tea and tuned the world out for a while.

The doorbell interrupted her thoughts.

Who in the world could this be? She looked at her watch as she got up and pressed the intercom. "Yes?"

"Hi, Gabby, it's me," Nigel answered.

"Nigel? I'll be right down."

A moment later she was downstairs and in his arms. They kissed in the foyer.

"Come on up." She took his hand.

"I wish I could, but I have a car waiting."

"Oh, okay."

"I came by to tell you how much I enjoyed meeting your mother."

"Good. She liked you, too."

"I'm glad." A serious look came over his face.

"What's wrong?"

"I had a chance to think while I was away . . ."

Gabby's heart went into her stomach.

"Maybe I shouldn't show at the exhibit, given our relationship. I know we started dating after you took my painting, but I don't want to blemish your reputation, and if any of the other artists who didn't make it in hear about it, that's just what could happen. I don't want to be responsible for that."

Gabby was beyond relieved. "Oh."

"What do you think?"

"Nigel, I really appreciate the gesture. Still, the fact is you're in the show because of your talent. Your painting is amazing and once people see it, they'll know why you're one to watch."

"Are you sure?"

"Listen, you are not getting any preferential treatment. I pick the artists and Victor sets the exhibit up."

He smiled. "Okay. Now I can get to the real reason I came here straight from the airport."

"Which is?" she asked anxiously

He wrapped his arms around her. "I missed you."

"I missed you, too."

"And more importantly, I love you, Gabrielle."

Gabby's heart leaped. "You do?"

"Yes."

"I love you, too." She melted into his arms again and they fell into a passionate embrace.

A car horn honked.

Gabby reluctantly pulled away. "I think that was for you."

"I don't want to go, but I have to."

She kissed softly. "We'll see each other on Friday."

"I can't wait."

"Neither can I."

Just as he was about to open the door, he pulled her to him. "How about one more to hold me over?"

"Sure."

They quickly fell into another ardent embrace until the car horn became more persistent.

"Okay, I'd better go. I forgot I have people in the car with me from the firm."

She laughed. "Tell them I'm sorry."

"The heck with them. You know how long I had to wait at the baggage carousel? I think we're even." He winked as he closed the door.

⁕

Still on air from the night before, Gabby walked out of her front door for the Starbucks a few blocks from her house. It was such a gorgeous morning that, after she ordered a venti latte, she decided to sit and watch the city go by at one of the outdoor tables.

"Excuse me." An attractive and petite African American woman with a cute bob stood there.

She looked up. "Yes?"

"Is anyone sitting here?"

"No. Go right ahead."

"Thank you." The woman sat down.

Gabby quietly sipped her coffee.

"You're Gabrielle Blanchard, aren't you?"

"Yes. Have we met?"

"No. My name is Deidre Simpson. I'm Nigel Jr.'s mother."

Gabby's jaw dropped. "How did you . . . ?"

"How did I know about you? I make it my business to know everything about my son's father's life, which apparently includes you now."

Gabby was uncomfortable. "Listen, this is between you and Nigel. I don't think it's appropriate to talk to me."

"Why shouldn't I talk to the woman who's in bed with my son's father?"

People were beginning to look. "I understand that you're upset, but this has nothing to do with me."

"Oh, really? You're not the one who told him to go for joint custody?"

"What?" Gabby stood up.

"Listen, I know you're some rich big shot, but I'm here to tell you that I'm prepared to fight for my son."

"This is between you and Nigel. I don't have any say in it." Gabby started to walk away and then she came back. "You know what, I hope you do what's right for your son, because he's the one who will get hurt if you don't work this out. That's all I have to say." Gabby turned on her heel and walked like she was on fire. She flipped her cell phone open to speed dial.

"Hello?"

"Nigel?" She was a little out of breath.

"I was just about to call you. Are you excited?"

"I'm excited all right, but not about tonight."

"That doesn't sound good. Did something happen at the gallery?"

"No, the gallery is fine. You'll never guess who I just ran into."

"Who?"

"Deidre."

"What? How in the hell did that happen?"

"Funny, I was about to ask you the same thing."

"I should have known. I served her with the court papers for the custody issue."

"It would have been nice to know that you decided to go for joint custody."

"I was going to tell you, but your mother was there, and I had to leave for that appointment."

"Okay, but you could have said something last night."

"I suppose I got caught up in making my declaration."

"Nigel, this isn't the kind of thing that should have slipped your mind. I was blindsided. More than that, how does she even know about me? She actually showed up at the Starbucks near my house. What are the chances of that happening by coincidence? You know how many Starbucks there are in Manhattan alone?"

"I know." He sighed. "She must have been tracking me again."

"What do you mean, tracking you again? She's done this before?"

"Her younger brother is a P.I. She used him to try to find dirt on me the last time we had a child support hearing."

"I wish you had told me."

"I'm sorry. What did she say to you?"

"It's not important." Gabby was annoyed.

"She probably thinks you're the one who put me up to going for joint custody."

Gabby was at her front door. "I really didn't need this today."

"I'm sorry."

She rubbed her head. "Listen, Nigel, I know you're sorry, but I've got a headache now. I need to lie down."

"Are you going to be okay?"

"Right now isn't the time to talk. I'll see you later."

Still flustered, Gabby went straight to her room and flopped onto the bed. Getting ready for her big night lost a bit of its luster, but the show had to go on.

CHAPTER 17

While Alicia waited for the car to arrive, she checked her reflection in the mirror. From the living room Harrison could see her checking the clock.

"It's about twenty seconds later than the last time you checked."

"Who asked you?"

"I'm just saying." He closed his book. "You're waiting for him, aren't you?"

Alicia and Nathaniel hadn't spoken since their fight. She'd been tempted to call to apologize, but her pride got in the way.

"If by him you mean the driver, you're right."

The doorbell rang. Harrison got up. "I'll get it." He walked past her to the door. It was Nathaniel. "Hey, Nate, it's good to see you. Don't you look spiffy."

"Thanks, Harry. Is the lady of the house ready?"

"Yes. Come on in and see for yourself."

Nathaniel stepped in. His eyes widened when he saw Alicia in a beautiful, curve-hugging black gown. "Good evening, Alicia. You look fantastic."

"Thank you. So do you."

Harrison looked out the window. "It looks like the car is here." He opened the door.

Nathaniel put his arm out. "Shall we?"

She took his arm. "Yes. I'll see you later, Harrison."

"Okay. Have a good time."

"Thanks, Harry."

He closed the door behind them and watched as Nathaniel helped Alicia into the car. "It's not that long of a car ride, Nate, so you'd better work quickly," he muttered.

Unfortunately the car ride was even longer, due to the silence between them.

∞

Gabby couldn't have ordered a better evening for the Sixteen to Watch exhibit. The evening weather was calm and elegant, just like the night's big event. The crowd was a mix of artists, collectors, art critics, the press, celebrities and even a couple of reality show refugees.

Nathaniel, Alicia, Lauren and Randy all arrived at the same time.

"Hey, Lauren," Alicia said as she walked over to her. "You look amazing. Is that a Darius Cordell?"

"Yes, it is." Lauren twirled around and showed off the beautiful black mermaid-style gown.

"I love it."

"Thanks." She took a long look at Alicia in her black T-back gown with a sweetheart neckline. "You're looking pretty fantastic too. Isaac?"

"Yes. It's his spider-vein lace dress."

"I'm shocked that you went some place other than a gourmet grocery store."

"He has a Web site, you know."

"I should have guessed." Randy walked over. "Alicia, this is Randy Rivera. Randy, this is my best friend Alicia Archer and her boyfriend, Dr. Nathaniel Becker."

Both Alicia and Nathaniel looked uncomfortable with the introduction, but they went along with it.

"It's a pleasure to meet you both." He shook her hand and then his.

"Good to meet you, Randy."

"Same here. I've heard a lot of good things about you and your restaurant," Alicia said.

"Thank you." He looked around. "This is some event."

The gallery at night took on a different look. It was bathed in a combination of soft white lights in the common areas, with brighter ones illuminating each artist's work. Soft jazz played in the background while the attendees mingled and discussed each work. Waiters and waitresses walked around with trays of champagne and hors d'oeuvres.

Randy and Nathaniel each grabbed a glass of champagne.

"Champagne?" Nathaniel asked.

"Thank you."

Randy handed Lauren a glass. "How about we toast the woman who put this event together?" He raised his glass.

"Yes. Here's to Gabby." Lauren smiled as they toasted together.

Alicia took a small sip. "Speaking of our hostess, have you seen Gabby?"

Lauren looked around. "No. I'm sure she's working the room."

"How about we check out the artists? I'm sure we'll see Gabby." Randy took Lauren by the hand.

Alicia took another tiny sip. "Sounds like a plan." She rubbed her head.

"Are you okay?" Nathaniel asked softly.

"I'm fine," she insisted.

"It was just a question," he grumbled.

The four of them walked through the gallery and saw a variety of artistic styles from postmodernism to a new take on the impressionists.

"Gabby certainly chose an eclectic group of artists," Randy noted.

"For her, it's giving people a chance to see both ends of the spectrum and everything in between," Lauren said proudly.

Nathaniel stopped. "Look at this one."

The four of them were in front of Nigel's painting.

"I recognize the city. It's Cotonou." Nathaniel studied the work.

"I think Gabby said the artist's mother is from Cotonou," Alicia said.

"I like it," Randy said.

"Thank you." Nigel said as he walked over with Gabby, who looked stunning in an asymmetrical blue pastel gown.

"You're welcome."

"Great exhibit, Gabby. You've done it again." Alicia kissed her cheek. "By the way, I love your dress."

"Thank you. It's a Lisette."

"Oh, I'm impressed. She's not easy to come by, either," Lauren observed.

"It's one of the benefits of being a Blanchard. Her mother moves in the same circles as mine."

"I see. Bunny made a call," Lauren said with a nod.

"Right."

Alicia looked over at Nigel and cleared her throat.

Gabby finally got the hint. "Oh, excuse me, where are my manners?" She turned to Nigel. "Nigel, this is Alicia Archer and Lauren Jones. Ladies, this is Nigel Clark."

"It's a pleasure to meet you both." He shook their hands.

"It's wonderful to meet you, Gabby. Congratulations on such a wonderful exhibit," Randy said when the introductions were completed.

"Thank you. I like to think the sixteen most talented artists in the city are under my roof tonight."

"Judging from what we've seen so far, I think it's a pretty safe bet that's the case," Randy agreed.

"Nigel, you really captured the essence of the city in your painting," Nathaniel observed.

"Thank you. Have you been to Cotonou, Dr. Becker?"

"Yes, it's an amazing city. Please call me Nate."

"Thank you, Nate."

"Well, ladies, why don't we let the guys get acquainted," Lauren suggested.

"In other words you want a chance to talk about us," Randy joked.

"Don't worry, we won't say anything bad." She waved. "Come on, ladies."

Alicia felt a little off balance when she took her first step, but she covered it quickly as they walked over to the chic reception area.

Alicia was glad to sit. "Victor did it again. The place looks fantastic."

"Thank you, my dear," Victor said as he sauntered over.

"You deserve it."

"Thank you. I did sweat the details."

"And now you're lapping up the praise," Gabby added.

"And a few phone numbers." He winked.

They laughed.

A waiter passed by and looked at Victor. "If you'll excuse me, I'm going to see if I can add another number to my collection." He quickly followed him.

"You can't knock his hustle," Lauren said as she finished her champagne.

"True." Alicia put the champagne flute down.

"You're not going to finish it?"

"No, you can have it if you like. I hate to see it go to waste. It is good."

Lauren picked the glass up. "Thanks." She finished Alicia's champagne and put the empty glass down.

"Good grief, girl," Alicia said.

"What can I tell you? I was thirsty."

"Before we go any further, Alicia, what's the deal with you and Nate?" Lauren asked.

"What do you mean?"

"Don't play cute with me. I can see something is off tonight."

"I thought so, too, especially when you introduced him as Dr. Becker," Gabby added.

"That's his name."

"But he's more than a doctor to you, isn't he?"

"If you must know, we had a fight. This is the first time we've seen or spoken to each other in a couple of days."

"What did you fight about?" Lauren asked, shocked.

"He tried to tell me what to do. You know how much I hate that."

"He probably told you to slow down. You hate that even more."

"What can I say, Gabby? I'm an independent woman."

"You're a hardheaded woman," Lauren stated.

"Hey, you two are supposed to be my friends and support me."

"That also means we should tell you when you're being a jackass."

"If the tail fits . . ." Lauren added.

"Thanks a lot. Can we change the subject? It's supposed to be a fun night, not *Dr. Phil.*"

"Fine, but I promise you we will revisit this," Lauren said.

"I think the evening is going well. I'm pleased with the turnout."

Lauren looked confused. "You're not going to ask us what we think of Nigel?"

"Oh, what did you think of him?" she asked half-heartedly.

"Now I know something is wrong. What happened?" Alicia asked.

"I thought things were going well between you."

"I did, too." She took a deep breath. "I really don't want to talk about it tonight. Okay?"

"Okay. We'll talk when you're ready," Alicia said reassuringly.

A flash of light caught their attention as a few photographers snapped their photo.

"Why in the world are they taking my picture?" Lauren asked.

"You are at the art event of the season," Alicia said with a smile.

"But I'm not a celebrity."

"Oh, you're full of it. Don't you know that you're Gelman to my *Regis and Kelly*?"

Gabby laughed. "Not to mention the fact that you were married to a New York Giants player." Gabby regretted mentioning anything remotely connected to Ken the minute it left her lips. "I'm sorry, Lauren."

"That's okay."

"What's going on? Has something happened you haven't told me about?"

Lauren and Gabby looked at each other. "You might as well tell her, Lauren."

"Ken's threatening to make me either buy him out or sell the apartment unless I help him become a desk commentator at *NFL Weekly*."

"What? He's a real son of a bitch. It's blackmail, plain and simple."

"I know, and I have no intention of helping him or losing my apartment."

"Have you figured something out?" Gabby asked

"I think so."

"You know if you need anything, money or whatever, I'm here for you."

"Thanks, Alicia." She rubbed Alicia's knee. "I know I can count on both of you."

"Gabby, is Bunny here?"

"No, my mother called at the last minute. Daddy wasn't feeling too well this evening and she didn't want to leave him with a nurse."

"I know you would have liked her to come, but I can understand why she didn't," Alicia said.

"I'd rather she stayed home with him than come here. She can read all about it in the Art Review section of the *Times.*"

"Don't you love how casually she dropped that into the conversation?" Lauren giggled.

"Oh, my goodness, you've got a buzz already," Alicia laughed.

"Why do you say that?"

"You're giggling. You never giggle."

"Good champagne, love and a sexy man are enough to make any woman giddy."

"Oh, my goodness, did I hear the L-word?" Alicia said sweetly.

"Yes, you did. Randy told me he loves me, and I love him."

"No wonder the champagne went straight to your head. You're in love."

"I am. Isn't that something?"

Alicia looked at her watch. "You know, Gabby, you should get back to working the rooms before they send a search party for you."

"You're right." She stood up.

When Alicia stood up and staggered forward, Gabby and Lauren grabbed her.

"Are you all right, Alicia?" Lauren asked, concerned.

Alicia couldn't get her bearings. Her head was spinning. "No, I think I have to go."

A photographer snapped a photo, and the flash made the dizziness worse.

Victor walked over. "Is everything all right here?"

"No, Victor. We need to get Alicia out to the car. Can you get her boyfriend Nathaniel? And see if you can get someone to run interference with this photographer. His flashbulb is making matters worse."

"Don't worry, Gabby, I'm on it."

Victor managed to get a couple of waiters to distract the photographer, while Gabby and Lauren helped Alicia through the reception area and out to the limousine. The driver got the door as they helped her in.

Nathaniel ran to the car, followed by Randy and Nigel. "What's happening?"

"I don't know, Nate. I think there's something very wrong with Alicia. You probably have to get her to a doctor or a hospital."

"Don't worry, I will." He got in the car.

"Call us as soon as you know something and we'll be right there," Lauren said.

"I'll let you know."

The driver closed the door and quickly got in.

Randy put his arm around Lauren as the car drove away. "I'm sure she'll be fine."

"I know. She's strong." Lauren put her head on his shoulder.

"She got so pale," Gabby said.

Nigel took her hand. "You heard Lauren, Alicia's a strong woman."

Unbeknownst to her, another photographer snapped a photo.

In the car Alicia tried to steady her head, but it didn't help. Her head continued to spin whether she closed her eyes or not.

"It's okay, sweetie." Nathaniel held her close to him. "We're going to get you some help. You just hold on. Okay?"

"Okay," she said weakly. "I'm sorry about before."

"I'm sorry, too, honey. But I don't want you to worry about that now." He put his arm around her. "We're not far from the NYU Medical Center. How fast do you think you can get us there?" he asked the driver.

"I can get you there in fifteen minutes or less."

"Let's make it less. Okay?"

"I'm on it." The driver sped up.

Nathaniel took his cell phone out and dialed. "Hi, I need Dr. John Hubert, please." He waited while they connected him.

"Dr. Hubert here."

"John, it's Nathaniel Becker."

"Hey, Nate, how are you?"

"I'm fine, but this isn't a social call. I'm on my way there with a patient who's in the midst of an exacerbation."

"What are the symptoms?"

"She's unsteady on her feet and very dizzy. She had to be assisted to the car."

"Is she on any medications?"

"She's taking Avonex."

"I'll meet you in the ER and we'll evaluate her."

"Actually, John, I need you to see her upstairs in the MS Center."

"Why?"

"It's Alicia Archer, and it's not common knowledge that she has MS."

"I see. We've had our share of celebrities here. Meet us in the front and I'll have someone there to take her upstairs."

"Thanks, John. I really appreciate it."

"Not a problem. Do you have an ETA?"

"How much longer until we're there?"

"About five minutes," the driver answered.

"We'll be there in five minutes."

"Okay. I'd better get off the phone so I can meet you."

"See you in a minute." He closed the phone and looked at Alicia, who seemed to grow paler by the minute. "Alicia, honey, are you still with me?"

"Yes," she said weakly.

"We're getting help."

Three minutes later the car pulled up to the front of the hospital. Dr. Hubert and two nurses were there with a wheelchair. The driver jumped out to open the door.

Dr. Hubert leaned down and looked at Alicia. "So this is our patient?"

"Yes."

"Ms. Archer, can you hear me?"

"Yes."

"I'm going to lift you out of the car. Okay?"

"Okay."

"No." Nathaniel got out of the car and rushed over to the other side. "I'll do it."

"All right." A slight man with graying hair, Dr. Hubert backed away as Nathaniel lifted Alicia and put her in the wheelchair.

"Let's get her upstairs, ladies."

As the nurses wheeled her away, Nathaniel was on their heels. They rushed into a waiting elevator.

Nathaniel held Alicia's hand. "You're going to be fine. Dr. Hubert is one of the best neurologists in the country."

Alicia nodded.

The elevator doors opened.

"Take her to room four."

"Yes, Doctor."

As the nurses wheeled her away, Nathaniel tried to follow them. Dr. Hubert stopped him.

"Come on, Nate, you know the drill."

"But I'm a doctor. I have privileges here."

"That might be so, but you have a personal relationship with the patient. You're not going to be able to be objective."

"Of course I will. I'm a professional."

"You're a professional in love. There's no way you'll be able to stand still in there."

"But I don't want her to be alone."

"She won't be alone. Listen, I'll keep you apprised of what's happening and I'll let you in as soon as I can. Okay?"

"Do I have a choice?"

"No."

"Then it's okay."

Dr. Hubert patted him on the back. "Good man."

Nathaniel watched through the window as Dr. Hubert and his staff assessed Alicia's condition. He felt his heart break as he stared at her pale face.

A nurse came out. "We're going to take her for an MRI."

"Okay."

"We do have some paperwork for you. Are you the next of kin?"

"No. I'm her boyfriend. I'm also a doctor."

"Well, maybe you can fill out some of the paperwork."

"I can try."

"If you go over to the nurses' station, they can help you."

"Thanks. You'll let me know when she's back from radiology, right?"

"Yes, Doctor."

He went over to the nurses' station and they handed him a clipboard. He filled out what he could and then he took out his cell phone.

"I can't use this in here," he lamented.

"You can use this phone. Just dial nine for an outside line," the desk nurse piped up.

"Thanks." He picked up the phone.

"Hello?"

"Harrison, it's Nate."

"Hey, Nate, how's the evening going?"

"I'm at the hospital with Alicia."

"Oh, God, what happened?"

"She had an attack, but she's being treated here at the MS Center at NYU."

"Are they admitting her? Should I come down?"

"I don't think so. They just took her for an MRI. I'm pretty sure she'll be home tonight."

"But you're not positive?"

"I'll know more shortly. In the meantime they've given me a bunch of paperwork to fill out."

"What do you need to know?"

He read the form. "I know some of the basic stuff but I don't have dates for her surgeries or anything like that."

"I have a sheet with all that information here. Do they have a fax?"

"I'll ask." He tapped the desk. "I'm sorry. Do you have a fax machine?"

"Yes. There's one in the intake area," the head nurse answered.

"I've got this stuff to fill out and there's a sheet with all the details I need for the form. Can he fax it here?"

"Sure. The number is 646-555-8956."

"Thanks." He wrote it down. "Harrison, the number is 646-555-8956. Put Alicia's name on it, along with Dr. John Hubert."

"Got it. I'll do it in a minute. Call me whether it looks like she's being admitted or not. If she is, I'll be down there as soon as I can."

"Thanks. In the meantime, can you call everyone? I'm on the hospital's line."

"I will."

"I'll call you back with an update." He hung up.

Just as Nathaniel was about to speak, the nurse stopped him. "I heard you. We'll check the fax machine and attach it to the clipboard."

"Thank you." Nathaniel walked down the hall and into the waiting area. It was a position he wasn't used to being in. As a doctor he was the one people waited for. He put his head in his hands, and, for the first time in a long time, he prayed.

After what seemed like an eternity, Nathaniel heard the familiar sound of a physician's wingtips coming down the hall. It was Dr. Hubert.

"Well," Nathaniel said nervously.

"It's an exacerbation. But something tells me you already knew that."

"I did." He felt guilty.

"These things usually don't come on all of a sudden like this. There are signs."

"I know, but she's Alicia Archer, superwoman. She's been running at full speed most of the week."

"I see that a lot with MS patients. They can be quite willful."

"You just described Alicia to a tee."

"That's probably why she's so successful. Still, she needs to slow down and listen to her body."

"I know."

"We're giving her a course of intravenous steroids, which should help."

"Are you admitting her?"

"No, she can go home tonight but she has to take it easy."

"She will. She'll be outnumbered."

"You can go in and see her now."

"Thanks. I should call her family. They're probably pretty worried. Do you mind if I use the phone at the nurses' station again?"

"No, go ahead."

"Thanks, John."

He went back to the station and picked up the phone to dial Harrison.

"Hello?"

"Harrison, it's Nate."

"Hey, Nate, what's the story?" Harrison was clearly distressed.

"I just spoke with the neurologist and she's okay. They stabilized her with IV steroids."

"Thank God. But we both know why this happened."

"She did too much."

"That's going to change." Harrison breathed a sigh of relief. "I guess I'll call everyone with the news and then I'll get her room ready."

"Thanks. I'm about to go in and see her now."

"Tell her I love her."

"I will. I'll see you a little later."

"Okay."

Nathaniel walked down the hall to the room. When he peeped in the window, he saw Alicia lying there while nurses adjusted the IV.

He took a deep breath and entered. "Hey there."

"Hi," Alicia said softly.

He pulled a chair up close to the bed and took her hand. "How are you feeling now?"

"I feel like a fool but physically I feel better. I also feel bad for the way I treated you."

"We don't have to talk about that now."

"Yes we do. I pushed you away. I was wrong to do that. You were looking out for my best interests. I should have listened to you and gone to the doctor. It was stupid of me."

"You're not stupid." He kissed her hand.

She looked at the IV. "It doesn't feel that way."

Before Nathaniel could say another word, Dr. Hubert entered the room. "I see you're looking better. How do you feel?"

"I'm definitely better now than I was when I arrived."

"Good." He looked at the IV bag. "You're nearly done, so we'll be releasing you."

"Great."

"Don't get too happy. You must follow up with your neurologist right away, at least by Monday."

"Consider it done, John," Nathaniel interjected. "Her family and I will make sure of it."

"Good." He paused. "I'm going to get your release paperwork started and you'll be able to leave."

"Thanks, Dr. Hubert," Alicia said gratefully.

Nathaniel kissed her forehead. "I spoke to Harrison and he told me to tell you he loves you and he'll have everything set when you get home. You realize you're going to be on house arrest when you get home, right?"

"I know," she conceded.

"I asked him to call Gabby and Lauren so they'd know what happened."

"Good." She took his hand. "I really am sorry." Her eyes filled with tears.

He wiped her cheek. "It's okay, Alicia." He kissed her. "It's going to take a lot more than just MS to scare me away."

%

Lauren hung up the phone. She and Randy had returned to her apartment after the exhibit.

Randy handed her a glass of wine. "How is she?"

"Thank you." She took a sip. "She's better, thank goodness. Harrison said Nate took her to the NYU MS Center and they treated her."

"Alicia has MS?" he asked, surprised. "I didn't know that."

"No one knows outside of a very select and small group."

He sat next to her. "I understand she wants her privacy, but it's MS and a lot of people have it."

"I know, but that's the way she wants it. She thinks people will look at her differently if they know."

"Do you think so?"

"No, but it's not up to me. I have to honor her wishes and I'd appreciate if you wouldn't mention it. Okay?"

"My lips are sealed."

"Thank you."

They kissed.

"Did I tell you how stunning you look tonight?"

"Yes, but I won't be too upset if you tell me again."

He lightly traced his fingers on her shoulders. "Yes, you are stunning in this gown. I felt like the luckiest guy in the world."

"Thank you."

"However, the sight of you of out of this gown will be more ravishing." He raised his eyebrows.

"Is that right?"

"Oh, yes." He unzipped her gown and began kissing her neck.

Lauren closed her eyes. "That feels nice."

"That's the idea, my love." A chill went up Lauren's spine as he pulled her gown down along with her bustier, to reveal her breasts. He caressed her breasts in his hands while he lightly kissed the nape of her neck. She turned to face him, unbuttoned his shirt and kissed his neck and chest.

His body tightened as she placed her kisses further south until he could take no more.

He got up and lifted her into his arms and carried her into the bedroom.

❧

With all the excitement about Alicia, Nigel insisted he stay for the night and Gabby was too tired to disagree. The next morning his ex was still the elephant in the room.

Eyes closed, Nigel reached over to find the other pillow empty. When he opened his eyes, he saw Gabby sitting near the window.

"Good morning," Nigel said.

"Good morning."

He sat up. "Why are you way over there?"

"I was just thinking."

"I know you're still upset with me. I'm really sorry. I should have . . ."

"I accept your apology."

Nigel looked surprised. "That's it?"

"Would you prefer me to yell and scream?"

"No, but you were pretty angry and you barely said anything to me at the exhibit. I thought you'd unload for sure."

"I planned to, but then Alicia got sick and it changed things for me." She looked out the window. "She told us that she and Nate had a fight. Yet when she took ill, whatever happened disappeared. Nate focused on taking care of her without hesitation."

"He loves her and that's what you do when you love someone."

She shook her head. "That's when I realized that maybe I shouldn't have gotten so upset with you. It's not like you have any control over what your ex does. But you have to admit you should have told me about the custody case."

He hung his head. "I know. I was going to tell you and then I just . . ."

"What?"

"I guess I felt like a loser. You're a beautiful, successful woman who could have any man, and you were interested in me. I didn't know how I was going to tell you my personal life was a complete mess."

"Whose personal life isn't a mess? Everyone has something to deal with. The point is, if you love someone, you take the good with the bad."

"There's a lot of bad right now."

"So we'll deal with it. I want to help you through this. I'm sure you'd do the same for me."

"I would."

She got up and sat next to him on the bed. "I know." She kissed him. "How about we watch a little morning news?" She picked up the remote.

"You want to watch television now?" Nigel had something else in mind.

"Yes. I want to check the weather." She turned the television on.

"You're heading up to Scarsdale, aren't you?"

"I have to see her for myself." She turned the volume up.

"And that's our local weather for today. We now turn to Doug Moriarity for the latest in the world of celebrity news. Doug?"

"Thanks, Jane. Sources say that domestic diva Alicia Archer looked like she'd been hitting the cooking sherry when she attended the Sixteen to Watch exhibit at the Blanchard Gallery Friday night. She's reported to have staggered out of the gallery early, propped up by two other guests to a waiting car. As you know, Alicia Archer just launched a cookware line with two major retailers . . ."

Gabby turned the television off. "Oh, my God. Alicia is going to freak out."

"But she wasn't drunk. She has MS."

"We know that, but other people don't and they've assumed the worst." She stood up. "Forget the weather report. I'm heading up."

"I'm coming with you."

"Do we need to stop by your place so you can change?"

"No need. I brought a change of clothes with me."

"Good. That saves us time. Okay, I'm going to hop in the shower now."

"It smells like the coffee is ready. I'll bring you a cup, too."

"Thanks." She went into the bathroom.

Nigel went to the kitchen and fixed the coffee. On the way back to the room he noticed the paper on the counter. There was a picture photo of Alicia, Lauren and Gabby. There were two empty champagne glasses near Alicia. "Oh no," he groaned as he picked the paper up.

Gabby was toweling off when he got back. He handed her the coffee.

"Hmm, smells good." She took a sip. "Is that today's paper?"

He handed her the paper. "You're not going to like it."

Gabby's expression said it all. "This is insane. Alicia didn't drink the champagne. Lauren finished both glasses and now they're making Alicia out to be a lush."

"Unfortunately a picture is worth a thousand words, even if it's wrong." He kissed her forehead.

She sighed. "This is going to kill Alicia."

"She has people around her who love her and know the truth who will help her get through it."

"I know you're right."

"Of course I'm right." He kissed her forehead. "I'll be five minutes in the shower and we can get on our way."

"Okay."

Gabby shuddered to think of the effect the paper and press would have on Alicia's well-being. She'd spent so many years carefully crafting her image, only to have it blown to bits by misinformation. Gabby wondered if this was the thing she needed to finally admit to the world there was a kink in the armor of a seemingly perfect businesswoman and domestic doyenne. She knew that the very thing she tried to hide from the world was the one thing that could save her. But would she reveal it?

CHAPTER 18

With Kurt Jr., Gabby, Harrison, Lauren and Nathaniel at the table, Alicia's elegant dining room looked more like a war room.

"Does Alicia know about any of this, Nate?" Lauren asked.

"No. She's been pretty out of it with the muscle relaxers."

"Well, it's not like she won't find out, even if we tried to keep it from her. It's news now," Harrison said, disgusted.

"My mother doesn't deserve this." Kurt pounded his fist.

Gabby rubbed his back. "We know, Kurt. It isn't fair."

"She's sick, and for people to think she's a drunk kills me. Can't we sue?"

"I'm not a lawyer, Kurt, but I doubt it's actionable. We have to convince your mom to come clean about the MS. That's the only way. In the meantime I'll do what I can to keep the network appeased. The magazine and company board is another story," Lauren sighed.

Nigel walked in. "Excuse me. I hate to interrupt."

"That's okay, Nigel. What's up?" Nathaniel asked.

"A Winnebago just pulled up in the driveway."

Kurt Jr. jumped up. "It's Grandma and Gramps."

"I think we know who's telling her now," Gabby said.

In walked Walt and Loretta Carlson. Walt was a tall, regal man with dark brown skin, silver beard and close-cropped silver hair. Loretta was a full-figured silver fox with light-brown eyes who wore her shoulder length hair in a bun. They were dressed casually in jeans and sneakers.

Kurt Jr. looked like a little boy again with his grandparents.

"Come here and give your Grandma a hug." She squeezed him tightly. "How's my boy?"

"I'm good, Grandma."

"You look good, Kurt."

"So do you, Grandma. I like your jeans."

"Thank you. I'm an old lady trying to keep it together."

"You're doing a good job." He turned to his grandfather. "Hi, Gramps."

"Hey there, son. How are you?" They hugged.

"I'm okay, Gramps. I've had better days, but overall I'm good."

"You're talking about this nonsense in the papers with your mother."

"Yes, Gramps."

"Well, you can trust that we'll get this straightened out." Mr. Carlson looked around. "It looks like we walked in on a meeting or something."

"Hi, Mr. and Mrs. Carlson." Lauren smiled.

"Hello, Mr. and Mrs. Carlson. It's good to see you," Gabby said.

"Lauren and Gabby, it's good to see you girls. I knew if anything was going down with my daughter, you two would be right here." Mr. Carlson hugged both of them.

"Hello, girls, it's wonderful to see you." Mrs. Carlson hugged them as well.

"It's great to see you too, Mrs. Carlson. You both look great," Lauren said.

"Thank you, dear."

"Hi, Walt and Loretta, it's good to see you."

"Harrison, my man, how's it going?" Mr. Carlson shook his hand.

"I'm hanging in there." He kissed Mrs. Carlson's cheek. "Loretta, you're as lovely as ever."

"Thank you."

"So where is our girl, and what is this rubbish we're hearing on the news?"

"That's what we were talking about," Nathaniel piped up.

"You're the neighbor, aren't you?" Mr. Carlson looked at him suspiciously.

"Oh, Walt, cut that out. You know he's the one Alicia's been seeing. Don't pay him any mind. He knows who you are."

Nathaniel laughed nervously.

"Well, young man, you're also a doctor. Can you bring us up to speed?" Mr. Carlson asked.

"Alicia had an attack. I took her to the NYU Multiple Sclerosis Center and they treated her. She's okay now."

"That's the real story, but the story in the papers is something else entirely," Mrs. Carlson said.

"Where is she?"

"She's in her room, Gramps."

"All right, Loretta, you know where we're going."

"I'm right behind you."

They went upstairs.

Lauren waited until they were upstairs. "Gabby, can I talk to you?"

"Sure."

"Let's go into Alicia's office."

Gabby looked puzzled. "Okay. I'll be back, Nigel."

"No problem, baby, I'll be right here."

They went to the office. Lauren closed the door.

Gabby sat down. "Okay, Lauren, you've got my attention."

Lauren handed her the newspaper. "I think you should look at this."

It was an article about the exhibit, with a picture of an artist and one of Gabby and Nigel holding hands. "I didn't see this."

"I didn't think you did."

Gabby read the article. She shook her head. "I don't know what bothers me more, the fact that this happened or knowing my mother was right."

"This isn't the time to second-guess yourself, Gabby."

"You're right. I made a decision and I have to accept all the consequences, good and bad."

"Who's the artist?"

"It's Ivana Andrik. She's been trying to get into the exhibit practically from the moment it began."

"I take it she's not good."

"What Ivana has is the mechanics, but that's not the same as talent, passion and feeling. Her paintings are cold. Even a still-life painting is supposed to evoke a feeling. Otherwise it might as well be a Polaroid or a mug shot."

"Apparently she feels otherwise."

"Personally I wouldn't let Ivana paint my toenails."

"Ouch. You know if this is in one art section . . ."

"It's in a dozen art sections."

"You're going to have to figure out how to handle this, and you have to tell Nigel."

Gabby groaned. "Can we have one crisis at a time, please?"

"It should be so easy, Gabby."

"I'm sorry you've got drama going on, too."

"Don't worry about me. I've figured out what I've got to do." She looked at her cell phone.

"You think Alicia's going to be surprised to see her parents?"

"Surprised is a little too mild a word. Shocked and stunned is more like it."

∾

"Alicia?"

"Five more minutes, Mom." She turned over. "Mom?" Alicia opened her eyes.

"Hello, daughter." Her father smiled down at her

"Dad." She looked over at her mother. "Mom." She sat straight up. "Oh, my God, who died?"

"Relax, Alicia, no one has died. Everyone is fine." Her mother rubbed her hand.

"Is Samantha okay? Are you sure?"

"Samantha is fine and happy in Milan," her mother reassured her.

"That's a relief." Alicia sighed. "So what brings you here? Did Harrison call you?"

"What would he call us about?"

"Come on, Mom. I know you know something."

"You tell us, dear."

"I had an exacerbation and I had to go to the hospital."

"I thought you were supposed to be taking it easy while you were on hiatus."

"I was taking it easy, Dad, but I had the cookware launch this week."

"I'm sure you could have just gone to Herald Square, but you made several appearances."

"How do you know that, Dad?"

"We keep up with you on your Web site. It lists your upcoming appearances."

Alicia was impressed. "I didn't know you bothered with the Web."

"We tried to avoid it, but we had to surrender," her mother added.

Alicia laughed.

Her parents looked at each other.

"So did you have this attack after the exhibit?"

"I guess you could say it happened during the exhibit, Dad." She stopped to think. "How did you know about the exhibit?" Alicia grew concerned. "Mom and Dad, what's going on?"

"There are reports in the paper and on the news about you. They're saying you were drunk at the exhibit."

"What did you say, Dad?"

"I think you heard me the first time."

Alicia felt sick to her stomach. "I'm being accused of being drunk in public?"

"They're running a photo of you with Lauren and Gabby. In the picture you have two empty glasses nearby."

"But that's crazy, Mom. I had two sips of champagne and I didn't even finish the glass."

"You know that's not the point, Alicia."

"You know what I'm going to say, don't you?"

"Yes, Dad. You're going to tell me that I need to let people know I have MS."

"Your father's right, Alicia. Keeping it a secret isn't doing you any good and this whole thing proves it."

"But Mom and Dad . . ."

"Oh no, you don't, young lady. There's more at stake here than just your name. You have the foundation to think about, too. All this negative press isn't going to help raise money."

"I can't let that happen. It's my tribute to Kurt."

"We know. Listen, you have a house full of people downstairs who are here to rally and support you."

"A house full of people?"

"Yes. Everyone is here, including our grandson."

"I had no idea. I've been a bit out of it."

"Granted. You need to rest and regain your strength. You're going to need it for the fight you have ahead."

Alicia groaned. "I really don't know if I'm ready to do this."

"Alicia, it might be too late to get in front of the story, but you can get the truth out," her father said.

"I know you're right, Dad." She paused. "My goodness, I didn't ask you when you got back."

"We came in from Pennsylvania Dutch country and we're heading back home. As much as we love the Winnebago, my back is looking forward to our Sealy Posturepedic." Her father smiled.

"I can't say I blame you."

"By the way, Nathaniel is one of the people downstairs." Her mother raised her eyebrows.

"He's seems like a good guy. He cares about you," her father said.

There was a knock at the door.

"Come in."

"Hi, Mom," Kurt said.

"Hello, gorgeous, you're a sight for sore eyes. Come and hug your mother."

Kurt hugged her tightly. "Are you okay, Mom?"

"I'm fine, Kurt."

"Grandma and Gramps talked to you, so you know what's going on."

"Yes, we did, son. Don't you worry, it's going to be fine. Your mother knows what she's got to do." He stood up. "We better get going. We've got to get on the expressway and you know how much fun that is, even on a Saturday."

"Okay, Dad."

Her father kissed her cheek. "You go get 'em, tiger. You know if you need us, we'll be there in a heartbeat."

"I know."

Her mother kissed her cheek too. "You listen to your doctor and take care, like you're supposed to. Okay?"

"I will, Mom."

"We love you." Her father smiled as he opened her bedroom door.

"I love you, too."

Kurt sat on the edge of her bed. "Are you going to bite the bullet, Mom?"

"I don't know that I have a choice anymore."

∽

With Alicia's parents gone everyone lolled around the kitchen while Harrison made something to eat. Lauren's cell phone rang. She looked at the caller ID. It was Randy.

"If you'll excuse me," she said as she left the kitchen and went into the living room. "Hi, Randy, I'm so glad to hear your voice."

"Hi. I just got a break here and I saw the paper."

"So you know what's going on."

"It's ridiculous. How's Alicia doing?"

"Physically she's fine. I haven't been up to see her yet. Her parents were here."

"Well, I'm glad you're there."

"So am I."

"You know, though, this thing got me to thinking about Ken."

"It did?" She seemed puzzled.

"Yes. It's all about the power of the press. Maybe you should take your story public. I have a friend at the paper . . ."

"I can see where you're coming from, Randy, but I don't think that's a good idea."

"Why? It would put him on the defensive. I already called my buddy and he's ready to talk to you."

Lauren couldn't believe her ears. "You called him without consulting me? Why would you do that?"

"You won't take my money. I had to do something, Lauren. You can't let this threat hang over your life."

"I don't intend to let that happen."

"So why don't you tell me what are you going to do?"

"This is my problem. I have it covered."

"I love you. I want to help. Why don't you let me in?"

"Because I can handle it. I need you to trust me. I don't need you second-guessing me."

"I'm not second-guessing you, Lauren. I just can't stand by and watch him do this to you."

"I get it. Just call your friend back and tell him there is no story." She paused. "Listen, I'm going upstairs to see Alicia. I'll call you on my way back to the city." Lauren closed her phone and went back to the kitchen. "Gabby, I'm heading upstairs. Are you coming?"

She got up. "I'm right behind you."

When they got upstairs to Alicia's room, she was watching the news report about her incident.

"What in the world?" Gabby went over and shut the television off. "Are you trying to make yourself nuts today?"

"I told her, Aunt Gabby, but she wouldn't listen to me."

"I had to see how bad it was." She rubbed her forehead. "I have a headache."

"See what good it did you?" Lauren went into the bathroom.

"I can only imagine the number of phone calls and emails that are coming in," Alicia lamented.

"You can't think about that now, Alicia." Gabby sat on her bed. "How are you feeling?"

"Other than knowing my whole career and company are in the toilet, I'm peachy."

"Don't say that, Mom."

"He's right, you know." Lauren returned from the bathroom with a couple of Tylenol and a glass of water. "Here, take this for your headache."

"Thanks." She quickly took the pills.

"Listen, it might be too late to get in front of this story, but you set the direction it takes from here." Lauren sat down.

"She's right, Mom."

"I know. I just feel so stupid. If I had slowed down this week, this wouldn't have happened in the first place. Gabby, I'm so sorry for ruining your big night."

"Please, you didn't ruin anything."

"Blaming yourself now isn't the thing to do. You have to look ahead."

"I know, Lauren." She chuckled softly.

"What's so funny?" Gabby asked.

"I was going to call you two about having a meeting today to discuss *Pride and Prejudice*."

"Who's to say we still can't. It might be just the thing to take your mind off all of this," Lauren suggested.

Kurt Jr. got up. "That would be my cue to leave."

They laughed.

"Come on, Kurt, don't you want to sit with me for one meeting of the Austen Aristocrats?"

He leaned down and kissed her on the cheek. "I love you, Mom, but I'm not into chick flicks, even when they're books. I'm going to hang out with the guys downstairs."

"That's okay, sweetie," she laughed.

Kurt began to walk out.

"So you mean to tell us Sally has never dragged you to a chick flick?" Gabby asked.

"No. She's an action/adventure lover like me," he answered as he left the room.

"It figures my son would find the one girl who would love that kind of movie."

"He is a charmer. I bet you she secretly watches *Lifetime* when he's not around." Lauren winked.

They laughed.

"Thanks, girls. I can always count on you to make me feel better."

"What are fellow Aristocrats for?" Gabby asked.

"Now where are the books? I know you have three of them in here." Lauren looked around.

"They're on a shelf in my closet."

"I'll be back," Lauren said, imitating the Terminator. "That's the closest I ever want to come to an action flick."

They laughed. Grateful for the distraction, Alicia spent two hours with Lauren and Gabby, engrossed in their favorite Austen book. It took Alicia's mind off the task she had at hand and she was grateful.

CHAPTER 19

Nigel noticed Gabby's reticence on the drive back into the city. He knew she was worried about Alicia, but after seeing her he'd expected she would be less preoccupied. For her part Gabby was trying to figure out her next move to save the exhibit's good reputation and hers. When they got back, she went straight to the kitchen to make some tea. Nigel followed her.

"Have I done something? You were so quiet in the car."

"No. Why would you say that?" Gabby asked as she put the kettle on.

He produced the newspaper. "I read the article in the art section."

Gabby's heart fell. "So you know."

"Do you want to talk about it?"

She got a couple of mugs from the cabinet. "What's there to talk about? This is about a bitter artist looking for her fifteen minutes and a reporter who wanted to sensationalize a story where there is none." She put the mugs on the table.

He sighed. "I knew I should have insisted on taking my painting out of the mix."

"You asked and I said no. People loved your painting and it got one of the highest bids last night."

"What about the other artists?"

"It's publicity. They'll benefit from being a part of the 'scandal.' "

"I just think you're being a little too casual about this. I'm more worried about it than you are."

"Of course I'm worried. As a beginning gallery owner I was a 40-year-old divorced woman with a degree in art history I hadn't used in nearly twenty years. I had to prove I belonged with every exhibit. Every artist I chose had to be the best. It took me years to build my reputation and get the backers and patrons I needed to make the Blanchard Gallery a success. Now someone wants to take that away in one night." She stopped to catch her breath. "I come from a background where it's all about keeping a stiff upper lip, so I'm sorry if you think I'm being too cool about it, but stick around. I'm pretty sure I can prove how broken I feel inside." Gabby fought back tears.

Nigel got up and put his arms around her. "I'm sorry. I didn't mean to upset you." He rubbed her back. "Okay, sweetheart, you can let it out with me."

Nigel held Gabby as she cried. She knew eventually she had to face Bunny and listen to her "I told you so" along with the crow she'd have to swallow for Sunday tea.

∽

It was a breezy summer evening and Alicia sat on the balcony off her bedroom to look at the evening sky as it turned into night. Harrison brought her a glass of iced tea.

"Enjoying the evening?" he asked as he handed her the tea.

"Yes. This is my favorite time of day, you know."

"It was Martha's favorite time of day, too." He gazed at the sky.

"There's something about the color of the sky that's so peaceful."

"You know what you've got to do to bring peace to your life."

She sighed. "Yes, I do."

"Nate's worried it's going to be too much for you."

"It certainly feels that way."

"You have to look at it this way. Secrets have a way of weighing you down and you're a woman who likes to move ahead and get on with things. Telling people you have MS will lighten your load."

"He's right," Nathaniel agreed as he walked onto the balcony.

"How long have you been standing there?" she asked.

"Long enough."

"I'm going to leave you two lovebirds alone now. If you need anything, you know I'm only a buzz away."

"Thanks, Harrison."

Nathaniel sat down in the chair next to hers.

"Are you enjoying the evening weather?"

"Yes. I've had a rather eventful day for someone who's been in bed most of the day."

Nathaniel chuckled. "That's life in the fast lane."

Alicia laughed.

Nathaniel took her hand in his. "I'm just happy that you're all right. That's the main thing."

"I owe it all to you. If you hadn't taken me to the NYU MS center, I don't know what would have happened."

"You give me too much credit. Dr. Hubert played a part, you know."

"And how did you know to take me there instead of another hospital?"

"NYU is one of the best in the city and John is one of the top neurologists specializing in MS in the country. He's also a good friend of mine from my days as a resident."

"You had the inside track."

"You could say that." He kissed her hand.

Alicia smiled. "We still haven't talked about what happened between us."

"Yes, we have."

"No, we haven't. We've brushed over it."

Nathaniel stood up, took her hand and pulled her to him. "How about a kiss?"

Alicia kissed him passionately. "Oh, that was nice," he said, rubbing her back.

Without a word she kissed him even more fervently. Nathaniel felt something stir inside of him. "Alicia, let's not get anything started we can't finish."

"Well, if you don't want to finish the conversation, we can finish something else. Unless, of course, you're not up to it."

He pulled her close to him. "Does it feel like I'm not up to it?"

"No."

"You were just in the hospital."

"Yes, but I'm not dead. I'm very much alive and I want make love to you."

That was all Nathaniel needed to hear. He picked her up and took her inside to the bedroom and laid her down ever so easily on the bed. He took his shirt off and slowly lowered himself as they kissed.

"I love you," he whispered.

"I love you, too."

Alicia pulled her nightgown down around her shoulders and Nathaniel took it off the rest of the way. Although he wanted to take her right then, he slowed down to savor every inch of her body as if she were a fine wine. Alicia's senses came alive with pleasure as he explored the breadth and subtly of every curve with his lips, teasing and tantalizing every inch of her body. The more he pleased Alicia, the more he fueled his own passion and longing. When neither could take any more, he removed the last barrier between them and then two bodies became one in the pure rapture of love.

∽

With a Starbucks coffee in hand, Lauren was stretched out on the sofa completely engrossed in her Sunday political programs when her phone rang.

"Hello?"

"Hi, Lauren, it's Joe."

"Hi, Joe, how are you?"

"I'm not bad. The question is, how are you?"

"I'm fine, Joe."

"When I got your message to set up a settlement meeting with Ken and his lawyer for tomorrow, I thought perhaps you had a fever or something."

"You're hilarious, Joe. Is this what I pay you $500 an hour for?"

"No. The stand-up is a freebie."

"Oh gee, thanks," she said sarcastically. "Did you set up the meeting?"

"Yes. We're on for tomorrow at my office at ten."

"Good."

"Are you going to tell me what this meeting is all about? I am your lawyer. I should know."

"Don't worry about it. You'll see tomorrow."

Lauren hung up the phone and glanced at the newspapers on her coffee table.

"Look at this nonsense." She picked up one of the papers. "They are just running wild with this story." She threw the paper back on the table. "I bet Alicia's place is a zoo by now."

✍

Harrison bristled at the sight of the reporters in front of the house.

"Look at these vultures," he huffed as he closed the curtains.

"What's going on?" Nathaniel asked.

"Look for yourself."

Nathaniel looked at the reporters, news vans and camera people camped out in front of the house. "Good grief, when did this happen?"

"They've been here since I got up at seven this morning and they've been proliferating ever since."

"I'm afraid to get the papers."

"You don't have to get the papers to see what's going on. All you have to do is go on the Internet or turn on the television. The phone hasn't stopped ringing either."

"It's a good thing we turned it off upstairs."

The phone rang again.

"I'll get it." Harrison went to answer the phone.

Nathaniel looked out of the window again. "This is unreal."

"Nate, can you tell Alicia that Barbara's on the phone for her? I know she'll want to talk to her."

"Not a problem." He went upstairs.

Alicia had the Weather Channel on. "I figured this was the only safe thing for me to watch today."

He walked over and kissed her. "You're probably right. Barbara is on the phone for you."

"Okay, thanks." Nathaniel left as she picked up the phone. "Barbara?"

"Hi, Alicia, how are you holding up?"

"I'm still here. So tell me what's happening?"

"Word has it that Taylor and the stooges are scheduling a press conference for Monday afternoon."

"Where they'll announce that I'm taking a leave pending a full investigation, no doubt."

"More or less."

Alicia decided she had to start with someone and it might as well be a friend like Barbara. "Thanks for keeping me in the loop, Barbara. There's something I want to tell you before I do my own press conference."

"What?"

"I wasn't drunk Friday night. I have . . ."

She cut her off. "You have MS."

Alicia was shocked. "Yes. How did you know I was going to say that?"

"I figured it out a while ago."

"How? I thought I was pretty careful about hiding it."

"Oh, you've done a great job hiding it from most people. But my sister has had MS for thirteen years."

"I didn't know that."

"I don't really talk about it."

"I feel so embarrassed. I wasn't ashamed of the condition or anything."

"You didn't want people to treat you differently. My sister was the same way. It took her a while to realize that she didn't have to let the diagnosis define who she was."

"It seems I've done that."

"Listen, I'm in no position to judge. Heaven knows what I would do if I ever faced something like that."

"Well, I'm glad I told you, even though you knew."

"Alicia, I'm honored that you felt comfortable enough to tell me first." She paused. "So where are you having the press conference?"

"I'll probably have it up here in my backyard, considering half the media seems to be in my neighborhood already."

Barbara laughed. "You poor thing."

"Tell me about it. Anyway, thanks for giving me a head's up."

"You know I always have your back."

"I appreciate it. I'll talk to you soon."

"Take care, Alicia."

"I will." She hung up and dialed again.

"Hello, Viola Sherwood here."

"Hello, Viola, it's Alicia."

"Alicia. I'm so happy to hear from you. What the hell is going on? Taylor's on the phone calling everybody about this press conference thing and she's saying you're leaving. The whole thing is crazy."

"I know. I need your help today, Viola. I need you to schedule a press conference for tomorrow morning here at my house in Scarsdale. I'm going to tell the world I have MS."

"Oh, my God, Alicia. I had no idea."

"No one knew except my family and close friends. I've had it for nearly three years now."

"Oh, honey, I will get on this now and I'll have everyone there by nine sharp."

"Thanks. I don't know how you're going to keep it from the others."

"Not to worry. I know exactly what to do."

"Thanks, Viola. I'll see you tomorrow."

"Yes, you will."

Harrison and Nate entered. "What's going on?" Harrison asked.

"I'm having a press conference tomorrow morning."

"So soon?" Nathaniel was surprised.

"I don't have a choice. Taylor and some of the board members of Archer Omnimedia are having one tomorrow afternoon. I need to get ahead of it."

"You have a doctor's appointment tomorrow morning," Harrison reminded her.

"I need you to contact Dr. Stuart and see if he can come here today. I'm sure he's back by now. We have his number at home, don't we?"

"Yes."

"Okay, then let's give him a call."

"Okay. I'll let you know what happens." Harrison left the room.

Nathaniel looked at her.

"What?"

"You want to call a press conference?"

"Yes. I have to slow Taylor's momentum."

"This isn't a game. It's your life."

"You don't think I know that?"

Nathaniel sighed.

"You don't approve?"

"It's not a matter of whether I approve or not. I just think this whole thing is a big-enough circus."

"I know, but the sooner I get this done, the sooner we can get back to a normal life."

Harrison entered the room again. "Dr. Stuart will be here at two."

"Terrific. Harrison, can you contact my parents and Kurt and let them know I'm going to have a press conference on Monday morning."

"You're having it on Monday. Here?"

"Why not? They're already camped out in front of the house."

"It's your party," Harrison acknowledged.

"See, Nathaniel, we are on our way back to normal."

"I hope you're right." Nathaniel smiled, but he didn't look completely convinced.

Gabby changed her clothes three times before she settled on an Empire-style black dress. She figured if she was going to meet her executioner, she'd be dressed for the occasion. As usual, Rosie had on her uncomfortable uniform and set the table up for tea.

The doorbell rang and Gabby took a deep breath while Rosie went to answer it.

A few moments later Gabby heard several voices. "What's going on?" She went to the top of the stairs. When she looked down, she saw two men bringing her father upstairs in his wheelchair.

"Daddy?"

He looked up. "Hello, princess."

"Be careful with him now." Bunny was behind them.

"Mrs. Blanchard, we really would prefer if you stay below until we get him level," one of the men said.

"I want to make sure you don't drop him."

"We won't, ma'am, but we really don't want to hurt you in the process."

"Fine, I'll stay here."

Finally they reached the top. "Here you are, Mr. B." One man caught his breath.

"Thank you. Hello, Daddy." She kissed and hugged him. "I'm so happy to see you."

"I'm glad to be here."

"Are you feeling better, Daddy? Mother said you weren't feeling good on Friday."

"It was nothing. You know how your mother likes to fuss."

Bunny got to the top of the steps. "Give your mother a hand, Gabby." She held her hand out and Gabby helped her up the last step. "Thank you. I had a reason to be concerned. He had a little fever."

"You did, Daddy?"

"It was 99.0. In my book that doesn't qualify."

Gabby laughed. "How are you, Mother?" She kissed her.

"Very well, thanks." She started to wheel Mr. Blanchard to the living room.

"I'll do that, Mother." Gabby took over.

Bunny took a seat while Gabby got her father situated. "How's that, Daddy?"

"That's good, princess."

Gabby took a seat while Rosie began serving tea.

She handed a cup to Bunny. "Thank you, Rosie."

"You're welcome, ma'am."

"I'll fix yours, Daddy. You take it with honey and lemon, right?"

"Yes."

She handed the tea to him.

"Thank you."

Gabby quickly fixed her cup.

"We were so sorry to see all this fuss in the paper about Alicia," Bunny said. "It's complete rubbish, we know."

"I know, Mother. Alicia's still recovering from her attack and now she's got all this to deal with."

"It's a shame." Mr. Blanchard shook his head.

"She's worked so hard to get where she is and to have people smear her name without knowing the facts is unfathomable to me." Gabby sipped her tea.

"Alicia's a smart girl. She's going to come out on top," Mr. Blanchard said confidently.

"I'm sure you're right, Daddy."

"However, we're here to talk about another smear job. The smear job this Ivana is doing to you and the gallery."

"I'm glad you finally said it, Mother. It was killing me waiting for you to drop the other shoe."

"Now princess, we're not hear to judge you or attack your decisions. Are we, Bunny?"

"No, we're not."

"You're not? Because I deserve it. You told me this could happen and I went ahead with it anyway." Gabby hung her head.

"It's all right, princess. We're here to help."

"You are?"

"Yes. Tell her, Bunny."

"Someone bought Nigel's painting Friday, right?"

"Yes. It was one of the highest bids of the night."

"Bernice Lawson was the buyer."

"How do you know that?"

"Bernice is married to Thomas DiGregorio."

"The *Times'* art critic?"

Thomas DiGregorio was the premier critic in every art circle. His word could make or break careers and galleries.

"One and the same," Mr. Blanchard said.

"She was so taken with the painting, she snapped a picture with her phone and sent it to him. The camera quality wasn't that great, he said, but the painting was."

"Oh, that's fantastic."

"He wants to do an article about the gallery's exhibit."

"Oh, my God." Gabby was floored. "How did this happen?"

"It happened because you're a talented gallery owner with a real gift for finding the city's best undiscovered artists," Bunny said proudly.

"Do you mean that, Mother?"

"Of course I do."

Gabby felt a tear roll down her face. She wiped it away. "I'm so glad to hear you're proud of me. I was beginning to think I couldn't do anything right to you."

"Gabrielle, we might have our differences, but I love you. You're my daughter."

Gabby got up and hugged Bunny. "I love you, too, Mother."

"Now this is what I like to see," Mr. Blanchard said

"Your Mr. Clark will be pleased, I'm sure," Bunny said.

Thomas DiGregorio is a very big deal. I don't think, though, Nigel will be leaving his day job anytime soon."

"He's a smart man," Mr. Blanchard interjected.

Bunny brushed the hair out of Gabby's face. "This article will also silence that Ivana woman. Didn't you say she isn't very good?"

No, Mother, she isn't good, I'm sad to say."

"It's sad if this is the only way she can get attention." Bunny shook her head.

"She certainly won't have it much longer, once word of the article gets out," Mr. Blanchard said.

"Mother and Daddy, I don't know what you did, but I'm grateful."

"We told you we didn't do anything. It was all you." Bunny smiled. "Now please tell me Rosie has made some of Alicia's scones."

"Yes, she has, Mother. Rosie?"

Rosie brought a tray over.

"Richard, these scones are amazing. You must try them." She put one on a plate and passed it to him.

"Thank you, my love."

Gabby watched her parents with complete joy. Deep down she hoped to have the same kind of relationship. With the whole exhibit scandal behind them, she realized she and Nigel had a chance at it.

❧

Even with his gym clothes on, Dr. Stuart still managed to give Alicia that scolding look of his. He wasn't much older than Alicia, but he already had a full head of white hair and the bluest eyes she'd ever seen, even behind his spectacles.

"You know what I'm going to say, don't you?"

"I need to get a tape recorder. That way I will save us both some time."

"I'm not kidding with you, Alicia. I got the reports from Dr. Hubert in my office yesterday. You had a close call."

"I know."

"You keep saying that, but you never change. Running around from Westchester to Long Island to the heart of New York City in three days is hard on people without a chronic condition."

"Okay, I won't do it again."

"Where have I heard that before?"

"I mean it this time."

"I've heard that one, too."

"Is there nothing I can say to satisfy you?"

"I'll believe you've slowed down when I see it for myself."

"Okay."

"Any other symptoms I should know about?"

"Just the usual suspects, numbness, tingling, creepy crawlies and walking around like a drunk."

"That's not funny, Alicia."

"Who's laughing?" She sighed. "How did you manage to get through the press barricade?"

"I parked at Nate's place and walked over through the backyard."

"Good plan."

"I thought so, too." He took her pulse.

There was a knock. "Can I come in?" Nathaniel asked.

"Do you mind?"

"No."

"Come on in, Nate."

He walked up beside Dr. Stuart. "What's the verdict?"

"She's doing pretty well, in spite of what happened."

"I told you I was okay."

"To be safe, I wanted to hear it from a neurologist."

"You heard him. You heard him, too, didn't you, Harrison?"

"How did you know I was there?"

"I have a sixth sense."

"Thanks, Barry. I appreciate your coming by in all this madness."

"Not a problem, Nate. Now if you gentlemen will excuse me, I have to get home."

"Thank you, Dr. Stuart."

"Try to be good."

"I will."

"I'll walk you out," Harrison said.

Nathaniel closed the door behind them. He had a serious look on his face.

"What's the matter?" Alicia asked.

"I wanted to talk to you about something."

"Okay."

He sat down. "I know you're going to have the press conference and I think that you should."

"But?"

"Don't you think you're doing too much? I mean you're the CEO of Archer Omnimedia, editor-in-chief of *Everyday Elegance*, the host of a daily syndicated lifestyle show and you're a part of running the foundation. I think you can afford to step back from something."

Alicia looked completely taken aback. "What? Are you saying you think I should let them push me out of my own company?"

"No."

"Then you need to explain your statement a little more clearly, because that's what it sounds like."

"All I'm saying is you don't have to wear so many hats. You have to take time out."

"What would you do if someone told you that you needed to drop one of your jobs?"

"That's not fair, Alicia. You know it's not the same thing."

"Isn't it? You love working with Doctors Without Borders on your missions to Africa. How would you decide between that and the work you do at the clinic?"

"You know about the clinic?"

"You're not the only one who does their homework. I know you provide free care to all five boroughs several times a month."

"It's not the same thing, Alicia. I don't . . ."

"What? You don't have MS. Isn't that what you were going to say?"

"Stop putting words in my mouth."

"Stop trying to tell me that I have to give up something I love and have worked hard for all my life," she shot back.

"I'm not saying this to hurt you, Alicia." Frustrated, he threw his hands up. "You didn't see what you looked like when I took you to the hospital. You were so pale and weak, it scared the hell out of me. All I could think was,

'Please, God, let her be all right.' " He took a breath. "You know, Alicia, as a doctor I've always been able to keep my emotions in check. Now for the first time in my life I'm in love and all bets are off. I can't be detached. I'm totally selfish, because I want you here with me healthy and I never want to see you like that again."

Alicia was rendered speechless.

Nathaniel was overcome. "Listen, I've got to go. I need some air. I'll see you a little later."

"Nathaniel!"

"I'll see you later." He rushed out of the room.

Alicia sat back on the bed. She'd never realized her episode had affected far more than just her. It had affected the people she loved.

Harrison knocked on the door. "Alicia?"

"Harrison! I didn't know." She began to sob. "I just didn't know."

He rushed over and held her. "It's okay, Alicia. You're okay."

❧

After her parents left, Gabby gave Rosie the rest of Sunday and Monday off. She put on a sexy little summer dress and invited Nigel over. She left the door open so he could come straight up when he arrived. As he walked up the steps, he heard soft jazz playing in the background.

"Gabby?" he called.

"Hello, there." She stood in the hall with two tropical drinks in hand.

"Hi. What's going on here?"

"We're having a special little celebration with an island theme."

"Really? What's the occasion?"

She walked up and handed him a drink. "I thought you'd never ask. Let's sit down."

"Okay."

He followed her onto the terrace.

"Have a seat."

He sat. "The suspense is killing me."

"My parents came over for tea this afternoon."

"Both your parents?"

"Yes."

"So how was it between you and your mother? I'm sure she saw the articles."

"She did. In fact, both of them did."

"Were they really upset?"

"No. As amazing as it sounds, the one time I expected my mother to chop me up into pieces, she actually told me she was proud of me."

"That's terrific."

"Believe me, I thought I was done for. But as it turns out they had some good news for me."

"What? Don't keep me waiting."

"It turns out the person who bought your painting is married to Thomas DiGregorio and he loved it."

"*The* Thomas DiGregorio?" He was stunned.

"Yes. Not only was he impressed with your painting, he's going to do a piece in the *Times* about the gallery and the exhibit."

"That's fantastic, Gabby. You know what that means, don't you?"

"Oh, yes. An article from him effectively cancels out all the others."

"So the gallery and your reputation are intact."

He raised his glass. "Here's to the Blanchard Gallery and its amazing owner, Gabby."

"Thank you."

They clinked their glasses and then took a sip.

Nigel put his glass down and got up. "May I have this dance?"

"Yes, you may."

They swayed to the music. Nigel twirled her around, then pulled her to him in an ardent embrace that lasted long after the music stopped. Gabby took him by the hand and led him from the terrace to her bedroom, where they continued to make beautiful music of their own all night long.

CHAPTER 20

All cried out, Alicia looked at the empty pillowcase next to her. She picked the phone up.

"Hello?" Lauren was at her computer.

"Hi, Lauren."

"Hey, Alicia. What's wrong? You don't sound like yourself." She stopped working.

"I don't?"

"It sounds like you've been crying."

"I have been."

"Oh, God, girl, did something else happen?" She got up from her desk.

"It did. Only it doesn't involve the media, if you can believe it."

"I'm shocked."

"I got into a fight with Nathaniel."

"Another one?"

"Yes, if you can believe it. We made up after the first fight. But I'm not sure if that counts, since we never talked about it."

"So this second fight was kind of a combo."

"Yeah, you could say that."

"Do you know what he's angry about?"

"Yes, and part of it has something to do with the press conference I'm holding tomorrow morning."

"Wait. You're having the press conference tomorrow morning?"

"Yes. I set it up for then so I'd be in front of the press conference the board has planned for the afternoon."

"That's a good move, PR-wise. Nate didn't have a problem with that, I'm sure."

"He didn't per se. He has a problem with me fighting to keep my many jobs. He thinks I can afford to let one go."

"I see."

"You think so, too, don't you?"

"Alicia, you know I'm just as driven as you are, but you have a lot of balls in the air to juggle."

Alicia's eyes began to well up. "He told me how scared he was Friday night." She paused to catch her breath. "Lauren, I never thought about it from his perspective. I guess I thought that since he's a doctor, he could separate himself."

"Of course he can't, Alicia. He's in love with you. You're not a patient. You're the woman he loves and when he sees you suffering, he can't step back."

"I know that now."

"Oh, Lord, girl, what did you do?"

"I threw his jobs in his face. I told him to choose between them."

Lauren groaned. "No offense, Alicia, but there's a big difference between delivering life-saving vaccines to children and coming up with new crepe recipes for the brunch section of the magazine."

"You don't think I know that? I don't think I've ever seen him so upset."

"Where is he?"

"He left a few hours ago. I'm really afraid he's not coming back."

"He's coming back, Alicia. He loves you."

"What should I do, Lauren?"

"I can't answer that. But I will say this. You have a man there who loves you and is willing to do anything for you. If you love him, and I know you do, you have to decide what you're willing to do for him."

"When did you get so smart?"

"I hope after three divorces I've learned something." She lay back on the sofa.

"Speaking of divorce, what's going on with yours?"

"We have a meeting scheduled for tomorrow morning. So I might not get there in time for the press conference."

"That's okay. Get here when you can. Oh, and will you call Gabby and let her know."

"Will do." She paused. "Do you feel better now?"

"Yes. Thanks for listening. I'm worn out and I have a big day tomorrow. I'm going to get some sleep."

Lauren looked at the clock. "I might decide to do the same thing. Randy has a very late night tonight."

"Okay. I'll see you tomorrow. Good luck with Ken."

"Thanks. Good night."

"Good night."

Before she turned the light out, Alicia sat and thought about what she should do. *Here I have a man that wants me to be near him always and I threw it in his face. What's wrong with me? I don't want Taylor anywhere near the editor-in-chief job in any way.* An idea hit her. *Brilliant. I know exactly what to do. I just hope it's not too late for Nathaniel.*

Alicia turned the light out.

❧

Lauren picked up her phone.

"Hello?"

"Hi, Joe, it's Lauren."

He looked at the clock. "What time is it? Is everything all right?"

"Everything's fine, Joe. I need you to call Ken's attorney and tell him the meeting has been moved up to seven-thirty."

"What?" He sat up straight. "You mean in the morning? They're not going to go for that."

"Tell them it's an offer they can't refuse. I guarantee Ken will get his butt out of bed. In fact, I bet they'll be there early."

"What's going to get me out of bed?"

"I'll pay you double your hourly rate."

"I'll bring the coffee."

"Good man. I'll see you tomorrow."

❧

Lauren walked into Joe's office with a bakery box filled with pastries. As she predicted, although it wasn't seven-thirty yet, Ken and his attorney were already there.

She put the box on the table as Joe handed her a tall Starbucks cup.

"Thank you, Joe."

"You're welcome."

She sat down. "Would anyone care for a pastry? I have bear claws, Ken."

"No, thank you."

His attorney, Raymond Collins, didn't look pleased. "We didn't come here early for breakfast. It's my understanding that we're ready to deal."

"Yes. Ken, I've considered your offer very carefully and I've decided that I'm not going to give in to blackmail."

Ken tried to appear offended. "Blackmail? Who said anything about blackmail?"

"You did, Ken. When you told me that I'd better help you get on *NFL Weekly* as a desk commentator or I should be prepared to lose my apartment."

Raymond looked at him. "My client denies doing any such illegal thing."

"I figured as much. That's why I brought a reminder for him." Lauren pulled out a tape recorder and hit the play button:

"Lauren, I know you think you're going to make me go away if you just ignore me. But I'm serious. If you want to keep that apartment, you will help me get what I want from NFL Weekly *and I don't want to hear any bull about you not having any juice. I know you've got pull. So you get me what I want or you can kiss the apartment goodbye."*

Ken sank in the chair.

"Clearly, that could have been a doctored tape," his attorney said.

"You know, I thought you'd say that." She took out her cell phone. "I have cell phone messages with date and time stamps. I can play those for you, too. I believe I've saved about thirty or so messages just like that one. Want to hear them?"

"No. That won't be necessary." Raymond whispered in Ken's ear. "If you'll give us a minute."

"Sure. Lauren and I will step outside the office."

Lauren got up.

"After you, Ms. Jones," Joe said.

"No, Joe, not Ms. Jones. It's Ms. Jules for now."

"Duly noted, my dear. Duly noted."

They stepped into the reception area.

"You're a sly one," Joe said in admiration.

"I told you I had something planned."

"Smart girl."

Raymond opened the door. "We're ready."

Lauren and Joe walked back in.

"After consulting with my client, he's decided not to contest the original agreement. Ms. Jones can keep the apartment and he'll make no claim."

"Great." Lauren got up. "You'll have him sign to that right now, won't you?"

"Yes," Raymond said.

"Okay, Joe will take care of that right now." She looked at her watch. "I've got to go. Just messenger the papers to me, Joe."

"Will do."

"I've got an appointment to keep." As she walked out, she stopped and turned to Ken. "You know, Ken, I always wondered why you loved being a defensive tackle and now I know. It feels good to sack someone." She patted him on the back.

Lauren got into the waiting elevator. "Yes!" She did a fist pump.

The minute she got off the elevator, she called Randy.

"Hello?" he said sleepily.

"Oh, honey, I woke you up. Go back to sleep."

He sat up. "No, I'm awake now."

"I know you had a long night at the restaurant."

"That's okay. What's up?"

"It's over."

"What?"

"I'm just coming from my lawyer's office. Ken agreed to drop all claims to the apartment."

"Great! How did you get him to do that?"

"I beat him at his own game. I had an ace up my sleeve."

"Aren't you going to tell me what you had on him?"

"Later. Suffice it to say it was a quality sack. I told you I'd handle it, but I appreciate all you wanted to do for me."

"Honey, I'm so happy. As long at it's over, it's cool with me."

"Now the divorce will continue unabated."

"We're going to have to celebrate. Why don't you come over? I'm not working today."

"Hmm, that sounds tempting, but I have to head up to Alicia's for her press conference."

"That's today?"

"Yes. That's not to say I can't come afterwards."

"Please do, my love. Let's not waste a minute."

"We won't." She walked out to a waiting car. "I'll call you after the conference."

"Okay, honey. I love you."

"I love you, too." She closed her cell phone. "We're heading to Alicia's place, Tony."

"You got it."

❧

It was pure chaos at Alicia's usually serene home. Viola brought a hairstylist and makeup artist to help her get ready for the press conference. She also brought a planner to the event, chairs, and a small table of pastries, bagels, rolls, coffee, juice and water for the reporters and camera people.

Just as Alicia was about to pick up her phone, there was a knock on the door. When she looked up, it was Ron Wilder.

"Can I come in?"

"Sure, Ron. How have you been?"

"Okay." He looked around. "I see you're quite busy."

"Big press conference."

"I heard about it. I came up to see if there was anything I could do to help."

She smiled. "That was awfully nice of you, Ron."

"I also wanted to apologize for what happened and my actions afterwards."

"No apology needed. If anything, I'm sorry for not being more sensitive."

"It wasn't your fault."

"Does that mean you're back from your leave of absence?"

"Yes."

"That's good to hear. We need you. Why don't you head to the kitchen and get some coffee. We'll talk more later on."

"Okay." He stepped out. Alicia made her call while the hairstylist worked on her in the guest bathroom.

Viola walked in. "How's it going in here?"

"We're okay." Alicia gave her the thumbs up. "Wait, hold on a minute. Viola, is everything set up in the back?"

"Yes. We're all set. The reporters are already back there drinking coffee and setting up their shots."

"Great." She went back to her phone conversation.

Meanwhile Harrison watched the madness from the kitchen window. "This is crazy."

"You can say that again. I thought I'd never make it up the street," Gabby sighed.

"Good to see you, Gabby. It's nice to have a friendly face here."

"How about two friendly faces?" Lauren walked in.

"Hey, I thought you were meeting with the lawyers today."

"Been there and done that."

"Well?" Gabby said anxiously.

"I'm keeping my apartment and Ken has agreed to make no further claims. The divorce is back on track and I should be officially rid of him by the beginning of fall."

"I'm so happy for you." Gabby stopped. "That does sound strange, since we're talking about a divorce."

"But it's a divorce from a creep."

"Yeah, we should celebrate."

"How about a celebratory glass of orange juice, ladies?" Harrison asked.

"Sounds good, Harrison. Line them up."

Viola walked in. "Hey, girls, I'm glad you made it."

"So are we. It's a madhouse on the street with all the trucks and vans," Gabby said.

"You can be sure the neighbors will complain." Harrison sipped his orange juice.

Barbara Folsom walked in.

"Hello, Barbara, how are you?" Viola asked.

"I'm good, Viola. I don't really know why I'm here, but Alicia asked me to come."

"Okay. We're certainly glad you're here. Do you know everyone?"

"Yes."

Lauren walked over. "Hi, Barbara. I believe we met at the holiday party. You know Gabby too, right?"

"Yes. It's nice to see you both."

"You, too."

"Hello, Harrison." She smiled.

"Good to see you, Barbara."

Viola looked at her watch. "It's getting close to show-time. I'd better see how Alicia's coming along. If you'll excuse me . . ." She quickly left.

"It's getting close to nine. I guess we should take our places outside," Harrison said.

"I thought Kurt Jr. and Mr. and Mrs. Carlson would be here by now," Gabby said, concerned.

"They might be stuck in traffic trying to get here. I'm sure they'll be along soon," Harrison explained.

"Has anyone seen Nathaniel?" Gabby asked.

"I'm sure he'll be along soon, too."

"Why isn't he here?" Gabby was perplexed.

"I'll tell you about it when we get outside," Lauren said.

∽

Alicia checked herself in the mirror.

"Hey, it's just about time."

"Thanks, Viola." She got up. "How do I look?"

"You look great. Are you ready to do this?"

She took a deep breath. "I'm as ready as I'll ever be."

They walked down the stairs and into the backyard. The reporters were in their seats and the camera people were ready to roll. Alicia looked around and saw almost everyone who really counted was there. Harrison, Kurt Jr., Lauren, Gabby, her mother and father. Then finally Nathaniel arrived.

Viola went to the podium they'd set up. "Ladies and gentlemen, if I can have your attention. We're ready to start. Ms. Archer will be reading a statement and will not be taking questions at this time. Now without any further adieu, Ms. Alicia Archer."

Alicia took a deep breath again. "Good morning, everyone. I'd like to thank you for coming." She paused. "As many of you know it's been reported that I was seen drunk in public last Friday. I wasn't intoxicated, as has been widely reported. Almost three years ago I was diagnosed with multiple sclerosis, and last Friday I had an attack that caused me to become quite dizzy. I was treated by Dr. John Hubert and the wonderful people at the NYU MS Center. As many of you know, MS is an autoimmune disease that attacks the central nervous system. There are about 400,000 people in the U.S. who are affected by the disease. I sought to keep my condition private, but I have since learned that it's best to be open and honest, which is why I'm revealing it. I'm also taking this time to announce that in accordance with simplifying my life, I am stepping down as editor-in-chief of *Everyday Elegance,* effective immediately. I'm pleased to announce that this morning our board of directors confirmed our production manager Barbara Folsom as the new editor-in-chief. Barbara has been essential to the magazine since its inception and I know I'm leaving it in capable hands. Thank you." Alicia walked off.

Reporters crowded around her to get a comment, but Viola and her staff kept them at a distance so Alicia could get back to the house.

Her parents hugged her first. "We're proud of you." Her father kissed her.

"Thanks, Dad."

"You go, Mom. You did great." Kurt squeezed her tight.

Harrison was almost speechless. "You're dropping a hat. I'm proud of you."

"You know that means I'll be around more."

"Bring it on." He kissed her forehead.

She walked over to Gabby and Lauren. "Surprised you, didn't I?"

"Yes," they said in unison.

"But I think there's someone who's even more surprised than us." Lauren pointed.

Nathaniel took her by the hand. "I don't know what to say."

"Then let me say it."

"Come on, everyone, let's go into the kitchen for coffee and give these two a chance to talk," Harrison said.

The room emptied quickly.

"Nathaniel, after you left I had a chance to think about why I always wanted my hands in every pot, and the answer was work allowed me to escape my grief and loneliness. I had a love once that I thought would never come again, and then you entered my life and suddenly I had love again. So I have three titles instead of four. As long as I've got you, it's like my son says. It's all good. "

He took her in his arms and kissed her passionately. "I love you, Alicia."

"I love you, Nate."

"Did you call me Nate?"

"Yes. I'm turning over a new leaf and trying to loosen up. What do you think? Was it too much?"

"Not at all. It's perfect." He leaned in and kissed her tenderly. "Say it again, please."

"Nate."

"Say the whole thing again."

"I love you, Nate."

"It's music to my ears."

They joined the others in the kitchen.

"Here's the woman of the hour," Harrison proclaimed.

"What do you mean the hour? She's the woman of the decade, maybe even the century," Mr. Carlson said proudly.

"Though I appreciate it, that might be stretching it a bit, Dad. "

"You're certainly the woman of the century to me." Nathaniel kissed her.

Barbara walked up to her. "My, you really know how to throw a press conference, don't you?"

Alicia put her arm around her shoulder. "I'm sorry I sandbagged you."

"I'm still in shock. How did you do it?"

"Let's just say it was a marathon session of phone calls and some not-so-gentle persuasion."

"I can't thank you enough."

"There's no need to thank me. You're the only one who is as interested in the quality of the magazine as I am. I have complete confidence in you."

"I won't let you down, Alicia."

"I know. By the way, Ron is back, so you'll have some backup."

"That's a relief."

The two women hugged.

"It's the changing of the guard," Lauren quipped.

"Yes, it is." Alicia looked over at Viola. "I think Viola's looking for you. I'm sure she's fielded a lot of questions about *Everyday Elegance's* new editor-in-chief."

Barbara took a deep breath. "I guess I'm on."

"Go get 'em, tiger." Alicia patted her on the back. She felt a little twinge as she watched Barbara walk over to Viola for her first official act as editor-in-chief.

"Are you okay?" Gabby asked.

"Sure."

"You're going to be fine. You still have three other jobs."

"I know, Lauren, but I think I might cut back a little."

"Excuse me? Am I hearing this right? You're going to cut back?"

"Yes. I'm going to take time for me. Now, Ms. Producer, I will continue to do my duties as a host, but maybe I won't do as many appearances. Can you live with that?"

"I guess we can swing it. I'll tell PR to spin it so we'll get more out of your doing less. It can work."

"Cool."

"I'm glad you understood that, Alicia, because that was Greek to me," Gabby said.

"That's because you're officially an art denizen," Lauren said.

"What's new about that? She's always been one," Alicia said.

"Oh, now it's official. Tell her, Gabby."

"Thomas DiGregorio is doing an article on my new artist exhibit and the gallery."

"You're in the big time," Alicia said, impressed.

"You can be sure the bad ink will dry up quickly," Lauren added.

"The bad ink? What are you talking about? What happened?" Alicia was out of the loop.

Gabby took Alicia's arm. "It's a long story. Oh, did Lauren mention how she sacked Ken today?"

"Wait a second. I'm really out of the loop here. You pulled a fast one on Ken?"

Lauren took her other arm. "Perhaps we should grab some sparkling cider and take to the gazebo so we can catch you up."

∽

The chairs were gone and so were the vans, cameras and reporters. Alicia, Lauren and Gabby sat in the gazebo with sparkling cider.

"Lauren, I wish you had taken a picture of Ken's face. I bet his expression was priceless," Alicia chortled.

"I know you're not supposed to gloat, but it felt good."

"After what he put you through? Please. You should have reveled in it." Gabby sipped her cider.

Alicia lifted her glass. "I second that."

"I just have to be satisfied that he'll never get what he wants from me or the show."

"Did you do something, Lauren?"

"No, Gabby. I just know karma has a way of leveling things out."

"Yes. I'm happy to say all's well that ends well. As it has for you, Lauren."

"Now that's the truth," Alicia agreed.

"My divorce is back on track and I've got a sexy chef waiting for me in the city."

"Wasn't that the name of a show?" Gabby said jokingly.

"My goodness, Gabby, you're still corny as ever." Lauren laughed.

"I know." She grinned. "Umm, I have a little news to share about Nigel."

"There's more?" Lauren asked.

"Yes. He and his ex agreed to joint custody of their son. I will be meeting Nigel Jr. during his first fall break from school."

"Oh, that's great, Gabby."

"Thanks, Alicia. I'm looking forward to it."

"It sounds cozy."

"Speaking of cozy, you and Nate looked quite cozy."

"Now that I've gotten out of my own way, Nate and I will have more time to spend with each other."

"Oh, my God." Lauren jokingly cleared her ears. "Did I hear you correctly? Did you just call him Nate?"

"That's his name, isn't it?"

"You're really in love, Alicia, and I couldn't be happier."

"Thanks, Gabby."

"I second that." Lauren looked up at the sky. "You know it's funny how at the end of the day, it's always the three of us."

"We're the Austen Aristocrats. Of course we're together," Gabby proclaimed.

"Thirty-two years and counting, ladies." Alicia grinned.

"Let's not mention that in mixed company too often."

"Why not? We look good." Gabby winked.

"You're right. I think we've lived far beyond Jane Austen's dreams of romance. We've found love on our own terms. Frankly, I don't know what could be sweeter."

"Indeed, ladies, we've each found our own Mr. Darcy, even if one of us didn't know she was looking." Alicia reflected.

"Let's raise our glasses to our patron saint of sorts, Jane Austen." Lauren raised her glass, as did the others.

"Here's to Jane," Gabby said.

"And to all the girls looking for their own Mr. Darcy. Happy hunting. We sure have had a good time," Alicia laughed.

ABOUT THE AUTHOR

A native of Amityville, New York, Chamein Canton is a freelance writer, author and literary agent with the small literary agency that bears her name. This longtime Jane Austen fan and all-around romantic holds a degree in business management from Empire State College and lives on Long Island with her twin sons, Sean and Scott.

ONE

Because you have shared in our lives by your friendship and love, we, Sherrie Mary Williams and Lance Clayton Phillips II, together with our parents, invite you, Leah Russell and a Guest, to witness the joyous nuptials Sunday, the seventeenth of May, five o'clock in the evening at St. Paul's Enon Tabernacle Baptist Church, Philadelphia, Pennsylvania

Reception to follow

The rush of memories overwhelmed me when I pulled the invitation out of the half-unpacked cardboard box. My hands stilled.

Sitting down on the hardwood floor, I reached up to wipe away the perspiration on my brow and allowed myself to be pulled back in time to the biting cold of that Saturday afternoon, the heaviness of the ivory envelope I pulled from the mailbox. I remembered dusting off snowflakes clinging to my wool coat.

Even the scalding bitter blackberry sage tea I'd prepared once inside my apartment couldn't warm me. The snow continued to fall gently outside the window as I stared down at the thick gold embossed letters.

Joyous nuptials.

He was getting married to *her*. The person I had known all my life seemed like a stranger. Each elegantly curved letter seemed to twist around his image, drawing him further away.

My Lance.

"No matter what, Lee, we'll always have each other." His voice rose like steam in my mind.

In my memory of the last time we'd met before the wedding, black and white images began to stack up one on top of the other like the snow on Chestnut Street. Every other day the big trucks would come through and push it to one side, and the mound would grow until it rose to my hips and turned grey from exhaust and salt.

Closing my eyes, I went back to that night, back to one of the worst moments of my life.

Lance and I sat close over the small wooden café table, clutching our glass mugs of coffee laced with Bailey's. I huddled more deeply into my jacket each time the door opened and the wind blew in small gusts of snow. I watched as snowflakes silently landed, then turned to shiny puddles on the marble floor. After getting the wedding invitation in the mail, I had felt winter's coldness everywhere. Even Lance's smiles couldn't warm me. The hole in my stomach lingered, catching everything in its darkness.

"Come on, Leah, it'll be the whole crew, just like old times," he said excitedly.

Lance's voice was deep and beguiling. His lips curved into a smile and his head tilted as though he were listening to some invisible voice. His earth-colored eyes shadowed by curling lashes drifted closed as his long brown piano fingers wrapped loosely around the mug.

I looked down into the creamy foam of my drink and struggled to push back the sound of denial in my head. Struggled to hold in that other person under my skin who wanted to cry, weep, gnash her teeth, and claw at this stranger sitting opposite me.

I took a cleansing breath and tried to drown myself in the thick smell of coffee beans, vanilla, and honey. I pushed back that other person within who stood on the edge of that black hole in my stomach, her screams lost in the jangling of spoons on glass and whispered conversations mixed with the whirr of the espresso machine.

"We've gone over this before, Lance. I'm moving out to California that week." My voice sounded hollow to my ears, but he didn't notice. Lance saw nothing but full lush life, happy endings, and rainbows. His optimism was a magnet that drew people to him like bits of metal. You found it next to impossible to separate. If you could escape, some part of you would always long to come back. Like coming home.

"Don't you think you should reconsider? California's a long way from Philly."

I heard the echo of my parents' words and shivered. "It's a great opportunity. I can't just ignore it."

"You'll be alone out there," he pointed out.

I was alone here, in this café, sitting with a man I had loved all my life.

"No, I won't. Rena's going to be moving out there in two or three months."

He sighed and sat back, placing his hands behind his head. "I'm not going to win this, am I?"

I shook my head negatively as I met his eyes, looking for the boy I'd grown up with. The man I'd spent half my life holding in my dreams. Just for a second, his eyes searched my face looking for something and I saw a glimpse of the boy I knew from around the corner. I saw him peek out from that stranger's eyes. The Lance I'd kissed on the cheek under Christmas mistletoe would have known I loved him, he would have understood, he would have chosen me.

"What happened between the two of you?" he asked.

The unexpectedness of his question brought the little girl back.

"Shouldn't you be asking your fiancée that question?" I responded.

"I did." He threw his hands up. "She just shrugged and kept telling me nothing happened."

"She told you the truth," I replied.

There was nothing between the two of us. The rage, jealousy, humiliation, and biting remarks had ended one night with the sharp sound of my palm striking her cheek.

I met his eyes steadily. "Look, Lance. I wish you the best. All I've ever wanted was for you to be happy, and you are."

"I really need you, Lee."

My throat closed and it was hard to swallow. Yet I smiled, despite feeling bitter irony mixed with melancholy dreams.

"You'll be fine." I smiled sadly. "Just remember to look before you leap," I cautioned, reminding him of the time he'd jumped into a shallow ditch while showing off.

He laughed and the deep warm sound reverberated in the small café. Just for a brief moment, everything went still. A surprising richness swirled in the air. It filled me with memories of summers spent at the pool, soccer in the park, and popsicles on the front stairs.

We finished our drinks and headed out the narrow door into the small, brightly lit lane. I stood on the sidewalk snuggled into Lance's side as he hugged me to him. I felt his reluctance to let go as I moved away. Smiling up at him, I turned my cheek for his kiss. His lips stung with cold. In the yellow haze, the falling snow looked like tarnished gold. The snowflakes caught in Lance's eyelashes and I wished him good night. I stood with my knees locked and grief stuck in my throat as he strolled in the opposite direction into the growing darkness, towards her.

2009 Reprint Mass Market Titles

January

I'm Gonna Make You Love Me
Gwyneth Bolton
ISBN-13: 978-1-58571-294-6
$6.99

Shades of Desire
Monica White
ISBN-13: 978-1-58571-292-2
$6.99

February

A Love of Her Own
Cheris Hodges
ISBN-13: 978-1-58571-293-9
$6.99

Color of Trouble
Dyanne Davis
ISBN-13: 978-1-58571-294-6
$6.99

March

Twist of Fate
Beverly Clark
ISBN-13: 978-1-58571-295-3
$6.99

Chances
Pamela Leigh Starr
ISBN-13: 978-1-58571-296-0
$6.99

April

Sinful Intentions
Crystal Rhodes
ISBN-13: 978-1-585712-297-7
$6.99

Rock Star
Roslyn Hardy Holcomb
ISBN-13: 978-1-58571-298-4
$6.99

May

Paths of Fire
T.T. Henderson
ISBN-13: 978-1-58571-343-1
$6.99

Caught Up in the Rapture
Lisa Riley
ISBN-13: 978-1-58571-344-8
$6.99

June

Reckless Surrender
Rochelle Alers
ISBN-13: 978-1-58571-345-5
$6.99

No Ordinary Love
Angela Weaver
ISBN-13: 978-1-58571-346-2
$6.99

2009 Reprint Mass Market Titles (continued)
July

Intentional Mistakes
Michele Sudler
ISBN-13: 978-1-58571-347-9
$6.99

It's In His Kiss
Reon Carter
ISBN-13: 978-1-58571-348-6
$6.99

August

Unfinished Love Affair
Barbara Keaton
ISBN-13: 978-1-58571-349-3
$6.99

A Perfect Place to Pray
I.L Goodwin
ISBN-13: 978-1-58571-299-1
$6.99

September

Love in High Gear
Charlotte Roy
ISBN-13: 978-1-58571-355-4
$6.99

Ebony Eyes
Kei Swanson
ISBN-13: 978-1-58571-356-1
$6.99

October

Midnight Clear, Part I
Leslie Esdale/Carmen Green
ISBN-13: 978-1-58571-357-8
$6.99

Midnight Clear, Part II
Gwynne Forster/Monica
  Jackson
ISBN-13: 978-1-58571-358-5
$6.99

November

Midnight Peril
Vicki Andrews
ISBN-13: 978-1-58571-359-2
$6.99

One Day At A Time
Bella McFarland
ISBN-13: 978-1-58571-360-8
$6.99

December

Just An Affair
Eugenia O'Neal
ISBN-13: 978-1-58571-361-5
$6.99

Shades of Brown
Denise Becker
ISBN-13: 978-1-58571-362-2
$6.99

2009 New Mass Market Titles

January

Singing A Song...
Crystal Rhodes
ISBN-13: 978-1-58571-283-0
$6.99

Look Both Ways
Joan Early
ISBN-13: 978-1-58571-284-7
$6.99

February

Six O'Clock
Katrina Spencer
ISBN-13: 978-1-58571-285-4
$6.99

Red Sky
Renee Alexis
ISBN-13: 978-1-58571-286-1
$6.99

March

Anything But Love
Celya Bowers
ISBN-13: 978-1-58571-287-8
$6.99

Tempting Faith
Crystal Hubbard
ISBN-13: 978-1-58571-288-5
$6.99

April

If I Were Your Woman
La Connie Taylor-Jones
ISBN-13: 978-1-58571-289-2
$6.99

Best Of Luck Elsewhere
Trisha Haddad
ISBN-13: 978-1-58571-290-8
$6.99

May

All I'll Ever Need
Mildred Riley
ISBN-13: 978-1-58571-335-6
$6.99

A Place Like Home
Alicia Wiggins
ISBN-13: 978-1-58571-336-3
$6.99

June

Best Foot Forward
Michele Sudler
ISBN-13: 978-1-58571-337-0
$6.99

It's In the Rhythm
Sammie Ward
ISBN-13: 978-1-58571-338-7
$6.99

2009 New Mass Market Titles (continued)

July

Checks and Balances
Elaine Sims
ISBN-13: 978-1-58571-339-4
$6.99

Save Me
Africa Fine
ISBN-13: 978-1-58571-340-0
$6.99

August

When Lightening Strikes
Michele Cameron
ISBN-13: 978-1-58571-369-1
$6.99

Blindsided
Tammy Williams
ISBN-13: 978-1-58571-342-4
$6.99

September

2 Good
Celya Bowers
ISBN-13: 978-1-58571-350-9
$6.99

Waiting for Mr. Darcy
Chamein Canton
ISBN-13: 978-1-58571-351-6
$6.99

October

Fireflies
Joan Early
ISBN-13: 978-1-58571-352-3
$6.99

Frost On My Window
Angela Weaver
ISBN-13: 978-1-58571-353-0
$6.99

November

Waiting in the Shadows
Michele Sudler
ISBN-13: 978-1-58571-364-6
$6.99

Fixin' Tyrone
Keith Walker
ISBN-13: 978-1-58571-365-3
$6.99

December

Dream Keeper
Gail McFarland
ISBN-13: 978-1-58571-366-0
$6.99

Another Memory
Pamela Ridley
ISBN-13: 978-1-58571-367-7
$6.99

Other Genesis Press, Inc. Titles

Other Genesis Press, Inc. Titles (continued)

Bodyguard	Andrea Jackson	$9.95
Boss of Me	Diana Nyad	$8.95
Bound by Love	Beverly Clark	$8.95
Breeze	Robin Hampton Allen	$10.95
Broken	Dar Tomlinson	$24.95
By Design	Barbara Keaton	$8.95
Cajun Heat	Charlene Berry	$8.95
Careless Whispers	Rochelle Alers	$8.95
Cats & Other Tales	Marilyn Wagner	$8.95
Caught in a Trap	Andre Michelle	$8.95
Caught Up In the Rapture	Lisa G. Riley	$9.95
Cautious Heart	Cheris F Hodges	$8.95
Chances	Pamela Leigh Starr	$8.95
Cherish the Flame	Beverly Clark	$8.95
Choices	Tammy Williams	$6.99
Class Reunion	Irma Jenkins/	$12.95
	John Brown	
Code Name: Diva	J.M. Jeffries	$9.95
Conquering Dr. Wexler's Heart	Kimberley White	$9.95
Corporate Seduction	A.C. Arthur	$9.95
Crossing Paths, Tempting Memories	Dorothy Elizabeth Love	$9.95
Crush	Crystal Hubbard	$9.95
Cypress Whisperings	Phyllis Hamilton	$8.95
Dark Embrace	Crystal Wilson Harris	$8.95
Dark Storm Rising	Chinelu Moore	$10.95
Daughter of the Wind	Joan Xian	$8.95
Dawn's Harbor	Kymberly Hunt	$6.99
Deadly Sacrifice	Jack Kean	$22.95
Designer Passion	Dar Tomlinson	$8.95
	Diana Richeaux	
Do Over	Celya Bowers	$9.95
Dream Runner	Gail McFarland	$6.99
Dreamtective	Liz Swados	$5.95

Other Genesis Press, Inc. Titles (continued)

Ebony Angel	Deatri King-Bey	$9.95
Ebony Butterfly II	Delilah Dawson	$14.95
Echoes of Yesterday	Beverly Clark	$9.95
Eden's Garden	Elizabeth Rose	$8.95
Eve's Prescription	Edwina Martin Arnold	$8.95
Everlastin' Love	Gay G. Gunn	$8.95
Everlasting Moments	Dorothy Elizabeth Love	$8.95
Everything and More	Sinclair Lebeau	$8.95
Everything but Love	Natalie Dunbar	$8.95
Falling	Natalie Dunbar	$9.95
Fate	Pamela Leigh Starr	$8.95
Finding Isabella	A.J. Garrotto	$8.95
Forbidden Quest	Dar Tomlinson	$10.95
Forever Love	Wanda Y. Thomas	$8.95
From the Ashes	Kathleen Suzanne	$8.95
	Jeanne Sumerix	
Gentle Yearning	Rochelle Alers	$10.95
Glory of Love	Sinclair LeBeau	$10.95
Go Gentle into that Good Night	Malcom Boyd	$12.95
Goldengroove	Mary Beth Craft	$16.95
Groove, Bang, and Jive	Steve Cannon	$8.99
Hand in Glove	Andrea Jackson	$9.95
Hard to Love	Kimberley White	$9.95
Hart & Soul	Angie Daniels	$8.95
Heart of the Phoenix	A.C. Arthur	$9.95
Heartbeat	Stephanie Bedwell-Grime	$8.95
Hearts Remember	M. Loui Quezada	$8.95
Hidden Memories	Robin Allen	$10.95
Higher Ground	Leah Latimer	$19.95
Hitler, the War, and the Pope	Ronald Rychlak	$26.95
How to Write a Romance	Kathryn Falk	$18.95
I Married a Reclining Chair	Lisa M. Fuhs	$8.95
I'll Be Your Shelter	Giselle Carmichael	$8.95
I'll Paint a Sun	A.J. Garrotto	$9.95

Other Genesis Press, Inc. Titles (continued)

Icie	Pamela Leigh Starr	$8.95
Illusions	Pamela Leigh Starr	$8.95
Indigo After Dark Vol. I	Nia Dixon/Angelique	$10.95
Indigo After Dark Vol. II	Dolores Bundy/ Cole Riley	$10.95
Indigo After Dark Vol. III	Montana Blue/ Coco Morena	$10.95
Indigo After Dark Vol. IV	Cassandra Colt/	$14.95
Indigo After Dark Vol. V	Delilah Dawson	$14.95
Indiscretions	Donna Hill	$8.95
Intentional Mistakes	Michele Sudler	$9.95
Interlude	Donna Hill	$8.95
Intimate Intentions	Angie Daniels	$8.95
It's Not Over Yet	J.J. Michael	$9.95
Jolie's Surrender	Edwina Martin-Arnold	$8.95
Kiss or Keep	Debra Phillips	$8.95
Lace	Giselle Carmichael	$9.95
Lady Preacher	K.T. Richey	$6.99
Last Train to Memphis	Elsa Cook	$12.95
Lasting Valor	Ken Olsen	$24.95
Let Us Prey	Hunter Lundy	$25.95
Lies Too Long	Pamela Ridley	$13.95
Life Is Never As It Seems	J.J. Michael	$12.95
Lighter Shade of Brown	Vicki Andrews	$8.95
Looking for Lily	Africa Fine	$6.99
Love Always	Mildred E. Riley	$10.95
Love Doesn't Come Easy	Charlyne Dickerson	$8.95
Love Unveiled	Gloria Greene	$10.95
Love's Deception	Charlene Berry	$10.95
Love's Destiny	M. Loui Quezada	$8.95
Love's Secrets	Yolanda McVey	$6.99
Mae's Promise	Melody Walcott	$8.95
Magnolia Sunset	Giselle Carmichael	$8.95
Many Shades of Gray	Dyanne Davis	$6.99
Matters of Life and Death	Lesego Malepe, Ph.D.	$15.95

Other Genesis Press, Inc. Titles (continued)

Other Genesis Press, Inc. Titles (continued)

Other Genesis Press, Inc. Titles (continued)

Still Waters Run Deep	Leslie Esdaile	$8.95
Stolen Kisses	Dominiqua Douglas	$9.95
Stolen Memories	Michele Sudler	$6.99
Stories to Excite You	Anna Forrest/Divine	$14.95
Storm	Pamela Leigh Starr	$6.99
Subtle Secrets	Wanda Y. Thomas	$8.95
Suddenly You	Crystal Hubbard	$9.95
Sweet Repercussions	Kimberley White	$9.95
Sweet Sensations	Gwyneth Bolton	$9.95
Sweet Tomorrows	Kimberly White	$8.95
Taken by You	Dorothy Elizabeth Love	$9.95
Tattooed Tears	T. T. Henderson	$8.95
The Color Line	Lizzette Grayson Carter	$9.95
The Color of Trouble	Dyanne Davis	$8.95
The Disappearance of Allison Jones	Kayla Perrin	$5.95
The Fires Within	Beverly Clark	$9.95
The Foursome	Celya Bowers	$6.99
The Honey Dipper's Legacy	Pannell-Allen	$14.95
The Joker's Love Tune	Sidney Rickman	$15.95
The Little Pretender	Barbara Cartland	$10.95
The Love We Had	Natalie Dunbar	$8.95
The Man Who Could Fly	Bob & Milana Beamon	$18.95
The Missing Link	Charlyne Dickerson	$8.95
The Mission	Pamela Leigh Starr	$6.99
The More Things Change	Chamein Canton	$6.99
The Perfect Frame	Beverly Clark	$9.95
The Price of Love	Sinclair LeBeau	$8.95
The Smoking Life	Ilene Barth	$29.95
The Words of the Pitcher	Kei Swanson	$8.95
Things Forbidden	Maryam Diaab	$6.99
This Life Isn't Perfect Holla	Sandra Foy	$6.99
Three Doors Down	Michele Sudler	$6.99
Three Wishes	Seressia Glass	$8.95
Ties That Bind	Kathleen Suzanne	$8.95

Other Genesis Press, Inc. Titles (continued)

Tiger Woods	Libby Hughes	$5.95
Time is of the Essence	Angie Daniels	$9.95
Timeless Devotion	Bella McFarland	$9.95
Tomorrow's Promise	Leslie Esdaile	$8.95
Truly Inseparable	Wanda Y. Thomas	$8.95
Two Sides to Every Story	Dyanne Davis	$9.95
Unbreak My Heart	Dar Tomlinson	$8.95
Uncommon Prayer	Kenneth Swanson	$9.95
Unconditional Love	Alicia Wiggins	$8.95
Unconditional	A.C. Arthur	$9.95
Undying Love	Renee Alexis	$6.99
Until Death Do Us Part	Susan Paul	$8.95
Vows of Passion	Bella McFarland	$9.95
Wedding Gown	Dyanne Davis	$8.95
What's Under Benjamin's Bed	Sandra Schaffer	$8.95
When A Man Loves A Woman	La Connie Taylor-Jones	$6.99
When Dreams Float	Dorothy Elizabeth Love	$8.95
When I'm With You	LaConnie Taylor-Jones	$6.99
Where I Want To Be	Maryam Diaab	$6.99
Whispers in the Night	Dorothy Elizabeth Love	$8.95
Whispers in the Sand	LaFlorya Gauthier	$10.95
Who's That Lady?	Andrea Jackson	$9.95
Wild Ravens	Altonya Washington	$9.95
Yesterday Is Gone	Beverly Clark	$10.95
Yesterday's Dreams, Tomorrow's Promises	Reon Laudat	$8.95
Your Precious Love	Sinclair LeBeau	$8.95

ESCAPE WITH INDIGO !!!!

Join Indigo Book Club©
It's simple, easy and secure.

Sign up and receive the new
releases
every month + Free shipping
and
20% off the cover price.

Visit us online at
www.genesis-press.com or
call 1-888-INDIGO-1

Order Form

Mail to: Genesis Press, Inc.
P.O. Box 101
Columbus, MS 39703

Name _____

Address _____

City/State _____ Zip _____

Telephone _____

Ship to (if different from above)

Name _____

Address _____

City/State _____ Zip _____

Telephone _____

Credit Card Information

Credit Card # _____ ☐ Visa ☐ Mastercard

Expiration Date (mm/yy) _____ ☐ AmEx ☐ Discover

Qty.	Author	Title	Price	Total

Use this order form, or call **1-888-INDIGO-1**	**Total for books** _____ **Shipping and handling:** $5 first two books, $1 each additional book _____ **Total S & H** _____ **Total amount enclosed** _____ *Mississippi residents add 7% sales tax*

GENESIS MOVIE NETWORK

The Indigo Collection

SEPTEMBER 2009

"**TERRIFICALLY ENTERTAINING**"

Starring: Robert Townsend, Marla Gibbs, Eddie Griffin
When: September 5 - September 20
Time Period: Noon to 2AM

While being chased by neighborhood thugs, weak-kneed high school teacher Jefferson Reed (Robert Townsend) is struck by a meteor and suddenly develops superhuman strength and abilities: He can fly, talk to dogs and absorb knowledge from any book in 30 seconds! His mom creates a costume, and he begins practicing his newfound skills in secret. But his nightly community improvements soon draw the wrath of the bad guys who terrorize his block.

Allied Media Partners
1629 K St., NW, Suite 300, Washington, DC 20006
202-349-5785